WATERSHED

Cilla Grain

Edward Gaskell
DEVON

Edward Gaskell publishers
Old Gazette Building
6 Grenville Street
Bideford
Devon
EX39 2EA

First published 2015

ISBN 978-1-906769-55-0

WATERSHED

Cilla Grain

Typeset, printed and bound by
Lazarus Press
Caddsdown Business Park
Bideford
Devon
EX39 3DX
www.lazaruspress.com

To Gaby

Edward Gaskell
publishers
DEVON

1

Surprise

She shouted to herself, 'This bloody war!' Not accustomed to utter profanities, Margaret Rooney continually swore inside her mind. Would her husband and son consider her unpatriotic and irreligious if they knew her thoughts? She must drag herself to the air raid shelter, even though it was Bernie's birthday.

Margaret gathered up the essentials for her sojourn in the shelter, thinking how stupid mankind was – forever at war somewhere, about something, which became lost in the hostilities. *When the battle's lost and won. . .* those memorable words came into her mind, as she remembered Bernie, enthralled as he watched Macbeth at the city's Royal Court Theatre, when he was studying School Certificate English Literature. He had said, 'I'll remember those words always.' Bernie was as proud of his uniform and his determination to fight for his country, as his father. She felt guilty all the time about her anti-war stance. Would her service men folk consider her odd?

As she pulled the ancient hand-woven blanket from the washing line, her thoughts were of violence – Macbeth's corpses on the stage compared with the mangled bodies on the beach of Dunkirk, which Patrick, her husband, had described so vividly. Literature should surely deter people from bloodshed. Blasted war! Patrick would think she should go to Purgatory for swearing!

It was late now, how long had it been since the siren; the early hour of the air raid was unprecedented. Had she been what Bernie called, *woolgathering*? It wasn't quite dark, but where was Gladstone her cat? Her frantic call received no reply and no ghostly form appeared. She thought to herself that even her cat was camouflaged, his grey mirror-marked tabby like khaki in the gathering gloom – her every reflection was tinged with reminders of war to-day.

The air raid warden was hovering by the entrance to the shelter.

'Hurry Missus, - it's early, but where's your friend?' he shouted.

'Daisy's gone to Chester to stay with her daughter.'

The awful wail of the siren alerted her from her reverie. She wanted to think about Bernie, especially to-day. It was his eighteenth birthday and he should have been at home in Liverpool where he belonged. Where was he? Did naval ratings train on board a ship or inland or even abroad – perhaps somewhere like Canada?

Margaret's dark frame of mind was halted. Just inside the entrance of the shelter were two children – a boy and a girl. *Hadn't all children been evacuated to places of safety?* Their anxious faces made Margaret think back to Bernie – he hadn't suffered war as a child. He'd been free to enjoy his childhood. She caught the eye of the boy who looked distraught, as he took his sister's hand and exhorted her not to cry but to go into the dark interior.

'I can't,' she sobbed.

'Come on - I'll go first.'

'Hullo, children, come and sit by me. We'll talk together. I'll put my torch on.' The light from Margaret's cycle lamp lit up the dark interior, where people were hunched on benches on either side. There were no other children.

'It's. . .' the girl, who must have been about six or seven started to say, but her brother whispered to her and she seemed to accept that she shouldn't speak. They both sat down reluctantly by Margaret, who sensed that they had not been in a public shelter before – the reinforced concrete, flat-roofed buildings must be forbidding to youngsters. They didn't seem to have their gas masks with them, but they had rolled-up towels tucked under their arms.

'Have you been swimming?'

'Yes,' said the boy. The girl opened her mouth to say something, but her misery made her silent.

He continued. 'We went to the salt water baths but caught the wrong tram home.'

'Where d'you live? I'll come with you to the main road after the raid and put you on the right tram,' Margaret said softly.

'Thank you. . . so much. We asked the warden to direct us to a phone box, but. . .'

'The nearest one got a direct hit last week.'

'David's cross with me, 'cos I made him go to those baths.' The girl's voice was choked.

'No, no, I'm not, Anna. I'm very worried. . . worried about Mummy and Daddy. What will. . ?' His words were greeted with hysterical sobs from his sister.

'It's so dark and it smells in here. I want to go home,' said Anna defiantly.

An old man spoke. His husky voice was gentle. 'All the children have been evacuated from our street. Our Bobby and Jimmy, our grandkids, gone to the Lakes. 'ate it, they do. All green, freezing water and quiet.'

'My Mummy says our house is safe.' Anna said by way of contradiction.

'Sit either side of me and talk,' said Margaret. 'You'll get used to the poor light and the airlessness, very soon. It does seem dank in here.'

There was a chorus of agreeing voices and faces, lit up by the glow of weak torches, which could be seen in the gloom, smiling. All but a couple of middle-aged women were old – all probably grandparents, having spontaneous sympathy with the two little waifs. The children were slim, dark-haired, with big eyes, sparkling in the half-light. Were they blue? The children were clearly well-cared for, but anxious about their unfamiliar surroundings.

'Where's your cat to-night, missus?' one of the old men asked the lady in the pinafore.

'He's hunting. I looked for him everywhere and couldn't find him. If the bangs start he won't like it.'

A jokey old man said, 'Praps e'll catch a Jerry.'

The children seemed to understand what he was saying but didn't realize that he was speaking in fun. They looked at Margaret for some explanation. She laughed and their faces relaxed.

'You've a cat, have you? We want a cat.' The girl's tears had stopped and her apprehensive face looked alive suddenly.

'Yes, he's a little more than a year old. His name's Gladstone.'

'That's the name of the large dry dock, isn't it?' The boy's accent was what Margaret called *well-spoken* but his expression was one of surprise and curiosity. Without being big-headed, he seemed to want to show that he was knowledgeable about the docks: after all Gladstone Dock was the pride and joy of the Liverpool waterfront.

'Why is it your cat's name?' he asked.

'My husband worked in the Liver Building before he joined up into the Royal Navy and he had to visit the dock in his work. A group of dockers were having a bet on a kitten climbing up the side of the dock,' she explained.

A middle-aged woman protested, 'Don't go teaching them children about gambling, Maggie Rooney.'

'They'll be knowing it was just a game, Flossie, they're sensible. Anyway, each man put money against the kitten managing to climb to a certain height – you see the dock wall was marked. Patrick said he knew that the kitten would get to the top.'

'And. . ?' Flossie asked.

'He won the stake – it was a pound. Then he said to the others that he'd take the kitten home for his son for his birthday. That was just over a year ago, at the beginning of the war.'

'Your man's got the luck of the divil,' she retorted with contempt.

'Is Patrick the name of your husband?' the boy asked politely.

'Indeed it is. Today is my son's eighteenth birthday. He's called Bernie.'

'Where is. . ?' Anna received another meaningful stare from her brother. Margaret thought how responsible he was for his sister. He seemed to be recovering from his initial terrible anxiety, keen to show that he was intelligent and alert about the city docks. His nervous state, evidently, made him want to talk. Wasn't that the best way to be?

Once assured that Margaret was a fellow cat-lover, Anna snuggled up to her, asking, 'What's *your* name?'

'Margaret Rooney.'

'Your pinny's got flowers on it. They are different colours of heathers.'

'Where've you seen heather? There's little in Liverpool.'

'In Wales; my Mummy and Daddy are from Wales,' was the sleepy reply. 'I like your pinny, but your. . . your name's so big, would you mind if I called you, 'Pinny'? The child appeared uncomfortable, as if she wondered what good manners were in an air raid shelter?

Her brother cried, 'Anna, you shouldn't. . .' But Margaret was quick to say, 'You must think me foolish, coming out in my coat over my pinafore, but I was looking for Gladstone in the garden. You lean against me, that's right. Try to sleep and call me whatever you like when you wake up, luv.'

The anti-betting woman said, 'You cuddle up to Maggie, she's good with kids even if her old man gambles.'

An elderly man added, 'It'll only be a false alarm, as early as this.'

The words 'false alarm' made Anna sit up, but Margaret hushed her. 'He means that it isn't a real raid.'

The garrulous woman explained to David that Maggie'd had plenty of experience with children because she'd worked in an orphanage before the war. David nodded.

'All the children have been evacuated to the Lake District or North Wales. I wanted to see my son off to do his training in the Royal Navy, so I stayed here and I work in a munitions factory,' Margaret told him.

'We've avoided evacuation till now, but our parents are talking about sending us to Wales,' David confided in a whisper.

'Whereabouts?'

'Breconshire, my grandparents farm there. . .'

'And. . .'

'I'll have to go to boarding school nearby,' he added.

'And your sister?'

'She'll have to go to the local school. Don't say anything, she doesn't know.'

Having exchanged polite pleasantries with Margaret, David turned to the man on his other side who was trying to attract his attention.

He appeared happier telling the male listener how he'd never been in a town shelter and asked about a recent disaster where many people had been killed due to a direct hit to a shelter. The man agreed that there had been a horrific tragedy, but it was considered to be a freak occurrence, not likely to be repeated.

He added, 'Yous'll be alright.'

'When we heard the air raid siren I looked for a telephone box, and. . .'

'Even that had been bombed. Are you keen on sport?'

The older man's question started a detailed conversation about cricket, soccer and rugger. They agreed that different local journalists pleased or annoyed their readers.

The huddled occupants of the shelter chatted quietly or dozed for a while, until a resounding bang/crash echoed through the little area where they were sitting.

Anna shrieked and threw herself across Margaret and David, sobbing uncontrollably. All looked shaken.

The air raid warden's torch shone round the door and its owner explained the deafening noise: a lorry carrying oxygen cylinders had been hit by an incendiary bomb on the main road, but the driver was unhurt because he'd taken cover in a pub cellar.

'That's 'is story, anyway,' he said as he winked at Anna, put a bar of chocolate in her lap and disappeared. She had almost certainly never had a whole bar of chocolate and surprised, passed it to her brother, who broke it into pieces and handed it round the shelter. None of the occupants accepted a piece but all commented on the children's generosity. Anna was obviously relieved when David put a big piece in her mouth and taking a smaller piece himself said, 'We may need the rest later on.'

The chocolate woke Anna and loosened her tongue, she seemed anxious to ask Margaret something.

'What is it, Anna?

Looking anxiously at her brother she asked, 'Your voice is different from people in Liverpool. Are you Welsh?'

'No, I'm Irish, luv.'

The child nodded but the chocolate had not stopped her shivers. The woman's mind reverted to the subject of war. It was cruel to children. *How could children possibly understand about their lives being disrupted by bombs, rationing, evacuation and the existence of a tyrant named Hitler?* These thoughts made her forget her own preoccupation about Patrick and Bernie being away in the navy. The irony was that she'd been directed to work in a weapons factory and was shunned there for being Irish: some accused her of being an enemy alien.

Anna seemed unable to go to sleep immediately, and hearing her brother's relaxed conversation she told Margaret about her family. Her father worked in the University in a 'served occupation'. David corrected her by saying, '*reserved* occupation'. She ignored his interruption and said that her mother was a doctor, too, but had not worked until the war made her work. They had a storeroom at home with very thick walls which had been looked at by a man in uniform, who said, 'It passes the crit. . . something for a shelter'. David put in the older brother comment, '*criteria*'. Anna explained, 'He's twelve, so he knows big words.'

It was Anna's turn to talk and talk. She told Margaret about her mother reading a book about a girl called Alice and a white rabbit, in the shelter at home.

'When we had a raid last week, Daddy carried me down-stairs and, through a pretty window on the way I saw beautiful sparkly lights.'

'They were flares,' said David.

'David! Then there were bangs, but Mummy went on reading 'Alice' – she's probably reading it now.' She seemed sleepy and relaxed at last.

'It's gone quiet; the raid seems to be over. We'll hear the 'All Clear' soon,' Margaret whispered to David. 'Try to sleep, you have a journey home to do, and it's late. I haven't got a telephone at home or I'd speak to your parents.'

2

Memories

Margaret wrapped the child in the hand woven blanket, which she'd snatched from the washing line when the air raid siren interrupted the search for her cat. Minutes had been lost as she had called Gladstone repeatedly; he was unusually and unexpectedly missing. As she tucked the warm fabric round the child's back, she remembered how it had been on her own bed, when she was young and her mother had often reminded her to care for it. She could hear the words 'hand made by your grandmother' in her Irish brogue, the twenty five year old words of her mother, who had almost disappeared from her memory; the person from whom she'd been estranged for many years, inexplicably. Why? Was her mother still living?

If only I'd been able to stay in Ireland, the bombing hasn't affected Cork or Dublin. Patrick and Bernie wouldn't have been caught up in this devastation and bloodshed, there. But, had I been able to stay on the Irish small-holding, I couldn't have had husband or son. I'd have gone for a nun and wouldn't have experienced the last half hour of closeness with this child, who's excited in me a sense of maternity, a feeling which has lain dormant in me for years.

She'd been destined to be a teaching nun, despite having no vocation because she'd been considered a scholar by the Reverend Mother at the convent school and by her family.

She gazed at the sleeping child, consciously making the image memorable. Working in the awful factory had made her cynical. There would be life after Hitler. Smiling at the little boy she whispered, 'She's fast asleep. It won't be long now.'

He returned the smile awkwardly, explaining where they lived. 'Our surname is Williams. We got late. We weren't really supposed to go into town. Anna so wanted to go because she had measles when I went to the salt water baths with friends.'

'I do understand how you feel.'

'You see I'm due to go away soon and I wanted us to have one last bit of fun.' His expression clouded, overcome with guilt. He was almost thirteen, he said, and was about to go to boarding school, but knew that he would miss his parents and sister.

'Boarding school will be fun, won't it?'

'Will it? I wasn't very keen on being away from home. It'll change everything. I hope my parents won't think that we've run away because I don't want to go to boarding school.'

'My son's ambition was to go away to 'boarding college' as he called it. He read books about daring escapades at that type of school.'

'Is it like that now? The war's changed everything, hasn't it?'

'I don't know. Children still make their own fun. Your parents and Anna will come to see you at school and there'll be the holidays.'

'Yes. I suppose so. Anna's too young to go away to school. She'd hate it because she's determined to have a kitten, but if the raids continue who knows what will happen.' He appeared downcast. There was a pause. Margaret wished that she could touch him. In a flash his expression lightened.

'Please tell me about your son, Mrs. Rooney. I overheard you say he was in the Royal Navy.' His anxious tone changed to one of excitement as he said the last few words.

'His name's Bernie. He surprised us by winning a Junior City Scholarship to the Jesuit School. I was frightened that he'd want to be a priest and I'd lose him - we're Roman Catholics, you see, but he got Higher School Certificate, early, and had applied to train to be a doctor.'

'A neighbour of ours went to that school.'

She nodded and continued, 'Then the war broke out and he joined up, so I've lost him, anyway.' Her face wore a rueful smile but the boy's expression was one of total admiration.

'That's marvellous. I want to go into the Royal Navy or the Air Force when I'm old enough. That may be after the war, possibly.' There was disappointment in his voice.

Did he understand what he was saying? Or had he, like Bernie and many others, been seduced by advertisements of valour, glory and victory? Naval uniforms with their braids and badges made war exciting and a welcome change to youngsters who had only known the labours of the class room and the thrills of swimming and diving, rugger and soccer.

Margaret sighed. She thought of war in terms of 'The Battle of Britain', capture and casualty lists. Hugging Anna's small body she found herself again looking back at her own life. It was a little more than a decade since her own son had been Anna's age. He had been free to play, swim, study, and enjoy hobbies with ever-loving parents helping him to grow up. The only thing he had missed was the company of brothers and sisters, which didn't seem to arrive, as in other Catholic families. *Where and how is Bernie now? Why didn't I conceive after Bernie?*

Cradling the sleeping Anna and seeing David relaxed, Margaret began to doze. She was back in Ireland, sitting at the riverside reading a book. What was its title? Poetry? It was always that clear bubbling stream. Then, a deafening explosion shook the building, rousing her, her charge, the brother and all the assorted people in the shelter. Shouts, groans and Anna's screams joined the dust and acrid smell in the stale air.

'That was near, a direct 'it,' mumbled an old man clutching an even older man next to him. All the stunned people looked nervously towards the doorway, which seemed immediately to be filled by the bulk of the ARP warden.

'You're all safe 'ere. Thank God! Two houses got 'it, I'm afraid. Tunnel Road's a shambles. Jerry's thrashed the city to-night.' David and Anna gasped as they gazed at the man who had helped them to safety a couple of hours ago. Then, his face had shone with good humour: his voice had been cheerful. Now, that face was covered in sweat and dirt. His helmet dripped water and debris cascaded down from his shoulders. Even his torch was cracked and dusty, making its light eerie and dim. He made a vain effort to be jovial. He hovered in the doorway, looking exhausted. Anna sobbed uncontrollably. David's face was white. Margaret comforted Anna, spoke softly to David, asking him for his address and assuring him that she would walk as far as the tram stop with him and his sister and give him her torch, when the raid was over. At that moment the 'All Clear' sounded and the coughing and spluttering was greeted with a resolute if subdued cheer. The momentary quiet that followed was unnatural.

The older people rose stiffly from the benches but Anna, David and Mrs. Rooney darted to the doorway, hardly knowing what they were doing, but rejoicing that they could escape into the open air.

Once in the street they stopped. The road was like a building site. All could see through the curtain of dust, by the light of powerful arc lamps shining brightly but apologetically, the smouldering wreck of two adjacent houses. The light shone on the adjoining wall where two wrought iron fireplaces, one ground floor and the other above suggested that there had been a floor between. Only half an hour ago the shell before them had been a house, a home. Hoses were still playing on the skeleton of the building. The water appeared as a grotesque fountain as it caught the light. There was a small fire burning, outlining the rafters but it smelt foul, as though some fiendish rubbish had been added to a harmless wood blaze. As the curious group gathered aghast, a cry broke the amazed silence,

'Jesus, Mary and Joseph, it's my house!' Margaret Rooney ran forward, tears running down her face. An ARP warden barred her way to the still smouldering building.

'You can't go any nearer. It's not safe,' he said sharply but his expression was kind and he put his hand on her shoulder. 'Was there any person in either house, madam? We need to know.'

'No, no - my neighbour's house was empty. . . she's with her daughter, but my kit. . . my cat. . . must have been in my house' She was shaking and pressing her hands to her head. . . 'Oh God, I couldn't find him. . . I take him to the shelter in a basket but he. . . he wasn't. . . couldn't find him. Oh Holy Mary, I've nothing. . . nothing left, now.' A woman took her arm saying that she was a WVS worker and would take her to the Casualty Clearing Station. Others stood around, shocked by the devastation.

No one spoke but the hoses hissed and spluttered. Anna's tears made rivulets down her dusty face, she was trembling violently. David wiped his sister's face with a grimy handkerchief. Catching sight of the two stricken children, Margaret's demeanour seemed to change. She wiped her tears on her pinafore, made an effort to straighten her shoulders and turning to the warden with a questioning glance, mumbling a weak, 'What do. . ?' The question was never completed because a man in fireman's uniform appeared out of the ghastly ruins with something in his helmet - an almost fully-grown cat. It blinked and shivered but hearing Margaret Rooney's whispered, 'Gladdy, Gladdy. . .' it stretched and made a pathetic mewing sound, only to be engulfed between the helmet and the flowered pinafore. In a second there was a purring sound which seemed bigger than the cat itself. Even the children were reassured.

'It's not a kitten, it's a cat. Wha. . . what did you call him?' asked Anna, still shivering but instantly distracted.

'This is Gladstone, Gladdy for short, named after the dock where he was born. Remember, I told you the story of how I came to have him.' Margaret's attention centred on calming the frightened ball of fluff, but she beckoned to Anna, who timidly approached the terrified animal and stroked it gently. Her brother too moved closer, and held out his hand to the purring creature.

3

Coming to Terms

The next hours, days, of Margaret's life were a nightmare. Where was she to go? How was she to communicate her homelessness to her husband and son? Since they had joined up, she had often sighed as she addressed letters to Paddy and Bernie. It was as though she was writing to a uniform or inanimate object – a ship or a camp, rather than to men, but at least her own address at the top of the page must have reassured them about home.

Now, she had to write from another address, explaining the air raid and its destruction of the house which they all knew so well. Patrick had lost his fishing tackle, Bernie his stamp collection and she no longer had the willow pattern plates or the Dürer print. Losing everything was something she tried to put out of her mind because she was alive and she was unscathed physically. The reports of the raid in the paper were horrifying. She remembered with discomfort the last week-end that Paddy had been home on a short leave and had persuaded her to stay in the house whilst a raid was on. *Was he taking risks at this minute?*

The horror of the Casualty Clearing Station, the eternal form filling and the endless cups of tea with their obligatory dollops of sugar had, mercifully, given way to a miracle. A colleague from the orphanage, where she'd worked pre-war, had rented her a room in her house in a garden suburb of the city. Jean, whose husband, Will, was the Headmaster of a Catholic secondary modern school, had been one of the WVS officials she had encountered when being allocated the necessities of life the day after the raid. Jean explained that she had room in her house for Margaret and Gladstone. Will had taught Bernie, in his first year at Grammar School. The boys had nick-named Will, 'the sadist'.

'The twins will willingly double up in one room. They're hardly ever home since they became WRENS and Will is away with his school which has been evacuated to Mold in North Wales.'

Margaret was grateful, and also relieved. She knew that Jean had an outhouse which could be home for the traumatised Gladstone and she wouldn't miss the domineering headmaster.

Jean seemed lonely and welcomed her old friend. She was better off than Margaret due to family money; her recently deceased father had been a successful bookie, so she had opted for voluntary war work for worthy reasons. Jean had always prided herself on being 'a good Catholic.' Margaret secretly thought that her friend considered her eternally damned because she read more risky novels and poems than most women – on one occasion, she'd shocked Jean by quoting from Donne's 'To His Mistris Going to Bed'. Worse still Margaret sometimes even missed Mass!

Gladstone was in his element. He lay curled up in front of the gas fire if any member of the household was in the house and was carried to the outhouse at other times where he slept in a stout cardboard box which was filled with an old jumper belonging to the awful Will. He had risen to the status of air raid survivor and was favoured by the fishmonger as a result.

Margaret made several attempts at writing to Patrick and Bernie about No. 29, their home. *Where were they when they read letters? How am I to explain the devastation?* She decided that she would concentrate on the good news first. 'I'm staying at Jean's house for the time being with Gladstone,' she wrote after the usual endearments. Having made a stark mention of her place of residence, she found it hard to state the reason for her move, but decided to continue by explaining that she was in the air raid shelter when a bomb dropped on the house. 'There were two children in the shelter; they'd got late at the swimming baths and then...' She wrote a paragraph about the children's fear and plight, knowing that Patrick had a soft spot for children, especially sporty ones. After five attempts at the first letter she felt that the final note was more like a news bulletin than a letter from a wife to her husband of twenty years. She ended with the reality of the situation. 'There wasn't anything to salvage, it was all rubble. I'm so, so sorry.' She thought it strange that she, an Irish woman, was apologising for the senseless destruction of her home by the enemy of England. She finished the letter to Bernie with as an amusing an account as possible of Will's alleged uncomfortable experiences of evacuation, the Welsh, their impossible language and customs. The enclosed *Liverpool Echo* photo of

Gladstone in the arms of an ARP officer would please Bernie. *I find it easier to write to Bernie. . . I wonder why.*

Patrick's answer was short but sympathetic, though it did list the possessions which he would miss! He was adamant that his wife should consider moving out of the city and take a job away from the munitions factory, immediately. Before the war he'd been slow to show any interest in, or concern for, where she worked. Margaret smiled at this, asking herself how she could possibly move unless she joined the forces. Such a change would make keeping in contact with her men folk more difficult than ever. There was no answer from Bernie, which worried her greatly. She wished she had his last letter, which had explained that he was to train as a medical orderly. Had he mentioned where? In future she'd keep all her correspondence with her Identity Card in her bag.

Margaret was on the ten till six shift. It was the shift most likely to be interrupted by a raid. Although they filed down to a deep shelter, all the workers knew that the factory was a target for Jerry and were edgy when they reported for work. She thought of the evening to come and it reminded her of the two children in the shelter on the night of the raid. The shop she was going to was a pork butcher's, some distance from Jean's, where the meat was not rationed. Margaret realized that she would be in the children's neighbourhood. As it was Saturday, might the family be at home? To ascertain whether they had recovered from their recent ordeal was something she had pondered often, despite her own pre-occupations. Anyway she could return the bathing costumes and towels which she'd crammed into her string bag in the shelter. The children had put them down and forgotten about them.

*

Anna and David, who'd said their surname was Williams, had given her differing accounts of where they lived but the descriptions together made the house on the corner of the terrace seem the correct one. She noticed several windows in the front of the building were boarded up and there were still remnants of broken glass at the edges of the pavement. The front door was down a side path and as she approached it she was relieved to see that the patterned glass in the inner door was intact. Margaret knocked tentatively on the brass knocker. Was she intruding in another family's war misery? Immediately, she heard footsteps, so her resolve to disappear was useless. She was trapped.

'Excuse me calling like this but I think I met your son and daughter in. . .' she was overcome by the memory of two bewildered faces in the dusty dark of her ruined street and leant for support on the door frame, but the woman before her threw the door open wide and said, ' Come in, please come in, I'm Mary Williams. You must be the person who befriended our children in that tragic air raid. Am I right in thinking that your name is Rooney? Let me take your arm, you're all in. Do I see our bathing towels in your string-bag?'

'Your children left them in the air raid shelter and I picked them up and put them in my bag and then I saw. . . I found. . . I want to return them.' She produced the two bathing rolls.

'I understand. . . it must have been horrific. Thank you for bringing them back, Mrs. Rooney. Anna's swimming costume was a present from her grandparents. She'll be so pleased to see it again.'

Soon the two women were sitting in front of the Esse stove in the kitchen at the back of the house, waiting for the black iron kettle to come to the boil. They had already exchanged the latest news of Mrs. Rooney's blitzed home and the lack of windows in the Williams's house. Both women fell into an awkward silence.

'I must apologise for being emotional when I knocked on your door, but I had a vivid recollection of the children's expressions - on that appalling night. Er. . . I feel an eejit. How are they? Was their journey home horrendous? I had decided. . . before. . . to walk with them and at least put them on a tram but then, then. . . I discovered that the house which had received a direct hit was. . .'

Her companion's face was concerned as she recalled that night, which had been so devastating for both of them.

'We were frantic when the children were missing and the raid began. Then we worried throughout the raid as to what was happening to them. The moment the 'All Clear' sounded, Rhys, my husband, telephoned all the emergency numbers to ask for possible information about the children. No news! Then we decided, by being frantic, we'd blocked any possible in-coming calls. So we went upstairs to check the roof for damage or incendiary bomb fires, knowing that we'd hear the telephone – there was an uncanny after-raid silence everywhere.'

'Was your house alright?'

'All the front windows were blown out. When we climbed the ladder into the roof all seemed intact. From there we heard a strangled cry, which we thought later must have been David.'

'What a relief, you must have been overjoyed.'

'We flew down the stairs and there they were. It was a miracle and a fright at the same time.'

'I've thought of their plight often since. Thank God they were safe.' Margaret found herself crossing herself as she called on the Almighty's name.

'Seeing them alive, if dirty and cold was such a relief.' Mary Williams paused to make the tea and sit down beside her guest.

'Fourteen months of war has changed our lives in such unbelievably horrifying ways.' The women exchanged understanding glances with each other. They were both mothers.

'Your house, David said was. . . What a terrifying time for all of us. You did your best to comfort our two during the raid. Thank you for being so kind to them.'

'It was nothing.'

'How thoughtful of you to lend them your torch! It's here somewhere. We made enquiries about you but we were told it was *Classified Information*. I'm so glad you've come. Were they. . . were they. . . in a dreadful state? We keep wondering whether they were dazed or hysterical or what? They have said so little about it. From what they did tell us, an ARP warden took them as far as the tram stop but David said. . . said that Anna had to be carried most of the way when they got off the tram.'

'She had been asleep until the explosion. It must have been well after her bed time.'

'David said that the roads were covered in debris.' She paused in some distress, 'garden walls had collapsed and there was glass everywhere.' It was Margaret's turn to look horrified.

'I did try to find out about them but the damage in my area resulted in the usual war chaos. Sometimes I wonder which side some of the officials are on.'

'Eventually, when they got on the tram it was the last straw for Anna' – she paused, 'the conductor jokingly said they looked like enemy aliens, silly fool. Not that she knows the meaning of *alien*, but the word sounds frightening.'

'Tram conductors in Liverpool have a strange sense of humour which is lost on children. The man should have seen that they were alone and alarmed.'

'Anna isn't sure what is meant by *enemy* or *Germans* for that matter. She just knows that they're to do with the war and the changes it's made in her life.' Mrs. Williams sighed.

A young Liverpudlian voice joined in the conversation, 'The conductor did redeem himself by saying, "Sorry, duck, it was only a joke. You two is 'eroes, so yous don't 'ave to pay".' David had entered the kitchen, and he added, 'Bloody 'itler, upsetting kids.' Fortunately, he said, Anna had been sobbing so hard that she didn't hear the swear words. His mother frowned at him as he continued, sheepishly, 'I beg your pardon, good to see you, Mrs. Rooney.'

He looked years older to Margaret than he had been on the fateful night. His articulate voice faltered, 'Dad. . . Dad was trying to find out what had happened to you. He'll be so pleased that you've come to see us.' David put out his hand as if to compensate for his interruption and his language. 'I haven't lost the torch. It was a godsend. I'll go and get it.'

'What happened when you got near home, then?'

'We got off the tram at the end - at the end of this road but the torch was getting dim. . . the pub on the corner had been hit. No light, no singing. . . no stink of beer or tobacco but dust and a smell of burning; just holes in the wall instead of windows and glass everywhere. It was – was, I. . . we. . . dr. . . dreaded. . .'

'But you did get home. . .' Margaret said softly, but the boy had gone. His composure had been short-lived.

His mother continued the story, clearly understanding her son's sudden exit. 'David must have half-carried Anna the rest of the way. He was in a state of panic when. . .'

'He must have been thankful to see you.' Margaret sensed the other woman's emotion.

'No. Apparently he shouted and yelled as he came in the open door, then he must have collapsed.'

'What a shock!'

'We found him in a faint on the stairs with Anna, asleep, on top of him. When we roused him he was confused and incoherent. It was a ghastly sight. . . they were lying on a heap of broken glass. . . not a cut between. . .'

'Is David alright now?' Margaret interrupted.

'We don't know. He seems to have bad dreams and then moments of bravado, like his reaction to you just now. We've decided that both children must leave the city and go to their grandparents in Wales or boarding school as soon as possible.'

The women looked at each other in silence for a long time.

*

Mary told her husband later that she'd had a feeling that she and Margaret Rooney had known each other always. 'Her accent's charming. She explained that she'd been convent educated. Passing her exams with credit, her parents and teachers had wanted her 'to go for a nun'.'

Rhys replied, 'Thank God she didn't do that. Did she tell you how she escaped?'

4

War Weary

The night shifts were terrifying. Margaret found it difficult to sleep after she got back to Jean's house. It helped her to smuggle Gladstone up to the bedroom where his presence reassured her. Now that he was allowed in Jean's garden he loved his new abode. His gentle purring acted as a rhythmic lullaby but his sharp claws through the bed clothes alerted her as she was dozing off to sleep.

Was he damaging the eiderdown? How satisfying it would be to have her things around her! *Will I ever again have a home of my own?* Owning a two up, two down had been a pre-war ambition realized when Bernie was small and Patrick's widowed mother had died. She had loved the old lady, who had been kinder to her than her own mother. It had been a privilege to nurse her through the few years of mortal illness, in old Mrs. Rooney's house, which was home but now no more.

Margaret had started to have a recurring dream. She was at sea, *'a sunless sea'*, not on the New Brighton to Liverpool ferry but on a ship of war, surrounded by sailors, scrubbed decks, hammocks and guns. *I can see the deck of the ship, smell the carbolic soap and hear the sailors singing old sea shanties. Did I see Bernie on that ship? Was he the man tending the wounded sailor or was he that man himself?*

Sleep was elusive but she tried to make herself get back into the dream to understand what was happening. The sequel was frightening – the ship had vanished and there was an endless stretch of water – a river – the river Lee, in the Cork of her childhood and she heard a voice - Sean's voice, her childhood sweetheart's lilting tone,

'Where Alph, the sacred river ran
Through caverns measureless to man
Down to a sunless sea'.*

*'Kubla Khan' by Samuel Taylor Coleridge

Margaret stirred and Gladstone mewed in alarm. His large amber eyes and alert stance seemed to say, 'I know.' On the farm where she grew up, cats were merely mouse and rat catchers!

The supervisor suggested that she visited the factory doctor who did a surgery each week. The doctor was a woman, dragged from her rose garden and out of her recent semi-retirement by the Public Health Department and the War Office. She was more used to diagnosing syphilis than depression. 'Doc' was said to be brusque and professional. It was rumoured that this medic had had a 'sweetheart', killed at Ypres, and thereafter devoted her talents to general practice and gardening. The doctor smiled and nodded at Margaret as she entered the first-aid room which doubled up as a surgery.

'My man qualified at Trinity College Dublin at the end of the last century. We met in Ireland, at a rugby football match. The supervisor tells me that your house was bombed. How are you managing?'

'I'm suffering from strange dreams. My husband and son are both in the navy and. . .' Margaret blurted out nervously, how lame it sounded but 'Doc' had shown a chink in her armour by mentioning 'the lover.' Did one confidence encourage another?

Soon she was telling the doctor her fears about Bernie. The older woman reminded her that each Gaumont British newsreel showed ships being blown up and sunk and had she seen the epic film about the Battle of Trafalgar? The doctor's tone was kind as she said softly, 'No wonder you dream about catastrophe. Go into the cinema, late, just before the big picture. Don't torture yourself with *The News*.' Margaret thought, as she went back to work clutching an iron tonic, that perhaps she should be doing something on the land. The factory and cinemas were alien to her. She had studied the doctor's hands and understood the cause of their roughness. She imagined that salads and vegetables had become a substitute for roses. *Was one of the medic's nails slightly dirty?*

The daily routine of the factory shifts might have given all the workers a feeling of stability but anxiety was becoming a problem. Some drank heavily; others frequented the dance halls where they picked up Commonwealth soldiers and sailors and sported silk stockings, cigarettes and perfumes as their prizes. How cheap it all was! The iron tonic didn't seem to be working. Margaret was battling with the bomb damage officials and thinking that the struggle against bureaucracy had similarities with the war itself, when Jean called her to the telephone. 'It's Dr. Williams.'

'Good morning, Mrs. Rooney. Anna has been nagging me, she would love to see you, she's worried about Gladstone.' The formal voice reflected some reluctance or apology on the part of the speaker.

Margaret laughed, 'He's the most contented cat in Christendom. He doesn't seem to have used up any of his nine lives. Perhaps Anna'd like to pay him a visit. I'd like to see her, though I can't compete with 'His much photographed Lordship.' His photo was in the paper, you know.'

They agreed that they'd meet at Jean's when both women were not working.

5

The Visit

Jean postponed her weekly shop for half an hour in order to meet Mrs. Doctor Williams, as she referred to Margaret's new friend, and Anna. She was curious to see Anna and impress the mother with her house. Children were few in the city though the city evacuees were gradually returning, traumatised by the space and silence of the countryside. Margaret was embarrassed by Jean's obsequious welcome of her guest. Jean claimed that her wealth – from her bookie father, whom she referred to as a 'commission agent' – and her teacher husband, made her belong to 'the professional classes'. She often alluded to this, and as a result, she had an excessive reverence for doctors, especially if they were female.

Once alone with her guests, Margaret relaxed. Anna was updating Gladstone with news of school, David and the coming Christmas, explaining her gas mask to the cat which made a dive for the strap. The kettle was boiling. Apologies were made for the reconstituted milk by the one whilst the other produced homemade biscuits, a present from a grateful patient.

'She's a darling. Never ate butter until rationing, has the appetite of a bird and when I examine her heart I wonder whether she will survive for another week. The nineteenth century made them tough, Mrs. Rooney.'

'I wish you'd call me Margaret. Since I've been a war damage victim the only people I come into contact with are officials. Thank God for Jean: she's one of the few people who are close to me and knows my Christian name.'

'Alright, but if you're Margaret then I'm Mary. I get fed up with people calling me *Doctor*, which seems to lead to an impromptu consultation,' she laughed. 'Usually about bowel irregularities, impotence or childbirth.'

With Anna playing on the stairs with the kitten, the two women sat together by the kitchen fire admiring the biscuits, then guiltily nibbling one each self-consciously.

Mary sighed, 'I wish I had the fortitude and generosity of spirit of some of my patients.'

There was a pause as Margaret poured the tea and hesitated to respond to her guest. The other looked up, sensing an unspoken emotion.

'We all try to be stoical but recently I've been having arguments with myself about war, good, and evil. I've even been whining to the factory doctor who's given me a tonic.'

'You probably need a tonic after what you've been through. I know, Rhys, my husband and I agonise over the safety of our children. They should leave the city. How is your son?'

'I had a letter from Bernie, this morning. He's due to take part in sea trials – on a new or re-fitted ship. He'd just come back from a training camp at an 'undisclosed location'. Probably North Wales. . .'

'So. . ?'

'My last two letters had been held up. He said he was excited about action at last when the trials are completed, adding that he'd like to get his own back on Hitler for the loss of Number 29 and his much-cherished penny black,' she half smiled.

'Was that all that he said about the blitz of his home?'

'Funny, it didn't seem to matter; as though he couldn't think about bombs, Liverpool and the future.'

'Could that be because of the pro-war, pro-victory propaganda?'

Margaret shrugged, 'He started the letter, *My dear Ma* though.'

Mary looked puzzled.

'When Bernie was about eight he read a book where the hero addressed his parents as *Ma* and *Pa*. In tender moments since then he has used those endearments. It was. . . it was as though he was sending me a coded message in this letter, it. . .' Margaret wiped her eyes as she passed the steaming cup to her friend.

The two women went on to talk about their pre-war lives. Margaret explained how bright Bernie had been at the Jesuit school and how he had a passionate desire to study to be a doctor. Mary talked of her childhood in Wales and how she had met her husband, Rhys, at Medical School in Cardiff, though he was several years older than she.

'We assume that David will be a doctor when he's old enough to choose a profession.' *Her attitude to her children is different from mine. She still has them, while I feel I've lost Bernie already. Am I envious?*

6

A New Start

'A telephone call for you, Maggie,' said Jean, using her telephone voice. Margaret rushed to the phone praying that it was Bernie. He had called her once in the past from a friend's house and she'd put Jean's telephone number on her last letter, but it was Mary Williams.

'One of the part-time technicians at the university knows your husband. Apparently they worked together in the Royal Liver Building before the war.' She gave the man's name and Margaret remembered an oldish man, Tom, who had been a gas victim in the First World War.

'He said that they have a room in their house if you'd like it. He told Rhys that your husband was very good to him when he had a prolonged illness in 1935 and he owes him a favour.'

Margaret thanked her and said Tom'd had a soft spot for Bernie and she'd write a note to him.

'Would you like to meet at the Kardomah, sometime? Anna has plagued me to ask about Gladstone. She's fallen in love with him.'

'Yes,' she replied absent-mindedly and arranged a day. Was there going to be more bad news from Tom? Patrick used to say that he'd been 'broken' by the 1914-1918 war.

Margaret thought about him, his yellow skin and his constant chesty cough. She went to see him. It was a ten minute walk from Jean's. She knew that he didn't have a phone or a spare room but he'd helped Bernie with his stamp collection.

'I thought you'd come, I'm so sorry about the 'ouse. 'Ow's Paddy taken it? Been in touch? Lost his fishin' gear and *The Still*? Tom had always teased Patrick about his attempts to make wine and his Irish connections. He grinned.

'He wants me to leave the city. How can I?'

'That's where I can 'elp yer.'

'You? How?' She saw a conspiratorial glint in his eye as the familiar fit of coughing took over.

'Maggie, did yer know 'ow 'elpful Paddy was to me?'

'I know you had the odd drink and walk together.'

'I suffered bad with me chest. Yer man arranged that I worked on the ground floor. On Monday evenins he walked me up the town to the tram stop. Each week 'e made me walk one stop further. I told 'im in the end that 'e'd 'ave me walking all the way 'ome, sadist that 'e was. But those walks saved me life.' The revelation humbled her. Margaret didn't know what to say. She nodded.

'Our kids are in Australia sheep-farming, we've no grandbabees. I owe Paddy and the wife agrees; we'd like to see you out of this bloody city.' He pressed a bundle of notes into Margaret's hand, just as his wife brought in a tray of tea. She wondered whether her muffled, 'Thanks' was seen as gratitude for the tea or the money.

Margaret had never had as much as £20 in her hand before. She felt embarrassed and ashamed that she'd not known her husband better. On reflection she wrote a long newsy letter of thanks to Tom and his wife and said she would look for more pleasant war work, perhaps she'd join the Land Army, when the house was sorted out. They'd made it possible! Their kindness was something she'd never forget. She'd keep in touch and Patrick had said he'd visit them next time he was in the city. He'd thought it was good of Tom and his *missus* to offer her a room.

She confided her good fortune to Mary when they met, without stating the sum involved. Mary in turn wondered whether she would be as lucky in having answers to her advert for a girl or boy Friday to help her parents. The *Liverpool Daily Post* man who took down the detail asked me why I didn't use a Welsh newspaper.'

'Why didn't you?'

'Dad has advertised and made enquiries locally but he's drawn a blank. The locals don't want to be isolated away from the town. Some believe that the countryside is full of enemy spies dressed up as nuns or itinerant musicians. Dad's making do with land girls but it's not the answer. The last one took a fancy to Dad's neighbour who's married. Oh, the time! I must go to meet Anna from school. Be an angel and give me a few bits of news about Gladstone.'

As the two women parted, both giggled about the hero worship which the cat received from the fishmonger. Mary put the photo of Gladstone in the arms of the ARP man in her bag.

'Don't tell Anna that the photo was taken a week after the air raid, please.'

7

Letters

When Margaret got back to Jean's after a night shift the following week, there was a letter on the kitchen table. The writing was unfamiliar. More forms from the Ministry of this or that, she thought, but realised that all official notifications were typed. The familiar dread overtook her. *Was it bad news?* Ripping open the envelope she found that it was from the Williams family. To be precise, it was a letter in Anna's hand to Gladstone enclosed in an envelope addressed by her mother! It was a request to see him again and the writer, Anna, thanked him for the cutting from the newspaper.

Margaret remembered the notes she'd had from Bernie, as a child - the large letters worming their way across the page and the very practised signature at the bottom of the grubby paper. The message was that Anna longed for another visit to her feline friend. Margaret hurriedly replied, saying she would be at home at Jean's on Saturday morning and would love to see Anna again.

*

Anna had made a toy for her beloved out of paper and string and gave it to him as they arrived at the house. The two women watched with amusement, but both seemed preoccupied. The one said she was concerned about her parents and the other was undecided about future work. Anna was in another world, showing off her reading to Gladstone, who purred approval.

'Thank you and Jean for letting Anna visit. Her fantasies about your cat and the two barrage balloons, called Zenobia and Victoria, in the park opposite our house, seem to take her mind off her terror of the next air raid.'

'I sympathise. There was another accident in the factory last week. One of the foremen is fond of drink, the other is great. The drinker was on duty.'

'What happened?'

'One of the girls was badly burned. Safety precautions had not been followed. She lost concentration. Apparently she was worried about her brother who'd been wounded in France.'

'How is she now?'

'She's in hospital. I went there with her. Thank God she's recovering and her face seems alright, but her arms will be scarred. I was a witness, so I had to fill in details on a form, while the foreman glared at me.'

'You won't be popular.'

'I'm desperately looking for another job.'

'Locally?'

'No, I'd love to get out of the city.'

'We're going to move the children.'

'I looked in the paper but there was nothing much there for me but I did see your advertisement. Have you had any replies, yet?'

'Not one and it's been in the paper twice now. Rhys says that David and Anna must both go to the farm and David must go to the local Grammar School, so he can help Dad in the evening and at week-ends.'

'What does David think of that plan?'

'He's seen the prospectus for a boarding school we talked about before and was excited to go there when he read how excellent the sports facilities were. Until then, the idea of boarding school had no appeal. As a result, working on a farm didn't seem as much fun as playing a lot of football.'

'Tell me about your parents' place. Why do they need farm help so urgently? Is it a very big farm?'

'No, but Dad and Mother haven't always been farmers. Though Dad was born on Cae Coch, he had a bachelor brother who was the farmer whilst Dad had a career in journalism and Mother was a teacher.'

'And. . .'

'It didn't work out like that. . .' Mary became overcome with emotion. Pulling herself together she continued. 'It had been planned that my brother would farm but he was killed in 1918, in the war. Uncle carried on with hired help until he died in a hunting accident in 1937 and Dad inherited Cae Coch.'

'So why didn't your father sell the farm?'

'I had David by then and Dad said perhaps David would like to farm when he was older. Perhaps he will.'

'Then the war came.' Margaret's tone was one of resigning to the fates.

'Maggie, what do you miss most from before the war?'

'I think the smell of a garden. Cabbages and tomatoes aren't a substitute for roses and lavender, in the summer. Now winter is here, I miss the light; the black-out is so dismal, isn't it?'

The visit was short because Mary had an evening locum surgery. Anna's father arrived to take her home and Margaret was pleased to see how tall and athletic Rhys was. He was as fair as his wife, son and daughter were dark. His face was sharp featured, but his expression was relaxed as he shook Margaret's hand, scooped up his daughter in a bear hug and said laughingly, 'Mary, you're cutting it fine again; you've barely half an hour before surgery. Please excuse us, Mrs. Rooney.'

As the mother and daughter said their hasty, 'Good-byes', Margaret asked herself some questions: *Would the Morgan family consider me as their Girl Friday? Would I still be able to do farm work after so many years away from the country? What will Patrick's reaction be if I apply for the position?*

Margaret felt that she'd established a friendship with Mary – they were on Christian name terms! Even so, she was surprised to see another letter on Jean's kitchen table, two days later, but noticed that there was an *A.A.Milne* book there, too, with a note from Jean. She opened Mary's letter.

Dear Margaret,
Thank you again for our visit. Anna has been full of Gladstone and his antics and seems reassured about things since she saw him so relaxed and frisky. Anna is sure that she left her 'When We Were Very Young' book somewhere in Jean's living room, it was a fourth birthday present from the grandparents; she has a habit of pushing things under cushions so that they don't get bombed! I'm sorry. Would you be an angel and meet again in town next week so you can bring the book? It's a slack week for me. Please say 'Yes', I'd like to see you. I'm in a state because there have still been no answers to my advertisement. Dad and Mother are worked into the ground because the land girl allocated to them is useless. She's a terrible flirt. She thought milk was made in a factory. The cows hate her!

I don't think I told you about my family, I became so emotional about my brother, Owen. I'm sorry.

Though Cae Coch is a farm which has been in the family for generations and Dad was born there, it was planned that my brother would run it, with his uncle, to breed horses – he was horse mad, when he came back from the First War. I think I told you this before. He didn't come back. So Dad moved into the house after his brother died, engaged a manager and a farm worker while he continued with journalism and Mother continued to teach at the local school. This war resulted in the workers joining up and Dad being left high and dry. Fortunately, Mother retired in 1938, so she can help but she is not good with the large animals, though excellent with the dairy work, thank God. Dad must've been making a joke, about the land girl's farming ignorance. However, she couldn't milk and wasn't prepared to learn; hence the need for help from Gwyn next door. I don't know why I'm writing all this to you, now. Sorry.

Rhys says I bore everyone with telling the tale of the Morgan family history. Please accept a bigger sorry. Isn't the news bad this week? It's so hard pretending that all's well to the children. I long for Christmas. I have a whole week off, so we plan to go to Mid-Wales to stay at the farm. Unfortunately Rhys can only be away from Christmas Eve until the day after Boxing Day.

Can you meet me at the Kardomah at 2.30 Tuesday, for me to collect the book? If that's impossible, please phone.

I had to write as I find it difficult to talk about Owen – we were inseparable.

Yours sincerely,
Mary Williams

The letter was odd, Margaret thought, but it made her consider the isolation of a woman doctor, who probably lacked a close friend and confidante. She herself mourned the enforced loss of her sister, Bridget. As children they had shared everything and when Margaret had been banished from home, she had experienced a feeling of emptiness due to her total separation from Bridget, for all time. Owen's death must have been similarly shattering to Mary at a young age. *How I envy the Williams family going to Wales - fresh air, new laid eggs, and possibly a log fire. Heaven! Even if it were only log and not peat. Oh! Will I ever smell a peat fire again? I wonder why Mary refers to her parents as Dad and Mother?*

8

The Kardomah

The Williams family was finishing lunch – corned beef hash with onions from the garden and their own potatoes. Their children had left the table and were listening to the gramophone in the sitting-room.

'If there hadn't been a war would we ever have grown vegetables? There's something good about bringing the country to the city.'

'It isn't all that wonderful for the poor man who has to do the digging. Next year, perhaps, you'd like to do the spade work. You're a daughter of the soil? O.K. Did the potatoes have any shrapnel in them?' Rhys's reply was preoccupied; he was more interested in the newspaper which he'd started to read.

'Rhys, what did Tom tell you about the Rooneys?'

'Can't we forget that family for a bit and concentrate on our own affairs?' He put down the paper.

'Mary, we need to think about David and Anna. David is going to boarding school after Christmas, whether you like it or not. There may be more raids here. London is having unspeakably severe raids. We can't keep pretending that we'll win this war. We could be invaded. I know we forced the Germans back in what has come to be called 'The Battle of Britain', but there could be a reverse of fortune. That air raid experience scared Anna. . .'

'I was thinking about Anna.'

'What?'

'I'd hoped that she could go to Dad and Mother's - go to the local school.'

His tone was irritable, 'They can't manage the farm at the moment let alone look after a child of six. Be sensible, Mary. It might be better if both children went to your parents: at least David could help on the farm. I did suggest this last week. It would prevent David taking up his place at Public School.'

'Margaret Rooney told. . .'

'Oh, here we go again. . .'

'Don't you believe in coincidence? My parents need help on the farm and Margaret. . .'

'Mary, you may have got on Christian names with a woman who was very kind to our children in an air raid, but that doesn't mean you can send her into the middle of Wales as a farm worker.'

'She wants to move from the city. Tom told you that she was born on a farm in County Cork. Come on, Rhys, that must have been more primitive than Breconshire.'

'What you haven't considered is the nationality issue. The Welsh yokels will think Margaret, as you call her, is an Irish foreigner, perhaps even a Nazi, *and* she's an R.C. Think, Mary!'

'Oh God! I'd forgotten what living and working in Liverpool does to you; it's like the League of Nations. Northern Ireland is part of Britain all the same.'

'And Eire?'

'I would have thought that an Irish accent is an Irish accent to the Welsh. Please let me suggest it to her?'

'Suggest it to your father first. Phone him this evening. He understands prejudice and will persuade you from your lunacy. Remember you only have three minutes to make your recommendation.'

*

Mr. Morgan listened to his daughter's proposition. He said he'd been sent to Cork in the early twenties to do research for an article on 'The Troubles' and felt rural Ireland was similar to Wales. 'Why not ask her?' The pips sounded and Mary turned triumphantly to her husband.

*

'Rhys says he'll help over Christmas and I've made butter and strained milk many a time but the parents need more permanent help.' Mary sipped her coffee. 'This is real coffee, it tastes good. Where on earth do the Kardomah manage to buy it? D'you think it's black market, Margaret?' She hesitated before she continued, 'I feel uneasy about what I'm about to say - Rhys says I have a bee in my bonnet and won't let go until it's stung someone.'

Margaret was puzzled but comforted herself with the idea that the blitz got to everyone in time. Even this seemingly competent professional woman was not herself. Perhaps she was having bad dreams too. She said quietly, 'The coffee's excellent.'

'I don't know how to put this. Let me try. You wouldn't, possibly, think. . . consider helping my parents? Tom told Rhys all about your childhood experience of living on a farm.' Mary blushed as she blurted out the words. She seemed to recite the words as though she had rehearsed the conversation, and as she spoke the words were a little patronising and out of place. She added, inconsequentially, 'We've decided to send Anna to her grandparents, so she'll be safe.'

Margaret laughed. 'I thought you were going to ask if I'd like a room in your house. Everyone who has a spare room seems to want to make it available to me. The idea of a person being bombed out appalls, but honestly I've got used to it. I'm alive but 'yes' I do want to escape the city but. . . I don't. . .' She hesitated.

'I'm sorry - you wouldn't consider it? You'd love Wales.' Mary was confused and embarrassed. Margaret replied slowly.

'It's difficult to say this but remember I'm an R.C. I've lived in Cork, Dublin and Liverpool, each place is Catholic. I understand that Wales is different. Another thing, Patrick and Bernie need a place to come home to, on leave.' Her tone of voice belied the words she was saying. It was as though she was considering the suggestion out loud.

'I think I understand.'

Margaret paused and added quietly, 'I'm a bit of a hypocrite. The truth is I only remain a practising Catholic because my husband and son are devout.'

Mary looked surprised and perhaps a little shocked as she voiced, 'Why?'

'Patrick was a Protestant when he married me, my parents didn't consent to the marriage, though it was in a Catholic Church. Patrick was English. . . to them our marriage was shameful. The whole family was and probably still is staunchly Republican. Cork, because of its history is very anti-British. My people never forgave me.'

'I know it's personal but you still attend mass regularly, don't you?'

'Of course I do, but often wonder why. It was strange. When Paddy and I married I was already disillusioned about my faith.' She paused, stirring her drink - which had no sugar in it - vigorously. Mary nodded.

'The family's reaction to Paddy was an added blow to me. Soon after our simple church wedding 'in the vestry,' Paddy was received into the Catholic Church and has been a fervent believer ever since. It was too late a conversion for my family to know about or accept.'

'And your son?'

'His religious faith was determined accordingly. He is a good Catholic and a good man. I was frightened that the monks at the school where he was a scholarship boy would encourage him to be a priest.'

Both women were silent. Mary said softly, 'I suppose I've never thought about religion enough. I've always taken my Anglicanism or Church of Wales faith for granted.'

It was as though a shadow fell across Margaret's face as she whispered, 'Perhaps you've never had your belief destroyed.'

The two women sat silently for some moments.

'Think about Wales. Do. Here's Dad's address. I must fly. I've a clinic in a quarter of an hour.'

Later, Mary told her husband about the strange conversation. 'It's as though she likes the idea of fleeing Liverpool but feels her men folk will somehow think she's renouncing her Catholicism by doing so, and will consequently disapprove.'

'To be an uncomfortable Holy Roman is not to be recommended. How do they come to have only one child?' Rhys commented as he wrote his letter of acceptance to the boarding school which had offered David a place.

9

Decision

Margaret went to work on the following two nights weighing up the pros and cons of Mary's offer. She had discussed the matter with nobody. The other women at the factory talked mainly of dates with servicemen, make-up, black market clothes coupons and the records played on *Music While You Work*. They would imagine that she was mad to think of going to live in the country. When back at Jean's house a wave of guilt came over her. Jean had been kind when she most needed friendship, but Will was coming home for Christmas!

She felt that she'd been non-committal in the Kardomah. Why had she blurted out all her concerns about religion? Perhaps it was because she was fingering her rosary while Mary was asking her about Wales. The rosary was a present from Bernie as he got on the train for the mustering depot. It was mother of pearl and he'd made a joke about its appropriateness as he hugged her goodbye. She thought to herself that she prayed more than ever now, like every other person who was separated from mother or children. Even so, she had developed an anxiety about the Catholic Church. *Why have I exposed this secret uneasiness to a comparative stranger?*

On the second night, looking for a cigarette in her bag she drew out the piece of paper with the address of the Morgans in Wales. It seemed odd for Dr. Williams to have given it to her. Or was it? Margaret's geography wasn't good. Where was Wales? Wasn't Will there? Where was Breconshire? Heroines in classical novels tended not to travel much and her knowledge of places was restricted to near Liverpool or the South of Ireland. She'd go to the library on the way back to Jean's and study a map of Wales.

Margaret found herself writing to Mr. Morgan that evening. Apart from her family she'd only written business letters to the Bomb Damage Department, hitherto. After several attempts she produced a short note, which read:

Dear Mr. Morgan,

As your daughter, Dr. Williams has told you, I have become home-less as a result of an air raid which destroyed my house. It was during that raid that I met your grandchildren, who had become stranded in down-town Liverpool when the siren sounded. I understand that you are looking for living-in help on your farm.

I was born on a farm in County Cork and lived there until I was seventeen. During my childhood, I worked a great deal on the land and enjoyed the outdoor life.

Though I had passed my exams in school I was sent by my parents to help a suddenly widowed relative in her business in Dublin. As a result, I lost the place which I had qualified for, in the convent, to train as a pupil teacher. Within a couple of years I met my husband, married and moved to Liverpool. Even so, I think I could still milk cows and sheep. I was told that you have Jersey cows.

I liked the information which I read in the library about Breconshire. The photographs of the Beacons were beautiful. There weren't detailed maps of the area available, (I suppose that's to do with the war), so I'm not sure where your farm is exactly.

I realize that if you decided to employ me, my duties would include helping to look after Anna Williams, whom I got on with well during that frightening raid and have seen several times since. She has taken to my cat, Gladstone. He was rescued from the ruins of my house by a fireman.

I now lodge with a generous friend, Jean Malone, whose house is a long way from the munitions factory where I work.

I've two worries about my suitability to work on your farm. The first is that I am a Roman Catholic and your family may consider that I might influence Anna away from your faith. My religious beliefs are moderate. The war and the factory have made me broad-minded about many things. My second concern is about my husband and son being able to visit me in Breconshire. Are there lodging houses nearby, where they could stay if they had leave?

Please let me know whether you will consider me for the position?

*

Margaret put Will's dictionary and grammar book back in the book-case as she heard Jean's key in the door, and ran to her room with the finished letter. It seemed both formal and adolescent when she read it through, but she decided she'd sign and send it. Once it was posted she agonised about certain words and phrases – 'sent by my parents', 'influence', 'broad-minded' and 'cat'. *Have I exposed the wound of leaving Cork and marrying soon after?* It was too late to worry. The cliché, 'there's a war on', comforted her.

There was a distraction the following day – a brief letter from Bernie to say that his ship was sailing to an 'undisclosed destination'. He was excited and expanded on his new responsibilities as a medical orderly. Margaret touched the beads in her pocket. She must dispel her misgivings and humbly ask God to look after Bernie.

Mr. Morgan's reply came in a couple of days. The envelope was addressed in a beautiful copperplate hand and aroused suspicion in Jean, who suggested that Margaret must have a secret admirer.

Mr. Morgan explained that there was a great deal of space in the farmhouse, though the accommodation was basic. There was a loft over the dairy which he offered Margaret as a bed-sit. It adjoined the house, so benefited from the range in the kitchen which was alight day and night. Her cat (why was he named, 'Gladstone'?) was welcome and would be allowed in the house, a status not permitted to the four farm cats. The farm was quite isolated, so had been turned down as a billet for evacuated children. To have their grandchild would be a delight to him and his wife but Anna would benefit from a younger woman in the household.

He wrote, 'There is plenty of room on the farm when the Williams family is not here for you to have your husband and son to visit'. The letter ended with a plea to Margaret to agree to be part of the work force of the farm, Cae Coch. 'Mrs. Rooney would be free to leave after a month,' he wrote, 'if she was not satisfied with the conditions. Why not come at Christmas and take a look at the place? As you are often at work during the cheap rate for telephone calls, just send a wire to say, *yes* or *no*.'

There was an explosion at the factory the next day. One of the young girls was badly injured. The pandemonium which followed left all the workers shaken. Margaret went with the youngster to the hospital in the ambulance. She knew that next time someone would be killed. The foreman, who had a problem with drink, was taking risks with the production of a new type of shell. Fear of a fatal accident removed any reservations Margaret had about Mr. Morgan's offer. She telegraphed Wales on her way back to Jean's.

YES STOP AGREE TO SUGGESTION AND WAGE STOP WILL
DISCUSS TRAVEL PLANS WITH YOUR DAUGHTER STOP M.R.

Explaining her decision to Jean was less difficult than anticipated
because Will had sent a long list of requests for his Christmas break.
Jean was distracted, 'How and where am I to find a melon and how
much will it cost?'

10

The Royal Scot

Margaret had a telephone call from Mary Williams in the evening before the journey to Wales, 'I've ordered a taxi to take us all to the station. My husband is not travelling with us because he has pressing meetings and interviews at the university. He'll join us on Christmas Eve.'

'You did say I could bring Gladstone, didn't you?'

'Indeed yes. I need to tell you that Rhys and I've decided that Anna is to stay on with my parents after Christmas. Liverpool is too dangerous for a child. David knows that he's to go to boarding school in the New Year.'

'How wise you are to take Anna away from the air raids. Is she looking forward to being with her grandparents?'

'That's why I'm ringing you. Anna doesn't know she's to stay in Wales. We think she won't like it.'

'Is she too young to understand?'

'Perhaps. She's being difficult to-day. Even for Christmas she wants to take all her belongings. There just isn't room in the cases.'

'I've very little to take. My luggage will take up a very small space.'

'I know that. Thank you. You won't mention about Anna staying in Wales, will you? Is it possible to give her some responsibility for your cat? It might compensate her for missing home and us when the time comes?'

'That's a good idea. I'll do my best. I'll be ready at ten o'clock sharp, in the morning. The train's at one isn't it? I've a stout Bovril box for Gladstone which he likes.'

*

'The taxi's here!' Margaret heard David's voice.

'Good Morning, Mrs. Rooney, we're nearly ready. I'll start taking the cases out to the taxi.'

'Gladstone's in a cardboard box under one of the seats, he can't escape.'

A tearful Anna climbed into the taxi, holding Fatty, her rag rabbit, under one arm and her doll, Gretel, under the other. She threw both down when she spied the box and heard a purr. 'Is Gladstone in the Bovril box? Is he coming to Wales?' The little girl was delighted. 'Can I nurse him, please?'

There was a chorus of 'No!'

*

After an air raid alert, which turned out to be a false alarm and caused a delay, they were at last on the train.

Anna whispered to Margaret, 'While you were talking to Mummy about the cases, David and I walked up the platform to see the engine, it's *The Royal Scot*! I've a picture of it in my *Book of Trains*. The book's in my case. I'll show it to you when we get to Granny's.' Anna was pleased for the second time that day.

The train journey was exciting and she was soon asleep on her mother's lap, only to wake when the engine's whistle blew as the train approached Shrewsbury, where they were due to change lines.

There was a big crowd on the platform and Anna made no fuss about holding Mrs. Rooney's hand, while her mother and David put the cases in the 'Left Luggage'. The train to Wales was delayed, the man in the luggage office told them. 'Stay in the Waiting Room. I'll have to examine your luggage, while it's here.'

Looking round the crowded room, Anna told Margaret that she hoped to see her war heroes, men with gold braid on neat uniforms with lots of shiny brass buttons. As though she'd magicked him a man covered in gold stripes and badges, tall and slim, smiled at her as he spoke to no one in particular.

'There he is, the man in the newspaper, The Admiral!' cried Anna.

'What platform's the train for Liverpool on?' The uniformed idol asked.

A man with a whistle between his teeth said, 'Platform Seven, sir.'

Margaret whispered to Mary, 'He's a Royal Navy officer and going to Liverpool. I'd like to speak to him. He may have up-to-date news.'

'Someone may be listening,' Mary replied, quietly. Anna said that *she* was listening but her mother put her finger to her lips, looking

as a mother looks when their child hasn't washed their hands before dinner. Margaret stifled a smile.

At last, the man with the whistle came into the Waiting Room and told those there that the Cambrian train was on Platform Two.

'That's our train - it's over the bridge,' said David.

'Would you mind, Margaret, taking Anna and Gladstone over to the train while David and I collect the cases? We've only fifteen minutes.'

'Of course.'

'Try and find a carriage with three or four vacant seats in it. Wave your newspaper out of the window to show us where you are. I don't know what I'd have done without you. Thank you, thank you.' Her tone was desperate and as they parted the crowd thinned. It was clear that Gladstone was scratching his box and yowling.

Anna ran and put her arms out towards her mother who was close to tears. Mary cuddled her explaining, 'Mrs. Rooney'll see us when we come over the bridge. Look after Gladstone, he needs you. Be brave, darling!'

To Margaret she said that she'd be as quick as possible and David added that the porter had been sure the Cambrian train was never full and they'd all be able to sit together. Mary hugged and kissed Anna as she hurried with David towards the Left Luggage Office.

Anna took Margaret's hand reluctantly.

'Why's Gladstone making that funny noise, Mrs. Rooney?'

'I think that he's not happy with all the unfamiliar noises of the station.' Margaret was concerned in case her beloved cat could somehow force the box open.

'Can I have him on my knee in the next train?' asked Anna.

'No, I'm afraid not. He might run away into the corridor of the train and we'd lose him.'

'He's probably thinking of his home like I'm thinking of Daddy.' The child's voice was pensive.

'He's lost his home but he's looking forward to living on your grandparents' farm.'

'I'm sorry. He was under that ruddle, wasn't he?

'Yes, it's *rubble*. D'you remember David telling you that?'

Anna was silent and Margaret wondered whether she had further upset the unhappy child by correcting her. She searched for a new topic, as they approached the bridge.

'I'm looking forward to seeing the mountains in Wales.'

'And the cows and sheep,' Anna said absently as she was counting aloud the number of steps up on to the bridge, banging her foot on

45

each one and stamping across the bridge itself. She gave a cry of delight when the stairs going down on to the platform were the same number as the ones going up.

'You can just see the engine - Look! Smoke and sparks are pouring out of its chimney. It must be *The Prince of Wales*.' Anna was pleased.

'We'll get in this carriage near the steps so your mother can see us. Look, I've wedged my newspaper in the window.' There were just four unoccupied places. Margaret lifted Anna up into the carriage and on to a seat, as she pushed Gladstone's box under it. She explained that cats liked the dark when they were frightened. At that moment the lights went out. Everywhere. An air raid siren wailed. Anna had never been in 'such a dark' as she told her grandfather later - much later.

Margaret sensed that Anna was alarmed. She grasped her hand more firmly, too late.

'Who's in the train? Are they Ger. . . Germans? I can't see. . . see Gladstone. I can smell sm. . . smoke.' Anna sobbed uncontrollably to Margaret, who was startled and embarrassed by the outcry.

'Isn't your doll called Gretel? That's a German name.' Anna fumbled for her doll, which she had neglected to hug in the horror of the moment.

'Um, the seat's scratchy,' she screamed. 'Mum! I want my Mummy!'

'Germans aren't bad. It's only their leaders who have caused these horrid air raids.' Margaret felt that she was shouting.

The other people in the carriage all murmured a sound, which might or might not have been agreement and an old man in the corner said. 'I've a torch, little girl, if I put it on you can see us all.' *Do these travellers want to examine me – the child abductor?*

'Ye-s', please turn your tor-ch on,' sobbed the child as the compartment was lighted, dimly showing three elderly men and a woman - all normal, not visibly 'German'. Anna's sobs turned to screams as the poor light created odd shadows.

'Torchlight is always strange until you get used to it,' the woman occupant said as she patted Anna and stroked Gretel's hair.

Soon Anna's crying turned to hiccups, as she climbed on to Margaret's knee and was soon dozing. Margaret apologised to the other people but any explanation seemed beyond her.

Thank God it's dark. I'm so relieved that Anna has gone to sleep. I was frightened that her sobs would never subside. I was beginning to panic. What's the matter with me? I used to work at St. Mary's Orphanage before the war and felt I was good with children. Has my time in the factory dulled my ability? Am I no longer sensitive to the terrors of the young? Has the war hardened me? Why did I have no more babies after Bernie? Oh God, where is Bernie? Has he received my address in Wales? What will I do if Mary and David don't come?

The fifteen minutes stretched to many more, perhaps due to the air raid and the black-out - Margaret, though anxious, couldn't see the station clock. Though the torch had been turned off Anna's features were just visible in the gloomy light as one of the men lit a cigarette. All children had something in common – that childhood innocence. She remembered Bernie asleep on her lap, the warmth of the soft little body had comforted her. Her memory went back to her own childhood. *Why did my Mam turn against me so violently? Why didn't we go to Cork to find the truth of the matter? But Cork had been a dangerous place in the nineteen twenties – not a friend to England. Perhaps, better to leave things alone. The family could have humiliated me in front of Bernie. It was right for our savings to be used on Bernie's school uniform and his games kit. I wish I knew where Bernie was.* Anna stirred and murmured the word, 'Pinny' with a smile, in her sleep. Margaret felt sleepy but held the rolled up newspaper in her hand, through the slightly open window. The other occupants of the carriage couldn't see her sudden tears, thank goodness. She was anxious not to miss the Williamses, so dried her face and peered out of the window into the dim light.

Suddenly the carriage door opened and David spoke through the murkiness. His whispered greeting dispelled her apprehension. The youngster gave a nervous laugh as he said quietly, 'That was scary. The crowd grew on the other platform and we thought we were going to be knocked over or miss the train, but here we are. How's Anna? Mum was pleased that she was with you.'

His mother was breathless as she heaved two large cases into the compartment behind him. 'The Luggage Van is so full that we'll have to have these two with us, I am sorry.' The torch-owner had lit the carriage and insisted on putting the luggage on the rack as the 'All Clear' sounded. The lights immediately came on in the carriage and the train began to move.

11

Cae Coch

There was not enough room in the carriage for comfort. They were not sitting next to each other so they couldn't talk but Margaret was near to the window and could look out into the gloomy darkness and imagine what the scenery was like in daylight. Shropshire was reputed to be flat but she longed to see fields, hedges and trees. County Cork had been less orderly she had been told, but perhaps farming had progressed since she had lived in Ireland, maybe at last it had moved into the twentieth century. The smell of the smoke from the engine mixed with the fresh winter air, rushing through the partly shut window was exhilarating and she felt excited at the prospect of being in the country. No air raids, no trams and mud replacing grime. Yes, she thought she had made a good decision to go back to the land. There was a secret pride in having made her decision. Throughout her marriage Patrick had decided things, not always wisely, never promptly, and often her views had been ignored.

After several stops Mary, Margaret and the two children had the carriage to themselves and they were able to converse. Mary asked how Anna had been.

'She's sleeping like an angel now; but at first she was distressed and cried because the lights went out as soon as we got into the carriage.'

'She's frightened of the dark.' Anna's mother gazed anxiously at her daughter.

'I soon made her comfortable,' Margaret said unconvincingly. 'When she went to sleep, she murmured the word "Pinny" and smiled several times. What or who is Pinny?'

Both mother and son laughed.

'When she came home after that terrifying air raid she couldn't remember your name and assured us that you were called "Mrs. Pinny".' Margaret was puzzled for a second and then her mind went back to the ghastly raid and she joined in the laughter, which of course woke Anna. 'I remember now. I think I like the name. I was washing-up when the siren went, couldn't find Gladstone anywhere and ran to the shelter in my haste, throwing my coat on over my pinafore, grabbing a precious blanket from the washing line and my bag as I went.'

*

'We're here!' shouted David. 'There's Grandpa, standing under the light.' Margaret and Mary had both been dozing, but Anna was wide awake and pulling Gladstone's box from under the carriage seat.

Soon, they were all on the platform with the suitcases stacked around them and Margaret was being introduced to Mr. Morgan. He was tall, dark, slightly bald with a fine bone structure and neat moustache; slim and younger than she had expected. His firm hand-shake was matched with a broad smile, reminding her of a comment a schoolmaster had made about her son's 'open face'. Margaret told herself that this man was to be her employer, but the prospect was not daunting.

There was a hired car outside the station with a driver. Mr. Morgan sat in the front seat with Anna on his knee, whilst the driver, Pete, helped the two women and David into the back of the car with Gladstone. Pete explained that he would collect the luggage when he made a further journey to the station to fetch two servicemen from a later train.

David was keen to tell his grandfather about the luggage being searched and the man in charge of the baggage office suspecting that the vase brought to Wales for safe-keeping was a bomb.

'The man said it was German and was annoyed when I insisted it was Egyptian with an engraving of Tutankhamen on it. Luckily he was alright when Mum pointed out that it was wrapped in a copy of *The Times*.'

'Please let Gladstone meet Grandpa?' begged Anna as the car sped along the country road. Mr. Morgan quietened her by telling her of the arrangements that had been made for Gladstone's comfort in the woodshed of the farm. 'I think Mrs. Rooney should take him to his quarters in his box; there is a saucer of milk, water and a bowl of fish waiting there for him. He'll remember that he slept in that box in Liverpool and it'll feel like home to him.' Anna accepted the explanation as the car wound its way up a rough track towards the stone farmhouse – *Cae Coch*. Hurricane lamps hung either side of the door, giving a warm glow of welcome.

The four adults went into the house whilst the children disappeared, with a hurricane lamp, to investigate the familiar out-buildings, their occupants and the changes which had taken place since their last visit.

*

Mrs. Morgan took Margaret's hand, as if she was shaking the vicar's hand after Sunday church but her words were welcoming. 'I hope you'll be comfortable at Cae Coch. Mary, please will you do the honour of showing Mrs. Rooney and Gladstone round the farm whilst I make the tea. You'll need to light another hurricane lamp. The farmyard is a little muddy, be careful where you walk. . . I hear the sound of an impatient cat.' The last few words were said with a smile. 'You know he is to be in the woodshed until he gets used to the farm. Use this knob of butter and butter his paws.'

The two younger women grinned at each other. The one, tall, red haired, fair skinned with broad shoulders and grey green eyes, the other slightly built with dark hair and blue eyes – Welsh-looking but having no accent. Both had ready smiles. Despite their physical and social differences, Margaret felt that there was an affinity between them. Mary whispered, 'Did you feel you were a pupil again? Mother was headmistress at the local school. She can seem a little stiff even to me but you see the famous Gladstone touched her stout heart.'

'She doesn't seem to be the typical farmer's wife. You are small like your mother but she is fair whilst your father is dark. You are fine-boned like him, don't you think? Does your mother milk the cows and help with harvest?'

'Yes, people say I favour my father. My brother was fair and handsome like Mother. The answer to your second question is *no*.'

'Your mother doesn't help on the farm then?'

'Since she moved here mother has looked after the dairy, made butter and cheese and cared for the hens. You remember it was my brother who was destined to be the farmer, but that wasn't to be. Dad took over things totally when his own brother died several years ago. He insisted that he continued to be a free-lance journalist, so they've always had hired help. Even so, Dad takes the animals to market and is in charge of the accounts.'

'Why did they have to advertise for someone so urgently?'

'Recently, the man who did most of the work with the cattle, and the other stock decided he wanted to join up, so things got out of hand. Evan Lloyd wasn't called up but felt being a soldier was his patriotic duty. I think he wanted to get away from Mrs. Lloyd. Before his marriage he lived in the loft above the dairy - which is to be your domain. I hope you will like it.'

Margaret laughed but decided that she mustn't ask too many questions. After all she was going to live and work here. 'The dairy must be a great deal of work for your mother, isn't it?'

'It is but she takes pride in it and gives talks to local Women's Institutes on occasion. Here's the wood shed. Poor Gladstone, go on, jump out of your Bovril box at last.'

Gladstone sniffed, climbed out of the box with a dignified air, stretched languidly as if he travelled by taxi, train and hire car regularly, but now his journey was at an end. The two women giggled as they smeared the butter on the cat's front paws. He walked to the water, first, ignoring his greasy fur and lapped thirstily, but smelling the fish he turned to it with purpose. 'He'll be fine,' said Margaret. 'Let's leave him to it. He'll be asleep in his box in no time.'

*

Tea was in the large farmhouse kitchen and Margaret was immediately reminded of her childhood: it smelt of hard work and cooking. This farm was clearly much more prosperous than her parents' small-holding in Cork. Mr. Morgan explained to her that he had put a doorway into the dairy from a lobby out of the scullery and managed to fit a bathroom there, too. The kitchen range had a back boiler and so there was always hot water available. He went on to say that the farm had a good supply of water from a copious underground stream running under the mountain behind Cae Coch.

'I've been fortunate to earn a modest income from journalism and Mrs. Morgan's been Headmistress of the local elementary school until recently. As a result we've been able to invest in Cae Coch, since my brother died. What d'you think of your quarters? Let us know if there is any problem. Evan was happy there until he married and rented a cottage.'

Mary interrupted, 'I haven't shown Mrs. Rooney her room yet, Dad. We were busy settling Gladstone, wiping shoes and washing hands for tea. She's seen the bathroom - your pride and joy.' She sounded nervous and Margaret was surprised to hear her use her surname.

Everything on the table seemed to be homemade. Margaret had never tasted welsh cakes, which were warm and their spicy smell lingered over the table. David spoke excitedly to his grandmother about their journey and the unexpected air raid at Shrewsbury, but broke off when he caught his mother's eye – he was talking with his mouth full! His grandfather took up the tale which he'd heard in the car on the way from the station and finished by saying, 'We're expecting another guest from the Cardiff direction, when your luggage comes. Good gracious! It'll be here in the next five minutes.' As he spoke the engine of a car could be heard outside. Mr. Morgan left the table went out of the door and returned to the amazed party in the kitchen, followed by a big man in naval uniform, with Pete carrying a kitbag and suitcase, trailing behind.

'Mrs. Rooney, allow me to introduce you to our mystery guest.'

'Patrick,' she gasped.

12

Patrick

'Well, aren't you pleased to see your husband?'
'Of course I am,' she murmured, after he had assured her that his sudden arrival was not connected to any bad news about Bernie. They were alone in the parlour of the farmhouse. Patrick put his arms, tightly, round Margaret's neck and seemed unaware of her resistance.

'What's the matter, Old Girl?' He gripped his wife more firmly.

Margaret mumbled, 'Nothing,' thinking it was strange that despite the fact that they had been married for twenty years, he had forgotten how she hated having anyone touch her neck. Footsteps from the kitchen made them both sit down, as Mary Williams opened the door, shouting, 'Hullo!' She came in with a tray laden with food and cups of tea for the new arrival at Cae Coch.

'You'll be safe in here for a while. Please forgive Dad; he loves giving surprises. At least this one turned out to be pleasant.'

Margaret had been grateful for Mary's self-possession, when the introductions had been made ten minutes previously. She, like Margaret, seemed taken aback at the sudden appearance of Patrick. *What was the connection between Mr. Morgan and Patrick? Which of them had got in touch with the other?* Fortunately the Tilley lamp on the kitchen table had shone downwards and Margaret felt that her expression of alarm and disbelief had been in shadow as she jumped to her feet in embarrassment rather than pleasure. Mary had guessed who the stranger was and sensed the discomfort of the woman sitting next to her. She had diverted attention from Margaret by asking the questions which were on the lips of all in the room save Mr. and Mrs. Morgan.

How had Mr. Rooney known that his wife had moved to the farm? How had he been able to make the journey to Wales from his base? Mary had demanded. Margaret had felt ill at ease. Mary went on to suggest that the Rooneys were made comfortable in the parlour whilst more tea was made for Mr. Rooney. Mrs. Morgan looked perplexed at her daughter's outburst.

'Yes, go into the parlour and my daughter will bring you some tea,' she had said, but Margaret thought her tone seemed cold.

*

'Well I'd better go and make my peace with mother. I must remember that I'm only the daughter of the house.' Mary said with a rueful smile as she closed the door behind her.'

Left, on their own again, Margaret said, 'How did you come to know that I was here? I've only been here a few hours. Your appearance was a shock.'

Patrick seemed unsure of himself. 'I believe that Mr. Morgan's a journalist on the local rag in the town here. His editor has a friend in high places, the War Ministry, I think, and the pal was able to contact my unit.'

'Is that in order? I didn't know exactly where your unit was.'

'It's a bit *hush hush,* but the message got through and I was given compassionate leave.'

'And. . ?'

'I phoned Mr. Morgan this morning and he said I was welcome here. I thought you'd be pleased.'

'Strange, that the Morgans didn't mention that you'd been in touch.'

'I asked them to let it be a surprise.' His expression was like Bernie's as a child and Margaret felt that she should show pleasure but she found it difficult.

She wanted to ask, *why now? Why not when you heard that the house had been bombed?* Instead, she asked, 'Did you think I was running away, back to my roots, to hew wood and draw water?'

'Maggie, don't forget you're my wife!'

She changed the subject. 'We can't see round the farm - it's too dark, but we can unpack our suitcases now the luggage is here. I haven't seen my room yet, I mean, our room, I should say. I was waiting for my cases, and then you appeared out of thin air.' She picked up the tray and collided with David in the doorway, who asked whether he could help with her cases and Patrick's kitbag.

'I have the key of your loft room. Grandpa keeps it locked when it's not in use. This way. The bed's made up, Granny says, but if there's anything you need, please tell me and my mother will sort things out.'

Both Margaret and Patrick were delighted with the quaint room, which was spacious, warm and private.

After excusing themselves to the family and bidding them, 'goodnight', they found they had access to the bathroom from a second door opening from the yard. They prepared for the night, then fell into bed, exhausted, all tension disappeared.

*

Margaret felt excited as she woke to the sound of a cock crowing and the bellows of cattle. For a moment she was back in Cork and there was no war. Soon, her daily anxieties came to mind: *why haven't I had any news from Bernie? Has he received the farm address? Does Patrick yearn for news of his son?* Perhaps he does but when they had discussed Bernie as they were trying to get to sleep, Patrick had said, 'Bernie'll be fine, he's a chip off the old block.'

Recalling those words, Margaret was not easy in her mind.

Hadn't Bernie been encouraged by his father to be adventurous? Would he take risks and be a danger to himself? Patrick had been a good father, in many ways. He'd taught Bernie to swim, to fish and to be a devout Catholic, but it was she who had encouraged him to read and study. The Jesuit school where Bernie was a scholarship pupil gave him glowing reports and he had already attained his Higher School Certificate before he joined the navy. He could have gone to university, but he wanted to do his duty and follow his father into the 'senior' service. Patrick had been in the navy as a young man in the 1914-1918 war and had told tales of the Battle of Jutland.

She dressed quickly and went down into the farmyard. The two Morgan grandchildren were there with a hurricane lamp as it wasn't light yet.

'May we visit Gladstone, please?' Margaret thought how odd the word *visit* sounded, but nodded enthusiastically. Between them they opened the door of the shed carefully, in case Gladstone tried to escape, but that precaution was unnecessary. All three of them laughed as they entered the woodshed to the accompaniment of a happy cat's purring. He rubbed himself against each one of them, his tail carried high, as he blinked at the strange light of the lamp. All the dishes were licked clean and Anna and Margaret felt his box which was still warm from his sleeping body.

13

A Wartime Christmas

It all seemed a dream as Margaret stood on the platform with Patrick, Mary and Rhys. The two men were going to travel a short way together, then change on to different trains at Shrewsbury. They had had two and three days, respectively, at the farm, which seemed to have passed quickly.

After the farewells the two women returned to the town in the hire car and walked along the river back to the farm. They agreed that it had been a good Christmas. Mary said it would have been perfect had Bernie been there, adding that his Christmas card - which contained a letter - was a testament to his continuing safety.

'For how long?' replied Margaret; her tone of voice was sad. Mary took her new friend's arm as she added her own fears about the future.

'Where will we be next Christmas? Will we be a vanquished nation? A year ago did we anticipate that Dunkirk would be evacuated?'

Margaret was uncomfortable. She felt a need to apologise for her husband's drunkenness of the evening before.

'I hear what you say but why does this terrible war have to bring out the worst in us?'

'What do you mean?'

'The whole family must have heard Patrick and Gwyn singing their way back from *The Wye*.'

'Remember that Mother sleeps at the back of the house. She's the only member of the family who might mind a Christmas carol at midnight. She didn't say anything. Rhys came back early because he'd promised the children to perform his bedtime ritual – a couple of silly Welsh songs. Oh. . . I'm sorry I didn't. . .'

Mary seemed to sense that her companion was thinking of childhood bedtime with her own son.

'No, I wasn't remembering Bernie. I was considering Patrick's irresponsibility. He and your husband cycled into town and when

Rhys came back on one of the bikes, the other two should have walked back not both ridden on the remaining bike.'

Mary laughed and quickly changed the subject. 'Patrick's account of his part in the brilliant organisation at Dunkirk is something I will hold in my memory and surely that courage must be an excuse for the occasional overindulgence and resulting irresponsibility at the local pub.'

'You're very generous, but will your parents look kindly on Patrick's drunkenness - for that's what it is - when he brings disrepute on the Morgan name? Your mother looked surprised when Rhys said that they were going into the town last night.'

'Dad will excuse it and Mother is more indulgent of the male of the species than the female. Your Patrick's manly confidence and rugged looks will charm her. Does Bernie take after his father? Has he that dark curly hair and those twinkling blue eyes?'

'No, he's fair, sandy, my height, not as tall or as broad as Patrick, and yes he has clear blue eyes. Bernie appears to be very serious, his features are classic, but he is quick to smile and has an infectious laugh. He's too young to drink in pubs, but I suppose the navy will change all that.'

'My brother was fond of joining Gwyn at 'The Wye', though they were both under-age drinkers. They must have charmed the landlord. Mother seems to see Gwyn through rose coloured spectacles. What do you think of our neighbour?'

Margaret felt uneasy but said evenly, 'I haven't seen much of him to have any opinion yet. I haven't met his wife.' Her mind cast back to Christmas Day, when Gwyn had brought several beautifully knitted gifts for the family including her. She had wondered why Nancy, who had worked the garments, had not been with him.

'Nancy's very shy and I don't know her well but she was taught by Mother, who seems fond of her. She hasn't managed to carry any of her babies to full-term, which is sad. I see the same sort of sadness in the slums of Liverpool in my medical work and of course there's a great deal of T.B., another killer, there. I often think Rhys is fortunate to work at the University. He's immunised from the wretchedness of poverty. Working with students must be motivating, don't you agree?'

'Yes. He's involved in research into embryology, isn't he?'

'He was. Now, it's getting as many doctors trained for the RAMC and other medical positions within the war. Dad said Patrick's account of the Battle of Britain was gripping. You were reading to Anna at that point in the conversation. We were all kept in the dark about the imminence of German invasion, weren't we? We thought the warnings were government propaganda.'

'In the last letter I had from Bernie before our house was destroyed, he described the occasion when his ship had picked up a German pilot, well off course, with horrific burns. Bernie seemed more interested in the poor man's medical treatment than the possible German threat. Do the authorities interrogate these injured men?'

'I wonder. We don't really know how much information the troops receive about prisoners and the progress of the war. It's good to think that your Bernie is so enthusiastic about his medical talents. Will he go into the medical profession when the war's over?'

Margaret's answer was an incoherent mumble. She wanted to shout, 'Stop this mad war, God! Don't let any more blood be shed.' The river, beside which they were walking, had a strange effect on her, half calming but half stirring chilling memories of her youth. What was the use? Everyone felt the same but pretended that *all would be well*. They sat down on an old rustic seat by the Wye; the only sound was the flow of the water. They were quiet.

'To-morrow, I have the worst task of all. I have to tell Anna that she's not coming back home with me. Will Fatty, Gretel and Gladstone be sufficient compensation for being without her parents? I think not. Maggie, I feel so dreadful, as though I'm abandoning her. You will write and tell me how she is. Please. I mean how she really is, won't you?'

14

Anna

After a little more than a week at Cae Coch, Margaret was put in sole charge of the cows: their mucking out, milking and feeding. The hire car had come whilst she was doing the milking and Mr. and Mrs. Morgan were in the vehicle as it drove away to the railway station with Mary and a defiant Anna. Margaret had a strange feeling of isolation; her life had changed profoundly in a week. She had been able to talk to Mary, a younger woman and she felt an affinity growing between them, but now Anna's mother had gone back to Liverpool, leaving her younger child to live on the farm with her grandparents. David was already at his boarding school. Alone at Cae Coch she made herself concentrate on the milking but her mind seemed to stray to the little girl of whom she'd become so fond in such a short time. To be busy in the dairy was the best plan when the Morgans returned with Anna. Anna might rush to her for comfort. That wouldn't do.

How would the little girl accept the separation from her mother? How will I be able to keep my promise to Mary? Margaret wondered how her Bernie would have reacted to her leaving him when he was six. Many children had had to accept evacuation; some had already only one remaining parent to relate to. As she strained the milk into the churns, and put her bovine charges into their field she pondered the fate of the two families of Morgan and Rooney whose futures seemed now to be connected. *Is my impetuous move to Wales going to be a disaster?* It was the first decision she had made for herself in her life. Patrick's being drunk the other evening still haunted her. It had to be forgotten. The absence of air raids was bliss, but she knew that somewhere the terror of war continued.

The dairy needed a little attention. Mrs. Morgan was a neat and competent woman, a good person to work with. Butter-making, with a hand churn was hard but satisfying. The two women enjoyed the work. There was always a basket packed with small parcels of butter for the grocer at the market each Friday.

She was washing the slate slab in the dairy when Mr. Morgan appeared unexpectedly. Margaret had never seen him there before and he startled her.

'I'm sorry, you didn't hear me coming,' he said, 'my wife's trying to comfort Anna but it's not easy. I thought she might find the bicycle a distraction. I didn't want to get it out of the hay shed without you knowing. I might have made a noise if I knocked bales all over the place.'

'I've just finished in here. I'll help reclaim the bike from the hay.'

Mr. Morgan wheeled the steed to the back door of the house and rang the bicycle's bell. Out ran Anna, her tear stained face beaming with pleasure.

'But it's too big for me to ride,' the child cried.

'Not a bit of it. I'll fetch a spanner and put the seat down. Then, Mrs. Rooney will go one side and I'll go on the other down the lane. By dinner time you'll be able to ride it.'

'Is it mine? I saw it at Megan's house, after church on Christmas Day. Is she letting me borrow it, really?'

'No,' said her grandmother. 'It's your bicycle. Megan's big enough to ride her mother's bike now and she asked whether you could have this one.'

Margaret had not met Megan but remembered that Anna had seen her in the town. *Was she the daughter of the doctor? Had Mary or Rhys Williams known him at school or Medical School?* She searched her mind to remember the friendships and ties of the family she now seemed to be part of. It was a bit like Ireland, but there it was the Church which bound her family, neighbours and friends together. They'd had little dealings with doctors; the rural community in Ireland had to be healthy, but she had disgraced herself by being ill.

There was a short delay while Mr. Morgan found a spanner in his tool box and lowered the bike's saddle. As they ran beside Anna down the rough lane, Margaret was surprised to notice how fit her employer was despite his age. *How old was he? He seemed younger than his wife – how strange!*

'Look ahead, not at the front wheel, keep pedalling!' The bicycle wobbled and Anna nearly fell as both the supporters let go at once. The little girl managed to stop with one foot dragging along the lane. She didn't cry.

'Try again!' It took an hour of gentle persuasion and then suddenly both the helpers let go of the bike and it whizzed past them with a very happy girl riding it.

After dinner Anna went for a short ride with her grandmother and at teatime she remembered her mother for the first time since the bicycle had appeared, only to say, 'I wish Mummy could see me ride.' Bedtime made her a little sad but her special poem read to her by the light of an oil lamp soon found her asleep, embracing Fatty with Gretel as a member of the audience.

Patrick, in his 'Thank you letter for Christmas at Cae Coch', had pleased all by enclosing a poem written by one of his sailor colleagues who had been a journalist in civilian life. This lad had been amused by Patrick's description of Anna's homemade patch-work rabbit, Fatty. He had immortalised Fatty on the page:

FATTY
'Fatty is a cuddly bunny.
'His tummy is big and his face is funny.
'He hasn't got a mouth you see,
'So how on earth does he drink his tea?

'Perhaps they pour it up his nose,
'And let it run down to his toes,
'Or else they pour it in his ear,
'But then poor Fatty couldn't hear.

'He doesn't seem to need to eat
'He doesn't like coffee, he doesn't like meat,
'But never mind it doesn't matter,
'Cuddly bunny gets fatter and fatter.' *

Anna had commented that, 'Uncle Patrick should know that bunnies don't drink tea,' but her smile lit up her whole face as she hugged the mouth-less wonder.

*A poem written by Patrick Adamson Press for Gaby Grain

15

Nancy

Since her arrival at Cae Coch, Margaret, sometimes with Anna's mother's help, had put Gladstone in the woodshed each night and the cat's bedtime had allowed his owner and Mary a few minutes of almost clandestine conversation together as the evening ritual was played out. Mary had foreseen that Margaret would be short of other women's company and had suggested that perhaps Gwyn's wife might like to be acquainted with her.

'You said you didn't know her well?' asked Margaret.

'No, I don't. She was a pupil of Mother's and she's a very accomplished needlewoman and knitter. Gwyn says she's shy. Mother wants to start a knitting group to help the servicemen at the front and Nancy would be a useful member of the group.'

Next day, Mrs. Morgan was taking Anna to the school to see the Headmistress and Mr. Morgan and Gwyn were going into town to buy drenches and feeding bottles in preparation for lambing.

After dinner, Margaret decided to call on Nancy as afternoons were the least busy time of day. She walked the half mile to the neighbouring farm and knocked gently on the shabby back door. As the door opened a shaft of light fell across the woman who must be Nancy and Margaret saw a frightened face which seemed to have a mark across the left cheek. The woman stepped back and Margaret explained who she was and how pleased she was to meet her new neighbour. 'You must be Nancy. I'm Margaret but my friends call me Maggie.'

'Do come in,' the younger woman said hesitantly, as she pushed her cardigan collar against her cheek. The kitchen was dark and, once inside, Nancy's face was out of the light from the small window. Margaret wondered whether she had been right to imagine a bruise. Was it a mark left by coal dust? There was a large coal scuttle next to the old fashioned kitchen grate. Nancy must have been embarrassed that the mirror near the door showed the large smudge on her face.

'I do my needlework in the front room where the light is better but we'll have a cup of tea here, if you don't mind, because it's warmer. I've had trouble all day with the fire. The chimney needs sweeping, I've asked Gwyn to sweep it but he's been too busy. It seems alright now and the kettle's boiling. How is Anna bach?'

Both women were concerned about the child who had been separated from her parents. Nancy knew of Anna from babyhood, when she'd made the Morgan grandchild a layette, which Mary had spoken of with pride. It seemed strange that Mary had never met her. Nancy explained that she had not long been married to Gwyn and they used to live in the town. She didn't go out much, she told Margaret because of poor health and her sewing, adding nervously, 'Gwyn is particular about meal times. You know he was a great friend of Owen Morgan, Cae Coch'. Margaret thought to herself as he was much older than his wife, shouldn't he be more 'particular' about bedtime and about his wife's welfare, in general? When the invitation to the knitting group was extended, Nancy looked pleased, almost excited, but said, 'I'll ask Gwyn whether I can. He likes Mrs. Morgan.' As they said, 'Goodbye,' Nancy's face was again in shadow but Margaret was sure that there was a mark not a smudge there and Nancy's hair was worn over the forehead in an odd way.

As she started the evening milking, Margaret's thoughts were critical of Gwyn. She decided to ask Mrs. Morgan to write a note to Nancy, to confirm the invitation, to give to Gwyn when he called in next day. Mrs. Morgan would be able to explain the 'war effort' to Gwyn Jones in terms that he would understand, after all 'he could do no wrong in her eyes'.

Margaret continued her musing about the only close neighbours to Cae Coch. Gwyn and Nancy lived so close to the Morgans, but were in very different circumstances. The Joneses seemed not to have a bathroom or inside sanitation. They had no children to support but Nancy had confided her three miscarriages to Margaret. Neither had mentioned the evening of celebration at 'The Wye'. Gwyn must earn a wage from Mr. Morgan for looking after the Cae Coch flock, on the mountain with his own sheep. Soon the whole flock would be brought down from the mountain for lambing, and the healthy lambs would fetch a good price at market. Gwyn had milked the herd at Cae Coch when Mr. Morgan had no farm help and would have received a good wage. Did he resent her taking over the milking? Nancy's handiwork was faultless and sought after so that would bring in some money and yet the couple seemed to be poorly clad and without the joy of being alive which was the hallmark of the Morgan household. The Joneses' basic existence reminded Margaret of so many Irish farms; but there the poverty was due to large families. Here there were no children to eat the profits from the land but even so these two wore an air of defeat. Did they long for children or was it Gwyn's love of drink? Margaret decided to turn her thoughts to Anna. How wonderful it was to read either to the little girl or to herself without the ever present fear of an air raid siren. Yes, she was glad she was in Wales. When at leisure, she took out her writing things to write to Patrick and Bernie. *I must concentrate, as I need to reacquaint myself with Pooh Bear and the Hundred Acre Wood before bedtime, when Anna might ask a profound question about the story which A.A. Milne would be better equipped to answer.*

16

Knitting

'Sit on the stool in front of me, Anna bach, and I'll show you how to knit,' said Nancy. Her unaccustomed confidence surprised Margaret. It was Saturday afternoon which had been set aside for the 'Knit for Victory' sessions, and Mrs. Morgan had decided that Anna should be introduced to the war effort. Margaret saw the tears in the child's eyes. Anna had confided that she couldn't knit 'at all' and Margaret was trying to think of some excuse to escape the good work and take the little girl with her, but Nancy seemed enlivened by the company. Or was it Mrs. Morgan's pride in one of her pupil's artistic gifts? Nancy seemed almost self assured. Obediently, Anna sat on the stool, chose some blue wool and a pair of needles from the box and even smiled.

'First we need to cast on,' Anna looked amazed as the arms encircling her wound the wool round the needles which she held firmly in her little hands. Stitches appeared on the needle in Anna's left hand and she found herself counting, 'one, two. . .' Had Margaret heard properly, 'Twenty'?

'Can't I have more stitches?'

'Not yet, Anna, you must learn to knit plain and purl before that. Put your right needle into the first stitch. . . furl your wool round the needle. . . pull the wool through and push the stitch off the left needle, like this. And again. . . It seemed ages before the stitches were transferred on to the needle in Anna's right hand. A shout from Mr. Morgan in the yard alerted Margaret and she ran outside.

'Be sure to see that Anna doesn't hear the six o'clock news to-night. There's been a twelve hour raid on Bristol and Rachael's parents live in Bristol. Rachael is a school friend.' Margaret's mind reverted to its usual air raid preoccupation, her thoughts revolving around destructed homes, lack of water and fear. *Isn't Bristol a port?* Could either of her men folk be there in the ruined docks, injured or worse? There had been casualties, of that she was sure. It was all so biblical – *The Slaughter of the Innocents.* Returning to the kitchen, she saw that Mrs. Morgan had come down from her bedroom and was asking Anna to show her the knitting she'd done and 'could she start another row?' The child seemed to panic and suddenly needles and wool became a tangle of tears and dropped stitches.

'We must make a start, decide on sock patterns and plan how many pairs we can supply in a month,' Mrs. Morgan said stiffly.

There was quiet whilst Nancy restored the stitches to their rightful place on the needles and apologized to Anna's grandmother saying, 'Perhaps, Anna could practise with Mrs. Rooney at our house next time Gwyn has to be with Mr. Morgan and the sheep.' Mrs. Morgan replied by putting a drawing book and a pencil on the table and beckoning to Anna to copy some drawings of animals. The three adults continued to knit on in silence.

After a long pause, the women discussed their campaign for making socks, balaclavas and patchwork blankets for the troops. Mrs. Morgan outlined the objects of the 'Comfort' organization which had been started by her husband through the local paper for which he worked. So far, she said, there were twenty groups within the town and outlying farms. 'Mr. Morgan is pleased with the response locally and the editor has devoted the leading article in this week's paper to the success of the project.'

Margaret was an expert knitter and her work was praised by both her companions, but her mind continued to be full of Bristol. Had her last two letters reached her men folk? She'd told Patrick about a trip to the next town where she'd been able to go to confession and mass. Brecon was a garrison town and services in the Catholic Church were numerous, as there were often different regiments in training there. The Morgans were pleased that she attended church with them but felt that they should allow her to follow her own religion. Margaret thought that Patrick had made some comment about there not being a Catholic Church nearby, when he was at Cae Coch. He had a habit of saying the wrong thing. For her part she was happy to worship with the family, but if he knew her true feelings, Patrick would consider she was becoming a 'lapsed Catholic'. That would never do.

These monthly outings were useful, for she was able to take a case full of completed garments to the 'Troops Comforts' headquarters and return to Cae Coch with more knitting wool. Seeing soldiers in the streets, near the Catholic Church, was a constant reminder to

Margaret of the war and her two men being part of it. The church visits did make her aware of her duty to her religion. She knew that to lapse from Catholicism would sadden Bernie; never had she missed saying her rosary at night time. Even so, the war had made her think that she was praying to the same God whichever church she attended. Weren't German mothers praying in the same vein as she? They were probably knitting socks and gloves as well.

On one of these days away from Cae Coch she noticed the offices of the weekly newspaper which Mr. Morgan worked for. The building was imposing and Margaret realized, as she peered into the window, that she worked in the household of a remarkable man. Apparently Dai Morgan had won a prize for a series of articles which he had written in 1938 about the history of farming in Wales. There he was smiling from a photograph receiving a certificate and medal from the Lord-Lieutenant of the county. No similar picture graced the walls of Cae Coch! Margaret smiled to herself, thinking that Wales was a pleasant country. It would be the best place to be if her family was there too and the war was over.

17

School

Anna continued to like school. Either Margaret or Mrs. Morgan took her there and brought her back to the farm in the afternoon. Sometimes they would cycle, other times they'd walk. The cycle ride by the road bridge was longer, but quicker, because the swing bridge was too difficult to negotiate with a bicycle. Mrs. Morgan's 'sit up and beg' bike's heaviness was an advantage when there was shopping to do. Margaret could use the large basket attached to the handle bars and the bicycle remained stable with the added weight.

One of the shops which Margaret went to on her way back from the town was the bakery. Davies' made prize-winning *bara brith*, which Mrs. Morgan liked to buy as a special treat for the family. As she walked into the shop Margaret heard a well-dressed woman, whom she'd seen in church say, 'Here comes the IRA.' Was she to run away or pretend she hadn't heard the insult? She realized that if she went back to the farm without the *bara brith*, she would have to explain what had happened in the bakery. She went to the counter whilst her detractor was paying for her bread and looked her in the face and said, 'Good Morning'. The woman chose to ignore her. Margaret hoped that the Morgans would decide to dispense with treats.

The grocer's shop was very different. Was it because Margaret had decided to do the shopping on the way back from the school, so Anna was with her? The very tall son of the proprietor always liked to joke with them. Margaret asked for split peas and he replied, 'You'll have to wait a few minutes because father's just splitting them.' Back at the farm the joke was explained to Anna, but her companion wondered whether this tall man had been teased at some time for being so lanky and having heard from town gossip of the insult to Margaret, had chosen to be especially well-mannered to her and her charge. *He knows the hurt that I experienced from a nasty tongue as an Irish woman in wartime Wales.*

The bakery incident was overheard by a new recruit to the church choir. She told the vicar. After church he took pains to introduce Margaret to the offensive woman who had made the IRA remark. 'This is Mrs. Rooney whose husband and son both serve the King in the Royal Navy.' This public exchange stopped any further insults or innuendos to be levelled at Margaret. Mr. Morgan was horrified when he heard about the nastiness and added a personal apology to Margaret, 'on behalf of all decent people.'

*

Anna didn't like her grandmother taking her to school. Margaret wondered why. The little girl didn't make any obvious complaint about her preference, but she confided to Margaret that Mrs. Morgan expected her to learn a short poem each day – a task which was almost impossible for Anna.

'I do try to get the words right but they often end up in a bit of a muddle. Rachael finds reading and learning by heart difficult as well.'

'Perhaps you should try practising with Gladstone. Pretend that he's a pupil and you're a teacher.'

'Do you think Gladstone likes poems?'

'Cats like music and often run down the keys of a piano, so I think poetry is something that they would enjoy as it has rhythm.'

This ruse proved to be effective. Anna would secrete the piece of paper with the poem written in Flo Morgan's neat script on it to the wood shed while Gladstone was having his morning milk. She read the words with great difficulty to start with but, in time, began to understand their meaning and cadence. Gladstone seemed to enjoy the experience.

I must be very careful not to undermine Mrs. Morgan's authority over Anna. I am only the employee, after all. How many children has Hitler caused to be living away from their parents, in how many countries?

18

The Messenger

It was February and the mornings were still dark. Margaret dressed quickly, forced her unruly red hair into its old-fashioned slide, tied her head-scarf and as she blew out the candle, took her torch from the dressing table drawer. Despite the difficulties of poor light and winter cold she enjoyed her time with the cows and the warmth of the milking parlour. There were four cows in milk, which were kept in at night, all Jerseys. After the couple of months she had been in Breconshire, Margaret felt that these beasts had become her friends. Lizzie had had an attack of mastitis, recently, so her udders were tender, but Susan, Kate and Jane were in good health and enjoyed being milked. To-day, however, Margaret was daunted at the prospect of bending over the cows. She felt stiff and had back ache. Perhaps she'd lost her belief in herself.

As she rinsed her hands and face under the kitchen tap, she sensed movement and thought she saw a faint light in the cow barn. Remembering the Home Guard officer ending his talk to the local W.I. with the words, 'Be vigilant at all times; there might be a German spy lurking, anywhere', there was need for caution. The emphasis on the last word had amused the cosy audience in the Church Hall, but Margaret felt wary as she entered the barn.

'Good morning.' It was the quiet Welsh voice of Mr. Morgan. She noticed that the hurricane lamps had been lit, the udders of the four cows had been washed and there was fresh hay in the mangers. 'I would have started milking but my rheumatism makes me slow and Lizzie seemed to need sympathetic handling.'

'Thank you, how kind,' Margaret mumbled as she sat down on the three-legged stool, with the galvanised bucket between her knees and her head against Lizzie's flank as she started to milk. 'Mrs. Morgan will be pleased. Lizzie's milk is suitable for the dairy at last. Your wife makes excellent butter.' He smiled. Margaret felt it necessary to mention Mrs. Morgan's expertise. Her gift of running the farmhouse and dairy had impressed Margaret, especially as Mrs. Morgan was not by birth a countrywoman. Mary had joked about 'Mother', saying she was a townswoman who'd married into the countryside. However, Margaret was never quite sure how Mrs. Morgan viewed her. She'd made an unnecessarily favourable remark about the abhorrent Black and Tans on one occasion but had smiled when she saw Margaret's nod as she quoted a line from 'Hamlet'. How thoughtful Mr. Morgan was to-day, or was he checking up on her? No, she was sure his actions were well-meant.

'Lizzie's the one who's had mastitis isn't she? She didn't like me touching her, but she has confidence in you. You've saved me a vet's bill. Where did you learn your old wives' remedies?'

'My parents' smallholding was rented and small. We had to do without a vet. My Mam had the 'Gift'. She knew all the traditions, curses and cures. She even treated other farmers' animals - even so she couldn't read.'

'D'you regret leaving Ireland?' The inevitable question rang in her ear, but her automatic reply rarely varied.

'I got married and left Ireland for England with my husband and enjoyed a bathroom for the first time in my life' she added with a smile. He left to feed the other stock; they seemed to like his beautiful tenor rendering of 'Cwm Rhondda'.

The repetitive rhythm of milking was reassuring. The mixture of smells, winter feed, cow dung and carbolic soap pleased her. Margaret thought of all the other jobs that were similar – scrubbing, polishing and checking equipment. Her thoughts were again with Bernie on board his ship. *Was he safe from the destruction of the sea and the war? What would he say if he saw her in these rural surroundings – the quiet, the farmyard odours, the overwhelming, sweet hay smell which she loved? Would he enjoy the pastoral beauty of Cae Coch?* He'd often suggested, when circumstances allowed, that they'd visit Cork, but there'd never been the money or the opportunity. She touched the only photo which she had of him in her pocket and imagined his perceptive but mischievous grin, chiding her for doubting his ability to defeat the Germans single handed.

When milking was finished the task of carrying the buckets seemed harder than usual. Perhaps the cows were gradually giving more milk. Untied, Lizzie and the others wandered towards the field near the house and trotted towards their friends when the gate was opened and the other cattle acknowledged them with welcoming stares.

Involuntarily, Margaret rubbed her back as she strained the milk into the churn in the dairy and made her way to the kitchen door. Self-consciously she straightened up. Mr. Morgan was behind her and asked whether she was doing too much, 'You're so willing, we forget. . .' They were both surprised by the approach of a telegraph boy cycling towards the house, his neat uniform incongruous in the muddy lane and farmyard. The farmer put out his hand, muttering, 'Another communiqué from the Ministry of Agriculture, I suppose . . .' His irritation turned to alarm as he read the name on the envelope, 'It's for you, Mrs. Rooney. I hope. . .'

With trembling hands Margaret snatched the yellow envelope from the boy, managing a feeble, 'sorry' remembering that he was only the messenger. She fumbled with the envelope as Mr. Morgan thrust a sixpence into the startled boy's outstretched hand. The opening words in capitals stuck on the fold of the official form were alarmingly clear in the light of Dai Morgan's hurricane lamp, 'THE ADMIRALTY REGRETS...' but she couldn't read on.

She dropped the awful message but Mr. Morgan picked the paper from the muddy step. He couldn't help seeing the three ominous words, as he handed her the telegram. Margaret managed a quiet 'Thank you' as she ran up the steps to her hayloft sanctuary, dreading to read the rest of the words.

19

The Message

She was in bed, soaking with sweat, glimpsing Dürer's 'Praying Hands' on the wall, as it had been in her childhood. The hands turned into claws, then fins. The claw-like hands seemed to swim in the river, a tributary of the River Lee, which became the sea, the waves sweeping along helpless youths, who had mangled and bloodied bodies. She dreaded opening her eyes in case the priest would be there, praying, or the blood-stained cap would be on the kitchen table.

Someone was touching her, speaking to her. It was not the unsympathetic voice of her Mam but a quiet Welsh voice. Margaret dared to open her eyes and thought that her companion could be Dr. Thomas. That was the doctor's name, she felt sure; he was a friend of some people called Williams or Morgan – Welsh names? She struggled to remember. A little girl, was her name Ann or Anna? For a moment her head cleared and she remembered that it was war time. Hadn't she moved to Wales to work on a farm where the people were called Morgan, and a boy on a bicycle had handed her a telegram in their farmyard.

She moved her head. Yes. The yellow envelope was there. It wasn't just a bad dream. The awful word, 'missing' was about Patrick not Bernie. What did it mean?

The man was talking to her again. He was asking her about the picture; telling her that a copy had been in his school chapel. Then, he put something into her mouth – a drink – no it was solid, but his action was gentle. It didn't frighten her. He said something about her temperature being 104 degrees. Was that good or bad? She made an effort to nod. She thought this man must be the doctor. He was trying to help her. If only she could be cool and dry and drink something. Each time he spoke she wanted to agree. He wasn't the priest. Thank God, the man wasn't praying. He seemed shadowy. His movements round the room in and out of the light from the window were fluid, like clouds crossing the sky on a sunny day. She wanted to tell him how thirsty she was and how unwell, but he disappeared. Instead, she collapsed back on to the pillows.

She awoke. Her mouth was dry still but recognizing her bedroom at Cae Coch, she remembered the telegram telling her that her husband, Patrick, was 'missing'. Was that this morning? Suddenly, Nancy was standing by her bed.

'I'm not well. I'm so thirsty and hot.'

'You've been delirious for over a day, cariad. Mrs. Morgan sent for Dr. Thomas. He's prescribed M&B tablets and aspirins to bring down your temperature. It was 104 degrees. He said it was shock.'

'I thought I saw him but everything was a haze.'

'Not surprising.'

'I must have lost a day. Have I?'

Nancy nodded. She was, like her sewing and knitting, dainty, in her late twenties and could have been attractive, but poor health had dogged her. She'd told Margaret about her several miscarriages. Always cheerful, even when exhausted by her hard life, she was full of sympathy and able to understand the needs of others, especially her husband Gwyn's selfish wants. She neglected herself, shamefully. Her gentle smile compensated for her untidy dark hair and rough skin. Soulful eyes and a generous mouth made her face pleasant.

When the patient was properly awake, Nancy was quick to change the sheets and produce a clean nightdress from the drawer for Margaret. Meanwhile the invalid sat on a stool by the bed and sipped a glass of water, having swallowed the doctor's tablets.

'Thank you, Nancy, I'm glad you were able to come down to Cae Coch, I'm being a nuisance. Could there be a mistake? Patrick wasn't at sea.'

'We thought it was your son. I understand now. Husbands are so precious,' was the strange reply.

Margaret didn't respond but wondered whether she'd have considered Gwyn 'precious' if he'd been her husband. She was about to say that she thought at first that the telegram concerned Bernie but stopped herself. Fatigue was overtaking her again. Her companion not noticing her hesitation, said, 'Gwyn and I will help out here until you're well. Don't fret about Anna bach, she'll be alright.

Mr. Morgan's put her in charge of feeding your cat. What's his name?'

'Glad. . . Gladstone, er. . . yes, good.' was the sleepy reply.

*

The doctor had paused at the kitchen door. He had to pass on bad news, but knew that as far as possible he must respect his patient's confidence. Mrs. Rooney's demeanour was worrying. 'Missing' didn't mean dead. There could be a second message which confirmed Rooney's death or otherwise. He should know more about the procedures of the War Office and Admiralty. He questioned what had brought on Mrs. Rooney's severe physical reaction, to the news – a delirium lasting twenty-four hours. He'd heard in the town that Mrs. Rooney was a tough Irish woman and a Roman Catholic!

She appeared to be someone who would grieve inwardly but would put a brave face on the possibility of widowhood. To have become hysterical and then delirious was out of character. Her temperature was very high and he wished he'd taken it again before he left the loft, but Nancy Jones was waiting to make his patient comfortable. The light had been poor because the window was small. Had he read the thermometer correctly? Yes, she'd been staring at that picture with rapt attention, as though she was demented when he roused her. Why?'

'Mr. Morgan, I'm concerned about Mrs. Rooney. It seems that yesterday's telegram was about her husband. He's missing. The shock has brought on delirium.'

'You're sure about the message being about her husband, not her son?'

'No it said Patrick Rooney, I read it and Mrs. Rooney confirmed it in a lucid moment.'

'Strange. As far as we know, Patrick's been working at a Naval Training School at Plymouth. That's what he told us at Christmas. I follow the 'News' and would have picked up on any recent air raid on Plymouth.'

'There is a son then?'

'Yes, he's a medical orderly, on active service, in training or at sea. I assumed the telegram was about him.'

'Tell me, Mr. Morgan, "missing" means what? That there is some uncertainty about the person, doesn't it?'

'Yes, that's right.'

'I know so little about service procedures. I wouldn't be breaking patient confidentiality by asking you how Mrs. Rooney took the news, initially?'

'She ran to her loft room. My wife asked Nancy to ask how she was in the afternoon. She was asleep, but obviously unwell.'

'That's when you rang the surgery. I should have come out last evening. I'm concerned.'

'Perhaps we should have shown alarm. I knew how one of those telegrams could affect you. We want to help Mrs. Rooney as best we can.'

'I've heard from your daughter that Mrs. Rooney was extremely competent. I know from gossip that she's Irish and a Roman Catholic.'

'Her nationality and religion is not relevant, surely, Doctor?'

'I'm thinking aloud. Sometimes gossip gives a doctor insight into a patient. Here it doesn't.'

'I understand. Yes, it may be significant that her house in Liverpool was bombed and that her two men are in the services.'

'Poor woman. Those details help. I must monitor her temperature. It is very high to-day. As I said a moment ago Nancy Jones was waiting to change the bed, so I might have read the thermometer incorrectly.'

'Oh!'

'No, I know from observation that her temperature was high and she was staring in a fixed manner at the picture, 'The Praying Hands' – odd! All reports suggest she's tough. I need to keep her under examination for the moment.'

'Thank you. We'd like that.'

'This war touches us all. Doesn't it? How are you and Mrs. Morgan finding things?'

'My wife has been relieved by having Mrs. Rooney to help. She's been invaluable, but seeing her with that telegram, brought back bad memories to Flo. The words 'OWEN MORGAN KILLED IN ACTION' jumped off the page in 1918 when our boy was taken.'

'I did think about that as I was driving here. I'm very sorry. My father reminded me the other day that you lost a son in France at the end of the last war.'

'My wife's been quite stoical since that time, but to-day I've seen a look of haunted memory in her bearing, but she can't speak to me about it.'

'That's understandable.' The doctor was taking pills from his bag and counting them into two bottles as he talked, noting down instructions about Margaret's treatment. 'I've given her the first two tablets.'

'Put them by there,' said Dai Morgan, indicating the dresser. As the doctor shook Mr. Morgan's hand in farewell, he warned him about his fears of some deep anxiety in his patient; she'd been through so much in a few months, adding that he could not disclose anything she confided in him. The older man looked grave but said that he understood, adding that he and his wife would co-operate with the doctor in all ways possible.

'I'll come by to-morrow, and possibly ask the District Nurse to pop in. This is the first casualty of the war I've treated. I feel a little guilty living out a world war in this peaceful part of the world.'

As Mr. Morgan took out his wallet, Dr. Thomas shook his head.

'No, there's no fee to pay. Let's pray for good news.'

20

Nurse Roberts

The medicines which Dr. Thomas prescribed had some initial effect, but in a couple of days, Margaret began to vomit, a complication which gave concern to the doctor. Nurse Roberts visited daily to check on the patient's temperature, comfort and recovery. She was conscientious and respected Margaret's courage in turning her hand back to farm work when she'd found herself homeless. The sickness was worrying, especially as it followed the delirium which had alarmed Dr. Thomas initially.

The loft hideaway had low beams, had Mrs. Rooney hit her head on something or fallen when she escaped to read the dreaded telegram? Had she some brain contusion? Margaret said that she had had no bump on the head. The nurse was puzzled. When, after two days of improvement, her patient was again rambling and delirious and the high temperature had returned, Nurse Roberts recalled Dr. Thomas' description of his first visit. He'd said, 'Mrs. Rooney was frightened. She was hallucinating about something – remembering some awful experience.'

Dilys Roberts was concerned. She must gain the confidence of Mrs. Rooney. They'd laughed yesterday about this being, only, the second time in her life that Margaret had been ill. She'd said, 'My sister Bridget nursed me then and she used to say 'Maggie, please don't die' and I'd reply, 'don't be so dramatic, I want to have a man and ten babies, don't let me go for a nun, Biddy'.' Was Bridget the key? As District Nurse, Dilys had always addressed patients, formally. 'But. . .'

She took Margaret's wet hand and whispered in her ear, 'Maggie, Maggie.'

An eye opened and a faint, 'Bridget?' could be heard.

'No, it's Nurse Roberts. You're in an awful dream, try and wake and tell me about it if you can.'

'Where am I? I feel so hot and wet. . . It must be the river. . . It was so beautiful. . . now it seems sinister. . . and frightening. . . I. . .'

'It would help if you tried to remember the thing that put you in a state of shock before. Try, Maggie. . . Mrs. Rooney. Try, please.'

Maggie stirred and tried to focus on Nurse Roberts' face. *I can see a blur. I must try to concentrate on her features and answer her. She's trying to help me.*

'It was the same awful dream. . . I saw terrible sights in the water. . . the sparkling water of the river. . . near my childhood home. . . suddenly. . . suddenly it became a hostile sea. Horrible. . . horrible! A man shouting as he fell on me. . . or was I screaming? Was it my fault?' Margaret was trying to make sense, but her account was disjointed. She trembled. . . seemed reluctant to continue.

Nurse Roberts prompted her patient. She asked tentatively, 'did something happen near the river by your home, something violent, when you were ill before?'

Margaret moved to get out of bed, giving the impression that the conversation had finished.

'If it is something which is very personal, it might help to unburden your memory. Is that hard?'

'I don't know. . . I can't. . . I don't want...'

'I'm not forcing you to disclose a confidence. Remember though, that doctors and nurses are bound by their professional honour to be discreet. Please?'

'I was. . . did. . .'

'It could explain these awful dreams and perhaps stop them; I've met it before in patients.' The nurse's tone was coaxing as she wiped Margaret's face with a flannel with deft but sympathetic hands.

'I'd been sitting in the dusk by the river. . . in Ireland, as I had done. . . so many times before...'

'When?'

Margaret was deep in rapt recollection, oblivious of the other.

'But my body seemed. . . I think. . . seemed to be soaking wet. Had I. . . had I fallen into the brook? - I can't remember...' Each sentence was hesitant, abstracted but Nurse Roberts was careful not to interrupt.

'There was the sound of gunfire. I'm sure. . . I. . . It was an exchange of fire. . . not just one person shooting. . . a rabbit for the pot . . . There were bright lights in the twilight. Probably lamps...'

'And?'

'I remember running. . . a man. . . taking hold of me. It was my Da. He said. . . he said, 'Don't look in the hollow. . . there's been an

. . . an accident'. He muttered 'British' under his breath. . . with an awful oath.'

'Then. . .' said the nurse quietly

'My brothers were carrying. . . it looked like. . . the body of a man . . . his clothing torn and covered in blood. . . I tried not to look. . . I couldn't. . . It was put in the outhouse. . . where we hung the slaughtered pigs.' Margaret shivered.

Continuing, she whispered, 'I stumbled. . . into the kitchen. My brothers. . . threw a blood-stained cap on to the table – it was Sean's cap. . . I recognized it. . . it was Sean's cap. I know. . . As she spoke the name she crossed herself.

'Margaret, I can hardly hear you.'

Margaret spoke slowly, 'I've turned it over. . . and over in my mind many times. . . It's so. . . so difficult. . .' Her hesitation was deliberate. She didn't want to share this memory.

'May I ask who Sean was, Mrs. Rooney?'

'He was everything, everyone and everywhere to me, it was our secret.' Her voice was choked, but defiant as she held back tears.

'Why secret?'

'He was the son of the. . . big land owner. . . my Da was a tenant of his father, who had a. . . a. . . British. . . British wife, Sean's mother. . . I read with Sean's. . . Sean's crippled sister. They paid. . . my Da. My family was. . . is active Republican.' Margaret's expression was questioning, but the nurse gestured that she understood.

Her tone lost its hesitance as she said, 'I think I've had this awful nightmare before. I was in it when Dr. Thomas came here.'

'Why were you wet?'

'I wasn't wet then, but the dream seems to recall what happened to me, later. It is a jumbled account. . . it's very confused. . . Being soaking wet with a high temperature. . . that was the following week, I think...'

'Go on.'

'I feel I must. . . must tell. . . someone what really happened. . . I've never. . . ever told anyone, but. . . but perhaps I should. . . now. It was so long ago. It might make me able to understand what. . . what has happened to Patrick. Sean's death led to my. . . my total humiliation. As a result I had to leave Cork. . . Cork and break. . . break from. . . from my family. . . forever.' Her resolution made her confidence return.

'I have to keep confidences or lose my job,' Nurse Roberts said.

'The family was there. . . I was part of it. I fell into a chair. . . in a corner of the kitchen. . . paralysed with grief. The men stood. . . caps in their hands. . . their heads bowed, with an air. . . an air. . . of reverence. Father Mark, our priest. . . my Mam's brother, knelt by the table. . . droning on, saying the prayers for the dead, but I was praying my own prayers. 'Please, God, don't let them find out. Don't let me be with child. Let me escape from fighting and these religious fanatics'.'

'And the following week?'

'I was found unconscious in the river; but. . . but couldn't remember. . . how I'd got there.'

'Who found you?'

'Bridget and her husband knew that I read by the stream in a small thicket. . . not far from our house. . . They knew about Sean too. It seems that my body was in the water, but my head had hit a rock and was cut. . . Look. . . look under my hair, you can see the scars. I was in a coma for some time. My Mam was so angry with me.' She said this as she exposed the back of her neck, as though she wanted to give some realism to the fantasy of her hallucination. There *was* a nasty scar.

'Why was she so angry?'

'Someone must have made mischief. It couldn't have been Bridget, we were very close.' Margaret said as she shook her head wearily. 'I don't suppose I'll ever know.'

While these confidences were being recalled, the nurse was gently undressing Margaret's soaking body and dabbing her tear-stained face, having put a fresh cotton sheet on the bed.

'Let's get you back to sleep. You'll be fine now you've got it all off your chest.'

Margaret looked relieved, but said. 'You won't tell the Morgans, will you? I need this job.'

'Of course I'll keep it to myself. Would it help though, if I told Dr. Thomas in outline, omitting any embarrassing detail?'

Margaret nodded, reaching to the basin by the bed. Was the daily vomiting going to continue? Suddenly, Nurse Roberts laughed.

'Do you think that you could be pregnant, now, Margaret, I mean, Mrs. Rooney?'

'I suppose. . . I. . . surely not. . . I'm too old, aren't I?' Margaret mumbled. She was exhausted.

At that moment they heard a gentle knock. 'How's the patient?' asked Mrs. Morgan as Nurse Roberts opened the door a crack. 'What do you need? Please take any linen from the airing cupboard in the bathroom. My husband and I insist that Mrs. Rooney is made as comfortable as possible.'

'Good news, she's much better I think. Yes, the best news, so far. She'll be up to-morrow. How's the knitting group?'

Mrs. Morgan said almost curtly, 'It's good.'

'I'll be singing on my way home that new song I told you I'd learnt at WI. I was too anxious to sing on my way here.'

'That is good news. Good night, Mrs. Rooney. Gwyn's doing the milking until you're well. Don't think of stirring until Nurse Roberts comes in the morning. You will come back in the morning, won't you, Nurse?'

Margaret heard nothing. She was in a dreamless sleep – a change from the last few days.

'I think, Mrs. Morgan, that, my patient has at last thrown off those hallucinations.'

'I hope and pray that you're right.'

21

Recovery

Margaret woke and looked out of her hayloft window. She could see the mountain and the sheep grazing there, which had been her daily delight since she came to live in Breconshire. It was early morning, the morning after her talk with Nurse Roberts. She felt weak but her head was clear, the delirium had passed. The light seemed to be fading. It must be a storm brewing. That was it. She felt disorientated as she saw cows strolling towards the cowshed. Had someone left the field gate open? She grabbed her mackintosh, seeing from the corner of her eye that the clock by her bed read that it was five minutes to five – it was afternoon milking time! She had slept through breakfast and dinner, now it was almost evening. Guilt seized her. Who had fetched Anna from school? Who was going to milk the cows? She dragged her breeches on under her raincoat and picked up her scarf from the floor and wound it round her head, tying it as she rushed down the steps of the loft. She must have slept in her jumper.

In the milking parlour Mr. Morgan was tying up the four cows.

'Good afternoon,' he said in the same tone he'd used each day for the last couple of months. He wore an expression of sadness almost of grief. Margaret tried to smile but a strangled sob escaped from her mouth instead of a greeting. She remembered that she'd been ill.

'I'm sorry I've let you down. It must have been the telegram. Thank you for sending for the doctor. Have I really been out of action for days?'

'Indeed you have. What are you doing here? It's good to see you up and about but Gwyn's been doing the milking. He'll be here in a minute. You should be in bed or at least taking things easily until you're totally fit,' the farmer said, leaving the cow and crossing the parlour to speak to Margaret.

She felt there was a slight admonishment in his tone. 'Dr. Thomas saw the telegram about your husband. My wife and I are very, very sorry. I am already making enquiries of the Admiralty about him, through my editor.'

'I'm not sure what the word missing means, do you?'

'Let's go into the house and have a cup of tea and talk about it?'

Margaret felt that she was in the company of strangers as she sat at the familiar kitchen table. She was aware that though she now felt calm, she had been on a terrible journey since the telegram had arrived – she had travelled through hostile waters, which had un-nerved her.

'Anna is having tea with her school friend Rachael. I will take the torch and fetch her soon,' said Mrs. Morgan.

Sipping her drink pensively, Margaret thought how the routine habits of life, dressing, washing, eating and drinking brought back normality to an unusual situation. She was thirsty and had normal appetites after all.

Mrs. Morgan spoke. 'I want to say something which I have given much thought to over these days while you've been ill, Mrs. Rooney.'

Margaret became alert. *Have I added, being an unfit human being, to already being a Roman Catholic in this woman's mind? Do the Morgans intend to terminate my employment on the farm?*

'When our son Owen was killed in the last war, I can't explain my shock, my disgust, my anger and my raw grief, when I read the telegram. I felt the same emotions when I saw that disagreeable telegram in your hands on Tuesday.'

Margaret murmured a 'Thank you.'

'Remember we're both women and we need to support each other through thick and thin.' As she said these words, she appeared as the kindly elementary school teacher that she must have been before her retirement.

Mr. Morgan wore an expression of utter surprise and Margaret noticed him spoon sugar into his tea, which he never had sweet-ened, as he added, 'Yes. This week the war has come to this farm, to this town and to this family. We must be resolute.'

Margaret felt astounded. Her muttered response of gratitude to such support was almost inaudible.

'The cows will agree. I'm sure. Come, Mrs. Rooney, you've drunk your tea, yes? Enjoy the fresh winter air and greet the animals who might have forgotten your tender care.' He smiled as he stood up. As she followed him to the door, Margaret felt a gentle motherly hand on her shoulder. She thought how her feeling of loneliness of half an hour ago had been replaced with a feeling of 'family'.

'Being with animals especially horses always gives me an optimistic feeling.' Dai said as they walked to the stable where the two horses were munching their hay.

'Yes. I know. The bigger the horse, the more gentle it seems. D'you think they understand our pain?'

'I'm sure they do. My wife may have forgotten this but this old fellow, Hywel Dda was a foal in 1918. Our son, Owen bred him from my father's mare, Blodwen. I always believe that he knows everything that goes on at Cae Coch.'

Margaret patted the large carthorse's neck as she agreed. He nuzzled her coat.

'You're right. Anna sneaked out here each morning to have a chat with him when she missed her mother so terribly.'

'Do the same, my dear. He knows.' There was a twinkle in Dai Morgan's eye as they turned back to the house.

How kind the Morgans are! When I was with Sean he used to say, 'The Leprechaun knows' in the same tone of voice.

22

Unexpected Visitors

Margaret was up and about, her pregnancy confirmed. All at Cae Coch were delighted, though the mother-to-be was anxious about how to manage her new situation. *If I'm widowed how am I going to bring up a child? What am I to tell Bernie about his father and now about myself?* Perhaps she'd not write until there was more news about Patrick.

Gwyn was milking daily in her absence, and was keen to continue. *Does he resent my employment at the farm?* This question went round and round in her mind.

It was Saturday and Anna was 'in charge' of the invalid, whilst her grandparents were collecting eggs and carrying out routine dairy duties. 'Be helpful to-day, Anna, I know you could wash the eggs and perhaps feed the chickens. Your grandparents look so tired. On Monday the district nurse says that I can start milking and feeding stock but until I'm fully better after my illness I mustn't do too much mucking out or carry the buckets of milk.'

Anna, who was practising her knitting, had just finished her second dish cloth. She was determined to knit bootees next and was eager to help all she could. Margaret recognized the child's delight at her recovery. She wondered whether the daily trips to school with Mrs. Morgan, instead of her, had been quite as much fun as hitherto. At that moment, the silence was broken - a car drove into the farmyard and out jumped David and his mother. Anna was ecstatic.

Mary explained, 'I was so concerned when Mother told me you were ill. As this is David's half-term week-end and he was due to stay at school, I decided that I'd catch the next train, and have a couple of days at Cae Coch with the children.'

'What about your practice?' Margaret indicated the kettle and tea caddy.

'A cup of tea made with Welsh water, heaven. There's an American post-graduate in Rhys's department nagging to get experience of British G.P. work, so he asked him to do a long week-end locum for me.'

'Will the patients mind?' The substitution seemed a little casual to Margaret, and she regretted asking the question as soon as she'd spoken.

'You're probably right, they will. I ask, will they understand a word he says and will he have difficulty with the Liverpool accent? Don't worry! He's the image of Clarke Gable so he'll certainly make them better.'

They laughed; after all he was a better bet than an air raid, thought Margaret, who wondered when she had found anything funny recently.

When the Morgans had come in and all had had some tea, Anna disappeared with her mother and grandfather leaving David to wash the eggs and the two women to prepare the mid-day meal. Then it became clear to all that Anna was showing her mother how she could ride a bike. Squeals and laughter were evidence of their mutual pleasure. When they came back into the house, Mary whispered to Margaret that she had been instructed by Anna to 'start knitting'!

*

Margaret and Mary decided to take a short stroll, in the late afternoon.

'Dad said we mustn't be long, because it'll soon be dark, but it's so lovely to be in the country, even though it's cold. The air is fresh. How are you? You're warm enough?'

'I'm fine. I've been itching to start my normal routine for a couple of days. It would help to be occupied.'

'I meant, how are you really? I'm so, so sorry about your awful news. I was going to write but the post is bad at the moment. I'm so glad I came. Anna is so upset. She did take to your husband at Christmas.'

'I thought when I received the wire that it concerned our Bernie. Then I couldn't understand why Patrick was missing, because he's not on active service. It's a mystery, but a baffling one.'

'I think I understand.'

'It was a terrible shock. I'm gradually coming to terms with the uncertainty, I think. I just wish I knew what had happened. It's the not knowing the 'where? ; the 'how?'; or the 'why?'.'

'Dad said Mother was in an awful state to begin with. Your telegram reminded her of the one they received about Owen in the last war. Until today, I've never seen her being so compassionate.'

'Perhaps my predicament has opened up a door which has been closed for years.'

'Your illness frightened her, I think. You appear so strong.'

'I was so distraught at first that I thought I was going mad. The shock of the news brought on a delirium, is that usual?'

'The brain is a part of us which is not yet fully understood medically. It seems that a fearsome event can bring a flashback from our deep subconscious.' Mary's tone was one of a professional speaking to a patient. It gave Margaret confidence to continue the account of her illness.

'In my delirium I felt I was back in County Cork at seventeen.'

'Why?'

'Then, I had. . . had a terrible experience. It was a week after the shooting of my first love. . . my Sean...'

'Oh yes! You've told me all about Sean. His being shot was bad enough. What dreadful thing happened after his death?'

'It was. . . was. . . unreal. . . awful. . . terrifying.' Margaret's demeanour had changed, she started to shake and Mary took her arm, murmuring soothing words. The two women walked on in silence.

'I can't think about it. . . it's too. . . too horrible.'

The doctor quickly changed the subject and after a few moments Margaret stopped trembling.

'You said you were delirious then, d'you know why?' Her matter of fact tone calmed Margaret, who continued to relate the memory of her previous illness, with a little more coherence, thinking to herself that Mary had a very good 'bedside manner'.

'Yes. I was found. . . in the river near. . . near our place, un. . . unconscious, half in the water with. . . with my neck bleeding from. . . from slipping and. . . and hitting a rock or that's. . . that's what my sister thought.'

'Did she find you?'

'Yes, she and her husband. . . carried. . . carried me home. They said. . . said I was rambling. Bridget looked after me. . . nursed me...'till I was better. I had. . . had developed pneumonia. . . it was hard for Bridget. Mam left the nursing to Bridget. . . alone. Mam . . .didn't. . . couldn't. . . understand. . . she was angry with me.'

'Why angry?'

'I talked to Bridget. . . but. . . but she said. . . I must. . . must. . . forget the whole. . . awful Sean experience.'

'And?'

'Bridget's words, 'forget it, put it out of your mind', repeated themselves over. . . and over again.'

'Then?'

'Then, I came round. . . to see...'The Praying Hands'. The Dürer. It'd been a. . . a First Communion gift.'

'I can see the connection now. Anna gave you another copy of the painting, because you had lost yours in the blitz of your house.'

'That's right. I'd. . . I'd only three things left. . . left from childhood – my bag, my missal and. . . and the handmade blanket from my bed at home.'

'And when you were delirious this time, there was the Dürer again.'

'Yes. I'd heard. . . heard. . . as I rambled. . . the same words, "put it out of your mind. . . forget" again and again. . . so clearly. . . but the. . . telegram. . . was. . . there.'

Mary spoke softly, 'In these horrific months of war, I've listened to patients who've had those near to them killed, injured or missing, recall past tragic events in their lives, similar to what you've just told me.'

'That helps. The bad thing is. . . is that I was relieved. . . yes. . . relieved that. . . that it wasn't. . . Bernie.' There was a hint of embarrassment in her voice.

Mary didn't comment but said lightly, 'Perhaps Anna shouldn't have given you the picture.' The mention of the child made both women smile and Margaret's uncharacteristic lack of self-control seemed to wane.

'The odd thing is that I love. . . love the picture and the beautiful story behind it. It should confirm my faith in human nature,' she replied without hesitation.

'Tea's ready,' Anna's voice called from the kitchen door.

As they entered the farmyard, Margaret felt her confidante squeeze her arm, walking towards the kitchen door, Mary said, 'If you feel you need to tell me anything else, remember I'm a good listener. There are ghosts in most people's lives.'

*

That evening, Margaret was pleased that Mary was firm about her fitness for work, when the adults were discussing recent events. 'Carrying an unborn child is a natural process. Mrs. Rooney will come to no harm if she continues to undertake farm duties.'

Mrs. Morgan protested.

'Lugging about heavy buckets and stretching too much isn't very good, but native women in Africa make no concessions to pregnancy.'

The Morgans didn't argue. *Do they find it difficult to accept that their daughter is now a professional woman and no longer a little girl?*

Mary spoke convincingly, 'In Liverpool, women try to go into hospital for a few days when they have a baby – it's for a holiday. Those who don't go into hospital get up the day after the birth and run their homes as before.'

'That's what it's like in Ireland. Pregnancy's not an illness; some women have seventeen or eighteen children! T.B. takes some of them. And here am I with just one child, who's, unfortunately, away in the war and another on the way.'

Mr. Morgan who had not spoken for some time, gestured to the others that he needed to say something, 'Mrs. Morgan and I, Mrs. Rooney, have decided that we're pleased to offer you and your unborn child a home for as long as you like Our invitation is extended to your husband and son as well.'

Margaret was astonished but Mary was quick to endorse her father's offer.

'I agree with my parents. At the same time I think Mrs. Rooney would be happier to accept the offer if she could continue to make a worthwhile contribution to the farm.'

She turned to Margaret, 'I have felt less concerned about my parents and the farm since you've been here, please agree to be part of the family. We all face an uncertain future.'

'I can't say how grateful I am. I know that I can do useful work. I'm basically fit and strong. Thank you all.' She was nearly in tears.

Margaret had wondered whether she had said too much to Mary. It had been easy to unburden herself to a person who was in the habit of hearing confidences. No, she thought Mary was bound to, and would respect her 'secrets'. The support she had given to her father's offer confirmed this.

23

The Concert

As agreed after the half-term holiday, Margaret resumed her walks or rides to school with Anna as well as her farm work. She left the heavy mucking out to Nancy, who despite her frail appearance was physically strong. Anna told Margaret that she had started to like poetry and demonstrated her ability by reciting some verses from *When We Were Very Young.*

She said, 'At first I found learning by heart difficult because I kept thinking about you, Pinny, Uncle Patrick and my Mummy and Dad.' It appeared that Mary Williams had agreed that Anna could call Margaret, 'Pinny' when they were alone, but Anna said that her grandmother was old-fashioned and expected people to be formal when she was present. *I would have loved to have heard the mother and daughter conversation.* Margaret changed the subject, quickly, mentioning the coming concert to be put on in the town for the 'war effort'.

'You and I are going to do a sketch together.'

'Granny said that it was a secret.'

'It was but your grandmother gave me our script this morning. It's called, guess what? ' Milking'.'

Anna had never been to a concert so thought that they would take Lizzie to the Church Hall and demonstrate milking a cow.

'No, Anna, it's a sketch, a short play, like the one we read about the other day. There'll be lots of different items of drama and song, some amusing. We'll read 'Milking' through to-night, after school.'

The concert was a distraction. Margaret's mind seemed to work on two levels. She was thinking and praying about Patrick incessantly, but she was able to concentrate on other things at the same time. She dressed in an old pair of Mr. Morgan's trousers as a youth, wearing a smart scarf and a rakish cap. While Anna was dressed charmingly in a pretty cotton dress with a lace-edged apron and cap. She carried a small pail.

On the stage there was a *Drink More Milk* poster sporting a caricature of a Jersey cow addressing children together with a large photo of the local dairy's pony and trap – the pony's head immersed in a churn of milk.

'Where are you going to, my pretty maid?' said the youth.

'I'm going a milking, Sir.' (She said)

'May I come with you, my pretty maid?' Little Anna simpered, prettily, and the youth grinned, broadly, and all in the hall giggled at the innocence and innuendo of the continuing sketch. Margaret and Anna were a tribute to Flo Morgan's theatrical direction. It was fun. The evening was fun.

The vicar, who was wigged and moustached for his debut impersonation of Adolph Hitler, had opened the evening's entertainment. He was oblivious of his non-clerical appearance. Jack-booted and in fake SS uniform, he exhorted all, in his sermon voice 'to do their bit for the forces'. He couldn't understand why the audience was stifling laughter and catcalls. His act was a great success and provided him with a sobriquet for the rest of the war.

The church choir sang wartime 'hits' with a beautiful rendering of the 'White Cliffs of Dover', which resulted in an *encore*. The last item of the programme was by the local Home Guard. The squad marched on to the stage goose-stepping hilariously and seriously out of time but falling into perfect step, posture and voice when the piano struck up the 'March of the Men of Harlech'. Two youngsters carried a recruitment banner reading, 'Join now at the Drill Hall' to thunderous applause, which only stopped when the English and Welsh National Anthems were played with everyone up-standing and determined.

Margaret heard Anna say to Mrs. Morgan. 'Granny, I know now what I want to be when I grow up – a conjuror. I know I could make rabbits come out of a hat.'

They went home to Cae Coch in a van belonging to the butcher to find Mr. Morgan excited to give them some news.

'Has the new calf been born?' asked Anna, exhausted, as her grandmother hurried her to bed.

'No, it's better than that, but you'll have to wait until morning.'

'I know it'll be twin calves. I'll see them before school.'

'Perhaps?' was the chorus.

*

Mr. Morgan asked Margaret to stay and wait for his wife to return to the kitchen. 'The news concerns you. I've been making enquiries,' he mumbled as he filled his evening pipe.

Margaret wondered whether he'd engaged more farm help and secretly she dreaded being made to feel that she was an invalid and couldn't do the work she was paid for.

Mrs. Morgan returned to the room and her husband spoke, 'I've had a good piece of news from my editor. I found out that he has an old school friend in the Admiralty. I gave him all the details concerning your husband, Mrs. Rooney. This friend is looking into the matter personally.'

'I'd be glad of any help with news of Patrick. It's the uncertainty of the situation which is so distressing. I imagine appalling things.'

'Be patient, my dear. It seems hopeful.' Mrs. Morgan smiled as she said, 'Good night', adding, 'Thank you for putting so much effort into your sketch with Anna when you had much weightier things on your mind.'

24

Reticence

Margaret had another appointment with the doctor at his suggestion. The Morgans were concerned but tried not to show it. Was she to have problems with this pregnancy? She was over forty and in an anxious state. Her husband was 'missing' and nothing had been heard from her son for several weeks.

She laughed off the need for another half hour with Dr. Thomas. 'He probably wants a discussion about the relative merits of Rhode Island Reds over White Leghorns. He seems to want to make a success of his poultry. I've made the appointment so it coincides with the time Anna finishes school, she loves helping the doctor's daughter, Megan, groom the pony and always hopes for a ride.' The older couple were anxious even so. They thought of the baby with joy, an oasis in the desert of war. There had been no fresh news from the Admiralty.

'Take this article from 'Farmers' Magazine' entitled, 'The Economics of the Egg'. That'll keep our medicine man happy,' Dai said with a chuckle.

Margaret was a little surprised about the need for seeing Dr. Thomas again so soon, because she had seen the District Nurse regularly. *Is it very dangerous to have a baby at my age?* Dr. Thomas was giving her his free time, before evening surgery! He greeted her with a smile and his daughter took Anna's hand as she steered her to the garden with its field behind.

'Two happy children,' he said. 'I'm not going to beat about the bush, Margaret, may I call you Margaret?' As his patient nodded, nervously, he continued, 'I sense something's very wrong. No, I don't think it's physical, but, understandably, you've had two shockingly horrible blows in a short time. There's a horrified look about you, sometimes, but I remember. . .' He looked directly at her. 'That day. . .'

'When I was ill in bed at the farm?' Margaret felt uncomfortable.

'Yes. I'd been summoned by Dai, a man who is most level-headed. He and his wife were distraught. They didn't know how to comfort and support you. It was too raw for them. I was concerned, when I saw your delirium.'

Margaret bowed her head.

The doctor continued, looking straight at his patient, 'Forgive me prying and I won't pass on any irrelevant confidences to anyone, but you don't seem at ease with the pregnancy. It's understandable in the circumstances. Is it because your man is missing, or is there some other horror?'

At the word 'horror', Margaret winced, 'Horror, what a strange word to use!'

'I remember your expression, when I was called out to the farm. Your words were all over the place. . . and fearful, I thought.'

'I was ill,' she said quickly.

'I know, but as a medic, I hear the news, I read the papers, but I am isolated, in a small market town from what, I know, are horrors.'

'Yes, I understand.'

'Were you so badly affected by losing your home? Is it the dreadful news of your husband? Or lack of communication with your son? Or is it all of those awful occurrences, together?' He pleaded.

'I suppose it's the unbearable combination.' Her expression was vacant.

'Nothing more?'

'No, yes. . . perhaps, I don't know.'

There was a pause.

'I want to help if I can.'

'It takes me back in a relentless way. . . to the pregnancy with my son.' Her voice was weak as she looked at her feet. He mumbled something inaudible, but his expression was encouraging.

'And perhaps before that. . . I feel so alone. It's a. . . long story.'

'And the other day, at Cae Coch?'

'I must have been disorientated. . . I. . . wasn't there...', she felt distressed. Dr. Thomas meant to be kind, she was sure, but she didn't want to recall painful memories, at the moment.

The doctor was unaware of her reticence. 'That happens with fevers, but there was terror in. . .'

She forced herself to reply, 'I, I was back in County Cork. . . I could smell the peat fire. I heard that awful sound. . . and there was the Dürer. . .'

'I remember, 'The Praying Hands', you were staring at the picture.'

'Anna gave me the picture for Christmas,' She sighed. . .'It was so thoughtful. . . I'd said I'd always liked the detail in the fingers'. She looked down at her rough hands as she spoke.

'So that was good.'

'The copy I'd had since my. . . my. . . First Communion had been destroyed. . . in that wicked raid. . . I was seventeen when...'

'Were you ill at seventeen?' His expression was one of understanding.

'Yes. I was. . . it's all. . . an ill omen. . . I must try to. . . I was back there. . . I discussed my illness with Nurse Roberts. . . she said she'd tell you. . . I think I've laid. . . the ghost. . . it's. . . it's out in the open. I...'

'What about the pregnancy with your son? How is that connected?'

'I don't. . . it's as though it's a substitution. . . it's mudd...'

The door flew open with a waft of horsy smell. 'Daisy tried to nibble my hair ribbon.' Anna was delighted.

'Thank you, for the advice on the care of my chickens, Mrs. Rooney,' said the doctor, deliberately moving between her and the two children. 'Next time wear an elastic band round your hair, Anna, ponies don't like eating rubber or chewing gum.' The girls laughed.

*

'Why does Mrs. Rooney talk oddly?' asked Megan as the door closed behind Anna and Margaret.

'The doctor's expression was gentle as he replied, hurriedly, to his daughter, 'She's Irish. Mrs. Rooney was born in Cork, where her life on a small farm was basic and hard. One of these days we'll study Irish history. Your mother's got a good book about the subject. We've lived a sheltered life here in this town, Meg.'

'Anna tried to tell me but got a bit upset. She's worried about Uncle Patrick, who's he?'

96

'We'll talk later this evening.' The doctor pointed to the grandfather clock and hugged Megan absent-mindedly as he opened the door to see his patients in the surgery at the front of the house.

'Let's go and see Cae Coch some time, Megan. Remember Anna's younger than you and living away from home. Your mother'll be back soon. Put the kettle on, cariad. I'm glad that you get on well with Anna.'

25

Rescue

Margaret couldn't believe that she was here, in the beautiful ante-room to the Office of the 'Wye Valley Convalescent Hospital'. Until last week, Mrs. Morgan had told her, this had been the stately home of the Lord of the Manor. Apparently, the family's lineage went back to Prince Llewellyn, but the present Lord and Lady Irfon had elected to move into the small west wing in order to make their house available as a Rest Home for the wounded. Their sons were away from home - both serving officers in the army. Margaret had never been in a house as beautiful as this. The Big House in Ireland where she had given English lessons to the disabled daughter of 'the squire' was modest in comparison. She shivered as she asked herself the question - *Why does my mind go back to Cork and those last couple of weeks there?*

Margaret understood that Lord Irfon spent his time recruiting for his regiment, whilst his wife was the local Chairman of the Red Cross. It seemed that war found occupation for all.

She thought back to the previous evening when Dai Morgan had sprung the news about Patrick's escape from death upon them. All her questions about Patrick's state of health were maddeningly referred by her employer to a Captain Smith. Now she was waiting outside a door with a discreet sign, reading Captain Smith, RN.

'Come in, Mrs. Rooney. I'm Charles Smith.' The bearded naval officer held the door open for her and shook her hand.

'Please sit down.'

Margaret sat on the chair he pulled out for her, wondering why serving officers should treat women with old world courtesy, whilst all the administrative people whom she had met over the blitz of her home had been casual and impersonal.

A young girl in army uniform put a tray of tea in front of her; she marvelled at the elegant china tea cups and matching teapot.

'Would you like to pour?' His voice interrupted her reverie on the beauty of the china and all the questions about Patrick which she'd like to ask.

Margaret was trembling but pleased that she had something to do with her hands as she listened to what this man had to say about her husband. He told her that Patrick's mission had been to test a new landing craft which had been 'top secret'. He explained that extraordinary conditions in the English Channel had damaged the vessel which had sunk without trace, concussing its 'skipper' as it went down. Though Patrick had been picked up, it was some time before his identity had been established. Treatment for his poor medical condition and exposure had been the priority. Even now his precise state of health was only known to the Naval Hospital, but, Captain Smith assured her, Patrick was certainly, 'On the mend'. His face had puckered into a conspiratorial smile as he uttered the words, 'Top Secret'. Margaret had tried to nod in agreement with the conspiracy.

'It can't have been easy for you, so far from home. You're Irish?'

'Yes, Captain, I was born in County Cork.'

'I fished in the River Lee before the war. Good fishing. Now, I've looked into the service records of your husband and son. They are both a credit to you and to the Royal Navy.'

'Thank you.' Margaret considered her words were trite but she felt out of her depth.

'I've arranged a travel permit for you to make a visit to the Naval Hospital, a night's stay at the nurses' quarters there and a letter for you to obtain access to the hospital and the service consultants.'

Margaret was nervous, but her voice was clear as she said, 'I'm very grateful to you and all those concerned in Patrick's rescue. Thank you.'

Out in the waiting room she wanted to shout for joy, but instead she listened carefully to the subaltern who explained the formalities of her impending visit. It could be arranged in a week.

*

Even Gwyn shook her hand, whilst Nancy hugged her affectionately. Anna appeared from the orchard with a large bunch of daffodils for 'Uncle Patrick', reminding everyone that it was St. David's Day. The hire car turned into the yard – that was the Morgans' contribution to the trip, and all waved to her as Margaret climbed into the car. She was anxious about how ill or how wounded she'd find Patrick, but knew she had support for any alarming thing encountered on the return from her visit to the Naval Hospital.

*

When Margaret walked into the ward, Patrick was sitting up in bed, his head bandaged and his left leg splinted. He looked whole. His face was gaunt and pale. Strangely, injury and illness seemed to have diminished his large, healthy 6 foot frame. The dressing on his head made him appear bald to Margaret, but, she thought, he'd probably been shaved during his medical ordeal. Immaculate starched nurses busied themselves between the beds. Margaret felt as though she was on a hospital ship, perhaps because naval ratings were helping the walking wounded towards the dining room and an air of service discipline seemed present despite the bath chairs, walking sticks, odour of anti-septic and the chalk smell from abundant plaster casts.

'Maggie, Maggie, is it really you? Nobody told me you were coming. Take my hand so I can feel it's you. How did you manage it?' She'd never heard his voice so delighted.

'Mr. Morgan's editor had a friend. . .'

'Say no more, just sit there and let me look at you.'

Margaret was glad to sit because standing she felt a little queasy, had she forgotten in her shock at seeing her husband that she had been unwell. How was she to tell this clearly sick man that he was going to be a father?

'You look well. Wales suits you. How's Anna?'

'Anna sent you those daffodils. It's St. David's Day.' An absurdly young-looking nurse smiled across to the couple as she arranged the wild blooms in an earthen ware vase.

'She's missed you terribly. I've been beside myself. Put me out of my misery. What exactly are your injuries?'

'Not good, a fractured skull, broken pelvis and compound fracture of my left leg. The rest of me's fine.' He added the last few words with a broad grin. As he spoke she felt very concerned, was this the right moment to blurt out her news? The ward emptied as all the patients walked or were moved into the dining room. The remaining man was wheeled through the door in a wheel chair by a nurse, who was clearly having a joke with her patient, who tuned his head to wink at her. It was a happy moment.

'Lost both his legs at Dunkirk,' whispered Patrick.

Margaret felt shocked but thought that it might be their only time alone so she moved closer to her husband, squeezed his hand and said softly, 'I've some news too. We're going to have a baby in September, Patrick.'

His reaction was immediate, 'Well done us. You clever girl.' He took her hand in both of his, leaned forward and bent his bandaged head towards her, intending to kiss her.

The gesture nearly landed him on the floor. Both of them laughed at his enforced clumsiness.

'Tell me about your ordeal.'

'The boat I was testing chucked me into the channel, giving me a beating as it sank. It was hell, but to be rescued was a miracle.'

'Then. . ?'

'I was picked up by a Merchant Ship. But, Maggie, tell me more about our child.'

'Not now, I'm a bit embarrassed. It isn't the place - too many people about. I must know the details of the rescue. Everyone at Cae Coch will want to know. I've imagined all sorts of dangers.'

'I had no identification on me, I'm told. The ship had a medic on board so I was patched up and made comfy until the ship reached port. I had very few periods of lucidity.'

'I suppose it must have been obvious that you were a sailor.'

'Yes. I suppose so, but I couldn't reveal the nature of my mission. I must have appeared to be barmy. I was taken to a civilian hospital, close to shore, and then here last week, where I was identified by that tattoo you always hated.'

They giggled.

'This place is wonderful. When I was in the water I heard Bernie's voice as a child saying, 'I want to be a sailor when I grow up.' It was what made me try hard to keep semi-conscious, and it worked. Have you heard from our boy lately?'

'He's at sea. He doesn't know you were posted 'missing' or about the baby.'

They were both silent.

An orderly brought a tray for Patrick and adjusted his pillows. Patrick took hold of his sleeve, 'Tar, guess what, my wife's having a baby.' The young man nodded but bowed to Margaret as he set a place for her at the table and pulled a chair back for her. 'Congratulations, Mam.'

*

She was in the train heading back to Wales, but her mind was full of the time at the hospital. Her night had been fun. In the Nurses' Home, the girls, most of them in their twenties, had cooked a meal – it seemed, without the restraint of the ration book. After the meal they'd chatted to her. All had had some time with Patrick and explained how ill he'd been on arrival, but how he was determined to recover in order to return to duty. Margaret realized how easy it was to talk with these educated and vocational women. Compared with the girls in the factory, who'd been basic and often crude due to their humble origins, these were bright and sympathetic without being sentimental, but it was the factory girls who were constantly in danger. Another paradox of war.

In the morning she had had an interview with the naval surgeon. He had explained that Patrick would stay in the hospital after his injuries healed, for physiotherapy. He would then have sick leave when regular checks would have to be made. 'It'll take time, every person is different, but it seems that he has a very special reason to be fit and well again.' Margaret had blushed. The surgeon had written his name, the ward details and telephone number on a piece of paper and had told her that she could have a brief visit to Patrick out of visiting hours before she took the bus to the station.

As the train sped along, she pondered on this second visit, for Patrick had been in pain and she'd been upset by his domineering attitude. Patrick's initial welcome, the previous day, had thrilled her. He had not been as demonstrative as that since Bernie was born. During her morning visit to him he had been irritable and forceful about the baby, 'My daughter mustn't lose her Roman Catholic faith. You've become woolly about your Catholicism, Maggie.' She winced as she remembered the rebuke.

The matron on duty had explained that the painkilling drugs often wore off and patients became restless and demanding until the next dose did its job. This world of wounds, fractures, and drugs was new to Margaret but she planned to talk it over with Dr. Thomas. She smiled to herself, thinking it typical of Patrick that he knew the baby was going to be a girl. Her major concern was having an invalid on the farm when the war was already requiring Mr. Morgan to be away from home more, writing articles about the war in Wales. *How long will I be able to continue to do my job on the farm? Patrick didn't answer that question.* As the train pulled into the familiar station which she now thought of as a gateway to home, she checked herself. She was not a widow nor was her husband without legs trapped in a wheel-chair for the rest of his life. That was all that mattered. Despite her scepticism, prayer had worked.

26

Reorganization

As she described Patrick's injuries, Margaret noticed that even the peaceful rural mood of Cae Coch had changed. In the intelligent face of Mrs. Morgan she saw determination and in her husband's expression there was purpose – an acceptance of challenge and resolve to overcome it. She realized that the war had invaded everyone. It wasn't just rationing but broadcasts and newspaper articles and now a casualty, had, after two Christmases of war, made their way into the very fibre and heart of society. Was it ever going to end? It seemed that Dai Morgan had been writing an article on the bombing of Cardiff and its docks, its destruction had appalled the whole of Wales, bringing the consequences ever nearer and a shortage of coal, in Wales and England. This precious commodity was taken from the Welsh Valley mines and transported by sea to other parts of the country. Margaret saw photographs of debris in the paper on the kitchen table and thought back to her hospital visit. As if to answer an unasked question she said, 'The hospital is protected by a powerful anti-aircraft battery.' She almost added, 'And prayer.'

Mrs. Morgan suggested Margaret went to bed early as she was keen to do the milking in the morning. 'You're right to continue your routine. It'll take your mind from your husband's injuries.'

'Gwyn will be around in the morning if you change your mind. I need to have a talk with him,' added her husband.

Margaret had given a full account of Patrick's injuries and treatment, stressing that he would be in hospital for some time in order to take advantage of the physiotherapy facilities there. She assured the Morgans that her husband was in good spirits and being a model patient. Had the events of the last few weeks made her dishonest? *I wonder with dread whether Patrick's dark side will come to the fore when he returns to the farm.*

*

On waking Margaret remembered Patrick's bullying tone when she had said 'Goodbye' and she found herself addressing the only photo she had of Bernie. Though it had not been tinted she saw the eyes very blue, the lips red and generous, the strong chin and attractive sandy hair; never had it been as bright as hers, but the smile, which dominated the picture, was encouraging.

'Well, Bernie?'

His expression seemed to speak, 'Just get on with it and then we'll go to the flicks.' No, she wasn't going mad - it was this blasted war.

*

Lizzie was restless as she started to milk, but soon settled as Margaret spoke to her. How reassuring were the simple tasks of life! She finished the milking in record time; put the cows back in their field and rejoiced as they all joined their friends with true affection. As she was pouring the milk into the churn, Margaret was aware of someone approaching but she was concentrating on not spilling the precious contents of the bucket. A man's arm gripped her round her breasts and another pinned her hair to the back of her neck – Gwyn!

'So you're doing me out of a job again, Mrs. O'Clever.' His closeness was stifling. His face was contorted with anger. Margaret used all her strength to push him away.

'How dare you. How dare you touch me?' She realized she was shouting as she shook with rage.

'Proper little Irish redheaded vixen, aren't you? Taking the bread out of a Welshman's mouth.'

'A mouth rinsed with alcohol.' Her voice was tremulous.

His oath in reply was unintelligible.

Having freed herself, Margaret was at the dairy door. Though distraught, she said in a more measured tone, 'Don't you touch me again, ever, ev-er.' The biting winter wind was a cleansing caress.

'Pinny, did you call?' Outside, Anna stood feeding a carrot to Rose over the fence, her attention on what she was doing. She was absorbed in keeping her thick school jumper clean.

'Are you taking me to school to-day? Please?'

'Yes, be a dear and tell your grandmother that I'm making myself respectable. My hair's untidy. I'll be five minutes.' Margaret hoped that the suggestion of hurry would allow her to recover her equilibrium. To walk into the town would be the escape she needed.

*

Anna attributed her Pinny's agitation to her time away, 'Was it awful seeing Uncle Patrick with bandages on his head? Rachael said that when someone breaks their leg people can write on the plaster. Did you write anything?'

Margaret found the remark amusing and pointed out that she didn't really think that the Surgeon Commander would be pleased if such antics took place. She explained how formal and disciplined the hospital had been and how it was like being aboard a ship. A starchy ship. They laughed.

'I've missed you, Pinny,' and Anna was running up to Rachael with lots to tell her friend.

*

Margaret wished that she could dawdle so that she might find some explanation for Gwyn's sudden outburst. She stopped on the bridge over the River Irfon to think. He had groped her once before but she'd brushed him aside with, 'Don't be silly, Gwyn.' On that occasion she hadn't been aware that she was pregnant. To-day she had felt revulsion, made more intolerable because of the baby. As she looked at the clear water and heard its sympathetic bubble, her mind became lucid. Because the child within her had been molested, she, now, wanted more than anything to protect it. What had been a horrible experience had introduced her to the baby, as a person in its own right. For the first time, since her pregnancy had been confirmed she felt overwhelming joy. What a strange man Gwyn was!

Had Dai Morgan said something, once, about Gwyn being a complication? Last evening she'd been uncomfortable. The Morgans were so fond of Gwyn. Had he been in some trouble with another woman or, worse still, were the marks on Nancy's face bruises after all? On the other hand, had Gwyn's advances towards her been observed, or had he told anyone that she'd encouraged him? Her thoughts went back and forth between Patrick and Gwyn. Margaret felt alone. If only she could confide in someone, but who? Sharing confidences could lead to further problems. The surgeon Commander had said, 'Life's one damn thing after another,' adding with a big smile, 'Take heart.'

Once in the warm kitchen of Cae Coch with a cup of tea in her hands, Margaret felt a little more herself.

'Dai, I think you should acquaint Mrs. Rooney with the facts of the situation.'

Margaret relaxed a little. The situation didn't seem to be anything of her making, or was it?

'We've been discussing the future running of the farm and how we'll manage things,' said Dai Morgan.

Margaret was quick to reply, 'I want to continue my duties up until my baby is born,' thinking to herself that a few hours in a naval hospital had converted work into duties.

'We know that but as I said last night we're in a bit of a dilemma. It's Gwyn.'

Had Gwyn's hostility to her been obvious? Her voice was little more than a whisper as she muttered, 'I see.'

Margaret tried to relax. She hoped that the dilemma didn't seem to have anything to do with her but perhaps it did.

'The new Convalescent Hospital for service personnel in the town needs a man to be in charge of the fabric. They want a local man. The powers that be have decided that a civilian will be best suited to the position.' There was authority in Dai's tone.

His wife added proudly, 'And Mr. Morgan considers that Gwyn would be an excellent man for the job and he has been appointed.'

Margaret tried to appear in agreement but her inner being rebelled at the description of Gwyn being excellent. She made a mental effort to concentrate on his carpentry, his dry stone walling and general maintenance of farm equipment – tasks which Gwyn had undertaken and discharged meticulously. She mumbled a, 'Yes, he would be.'

Dai continued, 'That leaves us short-handed with the dairy work, milking, mucking out and tending of all the other stock.'

At mention of milking Margaret's mind went back to Lizzie's discomfort after Gwyn had covered for her in the milking parlour. She thought grimly that Gwyn seemed out of sympathy with animals and women, excepting Mrs. Morgan. Perhaps he'd behave in an all male environment.

'How would you like to take on a pupil?' asked Mr. Morgan.

Margaret was surprised at the suggestion but nodded, imagining a schoolboy or schoolgirl, trudging out to the farm twice a day.

'Could you work with and train Nancy?' His question was tentative.

'I'd like that. I get on well with her. She's conscientious.'

'You're sure she's tough enough for the task?'

'I think so. She's gentle, she'll be good with the stock, once she gets used to their size. You know how I admire her beautiful sewing and knitting. She's dextrous. Is she happy to work with the cattle and horses? I know she's used to dealing with sheep.'

'She feels that her fine needlework is not going to win the war,' said Mrs. Morgan softly.

'I'll teach her all that I know and she's so good with Anna. I'm sure it'll work.'

The Morgans looked pleased.

'Now, I'm going to make Gwyn's day. The War Ministry is going to be a much better payer than I. Gwyn will continue with his shepherd duties, after all he's the one with the trained sheepdog. Mott doesn't like women that much. I wonder why.'

As Margaret went out into the yard Mr. Morgan turned to her and said in a confidential whisper, 'Perhaps a War Ministry job will get rid of the chip on that man's shoulder. He's never forgotten how his school friends gave their lives for king and country in the last war and he was captive on his parents' farm, penniless with no honour and no glory.'

Margaret was silent. Would it mean that Gwyn was still going to haunt the farm? She was determined to rise to that challenge. Anyway, Patrick's convalescence would be a distraction. She wondered whether Nancy would like being a milk maid. *Had she been consulted?*

The answer to that question was made a couple of hours later when a smiling Nancy appeared in the milking parlour saying, 'Will you really teach me to milk and feed the stock? I'm a little nervous you know.'

'Will you teach me to do cable stitch? I want to knit Patrick a jumper'

Both women laughed as they burlesqued a tune from the recent concert, 'There's a war on. Every little helps.'

27

All Change

Margaret was a little concerned about Nancy's ability to deal with the large animals. They needed different handling from sheep. She need not have worried for Nancy was a good student and soon lost her fear of the horses and cattle. They in turn seemed to be gentle with Nancy; did they sense her fragility and sensitivity?

'Remember that I was brought up in the town, Maggie.'

'I know.'

'I met Gwyn, fell in love and married him. Did you know it was Mrs. Morgan who introduced us?'

'I did know,' said Margaret flatly, thinking that, surely, a sweet and able young girl could have married someone more kindly and understanding than Gwyn. *Am I beginning to demonize Gwyn?* – She must begin to be more charitable and forget his lapses towards her. In her many reflections about him she had resolved to confide in Dai Morgan if he gave her more problems. He seemed to understand the reason for Gwyn's bitter nature. Strangely, she thought of her employer as Dai, but she always obeyed the convention of addressing him, as Mr. Morgan.

Gwyn, Nancy told Margaret, was pleased with the position at the Convalescent Hospital and he enjoyed the status which his ability and better income provided. To her surprise Mr. Morgan spoke to Margaret again about Gwyn after he had started his new job.

'I've told him that drinking in the town public houses is not advisable because of a security risk.'

She'd replied, 'Careless Talk costs Lives.'

'And livers,' was his rejoinder. They'd laughed.

While the problems at the front escalated, it was essential to make the farm run smoothly. The war provided enough miseries without making more. Recent bombing of Cardiff made the whole of Wales alarmed – Llandaff Cathedral had been hit early in January and other raids were giving rise to many civilian casualties. Margaret was glad but guilty that no-one she or the Morgans knew was a casualty in South Wales. But, were her men folk out of the way of air raids? She was apprehensive. Patrick was, she thought, safe in the hospital, which was tucked away from the sea port with a camouflaged roof and anti-aircraft protection but Bernie was at sea – his ship like others was a good target for Jerry. She had been happier when he was training. *Why hadn't she had a letter from him for such a long time?*

As the two women drove the cattle from one field to another they chatted companionably to each other. Margaret was pleased to hear that Gwyn was valued at the Convalescent Hospital. Nancy told her friend that he could take a short cut to work without walking through the farmyard and his shepherd responsibilities were taken into account should he require time off. Margaret made no comment; she was relieved. Lambing was under way and it was essential that there were as few losses as possible. The ewes seemed to understand that the war made a difference to their care and responded by being model mothers – Mrs. Morgan was caring for only two weak twins in the Cae Coch kitchen. Margaret was cheered by Anna's insistence in doing her share in bottle feeding the demanding little creatures.

*

The Knitting Circle had progressed from one afternoon to two and included women from the town. In addition there were a couple of new groups in the town. Socks, gloves and jumpers in khaki, navy and grey were taken to a depot in Brecon to find their way to their appropriate destinations. Despite the bad news from the BBC and the papers, the knitters remained cheerful and determined that their effort would win the war whatever the opposition. Anna finished her white bootees for Margaret's baby and was complimented on them by her grandmother who had been sure that they would never be completed.

When searching for the beloved Gladstone, who had taken to blood sports now he was a rural cat, Margaret found him asleep on top of a blanket, covering a pram, in a remote shed. She was pleased because time was passing and clothes and equipment for the unborn baby had not been as much of a priority for her as they should have been. She asked Nancy about the pram and was told it had been donated by the wife of the headmaster of the High School.

'I've never met her.' Margaret said.

'Well, that's country life.' Just like Ireland Margaret thought, and for a moment she longed to smell the smoke from a peat fire. Nancy sensed that the other was silent for a purpose and after a pause she said, 'I'm lining a Moses basket as well. Your baby will have plenty of clothes.' She didn't add that some were her own treasured baby garments made for her own babies.

Trying to put the war news aside, Margaret continued to take Anna to school and when necessary she'd go to the surgery to check all was well with her pregnancy. Dr. Thomas and Nurse Roberts were both pleased with her progress. Her nightmares seemed to have stopped. They smiled when she told them that Patrick knew the baby was a girl.

'It could be,' said Dilys Roberts, 'it has a fifty per cent chance!'

Margaret had less energy than hitherto and was glad of Nancy's help. She still dreaded a face to face meeting with Gwyn but she had a feeling that he was avoiding her. She had one bad dream about him which disturbed her. He was strangling her. It was strange but his boorish actions had awakened memories of her earlier life. Gwyn's behaviour was beginning to haunt her; that was wrong.

*

Within the month, Patrick arrived at Cae Coch in a naval vehicle. As he walked into the farmhouse he appeared years older than the day he went away. Margaret embraced him warmly, hoping that he would fit into the household and not disgrace her. She had been told that he might be depressed as a result of his injuries, though X-rays had indicated no substantial damage to his brain. Even so, his headaches continued and he had told her that he would be on sick leave for a couple of months. She told herself that she must support him and forget the errors of his past. The Surgeon Commander had warned her that Patrick might not be able to continue in the navy – what would he do? Would he receive a pension?

The Morgans had, unknown to Margaret, arranged a celebration tea for Patrick. There was even a cake, baked by Mrs. Morgan with ingredients supplied by the grocer, 'for the Cae Coch war hero'. Patrick was the first serviceman to come back alive. There had been two soldiers killed on active service; their funerals had been solemn, with full military honours. To have a man return battered and bruised but alive gave hope to all.

'What good sorts the Morgans are,' Patrick said as he and his wife were alone in their loft hideaway. Margaret gestured her agreement and stopped herself from saying anything about lack of news from Bernie, which was her current anxiety. Her husband's only reference to her pregnancy was a joking remark about her 'rather large waist'.

Margaret got up at her normal time but to her delight she found Nancy already milking Lizzie, 'I thought I'd surprise you. See, I have done all the things you've taught me and even Lizzie seems to be enjoying my inexperienced hands.' Margaret left her to her triumph and helped Mr. Morgan with the morning feeding so he could be early for his ride into the town and the newspaper office.

'I've a very busy day. The news is bad. Hitler is making ruins of Cardiff and my editor is saying that since the destruction of Coventry last November, there has been an official blackout on news of raids because of the effect on the nation's morale. The paper has to concentrate on good news. We must cheer the population on the one hand but on the other prepare for invasion.'

Patrick was sitting at the kitchen table with a broad smile on his face, 'Look, Maggie, a letter from Bernie.'

Anna squealed as she hugged her Uncle Patrick, who pushed her away gently, 'Remember, I'm an invalid. If you squeeze me too hard I'll vanish.'

Margaret's euphoric voice drowned the little girl's excitement, 'God be praised, a letter at last. What does he say? Tell me.'

'It's addressed to you, Maggie.'

'Quick, let's read it together, then if you don't mind, Patrick, I'll take Anna to school, as usual. I've promised to walk to-day to count the lambs?'

Anna ran to the parlour to tell her grandmother who was playing the piano, about the letter.

'Let's go up to our loft, so we're by ourselves.' Margaret said impatiently.

The letter burned in her hand as one lame man and his pregnant wife negotiated the steps to their eyrie, delighted.

As she opened the letter, Margaret said, 'I'm so excited. His writing is, as always, a little untidy. A medic's hand?'

Patrick smiled as he pulled her down on to the bed next to him.

28

Bernie's Letter

Dear Mam,

This epistle will not be posted for some time; it will be collected when the mail ship comes – that's a movable feast, so I'm going to write as and when I can. Sorry it has to be in pencil, but that's how it is. First thing to say is that I haven't been sea-sick once – it is one of the hazards apparently of joining the navy!

I love my ship; she's very beautiful, called HMS ****** – a grey lady, whose number is *********. Though she's a ship of war, she has all the elegance of a passenger liner. D'you remember seeing the Mauretania sailing down the Mersey? How exciting it was! We and others nearly fell overboard as the Wallasey ferry we were on, almost capsized as we leant on the rails of the deck to have the best view of the beautiful ship. I remember our Dad telling me that ships were always considered to be female because of their beauty. As my ship's bows cut through the swell, I think of Moses parting the waters of the Red Sea – her power seems biblical. Every part of her is alive but mysterious. Her coiled ropes like snakes sigh as the wind catches them, loose metal fittings tinkle like delicate musical instruments, and the sea spray caresses the deck with a fragile kiss, as she glides with dignity through the waves. I often glance behind my lady and her wake appears as a majestic train. Magnificent! Mam, I have written the last few sentences to show you how content I am on board ship.

As usual, I'm dressed warmly in a naval duffle-coat and I never have less than two pairs of socks on. I often, (mostly), sleep in my clothes between watches, unless they're too wet.

I'm so glad you've moved out of Liverpool. I long to visit Cae Coch. Perhaps my next leave will be long enough for me to travel to Wales. I remember we went to Chester for my tenth birthday and there were signs to North Wales but I was insistent that I walked round the city walls one more time. You pointed to the river Dee and told me that it came from Wales. I confused Wales with whales, d'you remember? - I was going to write something more about Wales. Oh, now, it comes to mind. How's the dreaded Will doing away from Jean's cooking?

Sorry to break off but there was an urgent call from one of the docs and I had to go to the dispensary – I'll be for it; I'd forgotten to sign one of the drug records!

I spend a great deal of time below deck, working in sick bay. I love being with the medics who are sometimes quite complimentary about my ability. They tell me to 'hold my horses' about being a doctor. 'Wait, after the war you may have different ambitions.' Have you ever been aware of an anti-septic called Mercurochrome? Here, it is splashed on every cut, wound or burn – it is bright red and is a de-rivative of mercury. I've been adept at using it and as a result the chaps call me Merk. At first, I thought they were referring to my murky past, for they think that anyone who has been to a Jesuit School must be odd! Yes, I've met more non-Romans on board and mean to tell Our Dad that they are just like the rest of us; they don't have two heads. It seems that I had mixed with a very narrow group of people before I joined up.

The ship's padre is an R.C. and a credit to our religion. He under-stands men when they are home-sick, frightened of cockroaches, just miserable or really depressed. Yes, one of our off-duty pastimes is cockroach races; we bet on the outcome. Often the race is interrupted by the command, 'All hands on Deck'. I daresay the Germans do the same on their ships.

When you knit for the forces, use very thick wool; think of us poor mortals who face but one enemy – the cold! Some days I long to be told to do a job near the engines, so that I can bask in their extravagant heat.

My Dad had so much foresight, showing me round the docks and taking me on board merchant ships when I was younger, so I know quite a lot about how a vessel sails. As a small boy I often got impa-tient with his explanations of marine archeology and construction. Now I look proudly at every nut and bolt and think of the ship-builders as sculptors and artists of unparalleled skill. It reminds me of Christmas 1939, when we three play-read that bit of Hornblower and laughed so much that Gladdy fell off my knee – what a look he gave me! How is he now he's a country cat? Sorry duty calls. . .

Food is very basic but I always seem to feel hungry and enjoy the time in the galley because we usually have a bit of a laugh and joke. Card games and writing letters are quite an occupation, but as you see the number of times I've added to this letter, nothing ever seems to get finished. Mam, I felt bad when one fellow asked me to help him write to his girl, because he couldn't read or write. I'll confess. I've never written to a girl, so when he asked what should we say, I had to rely on my love of English Literature (D. H. Lawrence, the Brownings and Jane Austen). He said, 'Well, Merk, you must have had a lot of experience with women.' I nodded. Now, I'm labelled as the ship's Lothario.

Send my love to Our Dad, and if his service address is permanent, perhaps you'd send on this letter to him. Oh, I shouldn't have written about his rigid religious stance – 'Sorry, Da'. It's stormy this evening with enormous waves. I can't tell you how much I love the sea, its moods, its beauty, its smell and its sound – even when it roars! Hope all's well at Cae Coch.

Love
Bernie

Margaret and Patrick lay on their bed together and studied the close written pages.

'Look, there's a sketch at the end,' said Margaret. Patrick was sniffing the paper and mumbling about the salty smell from the pages, which were covered with red blotches and oily marks. He commented on the censor's black pen striking out the name and number of the ship.

'It seems to be a prostrate sailor lying on a pallet with another man wearing a white surgical jacket, with a malevolent grin on his face, saying, 'Where did you say it hurt?'' Margaret murmured.

'Thank God, he's unaware of my little escapade. Not a word about guns, torpedoes, mines or bombs. Well I suppose that's our Bernie. Like you, Maggie, he's full of that bookish stuff and won't notice when a shell drops on deck at his feet.'

'Don't, Patrick. Don't. Please God, may this awful war end soon, before more people lose their lives. It's not something to joke about.'

Looking anxiously at the clock, as she pulled on her wellies, she added, awkwardly. 'I'll be about an hour. It would be good if you could show Bernie's letter to the Morgans. You know, they think of us as their family.'

'Yes, they'd be perfect, if they had the faith.' Patrick folded the grubby pages, carefully. Then he slipped them into the even grubbier envelope.

That evening, as Margaret carried out the task of feeding and mucking out, her thoughts concentrated on her son's letter. Bernie had referred to his father's fixated Catholicism. His words were almost conspiratorial. *Had Patrick noticed the implied criticism of himself? Margaret felt guilty.*

She remembered an occasion, when Bernie was about thirteen, when Patrick had gone fishing one Sunday evening, and she and Bernie decided to walk to the Pier Head to taste the sea air. Passing the Liverpool Parish Church of St. Nicholas, Bernie said, 'Look there're people going into the church for a service', and asked his mother if they could go inside and take part in the Anglican rite.

Afterwards, Bernie had commented on the service being in English and how he liked that. She'd replied that she was thrilled by being told that each week the congregation sang the hymn, which her informant referred to as, 'For those in peril on the sea'. Margaret found herself humming, 'Eternal father strong to save. . .'

Did either I or Bernie mention the service to Patrick?

29

A Strange Alliance

On her return from school and shopping for a couple of items in the town, Margaret found Patrick in deep conversation with Mr. Morgan, in the Cae Coch kitchen. There was a stack of ironing to do. She had put the flat irons on the fire before she went out and Mrs. Morgan had tended them, meanwhile, and stopped them becoming too hot. Margaret apologized to the men for needing the table where they were sitting. They moved willingly, but took their chairs near the range instead of going into the parlour. *Do they want to be companionable or are they cold?*

As Mrs. Morgan was churning, it was a pleasant change to hear conversation even though Margaret felt that she was not going to be a party to it. The two men seemed to be in a world of their own. When news had come that Patrick was to recuperate at Cae Coch, Margaret had been worried that he would air his extreme Catholic views and offend his hosts, who, though committed to the Church of Wales, were, even so, moderate and tolerant of individuals of different religions. *Was Patrick learning tact, at last? Was he becoming a less bigoted Catholic?*

The subject of their conversation was 'morale'. Patrick said that it was vital to raise morale if the war was to be won.

'So, how d'you do that, when Lord Haw Haw is telling the world that we are a defeated nation?'

'Well aren't you in a good position to influence people, at least local people, through your paper.'

'Go on.'

'I know how good the British worker is. In my Marine Insurance days, I was amazed by the skills displayed in ship-building, for example.'

'And. . .'

'These same workers are either honing their skills for the war effort or using their talents in the forces. I've been surprised by the ability of some of the lads that I've been training.'

Margaret was impressed and surprised by Patrick's serious tone. *Had his awful experience changed him?*

'Before the war I'd go into the docks to get information and I'd watch tradesmen working in their various areas of skill, as I waited for someone to help me with my query. Sometimes, I'd take our Bernie with me on a Saturday. He probably liked the lemonade and biscuits, but I daresay some of the expertise and commitment of the Liverpool docks rubbed off on him.'

Had Bernie's comment thrilled his father? It seemed so. Strange, that Bernie's letter had not moved from their bed. Abandoned? Or just not to be shared?

'Yes, go on.' Dai Morgan's voice was excited; he was sitting forward in his chair, listening intently.

'I was impressed by the precision of the work done. Dirty work often. Even so, they had pride in the task in hand. At tea breaks, the conversation was intelligent. I was always delighted by the humour, too. I could tell you a few tales, Mr. Morgan.'

Dai had been scribbling in his note-book, despite being attentive to Patrick. 'I've had it in mind to do some character sketches of servicemen, but your comments open up the subject to craftsmen within the services – men and women. I could start by writing about the women's Land Army, after all I've employed a couple of the girls.'

'Sounds good and it's rural. The more urban skills like ship-building could be woven in by degrees.'

'What about some drawings?'

'I used to do some sketches for our insurance mag. Maggie, be a darling and fetch the one I kept and showed you last night.'

Margaret dutifully went and produced the magazine. Dai looked ill at ease. *Mr. Morgan wouldn't speak to his wife like that would he?*

'They're good. Yes. When I've run out of local models, could you supply the technical material and the jokes to make the people realistic and the articles readable?'

'What about giving them names like, 'Sid, the boilermaker'; 'Tom, the welder'; 'Alf, the. . .'etc'. Your rustics could be 'Taffy'; 'Llewellyn' or 'Gareth''.

Margaret became a little nervous, was her husband putting on a Welsh accent? She felt Patrick's puckish wit might take hold and his mimicry might offend, but Mr. Morgan replied with a smile.

'I'm game, the idea's good,' he said.

Patrick, wisely, nodded. He'd realized that he was near to ridiculing the Welsh. Care reigned.

'Before 1939, I wrote about the countryside, the crops, hunting and shooting, but now everything needs to be related to the war and how it has changed people's lives.'

So the column, 'Morgan's Men' was born, which led to 'Women of the War', a month later. The editor enthused about the copy. No secrets were exposed. Dai didn't miss an opportunity to chat to the most extraordinary people in his quest for a morale boosting tale, even the 'Knitting Circle' featured in one edition, accompanied by a sketch of a kitten playing with a ball of wool, which had somehow become tangled around a table, chairs and a tractor. The man who sketched the 'Men' and the 'Women' had not hitherto known his cartoon capabilities. Perhaps they would make him famous after hostilities had ceased.

30

Collaboration

Morgan's 'Men' and 'Women' were an added column of the local paper and didn't prevent Dai from writing the articles and information which he'd provided for the paper hitherto. He was busier than ever, but as a consequence the paper's circulation and popularity were increasing. Each Friday there was a scramble for 'The Express' and patients in the Convalescent Home and the community elsewhere identified with the invincibility of the British Worker. It was he and his lady who were going to win this awful war. Nancy brought the news from the town to Margaret. Dai Morgan and Gwyn were able to spend less time at home and reluctantly delegated more of the farm chores to Margaret and Nancy. Sometimes Dai would take Patrick with him on his quests for news; having someone who had suffered and survived an accident of war was a person to be emulated and praised. It brought the war closer to home. When Patrick was at Cae Coch, he would lend a hand, though initially, he was better at feeding stock than handling some of the more lively animals. He did learn quickly to speak quietly to the two horses and on one occasion managed to catch Rose who felt 'the wind in her tail' and in her excitement pulled away from Nancy and made a dive for the track towards the road. 'You're my Knight in Shining Armour,' said Nancy, who was near to tears. Patrick who had until then thought Nancy 'a bit wet', forever after called her Sweet Nancy.

Luckily, spring had been late and cultivation had been completed as a result of Gwyn working extra hours, after his duties at the Convalescent Hospital were finished for the day. He loved driving the ageing Fordson tractor, which had been an inspirational second hand purchase made by Dai Morgan early in 1939. Sometimes the machine could be heard after dark. All the grassland had been chain harrowed and some areas had been re-seeded; potatoes, swedish turnips, carrots and onion sets were beginning to grow. Mrs. Morgan played her part like the younger workers, but she worried about Margaret's unborn child as if it were her own. It became a joke between Patrick and Margaret that she had said to Mrs. Morgan, 'I'm an Irish peasant. I can work until the baby comes.'

Mr. Morgan overheard and had retorted almost angrily, 'Please don't belittle yourself. Remember you're an educated woman.' Secretly, she felt touched and valued. Patrick had commented later, 'The Welsh put too much store by education, I think.' Margaret thanked God that her Bernie had passed a scholarship to an academic school, though what good was that now? *Mr. Morgan likes educated women. He must have encouraged Mary to leave home to study medicine, at a time when the family was suffering from losing a beloved son.*

After tea each evening the family talked, prior to the nine o'clock BBC News. Both Morgans and Rooneys tried to entertain Anna. There was an unspoken feeling that it was near bedtime that she remembered and missed her mother. All looked forward to Easter which was the second week of April when the Williams family would be at Cae Coch. Anna wanted to tell David about riding her bicycle and compare notes about school work. She asked Margaret whether she thought David had read about King Arthur when he'd been at school in Liverpool.

The week before Easter Anna had gone to bed one evening when the conversation turned to the topic of *Propaganda*. Dai Morgan asked Patrick whether, he thought that all the facts, good and bad, were reported truthfully, in the reputable daily newspapers and the BBC news programmes. Did Alvar Lidell read the truth?

To Margaret's horror, Patrick laughed heartily saying, 'Of course not. Granted that the residents of Coventry and Bristol, who experienced heavy raids last November, were aware of the colossal damage and the large number of casualties, but...' he paused, as if to edit his next sentence. 'I don't think the statistics were published nationally. The people of each area just got on with life as best they could. We will know the truth after the war.'

'What about news from the front and at sea?' It was Dai's turn to regret his hasty words.

'We seem to be told of general victories, advances and some tragedies, but all news seems to be filtered by censorship. Publishing the unedited facts can put our troops in danger.'

The two women were due to read a two part sketch to Anna so they disappeared. As they walked up the stairs by the light of a lamp, Margaret asked, 'Do you think that Patrick is right about information being suppressed?'

'Probably,' said Flo Morgan, sadly. 'I read somewhere, 'the first casualty when war comes is truth'.' Her expression was grave and her companion noticed how weary she was becoming – the light of the lamp emphasized the deep lines on her face. Despite her sober mood, however, she went on to expand her statement.

'The details of events must be kept secret for the sake of morale. We mustn't forget the strides that are probably, being made in the manufacture of armour, explosives, ship-building and the development of new aircraft. We must have divine hope, my dear.'

'I know, I know.' They were standing on the landing, but Mrs. Morgan paused to say, 'Forgive me for asking but did your son, did Bernie, seem in good spirits, as far as you could tell, from his letter?'

Margaret felt the light on her face, she couldn't prevaricate. 'I think he was putting on a brave face for me. There was a touch of bravado about the whole letter.'

'Letters from the front from our boy, Owen, always suggested that he was on some exciting holiday. He was missing us – yes, but the war was a million miles away. Remember, soldiers see the whites of the eyes of their enemies. Sailors and airmen are more remote from the forces of the other side. I wonder which is better.'

'I think Bernie believes that his beloved ship is invincible.'

They stood together at the top of the stairs, in silence. *Did they know each other's thoughts?* The eternal bond of motherhood enveloped them. They smiled shyly, in the flickering light.

'Our son's last letter. . .'

'I'm sorry. I didn't mean to resurrect painful memories. Please don't let me distress you, let's. . .'

'No, seeing you and your anxiety about Bernie, I realized that I shouldn't have bottled up my grief for so long. My bad experience may somehow help you.'

'What did he say in his letters?' Margaret's voice was gentle.

'It was his last letter which was him. Him. All his enthusiasms and sensitivities were there. He was speaking directly to us. He loved the country like his father - "a man of the soil". He was an excellent horseman – hunted and competed at point-to-point events. He and another officer had hired two thoroughbreds from a French Riding Academy, for a week-end's leave. He described, the *magnificent bocage*, I think the word is a description of the French countryside; what they said to each other; how the horses rode and what enjoyment the ride was. The horses were called 'Salt' and 'Sugar'. I wondered what colour the horses were but then when he was killed I realized that they were both greys. Oddly, he'd always chosen to ride chestnuts and bays, but now I think how other-worldly the colour grey is.'

'I understand. I want to know the names of all the sailors on Bernie's watch and what they look like.'

Margaret had lowered the lamp but wondered whether her companion was shedding a secret tear too.

*

There was so much to do, both in the house and on the farm, before the visitors arrived. Dai Morgan and Patrick had gone into the garrison town to meet the soldiers, destined to embark for the front, within two days. There was a rehearsal for a concert for the local battalion, and a young Welsh tenor, Gareth Davies, was to entertain the men. 'The Express' wanted a story.

'He's my idol, why don't we get to hear his *beautiful* voice,' Nancy's pronunciation of the word 'beautiful' amused Margaret who realized how young and naïve her workmate was.

'We're not going to the front, Nancy. They don't even know where they're going, poor souls. Patrick's going to do a sketch of Gareth, anyway, so we'll pin it up in the dairy.'

'It's not the same.' Nancy went into the house to make the beds and help Mrs. Morgan, while Margaret went to do the dairy work. She was straining the butter milk into a bucket for the calves when footsteps heralded the entrance of Gwyn. She froze.

'I want. . .' he started but Margaret moved quickly and the bucket tipped. A small amount of the liquid spilt.

'Please don't. . .' she thought that she might be shouting. He seemed to take a step backwards, at the same time he took hold of a mop standing by the door. *Are you going to hit me with the mop?*

'Please, Margaret, Mrs. Rooney, calm down, down. . . I've come to apologise. Let me. . ?'

Margaret took the mop from him and started to mop up the milk. Neither spoke. The awful memory of his hands round her neck and the fear she'd felt, suddenly engulfed her. *With hindsight, might I have been wrong? Was it entirely his fault? Had he just been clumsy? Did I overreact because I can't bear my neck being touched? No, he'd made a sexual advance to her. It had been unwelcome. How did he feel about her now?*

He seemed smaller somehow, like a child, who'd been caught taking a cake from the pantry. Taking or stealing? Which was it?

'Let me speak. Please? I've changed. I...'

She put the mop into the bucket of water and tried to stand up straight, appear to listen, though she wanted to run. Run past him? No. She must stay. Perhaps, Mr. Morgan and Patrick would return. Surely, Gwyn didn't know how long they'd be.

'You shouldn't...'

'What I did that day was vulgar, rude... I'm not good with words. Life had been so awful... no Great War for me, no children and...' he hesitated.

'At the time, you didn't know that I was carrying...'

'No, I dain't... I was mad. After... I thought you'd tell the Morgans. You had every right. I didn't know how Nancy... Nancy would've taken the disgrace.'

'You terrified me. I thought...'

'I'm sorry. I've always been a bit rough. I wanted to say how I admired you. It came out like envy. I didn't mean...' The little boy look returned. 'I'm so ashamed. At the time I felt you had humiliated me, now I see how angry I'd be if anyone touched Nancy.'

Margaret realized that whatever happened now, the incident had to be forgotten. For Nancy's sake; for Gwyn's sake; she thought of Bernie – he was safe she thought, at this moment. She was fit and the child within her stirred as much as to say, 'Forgive'.

'There's this ghastly war on, none of us are free from it. I'm so fond of your Nancy and I want, I really want to forget what happened.'

'You see. Now I've got the job down the Convalescent, I feel part of the war. I want to do what I can to win it. I felt cheated last time round when all my pals didn't come back and I had to go on. I've a chance now, 'aven't I?'

'Of course, I sometimes feel cheated when I think of Patrick and Bernie fighting battles that are British.'

Gwyn smiled and Margaret realized that he usually had a grim expression on his face. 'D'you know, Maggie. I can call you Maggie, can't I? Nancy does.'

'Of course you can.'

'D'you know, I feel closer to you being Irish than I do to English people. I get on with Patrick, too And...'

'No drinking, now Patrick has this head injury.' They laughed weakly but spontaneously shook hands.

Gwyn left as a car drove into the farm yard. Margaret spied Patrick as he leapt out of the car, brandishing a sketch of the famous Welsh tenor, his handsomeness exaggerated, his arms outstretched, with musical notes and stars showering from his lips.

'See, Gwyn, where's Sweet Nancy? But, man, he's got some voice.'

I hope Mr. Morgan didn't hear the mockery in Patrick's voice. As Dai jumped out of the car, how graceful he was; he had the fluid elegance of some feline negotiating a grassy bank. His boots might have been dancing shoes. As he moved towards the house did he catch my eye with an understanding smile?

31

Easter

'Why's today called Maundy Thursday, Pinny?' asked Anna, as she was brushing Gladstone, in preparation for her parents' visit.

Margaret said that she thought the word was derived from the French language and it had something to do with Jesus 'washing the feet' and giving money to the poor, *by command* from God. She was hesitant to explain Christian festivals to Anna. She feared that she would get the detail wrong and that Anna would forever believe a Catholicised version of her own religion.

'Remember, I'm a Catholic and Maundy Thursday does have significance in our church, but I think it's different from yours – in Catholicism, there is no distribution of Maundy money by the King. Lent is important and Easter and Whit are the central festivals of our faith. Ask your grandmother all about different religions.' Anna seemed to like to ponder the different models of Christian worship and how they affected the people of Cae Coch. *Was she like her father, who was proud to be sceptical if not cynical about all branches of Christianity? Was Anna, like children in general, a bit of a mischief-maker?*

'Anna, let's check to see if the painted Easter eggs are dry and hide them in our loft for Sunday.'

Anna's voice was enthusiastic, 'Yes, each one has its name and picture on it. Would it be alright if I did two more for the Joneses?'

'Yes, there is a basket of eggs on the dresser, use two from there, but hurry. Your grandmother will be pleased that you've remembered Gwyn and Nancy.'

*

Margaret had been told by Nancy that the Morgans' son, Owen had been killed just before Easter in 1918 – on the 10th of April; it was the ninth to-day. Did Anna know about the tragedy of her uncle in that other war? There was a plan for the Morgans and Williams family to walk to church in the town for the three hour service on Good Friday, the following day. Margaret felt she would like to accompany them – Bernie was alive still, *thank God*, but she mourned his absence. *How did Patrick feel? Did he have this feeling of grief?* She'd ask Mary about the niceties of the situation. The day was, after all, the celebration of the crucifixion of Christ – all denominations of Christians acknowledged that.

*

'They're here,' Anna shouted from the kitchen door. In a trice the room was filled with the family. The kettle boiled, the tea was brewed and homemade Easter biscuits and hot cross buns appeared miraculously on the table. Parents embraced children and the two children clapped hands with each other; Margaret's hand was shaken as it moved from kettle to teapot. Patrick appeared and more greetings were made.

'You look well after your ordeal,' said Rhys.

'I'm not very good at sprinting and I seem to need a great deal of aspirin for headaches. But I must say that Cae Coch is a great place to recover from an accident. The air is so pure.'

'And how's the expectant mother?' asked Mary as she sipped her tea. I hope you're not doing too much.'

'I have excellent medical care from Dr. Thomas. Wasn't he at Medical School with you, Dr. Williams?'

'He was a few years behind Mary, but he did a locum for her when David was born.'

Margaret became concerned that she was talking too much so she made an excuse about a dairy task and signalled to Patrick to leave the family to themselves.

*

When they were talking after supper two hours later, the conversation reverted to the trials of war – rationing, which was beginning to bite; farm produce having to be sold through the Ministry of Agriculture; and the consequences of the air raids, which had been alarming.

'As ever,' said Rhys, 'in Liverpool, the poor are the hardest hit. Better off people have gardens and can grow vegetables or keep chickens, but a great deal of Liverpool is back to back terrace housing with no gardens. The inequalities give rise to property damage and thefts.'

'Mother, you know that the Medical School has suffered bomb damage and the tidying up has delayed classes.' Mrs. Morgan shook her head at her daughter, trying to divert the conversation from bombing, but David and Anna had already vanished.

'Nothing is sacred' said Rhys.

'We're useless here,' said Dai Morgan, 'We feel as though we're watching some satanic sport – as on-lookers – with our friends and relatives playing on the hellish field.'

Mrs. Morgan added, 'we were told that the last war was the war to end wars and...'

Mary leant over the table and said softly, 'Mother, we mustn't lose hope. At least the bombing is over. Consider David and Anna; think of the Rooneys' baby.'

'The thought of a baby in the house has cheered your mother. We saw so little of your two when they were tiny, because we were both working with school and farm, and you were so far away,' Dai replied, looking at Patrick and Margaret.

'You've made up for it recently in school holidays,' Rhys was standing up and made a gesture of raising a glass. 'Let's make this Easter a happy time. It's a privilege to have you both with us, Margaret and Patrick.'

There was a chorus of, 'Amen to that.'

*

'It's the tenth of April, Owen's anniversary. Who's coming to church?' asked Dai Morgan, the following morning; all the farm chores had been done as all the visitors had lent a hand.

'I'll stay behind and do what jobs, if any, which are left to be done,' said Rhys.

'Would you mind the two children staying with you? There is so much gloom and doom in the news that to add Christ's crucifixion seems unnecessary.' Mary asked.

'I'd like to come with you, if that's alright?' said Margaret.

Patrick looked shocked. He'd never been into a Protestant church since his conversion, and he seemed doubtful whether his wife should be eager to go to St. Mary's.

'Maggie, are you. . ?'

Margaret explained that she liked attending the services in English, but not the Welsh ones at the church. They gave her comfort. She didn't miss the Latin mass as much as she'd thought she would. Her words had a dramatic effect on Patrick who seemed uneasy, jumping up from his chair and raising his voice he declared, 'I don't think you. . .' Fortunately, his outburst was left hanging in the air as Mrs. Morgan came into the room, which was hushed. Patrick moved to the back door motioning Margaret to follow. She reddened as she rushed out of the room, sensing the sympathy of all for her embarrassment.

*

The Rooneys were back in what they called their 'Eyrie'.

'Maggie, what happened to you just now, are you losing your faith?'

'No.'

'You and I are Catholics.'

'Yes, I'm still a Catholic, but I need to worship in a church. When it's possible to travel there, I go to the Catholic Church. But it's. . .'

'St. Mary's is Church of Wales. It is not your church.'

'I know, but I feel God's presence there.' Margaret felt that she must keep control. Her voice was little more than a whisper as she put on her coat, 'There's only one God.'

She was half way down the steps from the Eyrie, when her words became clearer, 'Why don't you and Dr. Williams take the children along the river to watch the salmon jumping, while we're at church.'

32

Bristol

'I don't know what to do, Mary?' Margaret and Mary were walking along the Wye in Spring sunshine, following a family breakfast at Cae Coch.

'You're not your usual self, what is it? Is there something amiss about the baby?' Mary's tone was professional.

'The letter I received this morning was from Bernie. It was from Bristol. He's attached to the City Hospital there, on a course for Emergency Medicine.'

'Well isn't that excellent, is there a chance that he could visit Cae Coch?'

'I was thinking that, but as your father rode off on his bicycle this morning, he said that he was in a rush because there had been a massive air raid on Bristol, last night,'

'Did he give you any details?'

'No, I was shocked and didn't want to delay him. I couldn't mention Bernie's letter to Patrick either. He was checking the sheep with Rhys and Gwyn.'

'Why on earth didn't you mention it to Mother and me back at the farm?'

'The children were there. After the sadness of yesterday, everyone seemed so relaxed and happy that I couldn't spoil the mood.'

'Maggie, you're family.'

'After being rejected by my own family, I suppose I'm reluctant to impose on. . .'

'My dear Maggie. . .'

'You've adopted us so wholeheartedly and Patrick hasn't always behaved as well as. . .'

Mary Williams's tone was serious, 'You being here with Dad and Mother's so important to Rhys and me. We can give our all to our jobs, knowing that Anna is being looked after well and the parents have support.'

'Thank you, I. . .'

'Has it crossed your mind that David and Anna could suddenly be orphaned?'

Margaret winced.

Mary's voice was soft as she said. 'Your involvement in the children's lives is of paramount importance to us. None of us know what the outcome of this wicked war will be.'

The two women had turned back to Cae Coch, automatically, and had quickened their pace.

'I felt,' said Margaret 'that it was selfish to think only of Bernie, when there could be many casualties and much destruction in Bristol. I was numbed.'

'I know, once in the quiet of this beautiful countryside, beside this ageless river, one's mind clears.'

'Yes, but, I had a vision of Bernie in uniform – he would have to play his part in the raid; there's a bit of Patrick in him. Would you call it bravado?'

'Yes, I suppose. . .'

'To think he's been in danger at sea and been safe – then he comes ashore and meets up with the worst raid Bristol's experienced in the war.'

Taking Margaret's arm, Mary added with a hint of bitterness, 'One of the ironies of war.'

They were in sight of Cae Coch. They could see the cows lazily chewing the cud in the field near the house and the sunlight casting shadows across the yard. All was peaceful. Here was tranquility! The only sounds were of contented farm animals and the voices of the two children busy in the stable, where the old draught horse, Hywel Dda cocked his ears as he spied the two women, over the half door of his box.

Margaret stopped and looked round, 'Do I have to bring my anxiety and fear to such a contented scene?'

*

Dai Morgan sat at the kitchen table reading the daily paper. His wife was preparing the mid-day meal. 'The news isn't good to-day.' His voice was flat.

'Dad, Margaret, I mean Mrs. Rooney is concerned about the devastation of Bristol. . .'

'I know, it's awful news. That's why I shot off to the office at the crack of crow. The number of dead is in the hundreds. . .' He was going to continue but his daughter interrupted. Mrs. Morgan turned from the stove, surprised at her daughter's lack of manners.

'Dad, Bernie Rooney's been sent on a course at the Bristol Hospital. He told his mother in his letter which came in this morning's post.'

The only sound was the bubbling of boiling potatoes. The three women sat down at the table, as if some better news could be relayed by the man who'd been in contact with journalists from the ruined city.

'I wish I'd known. I'd have asked the news agency to find out about the naval orderlies. I'll telephone now.'

On his return to the kitchen, Dai said, 'I've left a message. The duty officer will find some information, I'm sure.'

*

Margaret had things to do in the dairy. Her work was watched and 'helped' by David and Anna, who asked endless questions, which taxed her patience. The day dragged on and then the telephone rang. Dai Morgan leapt from his chair by the stove and ran into the dining-room.

'Is there news?' Mary was the first to speak.

'That was my contact in the news agency. He said it was pandemonium in the hospital, all night. Rescuers, servicemen and civilians were casualties. He'll keep me informed.'

'Did you ask about Bernie Rooney?'

'Mary dear, I couldn't possibly ask about any individual. It would've appeared unprofessional and also a breach of security.'

'Thank you for seeking information, Mr. Morgan,' was Margaret's immediate response. Her voice was strained.

'I'm sorry. It's this awful business of *Careless Talk Costs Lives.*'

Patrick and Rhys, rosy-faced and laughing, burst through the back door and Margaret managed to say, 'It's clear that you've enjoyed the mountain. How are the sheep?'

Both men smiled and nodded. Margaret waved Bernie's letter in front of her husband. 'Let's leave the Williamses to talk with their parents.

As they went through the door, Patrick grabbed his wife's arm, 'Maggie, you're shaking. What's happened?'

33

A New Job

It was Easter Monday and still no news came from Bernie. Both Patrick and Margaret were very quiet, but Patrick was heard, occasionally, to echo the cliché, 'No news is good news.' This irritated Margaret who spent extra time doing catch–up jobs in the dairy and the barns. Mrs. Morgan joined her on Monday afternoon and suggested that they did a spring clean of the dairy equipment. This was an unnecessary task but Margaret realized that there was a kindly motive in the suggestion. When all was sparkling clean, the older woman said that between them they had done a very good job and touched Margaret on the shoulder as she added, 'I know what you're going through, my dear, I'm praying.'

At six o'clock the telephone rang and Dai Morgan let it ring as he said, 'This may be for the Rooneys, I never have calls on Bank Holidays. Come with me, both of you, into the dining room.' Immediately, he passed the receiver to Margaret whose 'Bernie' could be heard over the whole of Breconshire. Both parents spoke and fired questions at the caller; about him, the raid, the hospital and the casualties.

Margaret's words were joyous, 'He's exhausted but exhilarated by his recent experiences. He hasn't been in bed since Thursday night but hopes to have a 'nap' in an hour's time. I'm sure we didn't have our three minutes.'

Patrick said, 'The pips never lie.'

The tension of the last couple of days evaporated and Flo Morgan joined the laughter adding, 'Anna has a habit of using the phrase 'little minute' and I keep explaining that a minute is a unit of time.'

Anna said solemnly. 'Time is sometimes slow and other times quick to me, Granny.'

Her grandfather hugged her saying, 'Time does seem to deceive, that's why we shouldn't waste it, cariad.'

*

'It's been a good holiday all things considered,' said Rhys as he squeezed into the hire car beside David and some of his luggage. 'We'll see you all again in the summer.'

Anna didn't cry, for the first time, when bidding farewell to her parents. Taking her friend's hand she whispered, 'I know it was horrid hearing about Bernie and Bristol's raid, but Hitler isn't bombing Liverpool anymore.' Margaret thought of her knowledge of history and wondered whether there were any certainties in times of war, but hugged Anna instead of giving a reply.

'Will you have your baby when they come next time?'

'I don't think so, the baby is due in September and they'll be here in August. By the way, my baby needs more than one pair of bootees.'

*

There had been no sickly lambs, only the one set of premature twins in the farm kitchen. The flock seemed to have responded to the need for production. There had been several sets of healthy twins and no black lambs. The latter were considered unlucky locally, so Gwyn, 'the shepherd', was delighted. If only Bernie could visit, thought Margaret. Surely he had some time off. He wrote short notes regularly, but then a longer letter arrived. It was a day by day account of his month's time at the hospital.

'Please keep these notes until the end of the war.' 'I'm more determined than ever to study medicine when hostilities end. I think at last that I really could be a doctor.'

Glancing at the neatly written pages, Dai remarked, 'Well if he doesn't manage to obtain a place in medical school with this as a testimonial, he would make an excellent writer. It is so neat. Thank you, Patrick, for showing it to me.'

Margaret grinned, 'I thought doctors were renowned for their illegible writing. Bernie's last letter wasn't neat.' They laughed.

*

It was the day when Patrick had an appointment for a medical examination at the Convalescent Hospital. Margaret knew that he was anxious to return to naval life, but she feared that his headaches might prevent him continuing his previous duties. *Was Patrick's sleeplessness caused by his injuries or was it just another consequence of war and worry? Would Patrick be honest with the doctors? He replied differently to questions concerning his health, depending on the person enquiring, but he seemed excited about the possibility of returning to his old post and his pals of a couple of years.* Meanwhile Margaret considered whether she would welcome being on her own again. Patrick had, since his time at Cae Coch, made her feel small in front of the Morgan family; something she had been at pains to hide. She wondered whether she wasn't good in her dealings with men, if so why? Perhaps it resulted from her doing a man's job. Margaret shuddered, thinking of the other possible course her life could have taken – the nunnery!

*

'Hooray!' Patrick's voice interrupted her reverie.

'Sorry, Maggie, I'll be going off again and you'll be all alone again. Poor old girl!'

'I'm so glad you've been passed fit. Are you A1?'

'No, I'm not going back to my old unit, but they've given me a shore job and it's in Wales. Sorry, luv, I can't tell you exactly where.' How well he was able to generate an atmosphere of mystery!

'I must tell Anna and the Morgans.'

The conversation with his wife was at an end.

*

As the Royal Navy van drew away with a cheery Patrick waving vigorously from the window, the Cae Coch 'family' were lined up, as if for a service inspection. Only Anna was visibly upset.

'I'll look after Pinny, Uncle Patrick,' she had whispered as her hero closed the van door, with a wink in her direction.

Margaret needed to plan ahead and without her husband's presence, she was able to concentrate on her farm work and establish a routine for when she left everything to Gwyn and Nancy, in September. David was to help on the farm during the summer holidays. The hay and wheat harvest were going to be a problem but a neighbouring farmer had been asked to help. A group of prisoners-of-war had been allocated to assist, too. May Day was a school holiday and it seemed that warmer weather was on its way. The longer days made everyone more content. Margaret was able to relax.

*

Returning from the town's Maypole dancing, Anna and Margaret were met by Mr. and Mrs. Morgan in the lane, anxious to tell them that there had been another air raid on Merseyside - Wallasey had been the target.

'We didn't want anyone else to tell you about it. Wallasey is far away from your home, Anna.'

'Yes, I do know that. Thank you, Grandpa.' Even so, she looked anxious, wondering about her parents and asking questions about news bulletins. Dai seemed absent from the farm much of the time. He confided to Margaret that he was in the newspaper office working but also monitoring news agency and B.B.C. reports of continual raids on Merseyside, throughout the following week.

'Don't let Anna fret. It seems that the docks have been hit badly especially the Bootle area where there have been extensive casualties. There's food shortage and a homeless problem.'

'What about the Williamses?' Margaret asked, 'Have you telephoned them?'

'There're no lines. It seems that the telephone exchange was put out of action. I've explained that to Anna. I'm worried but not alarmed. Carry on as usual. Anna must be kept in the dark until we receive reliable news.'

Mrs. Morgan looked distressed and had to rest, but reassured Anna by saying that she had a bilious attack. It was May 14th before a letter arrived. The envelope was torn and dirty. Mary described the war chaos. She and Rhys had taken in refugees from the bombing. A friend had had a leg amputated and the university had suffered considerable damage. As Margaret read the catalogue of miseries, she saw that the final page was a happy note to Anna, 'We're fine. We have spent a lot of time in the shelter; coming home at all hours; but everyone is so helpful and determined to fight on. The lovely St. Luke's Church is in ruins – it's just a shell, but that's the nearest bomb site to our house. D'you remember, Anna, running up all the steps to the church, last year? It was a beautiful sunny day. We still have the photo.'

'Mummy must be alright; that's her writing. Oh, Pinny. . .' She cried a little but was distracted by second letter to her from Patrick, from a SECRET LOCATION. 'He's in America, I know what he means.' No-one disillusioned her. Mr. Morgan had more reliable news. Rumours in press circles were rife. It was thought that there were developments on the Pembrokeshire coast.

'Pembroke Dock is an obvious place to use the harbour to continue to wage the 'Battle of the Atlantic'. I guess that's where Patrick is,' said Dai one evening to Flo and Maggie.

His wife's tone indicated some surprise, 'Dai, should you be speculating on such a sensitive matter? What about, "Careless talk"?'

Margaret looked amused, as Mr. Morgan replied, 'My dear Flo, neither you nor I nor Mrs. Rooney are likely to be conspiring with the enemy.'

'I suppose not. This war makes us lose our common sense sometimes.' All three saw the joke.

*

Weekly phone calls to Liverpool were resumed at the end of May and the bombing seemed to ease. The BBC news was full of Hitler's assault on Russia. Mary and Rhys reported that they and the Liverpool population were kept busy, every hour of the day, keeping well and making the best of a meagre diet. Their ruined city was recovering and rejoicing.

34

Summer at Last

The families in Liverpool and Cae Coch struggled through June and July, 1941. Mary became weary and Margaret grew fatter and tired but excited. Dr. Mary revealed the reason for her fatigue to Margaret in a short letter - Merseyside casualties of the May blitz, had added psychological symptoms to their physical ailments; she was working long hours, conditions were poor. She'd added that she felt a need for a break and had asked Rhys' colleague to do a locum for her, again, in August.

The war had toughened the nation and every person, except a few despised spivs, who operated a black market in food, drink and clothes, worked hard for a victorious outcome. The question, 'When will the war end?' had been replaced with, 'The war will end with our hard work and determination.' The people of Wales, like most of the country, were resolute in playing their part.

*

August brought the Williamses to the farm and David from boarding school. Mary and Rhys had the unenviable task of acquainting Anna with the news that she was to go to boarding school from September. Rhys had to return to his post after less than two weeks, promising to be in Wales, again, for a quick visit when Anna and David were setting off to school.

'Mrs. Rooney will not be able to take and fetch you to and from school, when she has her baby.' Mary was helping her mother with the washing-up, whilst explaining about boarding school to a disgruntled daughter.

'But, Mummy, she won't have me to help her look after the baby,' Anna exclaimed, near to tears.

'You're only going to Brecon. Mrs. Rooney may bring the baby to see you one week-end. There will be half-term and two other week-end breaks during the term. We've left enough stamps at the school, for you to write each day, if you think you need to tell us anything.' Margaret concentrated on the ironing and said nothing.

'I've got the holidays,' Anna told her 'Pinny', later, and I'm not going to think about school. Anyway, the war will be over by September, so I will be able to go home to Liverpool.'

*

The hay was in, dry and rich. The wheat was harvested. Both carthorse and tractor had behaved well. The fruit, from Dai's garden, had ripened and been bottled in Kilner jars. Jam had been made and apples stored in Gladstone's outhouse. News from Patrick was good; he was enjoying his new job. He asked for his artist materials to be sent to him *via* a naval depot address. This request gave rise to some dismay!

'God's in his heaven and all's right with the world.' David said at supper. The whole family was so exhausted that no-one had the energy to comment.

Then a cloud gathered in the form of a telephone call from Bernie, who had returned to base for yet another training course on anaesthesia, having passed his Sickbay Attendants one in Bristol with flying colours. He had received a letter from the Admiralty, informing him that he was to join a ship in Plymouth, the following week. There was to be no embarkation leave!

Mary insisted that they found a way for Margaret to travel to Plymouth to say, 'Au Revoir'.

The surprise came the following day.

'Dad's editor has to make a trip to Plymouth to interview a naval Commander, who is interested in 'Press Influence on the Public'. He's willing to take you with him as company for his secretary on the journey.' It turned out that the secretary had been at school with Mary and the two women had schemed to arrange the trip. Margaret was ecstatic. Her only reservation was that Patrick could not get leave to bid Bernie, 'Bon Voyage.'

*

'We had a picnic on the Hoe. I had bought some cherries, black market, probably. I planted a stone in the grass. Bernie was unhappy to leave me but excited about putting his training to the test.

Afterwards, I saw him lined up with his watch on the deck of the ship before it set sail. All those sailors and marines were wearing their best uniforms and standing at attention. They looked like statues. What a sight! Mr. Morgan, your editor loaned me his field glasses so I saw all the sailors clearly. Bernie looked so smart. I was so proud. I wished that I could touch him. The marine band was playing – *Rule Britannia* and *Life on the Ocean Waves*! It was only when the tug pulled the vessel away from the landing-stage, that I realized that he was sailing goodness knows where.'

The Cae Coch audience had never before heard Margaret carried away by her recollections; she had lived and re-lived her day in Plymouth, a thousand times. She appeared as if in a trance. All present including the Joneses listened with riveted if sombre attention. Anna touched Margaret's hand asking, 'Have you a photo?'

Margaret explained, with sudden emotion, that photography was forbidden, even by the press but the image of her son, on that deck, would always be in her mind and her heart.

'We all shouted, 'God Speed' and no tears were shed until the ship was out of sight.' Margaret's voice faltered.

'I wish I'd been there,' said Anna, 'but can I come with you when he comes back?'

There was no answer. Margaret had fled from the room.

35

Emergency

The government advertisement, 'Don't delay, Plough to-day,' had encouraged Dai Morgan to consider maximum crops. He had invested in good hay seed and prepared the ground carefully enriching it with farmyard manure. As a result it seemed that Cae Coch would have a second hay harvest, in late August. The family were discussing this when Margaret came into the kitchen early one morning, seeming anxious.

'I've left Nancy finishing the work in the cow barn. Is it possible for me to have a quick word with you, Dr. Williams?'

Mary jumped to her feet and told Anna to finish her breakfast, because there was a great deal 'to do today' on the farm. 'Rome wasn't built in a day, Gladstone will survive without being brushed,' she said as she followed Margaret with some apprehension.

'I've awful pains in my stomach, Mary. Did we walk too far yesterday or. . .'

'Walking never did a pregnant woman any harm. Let's have a look at you.'

The two women hurried up the steps into Margaret's loft – now officially called, 'The Eyrie'.

After a cursory examination, Mary spoke authoritatively, but kindly.

'To avoid any alarm, it would be a good idea if we took a trip to the Cottage Hospital – that's where you plan to give birth. Isn't it?'

'Um, yes, it is.'

'I'll tell mother that you've asked me for advice on things you need for the baby from the chemist. I'll suggest we phone for a hire car in the circumstances. It might be advisable if you packed a bag with essentials, too.'

'Won't she think the car unnecessary for just shopping,' murmured Margaret.

'Mother will probably know what's going on, but she'll have a lot to do anyway. Nancy will reassure her. My mother does look her age suddenly, doesn't she?' Her words were anxious.

Margaret, wondered how old Mrs. Morgan was but nodded, feeling some concern.

*

Nurse Roberts was ready, waiting at the hospital Reception Desk. Margaret imagined that Mary had phoned the hospital at the same time that she phoned the garage, while she'd been gathering the things Mary had suggested she secreted into the car before they set off.

'Dr. Thomas is on his way. He'll be surprised to see *you*, Dr. Williams. Are you going to give a second opinion?'

Mary looked a little embarrassed. 'No, Mother has asked me to buy some things at the grocer and see what fruit is on offer, if any. I'll leave you obstetric experts to look after Maggie.'

'It's probably a false alarm,' said Margaret, hating the fuss she was causing.

'Well, I've got a nice room for you if baby decides to be born. You're the only maternity case here at the moment. The war's put the locals off having babies.'

As they laughed at the weak joke, Margaret doubled up in pain and sat down to regain her breath.

By the time Dr. Thomas arrived Margaret was on a well-prepared bed with Nurse Roberts scrubbed up for a delivery. The doctor looked at Margaret's records and scratched his head.

'It must be a false alarm, Nurse. Margaret has three weeks to go.'

'I hope you're right.'

After an examination he assured the patient that all was well. The foetal heart was fine and Patrick's daughter seems big enough and fit enough to arrive in war-time Britain. 'We'll await developments.'

'She doesn't know about rationing and her father being at a secret location,' said the nurse, but Margaret saw the anxiety in her expression. 'I'll instruct the orderly to prepare a heated cot while I do the real work.'

*

It was noon, when Mary returned to collect Margaret from the hospital. Dilys Roberts was emphatic that her patient was to stay put – that the baby would be born before to-morrow.

'Don't worry, Maggie, I'll reassure all the family. I wonder how Anna will react - Cae Coch without Pinny.'

'She'll be delighted to think that the baby will be home before she goes to boarding school. Oh, I've been presumptuous in using the word home.'

'Cae Coch is your home, Maggie. Please don't ever forget that.'

'I'm so grateful. But, Mary, don't let Anna take Gladstone to bed with her. Did you know she did one night when she was homesick? Your mother was so cross with her. I don't want to be the cause of friction.'

The two women embraced and Mary put her head on one side, as she said, jokingly, 'Will I have a little of my baby back when you are engrossed in new motherhood?'

*

The doctor had long gone when Nurse Roberts popped in with the Night Sister to say that the hospital was not very busy and all Margaret had to do was ring her bell if she needed anything. Her pains seemed to have stopped completely.

Margaret was informed days later that at 4 am, the Sister reported to Nurse Roberts at home, that she was very concerned about Mrs. Rooney, her temperature was high and she was very restless. 'Please will you come into the hospital? I'm not a midwife.' She had shouted down the phone.

*

Margaret woke in pain, her back hurt and she felt so hot, only to find a person who seemed to be in some sort of uniform, standing over her. She wasn't Bridget, who was she? She dozed a little. People seemed to be talking to her but she didn't understand them. She drank things: she smelt something – whatever it was it made her sleepy. The pain went away and she slept. As she slept she was in good company.

It was so good to be by the river, walking with Sean and Bernie. Was it the Lee or the Wye? It was a sensible conversation. The men were discussing the relative merits of Trinity College, Dublin and University

College, Aberystwyth. But why are they ignoring my comments as though I'm not here? The river is flowing rhythmically like a tap. It is so good to hear. Suddenly the voices became quiet and another man was speaking with authority, 'It's a boy and after all this time he's still breathing – thank God.' *Margaret could not understand.* Then, a woman's voice, it wasn't Bridget. *Where was Bridget?*

'Welcome young man. You'll have to bawl your way into wartime Wales.'

Margaret heard the words but they made no sense. *War and Wales? Where had Sean and Bernie gone?* 'Come back'. She called their names but there was no answer.

She heard the man's voice again, 'While I tidy up mother, take the little fellow into the waiting-room to show him to Mrs. Morgan. She needs some reward for her twenty-four hour vigil.'

'But he's all mucky.'

'She's used to new born lambs. A little muck won't worry her.'

At last Margaret understood. She remembered that they were introducing a new cross breed of sheep on Sean's father's estate. It was so important to have all the lambs born alive. Why couldn't she see the lamb? How hot she felt. She seemed to be in a bed. How odd! She must make herself heard.

Her voice was a whisper but she muttered the words. 'Where am I?' She smelt a faint smell of soap. No answer.

'What are you talking about?' She heard. It was she who was speaking – it was her own voice.

'You gave birth to a beautiful baby boy.' A woman spoke these strange words.

'Yes, I know. His name is Bernie. He's been chatting to Sean and me for hours and it must be teatime.'

'We'll soon have you comfy, try to sleep.'

*

'It's been nearly two days since you went into labour and gave birth to a lovely baby,' Nurse Roberts said.

'You're teasing me. I came here on Monday. Isn't it Tuesday?'

'It's Wednesday, Maggie, I mean Mrs. Rooney. You're back from the brink.'

'I did feel very hot and I had a very odd dream. I was cradling and feeding Bernie. Can I see my baby, please? Is it a boy or a girl? Tell me.'

'You've been in a strange world. Totally unintelligible. *He* is lovely.'

'I can see the cot, now. Let me see my son, please?' She put her feet to the ground, faltered, and nearly fell.'

'Here he is, hold him carefully. You're not well enough yet to get out of bed. You have a fever – *puerperal fever*, to be exact.'

Margaret wasn't interested. She was gloating over the little bundle, dazed but overjoyed.

Nurse Roberts continued her narrative, 'It's a form of septicemia – caused by some infection during labour. You were in labour for over twenty-four hours.'

The mother still wasn't listening.

The nurse sounded angry. 'This hospital is clean, very clean. It's not our fault. The laundry mixed our clean linen with soiled sheets from the Convalescent Hospital.'

'Well, I'm alright. Does it matter?'

'Yes. It does. It does. You've been very ill and without the new drug in trials that Dr. Thomas obtained from Cardiff, you might not have recovered.'

An ecstatic Margaret and her child were left alone for the first time.

36

A Rose by. . .

'You're ten days old to-day and. . .' Margaret whispered to her baby as he fed greedily from her. She wanted to tell him about his brother, his father, the farm, and Ireland but the memories of all were muddled in her mind. She felt almost well at last. What a nuisance she'd been to the Morgan family and to the hospital and medics but all seemed so pleased with her recovery. Patrick had been officially informed of her critical state of health but as yet had not appeared.

As if by telepathy, the sister came into the little room, smiling broadly as she escorted Patrick through the door. 'Daddy has come to see his son and heir.' Margaret was surprised at the comment. A photograph of Bernie had been on the front page of 'The Express', last week. The headline had been 'Sailor Bernie Rooney Has New Baby Brother'. Margaret didn't correct the sister.

'I knew that the baby'd be a boy.' Patrick said with pride as he took the now sleeping baby from his mother's arms. The baby protested weakly but allowed his father to almost smother him as he reached over to peck Margaret's cheek.

'I don't know Maggie, old girl, why d'you have to have another fever? When we were in Liverpool you never had fevers. It must be the country air.'

'I'm quite old to give birth,' Margaret said nervously, wondering if the baby was comfortable or even safe. She couldn't dispel her earlier thoughts. Had she really seen Sean and Bernie? It must have been a dream or was Bernie dead too and were both men appearing to her in spirit form? She shivered. She was sure that she'd felt the Leprechaun scratching her neck causing inescapable fear to envelop her.

Patrick was studying his son. He took hold of his tiny hands from within the shawl and counted the fingers. He looked transfixed by the feel of the small form. Margaret's dark thoughts vanished. Patrick had behaved similarly when he first held Bernie. He'd said solemnly then, 'I hope these little fingers will be the instruments of greatness in years to come.' This time Patrick said, 'Shall we call him Bryan after my father? Remember Bernie had a mate called Bryan?'

How did he do it? Margaret wondered. He exasperated one minute and amazed the next.

'Yes I like the name and I liked the friend of Bernie's. But I. . .'

'That's settled then. We'll have him baptised in the church in Brecon on my next leave.'

Patrick kissed Margaret abstractedly, almost dropping the sleeping child, sensing that their conversation was at an end. Her voice was timid as she forced her words out.

'Patrick, you must realize how well I've been looked after in this hospital and in this town. Mrs Morgan sat up all night, alone, when the baby, I mean Bryan was a long time being born.'

'Don't fret, I'll say thank-yous all round.'

She continued doggedly, 'The Cae Coch people and the medical staff have shown me and our baby extraordinary kindness over the last week or so, and I thought. . .'

'I know, I know. I'll make a point of remembering to thank the doctors and nurses here, too.'

'Good. Thank you.'

'Just now I'm going to meet Gwyn at *The Wye* to wet Bryan's head. I promise we'll toast you, Maggie.'

Margaret muttered, 'Wait a minute, please, Paddy.'

'I'm running a bit late. Can it wait?'

Her voice was stronger as she said, 'It would please me and the Morgan family if we gave Bryan a second name, a Welsh name, preferably Glynn.'

'Why Glynn?'

'It is the Christian name of Dr Thomas. Nurse Roberts has told me that without his care and commitment I might have died. He managed to get hold of a new drug, 'penicillin', still in trials, from Cardiff, to fight the infection I had.'

'Well it looks strange, doesn't it? I mean a Liverpool Irish baby having a Welsh name?' He replaced his son in the cot beside Margaret and after a pause said, 'Bryan Glynn it is then. Second names aren't that important anyway.' Margaret nodded her pleasure and didn't mention the Welsh custom of using first and second names together. After all Mary Jane was the barmaid at 'The Wye' and Lizzie Ann was the licensee. Bryan Glynn became a person in his own right.

*

'Only a couple more days and I'll be back at the farm.' Margaret told Nancy, two days later as they sat together. 'Patrick goes back to-morrow.'

'He's brightened up the farm. Gwyn gets on with him great.'

'Um yes, it was good that he was given compassionate leave.'

'He seemed quite soppy over the baby, didn't he?' Nancy loved the 'romantic'.

'Patrick will get used to the name. If the war goes on much longer, Bryan Glynn will be bi-lingual.' Both women laughed.

'He's been telling us about his latest painting. He was full of it when he and Gwyn came back from 'The Wye'.

Margaret was concerned. 'Do you think he's alright since his accident? Shouldn't he be getting on with his job and not sketching?'

'No, no. It's a naval commission - a town from the air, Maggie. D'you know, I'd love to go up in a plane.'

'Nancy, you and Gwyn must keep that information to yourselves. It may be one of Patrick's stories but it could be Top Secret information. Make any excuse but don't let them go to 'The Wye'. Bryan Glynn doesn't need a father in prison for treason.'

'He told us about his painting at our place. P'raps he shouldn't 'ave...' she broke off in confusion.

'Nancy dear, don't repeat what he said - not even to the Morgans. Drink gets to Patrick. Tell me about the farm. Has Susan had her calf?'

'A beautiful heifer. We'd like to call her Meg.' Nancy put the baby gently in Margaret's arms, saying, 'Nos da, cariad'. Dr Thomas likes your name, little one. Come home soon.'

148

37

A Different Christmas

Bryan Glynn was beginning to sit up and gave all at Cae Coch a new enthusiasm. When any decision had to be made, it became a farm joke to say, 'Have we asked Bryan Glynn?' He in turn would look baby-wise and smile.

Margaret's second Christmas at the farm was more sombre than the first. The war was no longer about to finish, but there were fears that it would not be won and Britain would succumb to a Nazi dictatorship. Norway and Denmark had been overrun, France had fallen and there were worries about the Japanese and their activities in the Far East. Even so there was a need to make the celebrations as pleasant as possible, for Anna and David. The baby, who was oblivious of all but his own comforts and loving audience, lightened the mood of the household. It was decided that as the Williamses were arriving on Christmas Eve and departing on Boxing Day that Christmas Day itself would be very special.

'We will go to church, this morning, won't we? I want to sing carols,' said David. Anna seemed ebullient too. She wanted to meet her friends from the school, which she'd so recently left.

Their grandmother said, 'Of course, brush your teeth and comb your hair and help Mrs. Rooney with Bryan Glynn's pram.'

No effort had been spared at the Parish Church. Every attic within the district had been scoured for the most beautiful array of decorations, which adorned the cypress tree in the porch. Holly and ivy were liberally displayed in every nook and cranny of the historic building. All the children's faces shone to match the ancient brass and silver church vessels and plate. Margaret thought to herself that probably in former days most people there would have been considering possible Christmas gifts. Perhaps to-day, all were praying for peace. Her reverie dwelt on prayer. *What is it? Is there a God or Gods? Was there a basic human need to reach out beyond self to some omnipotence?'* She realized that she was so busy thinking about prayer that she was not praying about either Bernie or Patrick.

Why did she always consider her son before her husband? Was she a strange sort of wife? Anna was having difficulty in finding her place in the creed, so Margaret pulled herself together, helped Anna and read the printed words with a sense of shame. She stopped herself saying, 'War without end' and joined the rest of the congregation in the possibility of a 'World without end' – she'd cling to that. The concept of 'everlasting life' comforted her. The children began to sing, 'Away in a Manger', standing around the younger ones in their prams and pushchairs and Margaret's introspective mood vanished. Instead of serious thoughts she marvelled at the created world, especially the human voice – the child's voice. *There must be a God.*

The celebratory Christmas meal was fun. All presents were necessities instead of the luxuries of former days. Anna loved her handmade pyjama case with its beautifully embroidered name in the shape of a cat. David grinned at his knitted naval gloves and socks. 'Will they last until I join up?' he joked as he pulled on the navy gauntlets and shook Patrick's hand, with his gloved hand.

'Perhaps, Anna, you'd open a special letter that came yesterday, from a long way away, for Master Bryan Glynn Rooney,' said Dai Morgan. Anna took the rather grubby envelope in her hands and gently prized it open. A piece of card emerged – the card was white but on its front was the charcoal representation of a ship – a ship of war, without its guns. On her bows were the words 'HMS Bryan Glynn'. She was sailing through calm seas and a turtle had its head above the water, where the two words, 'Love Bernie' were written.

Everyone gasped at the beauty of the picture and Dai Morgan said to the baby, 'So your brother has inherited his father's talent. What d'you think of your ship, Bryan Glynn?'

There was a whoop of approval, but the card was wrested from the eager grasp of the little fingers, just in time.

'Frank the Frame was at school with me,' said Mary. 'He has a shop in the town. Please let me have the ship framed for Bryan Glynn.'

It was agreed.

*

New Year's Day, 1942 was just another day. The guests had returned to their professional duties and their schools. Mr. Morgan commented that it was Mary and Rhys's sixteenth wedding anniversary, adding that perhaps they would celebrate their silver wedding anniversary in wartime.

'Make do and mend', 'Careless talk costs lives' and 'Waste not want not'. On the farm, Margaret, Nancy, and Mrs. Morgan worked from dawn to dusk squeezing every ounce of production from the stock and the arable acreage. Silage had been made for the first time ever and proved to be an important winter feed. Mr. Morgan and Gwyn helped when they could – Gwyn maintained the farm tackle and Dai ordered animal foodstuffs and kept a weather eye on the whole enterprise. Margaret fell into bed at ten o'clock each night and prayed that Bryan Glynn would sleep through the night. When teeth or colic disturbed him, Margaret reacted, automatically, by lighting the lamp, changing the baby, feeding him and singing him back to sleep, only to leave herself wide awake and thinking. *I'm anxious about Patrick, his drinking and his garrulous tongue. Will it get him into trouble? Were his words to her about Bernie's ship sailing to the Far East gossip or news? If it was top secret information will Patrick blurt it out in the wrong place? Will either Bernie or Patrick survive? Will Britain be invaded?*

There were so many things Margaret had wished she'd said to Bernie. She'd always adored him but had never told him of the depth of her feelings. The war seemed to have overtaken events. She was stunned by the changes in her life, but at least she and her second child were safe on a day to day basis. Never since her marriage had her thoughts returned to Cork so often. She dwelled on her family's estrangement from her; was she to blame? She remembered her broken-heartedness over Sean. But there was shame, guilt and fear connected to her accident in the river, which her mother had treated with such scorn. *If only I could remember the detail. Did Bridget know the true story? Will God take Bernie from me because I have disgraced my family? Have I been given Bryan Glynn as a consolation prize?*

Margaret smiled to herself as she watched Mr. Morgan ride out of the farm on his bicycle. Despite his taxing work for the newspaper and his overall responsibility for Cae Coch, his attitude was one of youthful determination; he was on a mission to avenge an enemy, which had robbed him of a son. *I do admire him.* As she entered the kitchen she was pleased as she saw Mrs. Morgan with Bryan Glynn on her knee, explaining that Gladstone was 'a cat'. The baby's joy and even temper engaged his adopted grandmother, who adored him. She had been showing the strain of over work, lately, and looked older. Margaret and Nancy had been anxious about her health. Nancy had explained that Flo Morgan didn't only look older than her husband, but she was older.

'Oh, Maggie, there was such a lot of gossip when Dai took up with Flo. He was only eighteen and she was the school mistress! She put on a Miscellany at the Town Hall for Christmas and it was love at first sight.'

Margaret didn't want to discuss her employers so asked, 'Did the locals know what a Miscellany was?'

'No,' said Nancy, 'I'm not sure what it is myself.'

They both laughed.

They'd started playing Consequences, recently, when the family was together, so they both cried, 'And the world said. . .'

'Well it's been a good marriage whatever anyone says.' They were silent.

'Gwyn's a lot older than me so it works both ways,' said Nancy. Margaret thought to herself that she'd had no reason to worry about Nancy's bruises lately. Another paradox of war?

The two women had been cleaning the horses' tack – a job which had been put off and was necessary because Mr. Morgan had to drive Rose to market to buy some essential supplies for the farm. Margaret sighed, wishing that there was more time to spend on the two horses.

'Did I ever tell you that two of my brothers left farming for a racing stable in County Kildare?'

'No, Maggie, you've never said anything about your home to me. I want to know but daren't ask why you left Ireland. If it's a secret, I won't tell.'

'You're sure, Nancy bach?'

'Promise,' was the prompt reply.

'I'd been ill and was sent to Dublin to help Aunt Theresa in her shop in the docks there, where I met Patrick and married him, some time later.'

'How did you meet him?'

'It was just after the last war. Dublin was in turmoil. Ireland wanted independence from Britain and there was anti-British feeling and civil violence in the country.'

'Maggie, you're so clever about history. No wonder Mrs. Morgan likes talking to you. I'm a bit of a dunce. Go on.'

'Because it was a bit hazardous in Dublin, Patrick, working for a company in Liverpool, volunteered for the job of dealing with his firm's office there – you know how he loves danger and anyway he earned more money as a result.'

'And. . ?'

'He bought his cigarettes in Auntie's shop.'

'That all. I imagined brave escapades. Fill in the details. Please?'

'I heard him ask one day, "where's the lady with the lovely red hair?" Auntie was short with him, because she noticed he wasn't Irish. He persisted in coming to the shop each time he was in Dublin. Then he asked me to walk round the docks and meet his colleagues.'

'And. . ?'

'Soon we were having coffee in O'Connell Street, in the centre of Dublin, very posh, where he told me he'd fallen in love with my wavy red hair and my Irish brogue. He apologized for being a Protestant.'

'How romantic! Why are you so mysterious about such adoration?'

'A month later he asked me to marry him and escape "The Troubles", live with him in Liverpool in his mother's house and have lots of babies.'

'There's very romantic!'

'I was thrilled. He was such fun and the future seemed wonderful. My aunt surprised me by being pleased – she feared more violence in Dublin and was thinking of closing the shop.'

'It's like a fairy story, Maggie.'

'I wrote home with the news. My sister wrote the reply from my parents. The message couldn't have been clearer. My marriage was a disgrace to Family, Church and Country. Patrick was from England and a Protestant. I was to be an outcast.'

'Oh Maggie, how unfair! I understand your secrecy about Ireland. Has there been any contact since?'

'I became a little out of touch. Just before Bernie was born, Michael Collins - a popular Irish politician - was murdered near to my home in Cork.'

'Did you know him?'

'No. Michael Collins was killed by another Irish nationalist in an area of fervent "Home Rule for Ireland". So any communication between Cork and Liverpool would have been dangerous, then or for a long time afterwards. Britain was disliked.'

'You had Bernie though.'

'Yes. I adored him and Patrick, but I too felt a failure. Patrick had ambitions to have a big family – to start a Rooney dynasty. His pals used to tease him by saying that his wife was too stuck-up and clever to produce babies. I think that's why he started to drink.'

'And now you have Bryan Glynn,' Nancy whispered wistfully.

38

St. David's Day

One morning in February Mrs. Morgan decided to confide in Margaret and Nancy that she was not fit enough to continue doing so much and felt that she should delegate the dairy work to Margaret and concentrate on the cooking, the farmhouse, and helping with Bryan Glynn.

'I have had a letter from a former pupil who is doing her Higher Certificate at the County School and is keen to go to Harper Adams Agricultural College. She would like to learn about making cream, butter and cheese. I think we could use her effectively. Her name is Bronwen.'

It was arranged that Margaret would interview her and make it clear that she would have to do menial tasks at first for the farm was short staffed. Bronwen was engaged and learned quickly. She was a delight to have around. Her lovely soprano voice rang out over the farm and Margaret realized she was a member of the church choir and no stranger to her or the rest of the Cae Coch folk.

The dark days of winter passed and the first signs of spring arrived to everyone's relief. To celebrate, Margaret and Nancy booked tickets for a St. David's day concert at the Town Hall. A male voice choir had come from South Wales to enthral the local audience. They sang ballads, hymns and Welsh songs, enjoying their break from the mining community of which they were part. It was a delight and the two women returned to the farm, ecstatic. The Morgans were pleased to see their enjoyment and wished that the women who worked so diligently had more time to relax.

'Before the war, we had concerts and eisteddfodau regularly. You know, Mrs. Rooney, Wales is like Ireland, a musical nation. Let us hope we return to being a cultured society after the war.' Mr. Morgan said. He and his wife had been filling in forms all evening for the Ministries of Food and Agriculture.

*

A day later the nine o'clock BBC Home Service news bulletin reported a naval battle in the Java Sea. Margaret gasped. 'Patrick has told me that he had been given reliable information that Bernie's ship was destined to sail to that region from Singapore.' There was a tense silence as they all listened for more news of the battle, but the announcer did not give any further detail. Margaret had a sleepless night and told Nancy of her terrible fears in the morning.

'I have slept little, cried a lot and tried to pray. There's no word from Patrick. He might know more.' Nancy was unable to reply. All crowded around the wireless at the time of each news bulletin but there seemed to be a black-out on naval battles. It was a relief to feed and care for the animals, as they had no involvement in the war crisis, but Bryan Glynn sensed the atmosphere and watched his adopted family warily as though he had done something wrong. Despite his restlessness the adults tried to act normally. It was impossible.

On the third day, Dai Morgan, who had been on edge all morning, saying he was writing an article at home, and must meet a deadline, received an urgent phone call from a reputable News Agency. His conversation was short and his face ashen as he walked into the kitchen. 'The news is bad. Mrs. Rooney, I have to tell you that the most horrific thing has happened. Try to be brave. We're all with you, but the latest news is that the ship, which your son was so proud of and served so well, has been sunk by the Japanese in the Java Sea. I can't keep the news from you. I wish I could.' He sat down with his head in his hands.

Margaret looked at him with wooden acceptance but managed to whisper, 'Did the News Agency indicate whether there were survivors?' *After all Patrick had survived his ordeal.*

He sat up erect saying, 'First reports suggest the ship might have been scuttled – meaning that the captain realized his vessel would be boarded and confiscated by the Japanese and took steps to see it sank instead. That might be a good sign.'

Margaret sat in the kitchen of Cae Coch mute, cold and motionless. No-one spoke. She was in a world of mental torment. Mrs. Morgan seemed in shock. Margaret noticed Bryan Glynn as he crawled towards her and tugged at her breeches. He was the perfect image of Bernie at the same age. His expression was contrite, 'I'm sorry, I'm not Bernie,' it seemed to say. Margaret's eyes filled with tears. It was too much. She had to escape.

'Please excuse me. Bryan Glynn and I need some fresh air.'

Mr. and Mrs. Morgan rose to their feet, 'We'll be here when you come back. Take your time.' They uttered together.

As she put Bryan Glynn in his pushchair, Mr. Morgan opened the back door for her with bowed head, and his wife tucked a thick rug round the little boy lovingly, grabbing her own warm scarf and gently putting it round Margaret's neck, saying, 'You mustn't get cold, my dear Margaret. We'll wait tea for you both.'

The word, *sunk* was ringing in her ear and wouldn't go away. How deceitful words could sound. She'd seen Bernie's ship. That that beautiful piece of engineering could disappear under the sea seemed impossible. But the sea wasn't like a river. It was fathoms deep. Was Bernie in that sunken ship? *Please God no.* Where was he? She imagined all those brave sailors she'd seen at Plymouth jumping into the water, escaping not drowning. *They had been so alive. They must all survive. I can't deceive myself - even if those indomitable sailors had not gone down with the ship, what other hazards would they face?* Thinking about the sea and its dangers and its destructive force made Margaret preoccupied and she walked down the road to the town with no particular aim. She noticed Bryan Glynn's face was expressionless. His gaze was almost fearful. The cold and the wind gave her a determined energy to move. Movement was helpful. As an active woman it enabled her to consider what she could possibly do. Meanwhile her child had to remain quiet and still, as though he knew that he must not impinge upon his mother's thoughts.

She needed to find out all she could about this awful sea battle. Of course, Dai Morgan was probably doing that at this moment. What about Patrick? He must have received news through the navy about the battle. Her walk had taken her to the River Wye and she looked at the water with a new respect, tinged with hate and despair. *Have I ever understood the treachery of water as I and others enjoyed ferry trips on the Mersey and journeys across to New Brighton to see friends? Wasn't it my accident in the river, which resulted in my isolation from my family and Ireland? Bryan Glynn, I vow that you will not grow up to be a sailor.* As she turned back towards Cae Coch, the baby gurgled at the water in the river as it swirled and splashed over the multi-coloured pebbles. *It beckoned. Was it casting a spell on an innocent child?*

The phone was ringing as Margaret and Bryan Glynn reached the farm. It was a very chastened Patrick. He apologised to Margaret for encouraging Bernie to be a sailor. He had never been sorry for anything before. Margaret felt a great wave of affection for him. Despite his drinking and his obsessional nature, he did care. 'Give Bryan a kiss from his Da,' were his final words before the relentless pips sounded. He had lost his jocular manner. Margaret wished he was at Cae Coch, but was relieved that he was on a forty-eight hour, home leave, pass when the dreaded telegram arrived, confirming that 'Bernard Rooney was missing'.

Some of the local people lowered their eyes and shook Margaret's hand murmuring words of condolence or sorrow, others avoided her, their feelings were mixed – anger and regret had begun to envelop friends and relatives of servicemen. The local paper recorded army casualties each week. Bernie was the first sailor to be missing. One heartening thing happened to Margaret. The woman, who had spoken loudly, in the grocers, about the Irish in Cork re-fuelling German submarines, stopped her in the butchers and said she was sorry about her previous remarks. 'We're all in this together, an American cousin of ours was killed at Pearl Harbour last December, but at least we have the Yanks as allies at last.'

At Cae Coch there was a quiet reverence shown by all. The Morgans understood. Mary Williams's letter comforted Margaret, who was grateful for the well-chosen words of sympathy. *Did the tragedy bring back memories of her brother?* At half-term the Morgans told David and Anna about the grim battle and its consequence to Mrs. Rooney. 'Are you sure?' asked Anna. No one answered her question. To show her support for the war effort she told the family that she had decided to like boarding school in future.

As the days became longer, Margaret threw herself into the chores of the farm. She considered, like many, that the harder she worked the sooner the war would come to an end. At least it took her mind from her loss. *Was it of use to pray for Bernie? Was there a God?* At church the words 'life everlasting' came into her mind and when she reflected in private she sometimes felt Bernie's presence or heard his voice. She remembered her dream of Sean and Bernie discussing universities and felt a chill throughout her body. These moments she kept to herself but they disturbed her. Patrick's 'secret location' kept him from the farm, but he sent Bryan Glynn cartoons of the Cae Coch animals now and then. Margaret glued them into an exercise book, which the baby learned to recognize. He was approaching his first birthday and beginning to walk – a pair of Wellington boots appeared, by post from Patrick, to delight him and his mother.

The Morgans continued to be close and understanding. To lessen the work load Dai Morgan applied and was allocated some German prisoners to help with shearing, harvesting and other labour intensive tasks on Cae Coch. They were well supervised and courteous. *I wonder do British prisoners work in Germany and Japan?*

On the evening before David and Anna went back to school, the telephone rang. Thinking it was his mother David answered the call and shouted to his grandfather who was in the yard, 'it's your editor, Grandpa. He has been given some good news, which will please you.'*Was the call anything to do with Bernie?*

39

Aftermath

As a journalist, Dai Morgan was working harder than ever, through The Express, to give the public information about what was really happening on all the war fronts. Margaret considered that he was a journalist with integrity who hated scaremongering. News Agency reports were always vague and passing on their message could be misleading, but Dai made his own investigations. He had pre-war services contacts through the British Legion which enabled him to interview retired service personnel. It seemed that there was always a problem when writing an article to balance political and military points of view. Government experts worked, of necessity, by standards often dictated by secret information sources and Margaret often heard him say, 'where does the truth lie?' It was clear to Margaret that to this fair and compassionate man, the morale of the troops was paramount. Patrick, on one of his rare leaves, was reading one of Mr. Morgan's articles, which was on the health of personnel on active service.

'He's right you know, Maggie, the service medics do a grand job and they get men back into combat duty in an amazingly quick time.'

'He knows about fitness from having a daughter who's a doctor. I thought the part about civilians and service families suffering as a result of anxiety, was important.'

'The doctor whom I saw last week said that he'd heard on good authority that there were survivors from the Bawean campaign.'

Margaret was rooted to the spot and put the iron back on the hob rather than scorch Mr. Morgan's shirt.

'Why haven't you told me this before? Why did you have to see the doctor anyway? Patrick, don't play with my emotions, please.'

'You're so virtuous, Maggie. You can deal with whatever the Good Lord gives you. Fact is I've not been sleeping. I've been grieving about our boy. . . and. . .'

'And what. . ?'

'My hands have started to shake. I can't always sketch or paint as I used to.'

'Is that the drink?' She uttered the words before she gave thought to what she was saying.

Tears ran down her husband's face as he choked on the word, 'Yes'. She'd never seen a man cry. Margaret was horrified.

'I can't stop thinking about Bernie, his ship and all those brave sailors,' he sobbed.

Margaret sat down beside him and learned that unless he stopped drinking he would lose his rank and maybe be cashiered out of the navy. How differently men and women dealt with misfortune. She was eaten away inside with misery and drove herself, physically, to overcome her grief but he was unable to do his work because his solace was alcohol. Her sympathetic reverie was broken as the door opened and Nancy appeared with a toddling Brian Glynn, carrying a brown egg – it might have been a cherished teddy or a diamond.

Patrick pulled himself together and lifted his son on to his knee, saying, 'you're only one and making a good job of walking, Bryan.'

Margaret told Patrick how lucky she had been, having Bryan Glynn to look after every day and, as a result, she didn't allow herself to give in to overt grief.

'I'm determined that this son of ours will grow up happy and fulfilled.' Had Bernie been happy? – Yes. She thought he had. Had he been as committed to being a sailor as he suggested? Re-reading his last letter she had been certain that no-one had influenced him to join the navy.

That evening Patrick told Margaret about his 'top secret' work. She thought it was better for him to unburden himself to her rather than to anyone else. Apparently, he was in charge of camouflage for a hidden port in Wales, soon to give harbour to flying boats operating across the Atlantic by the RAF. Due to clever painted markings on the roofs of the hangars, the whole area appeared to be terraces of cottages and houses, from the air. The nets covering vehicles looked like fishing nets, he explained. Patrick had, she was sure, excelled in his art. He had also seen RAF casualties, but heard of more who just didn't come back to base. No wonder he had been warned about his drinking.

'Telling me about your work is one thing but you mustn't develop a loose tongue.' Had the husband and wife roles been exchanged? Was know it all Patrick really vulnerable?

Margaret's guard was down one morning and she found herself making an anti-war remark, bordering on the anti-British, to Mrs. Morgan. Understanding that she had breached the parameters of their relationship, she apologised. The older woman gestured to her and said, 'Go on.'

'I'm sorry but I feel sometimes as though all this killing madness is a dream and that I'll wake up. A moment later I know that Bernie is dead and I feel doomed.'

'I know. It's all so unnecessary. Acceptance comes with time, with a long, long time.'

'Will I ever accept it? Some days, it seems worse than the day before.'

'I understand. I hope you don't mind me saying this, but you being part of the Cae Coch family and allowing us to be involved in Bryan Glynn's life has made me happier than I've been for a long time.'

'How? Please explain.'

'I was bitter. I hid my feelings, but seeing this war, from a different perspective, made me understand more about life, sacrifice, love and death, too.'

'I see or I think I do.'

'Dai always had a way of dealing with his sorrow. He had a firm belief in something beyond the finite – call it God or some powerful being.' Hitherto Mrs. Morgan had always referred to her husband as Mr. Morgan when speaking to Margaret.

'I felt like that, at seventeen, when I was back in Ireland. I believed, I trusted, I had faith. Then my life seemed to go wrong. I had to leave home.'

'You grew up, my dear. You became a realist.'

'You're right, I wish that. . .'

'Believe me, that faith and trust is still there underneath. I've regained my reason for being, now, when my life is nearing its end.'

Margaret remembered that there was Mrs. Morgan's age and apparent failing health hovering between them and hesitated. She was embarrassed.

Mrs. Morgan, however, smiled as she said, 'I'm glad we've had this talk. We've just got to go on.'

'Thank you and that means waking Bryan Glynn from his nap or he'll not want to sleep to-night.'

Margaret wondered why she had ever thought of Flo Morgan as being unfriendly.

Throughout history, hadn't women waited, wanted and been left wishing that fate had served them better? Men had a certain comradeship in war, while women relied on consolation in each other. Patrick had mentioned, Bawean in the Java Sea, so casually; could she re-open that topic? Had the person giving him the information only wanted to give him hope? No, Patrick was so unsure of himself suddenly. She mustn't broach the subject: anyway he'd had to go back to his base. He hadn't visited 'The Wye' once, while he'd been on leave! Gwyn had been bereft of his company, too.

With her new confidence in the Morgans, Margaret asked them one morning about the activities of the Red Cross. Could she make an enquiry through the charity about Java survivors?

Dai replied that the charity tried all means to obtain information and send supplies to places and people where there was humanitarian need, but it depended on information filtering through official channels. 'Japan's a bit of a closed book,' he added.

Margaret asked, 'Do you think any of those sailors whose ships were sunk, could still be alive?'

'It's not impossible. The truth is that news from the Far East is spasmodic – it's different from Europe, there are cultural differences.' Dai's voice was understanding; he knew the meaning of the awful word, missing.

40

Christmas 1942

At the start of the war, Mrs. Morgan had bought a wall map of the world. She had said to all who were breakfasting in the kitchen, 'It will tell us at a glance what's happening.' All present thought that a map of Europe would be sufficient to serve the purpose.

In 1941 Hitler had invaded Greece, Yugoslavia and North Africa, and the map in the passage between the kitchen, parlour and dining-room had recorded the advance. 'Where will Hitler go next?' Margaret had asked; her geography had been sorely tested by the detail on the map.

'There is German activity in Russia, which will probably be unsuccessful, due to the bitterly cold winter there.' Mrs. Morgan read from the newspaper. The surprise development was at the end of 1941, when Mrs. Morgan had announced to Margaret and Nancy, 'The Japanese have attacked Pearl Harbour in Hawaii, which means that America has become our ally against Japan and Germany.'

These conversations were in Margaret's mind when the war had escalated, Singapore had fallen and the Japanese navy had become victorious in the Far East. Bernie's ship and many other allied naval craft had been destroyed and the Philippines, Burma and Hong Kong had fallen to Japan. One morning, when it was announced that Borneo, Java and Sumatra had fallen into Japanese hands, she gazed at the map and felt overwhelming fear. *How could the allies win this world war? Had they sufficient resources?*

'Don't be discouraged by the expansion of the Japanese empire, Mrs. Rooney. There has, recently, been an article in The Times pointing out that with the Americans on our side, with that country's vast wealth, peace is bound to come in time.' Mr. Morgan was passing from his typewriter in the dining-room to the warmth of the kitchen for the midday meal. Margaret found his usual optimism heartening and hugged Bryan Glynn who was struggling out of her arms to touch the brightly coloured map. *How old will Bryan Glynn be when the war is over and Patrick and I take him to Ireland?*

In June of 1942, when talk of harvesting the hay was a Cae Coch preoccupation, Mrs. Morgan had cheered the workers by quoting from, *The Times*, 'The American air force has reversed the Japanese supremacy in the Pacific war at the battle of Midway; five enemy warships were destroyed in the battle.' *Will this bring the war against Japan to a close? Whatever happens will I ever see Bernie again?*

With harvest, Bryan Glynn had his first ride on a load of hay. It had been a good harvest, providing much animal feed for the winter. The herd had become profitable – the calves had brought good prices at market. One morning, early in November, when Margaret and Nancy had helped at a difficult calving and the emergency was over, they decided to name the new calf Montgomery after the victorious Field-Marshall, at the battle of El Alamein. After settling the mother and calf, they went into the farmhouse to tell Mrs. Morgan about the new arrival, but she was glum and unable to join their jubilation.

Her words were full of news of the war. 'Though the Russians are counter-attacking and repulsing the Germans, as we were told they would, there was an item which horrified me on the one o'clock bulletin. There are rumours of murders of Jews and Gypsies by the Nazis in prison camps. I find I have no appetite for my dinner.' The two younger women were aghast. *I have a strange feeling of guilt at this news; whenever I hear about any atrocity I feel that it is my fault. I wonder why?*

'We must trust that our leaders are more humane,' Mrs. Morgan whispered to Bryan Glynn as she strapped him into his high chair. His smile defused the gloom of the occasion.

Patrick was on leave for three days at Christmas and helped on the farm and drew and read with Bryan Glynn, whom he, steadfastly, called, Bryan. He was still edgy, but wasn't drinking so much. Out of the blue on Christmas Eve he said. 'Maggie we had an adviser on explosives visit the unit, last week. He's a naval officer with a brother who was lost on one of the ships which the sank near the Celebes Islands.'

'Don't, Patrick. It upsets me too much.'

'Listen, please, don't go out of the room.' His voice was pleading.

'Remember I only have ten minutes before milking.'

'This explosives expert – he's a commander, was at a meeting at the Admiralty, where some top secret guy blurted out that after the battle there had been many sailors picked up from the sea and taken prisoner by the Japanese.'

'He told you this? Was he drunk or what at the time?' Margaret was alert.

'The Red Cross is trying to confirm the information.'

'I've been asking Mr. Morgan about the Red Cross.' Margaret nodded her approval.

'The Japanese aren't keen on the charity's policy of interfering in a country's internal affairs.' Patrick added aggressively.

Margaret smiled to herself. *Patrick thinks that because they're not Europeans, they're not Christian like the Germans! Sometimes, Patrick pontificates on 'the just causes of war', he cannot justify Japan's bellicose stance.* Even so, she washed her hands and went out to milk Susan. She must keep her head. Being with the Cae Coch cows, always made her optimistic. They were so accepting of their fate, knowing that they would be treated kindly even in death. *Animals don't go to war! However, didn't five million horses die as a result of the last world war! What cruelty! What awful tragedy!*

*

*It wa*s destined to be a sober Christmas. The Williamses described the shortages in Liverpool. Housing was a big problem. Doctors were still being trained in just over four years. There was a shortage of medically qualified personnel, both in the services and on the home front. This was made possible by reducing the long peace time vacations and overworking the University Medical School staff, Rhys told the family. There was no news from Bernie this year, but no-one commented.

David and Anna were happy because it was a chance to be with their parents for a short time. David loved his Public School and talked about his academic work, his games and the Officer Training Corps (OTC), but Anna was not keen on being away from her parents and grandparents. She hung her head and talked to Bryan Glynn and Gladstone, but said nothing about the convent to them or the adults.

On Christmas Day morning, after Church, the Williams family decided to go for a walk. Margaret and Mrs. Morgan were to stay with Bryan Glynn. Mr. Morgan and Patrick had gone with Gwyn to see whether the first lambs had been born. However, Bryan Glynn made a scene, insisting, to Margaret's annoyance, on going with the Williamses. He wanted to be with David and Anna and they with him; the Williams parents agreed to humour all three children. *After all it was Christmas.*

'Take him by all means, but you won't be able to negotiate the push-chair on the styles and narrow footpaths. He likes to walk but he's very slow.' Margaret warned.

'We'll carry him if need be.' Rhys said, flexing his biceps in fun.

*

While they prepared the Christmas fare, the two women chatted companionably. Mrs. Morgan asked Margaret about her views on the benefits of Public or Private Education. Her reply was hesitant. She explained that one was educated in Ireland if you were able enough to pass an exam into a convent or seminary, but the less able pupils left school with poor qualifications. She added, 'British Public schools and boarding schools appear to give pupils confidence, don't you think?'

'Yes and no. David is so sure of himself now he's at his school, which has such an unblemished history. Yet Anna is clearly unhappy at her convent boarding school. The Welsh County Schools, where my two went, provided a good all round education. It must be hard for Mary and Rhys to be separated from their children'

'Yes, it must be. I'm sure.' Margaret replied.

'Remembering the awful air raids on Liverpool, it's such a joy to see David and Anna alive and well.' Flo Williams dropped the potato knife, which she was using, as she corrected herself with embarrassment.

'I must apologise, for one moment I forgot your son. I'm so, so sorry. How could I?'

'It's alright. You only used a common turn of phrase, 'alive and well'.'

'Even so, I must have seemed insensitive. After that lovely picture your Bernie sent to Bryan Glynn last Christmas, and what has happened since, you must feel extremely low as well as sad, I regret my thoughtless words.'

'I'm unhappy most of the time. I try hard not to think of the possibilities. I reconcile myself to him being missing. I have to. But each time I walk through the churchyard, I think that if he has to be dead, it would have been better to have had his body back in Britain and know his resting place. I cling to missing not being dead, though.'

'I understand what you mean. We went over to France in 1920 to see Owen's grave – a journey arranged by the British Legion. I thought it helped a bit, but how did I know it was Owen there? I needed to see him, or at least his body.'

'I know.'

'We must try to be cheerful. Remember, we have oranges, three bananas and the Christmas cake, made by Nancy and decorated with that beautiful snow scene. That will be a big surprise for the three children.'

*

The Christmas walk had been enjoyable. The two older children had enjoyed playing with Bryan Glynn, who'd never had such attentive and amusing company – the best of gifts. As the Christmas cake was being cut and the whole Cae Coch family was chatting happily with Gwyn and Nancy about the first lamb, born in the night, David stood up and announced with some command. 'I have made a decision. I'm going to join the RAF immediately I'm old enough. I mean to become a pilot, and avenge the loss of worthy people like Bernie Rooney and others.'

The statement was met with blank faces and silence all round the table.

41

A Visitor to Cae Coch

One morning in the New Year, Dai Morgan asked Margaret if she would come and talk to him in the dining room.

'Is it about Mrs. Morgan's health? What did Dr. Thomas tell you? Nancy and I were concerned when she was clutching her chest yesterday. We had to ask him to visit as you were away at the time.'

'You did right and my wife was touched by your concern. The sedative which the doctor administered ensured that she slept well. I wish, though, she'd not come down to breakfast.'

'What caused her terrible pain? She said it was indigestion.'

'I'm afraid it's quite serious.' His voice was grave.

'I'm so sorry, we thought it was just bad indigestion.'

'The doctor has diagnosed her condition: it's *angina pectoris*. The symptoms she has, point to no other illness or disease.'

'Is there an appropriate treatment? What can Nancy and I do to help?'

'We'll take each day as it comes. As it is written in the scriptures, 'Sufficient unto the day is the evil thereof'.'

'You, Mrs. Morgan and the Williamses have been so good to me, Patrick and Bryan Glynn, that I want to assist in any way I can. Please remember that always.'

'Just see that she rests. Dr. Thomas suggests that she has a sleep each afternoon. It would be excellent if you saw that she went up to lie down after dinner each day – say at two o'clock, at the time that you put Bryan Glynn in his bed for a nap. She may need some persuading.'

'Of course.'

'There was something else which Glynn Thomas said, which will interest you, Mrs. Rooney. He'd had a letter from a medical colleague from University days, who'd gone over to Darwin, Australia after qualifying.'

Margaret wondered whether Mr. Morgan had confused her with someone with relatives in Australia, but she replied politely, 'What did this friend specialise in?'

'This doctor did some general medicine as well as accident work in the hospital. He did a post-graduate qualification in resuscitation. He's recently been commissioned as a surgeon commander in our navy.'

'Is this doctor coming to the Convalescent Hospital?' Margaret's words were tentative.

'No, no, but he had an extraordinary story to tell. He asked for a document in his possession about your Bernie's ship, to be scrutinized by the Admiralty. D'you remember the naval officer whom you met when my editor took you to Plymouth to see your son off to the Far East? Well, he wants to have a chat with you about some of the writing on this document.'

'I don't suppose I can be of any assistance. I did see the ship and met some of Bernie's fellow seamen. I don't suppose any of them are still alive.'

Dai didn't comment but continued his story.

'That officer is coming here to-morrow at eleven o'clock. You'll speak with him, won't you? Will you be happy to talk to him, on your own, in this room?'

'Yes, certainly I will. Are you and Mrs. Morgan happy for this meeting to take place?'

'Indeed yes. We'll be in the house and take care of Bryan Glynn, so you and the Commander have privacy.'

*

Margaret thought that the officer must be trying to tie up some loose ends. Had one of the sailors on Bernie's watch jumped ship before the cruiser sailed and was now on a charge?

Margaret got up earlier than usual, did her farm work speedily but efficiently and made herself presentable for the important visitor. He was punctual, put her at ease and extended sympathy about Bernie's ship.

'By all accounts your son was an exemplary sailor. I'm so sorry about his ship. I hear you have another small son. How is he?'

Margaret mumbled a few appropriate words about Bryan Glynn. Then she asked, 'How can I help you to-day, Commander?'

His tone was soft, 'I'll explain. It's a complicated story.'

Margaret nodded and looked attentively at her companion, who told his tale.

'A Dutch fisherman was sailing his boat near the Celebes Islands. As a result of the naval hostilities in the area, his crew was at pains to avoid having the boat sunk by the Japanese and was keeping an intensive look-out for trouble. They picked up a man from the sea, in a bad way, near death, who turned out to be a fellow Dutchman. Let's call him *Harry*. He was a fugitive from the crew of a Dutch hospital ship sailing in the area, which had been commandeered by the Japanese. He hated the Japanese. His home in Java had been destroyed in an air raid. These details only became known when poor *Harry* was stabilized in the Darwin hospital, where your doctor's friend worked.'

'I see,' said Margaret, she became curiously alert. The word 'Japanese' might have some connection with Bernie or his ship.

The Commander went on to say, 'The fishing boat reached the port of Darwin after an eventful journey and the sick man, *Harry*, now unconscious was taken to the hospital. When he was stripped for X-rays, the nurses found taped to his chest an oilcloth tobacco pouch. It was wrapped so carefully that no water had penetrated the tobacco or the paper around it.'

Margaret was bemused, but tried to appear interested. *What was the relevance of tobacco?*

'This is the amazing part of the story. The wrapping paper had writing on it. The nurses, thinking the words might identify the patient, put it aside for consideration later.'

Dramatically he pulled a piece of paper from his uniform pocket. A strong smell of tobacco filled the room. Margaret became excited.

'There, not the name and address of the patient, but a list of names in faint pencil. Mrs. Rooney can you read the names?'

Margaret held the paper as though it were some precious ancient manuscript, and two words spoke to her from the page, *Bernie Rooney – in writing which she had treasured from his childhood!*

'It's his writing; it's our Bernie's writing. I can't bear it. When? How? Please tell me?'

'It transpired that some hundred or more sailors and marines had been rescued from the sea after the battle where your son's ship was sunk. They were picked up by the very same hospital ship which the doctor's patient, *Harry,* was planning to escape from rather than be a prisoner.'

'Why write the names? *Harry* had little chance of surviving, surely. What does it mean? Where are these people now? Where is Bernie now? Can he possibly be *alive?*'

'The Admiralty considers that together with other reports from Dutch personnel, who had escaped from the area, there is little doubt that these men have been taken prisoner by the Japanese.'

Margaret whispered, 'Does this mean that my son has survived and is a prisoner? What an odd story, but I want to believe it. I feel that Bernie is alive. I recognized several of his comrades' names on the list.'

'Let's say that your son was definitely not drowned when his ship went down. The Admiralty has scrutinized the names on the list and all were sailors or marines serving in the waters of the Far East.'

Margaret felt sick, happy, surprised and out of her depth, all at the same time. Her visitor had not finished his tale.

'*Harry* – we found through the free-Dutch working with the British government, was an agent – an expert in espionage. No wonder he dreaded close examination by the Japanese. To continue, when he recovered from his exposure, he gave an account of his time with our prisoners. Under the supervision of an armed Japanese guard, he was ordered to distribute the rice and water rations to the prisoners. He mumbled words of English to them as he served the modest rations of food.'

Margaret was so emotional that she found it difficult to concentrate on the detail of the story, but made herself commit every aspect to memory. *Was this all happening or was it a dream?*

'He whispered, in English, as he doled out the food that he needed to escape as he was on a secret mission. Would the lads agree to stage a loud singing session as the light faded, so that he could disappear into the sea in the dark?'

'I suppose the Japanese weren't aware that he could communicate with the British prisoners.' Margaret thought aloud.

'Indeed, no. In return for the uproar he suggested that they all, clandestinely, wrote their names on this piece of paper. He told them that he was certain to escape to a small island where Dutch fishing boats took shelter in squalls. The sea and islands, in the vicinity, were familiar to him.'

'So what happened to *Harry?* What went wrong?'

'The weather changed, a mist came down; he missed the island and was drifting - almost dead - when he was hauled on to the Dutch fishing boat.'

'And. . ?'

'Before you ask *Harry* was and probably still is a heavy smoker.' He smiled as he opened the door for her, as she sobbed her thanks to all the people involved in the extraordinary story.

'Keep this information to yourself, Mrs. Rooney. Your husband is being told of the details by his commanding officer, this morning.'

*

On her return to the kitchen and Mr. and Mrs. Morgan, she realized that they were party to the secret. Both smiled. Flo Morgan had, recently, found an illustrated children's adaptation of *The Mabinogion*, which Bryan Glynn adored – he always rolled his eyes at the lovely Welsh word of the title. To-day, however, the woman with the beautiful voice had a new child's book in her hands, *The Tale of the Leprechaun*, and the delighted Bryan Glynn was enchanted by the picture of the diminutive fairy shoemaker, with his tiny purse holding a shilling.

'I haven't seen that book before, Mrs. Morgan. The story is one I treasure from childhood and adolescence.' Margaret's mind reverted to the normal. She understood that there would be no conversation about the visit until the three people party to the news had thought about its significance.

'Bryan Glynn must be brought up on both Welsh and Irish folklore, don't you think?'

'Definitely, how I love *the Leprechaun and Pryderi*.'

'The officer seems a good sort of man, doesn't he? Dai has been in touch with him for some time.' Mrs. Morgan said as she passed her charge back to his ecstatic mother. *I can't believe my good fortune – Bernie has escaped drowning, however I feel guilty that the Morgans face an uncertain future. Will this drug digitalis cure or improve Flo Morgan's heart problem?*

*

Later in the week Margaret visited Dr. Thomas to thank him for his involvement in the news of the prisoners of war.

The doctor replied by saying, 'Maggie, we medicos have an advantage in life. Wherever we go, our skills seem to be recognized.'

'I don't understand.'

'A doctor or nurse treats 'the patient'. That patient may be any colour, any nationality, male or female or believe any creed.'

'I remember Bernie telling me how his ship picked up a German airman in a bad way in the North Sea, at the beginning of the war. They treated him as well as a British serviceman.'

'Your Bernie's skills will be more use to the Japanese than a prize-fighter's. They would fear any person who appeared aggressive.'

'I trust so.'

'Be hopeful. Don't give in. Remember to keep the information that you received this week from others, Margaret. You could bring much curiosity on yourself if you confided in friends.'

What wise advice! Silence. If told - Nancy would be all concern; Anna would ask question after question; and the town would be full of speculation. As time passed she might suggest that there could have been survivors taken from the Java Sea, or official news might acquaint the world of the situation. She must keep hoping and praying that Bernie was alive and would endure.

'To change the subject, how is your younger son doing? I gather he's already bi-lingual.' The doctor smiled as he said this.

'At present, he's with Mr. Morgan and Nancy in the market. I wanted to have this quiet word with you. He's getting very boisterous.'

'He'll learn his numbers in Welsh at the market. How will Patrick cope with a Taffy in the family?'

Margaret laughed as she said 'Goodbye' to Dr. Thomas. *How was Bernie? Was he chained, starving or worse? She must believe that he would use his ingenuity to survive. He wasn't at the bottom of the Java Sea!*

42

Margaret Reads about Japan

The almost certain news that Bernie had not been drowned when his ship went down thrilled Margaret. However, her elation changed to dread when she dwelled on the matter of the prison camp. *Are prison camps as inhumane as concentration camps? Where is Bernie? Please God protect Bernie and all his fellow prisoners?*

Margaret had a sudden curiosity about the news of the war at first hand. Hitherto, she had been content to hear a report of what was happening from Mr. Morgan at the mid-day dinner table. Since the report of Bernie's ship being sunk, Margaret had wanted to distance herself from the horror of war; but after hearing the news of sailors surviving in the Java Sea, she was consumed with interest about the possibilities of Bernie being alive still. *Where are you, Bernie? What are the Japanese like? Are you being fed? Are the men I met in Plymouth with you?* When she asked to borrow Mrs. Morgan's atlas, her request was met with kindness and compassion.

'Use it and any other book in the house as often as you like, Mrs. Rooney.'

Seeing how tired Mrs. Morgan looked, Margaret suggested that she went to her bedroom for a rest. 'You'll be quieter there if Bryan Glynn wakes early from his nap.'

'He'll probably wake before I come down to have tea, would you mind bringing him up to my room? I'd like to read to him. He seems to like a story.'

'If you'd enjoy that, it seems a very good idea. There are some chores that I can do which are difficult if his lordship is around.' Both women smiled: they shared a common bond with the toddler.

A precedent was established. Flo Morgan would secrete a story with her at her rest time and when he had woken from his sleep, Bryan Glynn's request was, 'Ranny Morge's 'tory.' On the first day Margaret had spied on her son to see that he was behaving and there he was sitting attentively on a milking stool by Mrs. Morgan's bed and his mother heard the words:

'Do you not catch the tiny clamour,
Busy click of an elfin hammer,
Voice of the Leprechaun singing shrill'
As he merrily plies his trade.'

Margaret crept into the room after knocking quietly on the door and stood transfixed by the scene. Flo Morgan's voice was her most lovely attribute. *No wonder, Dai had fallen in love when he saw and heard the school teacher playing her part in the Miscellany of Nancy's mother's recollection, all those years ago.*

'This Irish woman doesn't know that rhyme, Mrs. Morgan. Who wrote it?'

'William Allingham. Dai found this book of Irish folklore in 'The Second-hand Shop' in Brecon, last week. Do look at the picture, Mrs. Rooney.'

'It's charming. And Bryan Glynn understands the 'click' and the 'clamour'.'

'You don't always give yourself the credit you deserve, my dear. Your son has inherited his ear for the music of words from his mother.' Margaret felt herself flush with a strange sort of embarrassment – her employer's wife had never given her such unambiguous praise before. She was touched.

Walking down the stairs, Bryan Glynn practised the 'cl' sound. He seemed, instinctively, to know it was the metallic noise of a hammer hitting an anvil, as he mimed the movement. *He remembers seeing one of the horses being shod at the forge. I wonder whether he is imagining the sparks flying too.*

As the days, weeks and months followed, Bryan Glynn continued to anticipate and delight in his time with Flo Morgan and she in turn went to endless trouble to find some tale or poem which would enthrall him. Margaret made use of the short time without her mischievous child, either doing some unpleasant farm job or pouring over the atlas. An encyclopedia was another object of study, at these private times. Margaret realized that her *good education* had been lacking in Geography and General Knowledge. She knew very little about Japan. To her, the word referred to a certain type of lacquer. She knew that Japanese women wore kimonos and rich European people owned lovely china of eggshell thickness, bearing scenes reputed to be sights in Japan – often depicting a mountain, which research informed her was named Mount Fuji. These treasured things were not part of her Cork childhood, though Sean's parents had had a couple of silk pictures. Perhaps they had been Japanese. As she increased her knowledge of Japan and the Japanese she became aware of a culture very different to any she understood. Until now, she hadn't even read about the country which was at present at war with Europe and America – in one concert at the Church Hall there had been a scene from 'The Mikado'! Her thoughts flew to the Lord High Executioner, and to Yum Yum's love of her own beauty. *My Bernie is living among aliens. How will he manage? Patrick's right - the Japanese are not Christians!*

Sometimes Margaret thought she was going mad with anxiety and misery. It was the routine of the farm and Bryan Glynn which steadied her. All the people around her at Cae Coch seemed to sense her dreadful worries and made every effort to alleviate them. The Morgans understood her preoccupations better than anyone else and Margaret became aware of a new closeness with her employers during this period of the war. Patrick found it difficult to put his grave concerns in writing and his leaves became spasmodic as his naval responsibilities increased. The tensions of war were becoming acute and Patrick's temperament was being tested. He was finding life without the prop of alcohol hard. When at Cae Coch, everyone indulged him with good food and conversation.

'You're fighting in the war and need special treatment, not living in the safe seclusion of rural life like us.' Nancy told him.

Meanwhile Margaret and Nancy, themselves, found rural life very hard work, even if it was secure. Mrs. Morgan did little work on the farm but continued to cook and clean.

'My wife looks ill,' Dai said one morning. 'On my way to the newspaper office I'm going to look in on Dr. Thomas. Perhaps there's a heart specialist who might take Flo as a patient to monitor her angina.'

Despite his domestic concerns, Dai continued to write his articles and oversee the farm, finding time to attend the market to sell and buy stock when it was necessary. Gwyn maintained and drove the ancient tractor for harvesting helped by prisoners of war from the nearby camp, in addition to his duties at the Convalescent Hospital. Even the older children from the County School 'lent a hand' picking medicinal herbs one week-end. All moved from one crisis to the next. Cae Coch survived through the conscientiousness of all who were part of and loved the farm. Even the German prisoners cheered when they heard from Nancy the news of Italy surrendering to the allies published in the daily newspaper. Mr. Morgan pointed out the irony to the family. The allies still had to overcome the German forces in Italy.

'Mr. Morgan, I find all the news dispiriting. There are so many fronts. Do tell me whether it can ever end. Please?' Margaret immediately regretted lowering her guard, but she saw a new sympathy in her employer's expression.

'Don't despair. I know you have great anxieties. We feel for you. I'm of the opinion that the American advances in the Pacific and the Russian successes on the Eastern front are heartening and will lead to a victory within the year.'

'That is good but when you mention the Pacific I think of my son. If only I knew he was alive.'

'I know. You said to me once that he was a good Catholic: that he had a deep and strong faith. Believe me, he will have that whatever circumstances he finds himself in. God is a power within us, not necessarily in Church Services.' He looked embarrassed, but Margaret murmured her thanks and tried to smile an acknowledgement. *The Morgans humble me. I know there is some power forcing me to persevere. I am so strong physically. Have I lost that profound spirituality of my childhood? I must look for and find strength or God within me.*

In one unguarded moment Margaret exclaimed, 'I feel at such a distance from the war, especially as Patrick is so rarely on leave from his unit to be with me and Bryan Glynn.'

'Your husband's war work is, I think, evidence of things, in Europe at least, coming to a climax.'

'Please God, I hope so. I must rescue your wife from my son. He does so enjoy his time with her.'

'She loves to read to him. If she had her way she'd make him a Shakespearian actor. My wife speaks of him a great deal when we are alone.'

'He doesn't tire her, does he?'

'On the contrary, I think he takes her mind off her illness.'

43

Granny Speaks

L etters to Cae Coch from Liverpool were full of the hardships having to be endured because of shortages due to American supplies being lost in mid-Atlantic. German U-boats were sinking merchant ships – Rhys' cousin was one of the many merchant navy casualties. The British Government was using a new system for ascertaining direction and range of enemy aircraft and shipping, known as radar, to repulse this onslaught, but losses continued to occur. However there had been no air raids on the city for a long time.

The Williames were working long hours in difficult conditions and were not able to visit Wales as often as they would have liked. Housing in Merseyside was a problem. As a result of so much bombing in 1941 whole areas were devastated. Rhys and Mary had been asked to let rooms in their house to doctors working as demonstrators in the Medical School. The RAMC needed more and more doctors, nurses and physiotherapists, both at forward positions and at Naval and Military hospitals.

There had been a development in life at the farm. Margaret had agreed to accompany Mrs. Morgan to see a heart specialist once a month in Brecon. Consequently, she was able to go to confession and mass at the Catholic Church, whilst Mrs. Morgan was at the town hospital. Meanwhile, Nancy was left in charge of things at Cae Coch. Bryan Glynn went with his mother. Mrs. Morgan's heart condition was being monitored at a special unit in the town. Mr. Morgan had said, 'It may be mutually beneficial for the pair of you. Glynn Thomas has great faith in this specialist, but I can't take the time off to be with my wife. Will it be a problem for you to go with Mrs. Morgan?'

'It will be a pleasure. Bryan Glynn loves the short train journey and Father Anselm is pleased when I manage to attend his services. He loves to make Bryan Glynn laugh.'

'I'll ask for a regular slot for Mrs. Morgan's appointment to coincide with the time of your service. Perhaps sometime we could arrange for you all to see Anna.'

On the third excursion, the Convent arranged for Margaret to pick Anna up and take her to a café for an early tea with her grandmother and Bryan Glynn. Anna seemed listless and looked pale. As they walked to the café, she told Margaret how she had tried to run away from the school and had been found by the parent of a day girl at the railway station. She had been in a lot of trouble when she was returned to what she called 'The Prison'.

'Will you post this letter to Mummy, Pinny, please? Don't mention anything to Granny. I don't want to worry her now she's not well. It is good to see you and my little 'boy mascot'.'

At the café Anna seemed to throw herself into the conversation and Margaret's fears lessened. *What had she written to her mother?*

Mary telephoned her parents, telling them that her family would not be able to spend Christmas at Cae Coch, because Rhys was needed for a couple of meetings and she had to be on duty over the Christmas holiday.

'Instead we will come to see Mother over the half-term in November,' when she hoped it would be convenient for David and Anna to stay at the farm. *Anna's letter has worked to alert her mother to her misery.*

'Nancy and I will do the beds to-morrow.' Margaret was pleased at the prospect of company.

'We will miss the family at Christmas, but we'll have plenty to do prior to the festival now we are selling Christmas chickens, ready for the oven.' Dai Morgan said with a tinge of disappointment.

'Let's have two celebrations: one with the children and another with the Cae Coch work force on Christmas Day,' his wife added brightly.

*

David and Anna were delighted and surprised when they were met at the station by their grandfather, and driven back to the farm to find their father waiting in the farmyard. He explained that their mother was with Granny checking on her health. Anna was ecstatic to be at Cae Coch and David too seemed to be delighted to have this unexpected visit from their parents. He wanted to discuss the

OTC with Patrick who unfortunately was not at Cae Coch and wouldn't be there on Christmas Day either, Margaret told him.

'This must mean that Mr. Rooney's involved in the 'Big Push'. Our OTC officer has told us cadets that the allies are about to invade France.'

'Perhaps we shouldn't speculate about such serious matters.' His grandfather commented gently.

That evening, Anna was safely in bed; Rhys and Mary were with Mr. Morgan in the dining room, when Mrs. Morgan attracted David's attention with the words, 'Will you have a serious conversation with your Granny, David? It's so good to see you so grown up and happy but I'd like to confide in you about a little family history.'

David sat at the kitchen table attentively. His grandmother produced a bottle of ginger beer and two tumblers; she poured the drink into the glasses.

'It's ages since I tasted this stuff. Where did you manage to get it?' asked David.

'Never you mind. I bought it specially for you. I know it is a favourite of yours. Just listen to what an old granny has to say.'

Margaret was rocking Bryan Glynn to sleep. He'd been so excited to see David and Anna that he didn't want to go to bed. His mother signalled to Mrs. Morgan, gesticulating about her presence and nodding at the door, but the other shook her head and frowned. *Mrs. Morgan must want me to hear what she's going to say to David. I wonder why?* David seemed unaware of Margaret's presence.

'The OTC is interesting and important to you, isn't it David?'

'Yes it is, Granny. I have told the officer that I intend to join the RAF as soon as my age permits. I must do my bit for Britain against The Bosch.'

'Have you discussed your plan with your father?'

'No, I haven't.'

'Have you mentioned the matter to your mother?'

'No, I haven't, yet. Isn't it up to me to make my own contribution to the war, Granny?'

'Yes. That's true. What could be the outcome?'

'I might fly missions without any problems. I might be shot down. I might even be decorated for gallantry.'

'Explain. . .' Mrs. Morgan seemed hesitant.

'You know, Granny, that poem by Wilfred Owen *'Dulce et Decorum est'*. I think it ends *Pro Patria Mori*. Doesn't that mean that it is right and honourable to die for your Country? One of the OTC chaps said it did.'

'David, I want to say this gently to you. Patriotism has its place in all countries and in all cultures, but the lives of patriots are precious. Don't you need to be more circumspect about deciding to be a pilot in the RAF at such a young age, without discussing it with your parents?'

'I don't understand. Isn't it important to do one's bit to win the war? We may lose the war the way things are going. Didn't a poet write this in 'Who's for the Game?'

Your country's up to her neck in a fight,
And she's looking and calling for you.

David's tone had a hint of triumph in it.

Mrs. Morgan took a book from a pile on the dresser.

'You're quoting from Jessie Pope. I have Wilfred Owen's poem here, David. He didn't agree with Jessie Pope's sentiment. Would you read it quietly to yourself? What do the words of the poem mean?'

David studied the page and looked chastened as a result. 'It describes the horrors of the battle field. The final words say one thing but mean another.'

'Exactly. Owen is telling 'his friend' that the Latin tag is 'The Old Lie'. Jessie Pope had used, *'Dulci et Decorum est'* as a caption for an enlistment poster. So, before you rush into a war, should you perhaps think of another concept – peace?'

'I suppose so.' A hint of doubt was creeping into his voice.

'Your Uncle Owen died for his country. And we thought the sacrifice would mean the end of war itself, but here we are again.'

Margaret noticed David flinch. He was uncomfortable. His grandmother continued.

'David, your beliefs are, I know, genuine, but remember there are other things beside glory and sacrifice, like duty and hard work. The spectacular is often disappointing or disastrous.'

David was silent.

After the pause he said, shamefacedly, 'I understand. Perhaps, I should think about it.' He suddenly noticed Margaret and Bryan Glynn and stood up saying, 'I haven't been sens. . . sensitive to you and your pos. . . position, either. I'm so sorry, Mrs. Rooney.'

With no pause at all, Margaret replied with the words, 'Your grandmother beckoned me to stay and hear what she had to say. I hope you don't mind, David?'

'No. You're family or like family. School sometimes carries one away. Being back here at Cae Coch is so normal and comfortable.'

'I feel the same. The war seems to be far away, yet we know it's inescapable. Thank you for playing with Bryan Glynn. Look! He's dreaming, probably about 'Hide and Seek'.'

The door into the passage opened and they all stopped talking as they saw the sleeping child.

*

When Margaret returned to the kitchen, after putting Bryan Glynn in his bed, the family was talking about David's future. 'Please join us, Mrs. Rooney,' Mr. Morgan was in the middle of explaining The Peace Conference of 1919.

'I had the honour of representing a Welsh group of newspapers at this historic conference. Though I was a junior reporter, it was thought appropriate for me to attend some of the open meetings. After all, hadn't I lost my precious son?'

'Our history master has told us that the President of America, Mr. Woodrow Wilson attended and influenced the discussion and then didn't sign the treaty of Versailles. Was that true, Grandpa?'

'I'm afraid so. He didn't support the setting up of The League of Nations either. In my opinion Mr. Lloyd George and Mon. Clemenceau, the French President, were the leading lights of the debates.'

'Didn't they re-draw the map of Europe?'

'Indeed they did and there was criticism of that after the treaties were signed. Also, they made Germany compensate heavily for their part in the destruction of France and Belgium.'

'That was fair, surely,' said David.

'Perhaps it resulted in the rise of Nazi-ism; many writers have stated that the reparation was unjust. I was so shocked at seeing the battle fields that I just wanted to come home. Other participants and observers might have felt the same. Some seemed moved by the devastation.'

'The Conference must have been good for the economy of Paris and France.'

'I dare say but it saddened me to watch some delegates enjoying the delights of the city – dancing and drinking to all hours, when others were finding it difficult to forget the horrendous human sacrifice and were determined to forge a lasting peace.'

'It is for my generation to see that this time there is an enduring peace. I realize that we should learn by the mistakes of history. This evening, Granny explained to me the importance of duty and sensitivity.' David sighed.

Mr. Morgan continued his recollections of The Peace Conference 1919, 'It is said that Mr. Lloyd George, who was nick-named the Welsh Wizard by the way, said, in dismissing the claim of the Treaty of Versailles that it would bring about the end of war itself:

'We shall have to do the whole thing again in
Twenty-five years at three times the cost.'

If my Mathematics are correct, it took only twenty years.'

44

The War Rages

'Everyone looks old, since the war has begun,' Nancy said, one morning, whilst they were feeding the stock.

'I feel older,' replied Margaret. 'Mrs. Morgan looks as though she feels poorly too. If it weren't for 'Our Mascot', Anna's name for Bryan Glynn, we'd all give up I feel sometimes.' Both women were amused as the toddler appeared with an arm full of hay for the horses. They in turn took a small mouthful from him, sensing his vulnerability but keen to please a good friend.

'How gentle they are with him. D'you remember how scared I was of the horses and cows when I started to help with the animals?' Nancy picked up the wisps of hay Bryan Glynn had dropped and shared them between the two horses.

'Nancy, Mrs. Morgan asked me to tell you that the Williamses are not coming for Christmas, this year. They came for half-term to explain; that was when you and Gwyn went to your great-aunt's funeral. Apparently, Dr. Mary has to cover Christmas Day and Boxing Day for her practice. It seems that the American doctor who has been so helpful to her is getting married on Christmas Eve.'

'I hope he'll help her when he's married. It's a pity, I missed the Williamses. I have made little gifts for them, but they weren't ready then, anyway.'

'We thought that we'd send one parcel next week before the children go back to Liverpool from school. Your things are ready now aren't they?'

'Yes, I'll give them to you to-morrow.'

Margaret looked serious as she said, 'It seems that there have been no air raids, in Liverpool, for some time and Anna is unsettled at school, seeing her home might be good.'

'I'd have hated to go to a boarding school. Wouldn't you, Maggie?'

'I loved my convent and studying. I think I'd have enjoyed concentrating on school work without all the farm jobs I had to do after school. The daily bus journey was a waste of time too.'

'I've made Bryan Glynn a sailor suit; it won't upset you, will it? He does like to wear his Dad's naval cap.'

'That's fine. By the way, Patrick won't be here. He's on duty. Mrs. Morgan hopes you and Gwyn will be with us.' Margaret said as she rescued Bryan Glynn from the hay shed where he was about to gather a second ration of hay for the horses.

'That'll be grand. Thank her, won't you?'

Margaret was pleased that Nancy had not asked her more about Anna's unhappiness. The two mothers hadn't managed to have a private talk at half-term, because Anna had monopolised her mother. Margaret had understood that there were difficulties about school as a result of Anna's demeanour and her confession, when they all had had tea together in Brecon. Mary had confided the problem to Margaret in detail, in a note which came with a tube of cream she had posted for a rash that Bryan Glynn had had for a couple of weeks. *Would a visit home make boarding school more tolerable for Anna? If not what would be the solution?*

Margaret wondered about the future. Would the next year bring victory or defeat? She thought of the plight of women – mothers and daughters. Her mind reflected on her own mother. Was Mam still alive? She had a fleeting memory of her mother applying a salve to the hoof of a farmer's workhorse with a tenderness which had surprised her at the time.

Boarding School

Margaret had read Mary's letter very quickly, when she received it, but it worried her. After her chat to Nancy she studied it. The letter reflected a mother's concern.

Dear Maggie,

Dad told me about Bryan Glynn's continuing rash on the phone. He said he'd tell you that I'd put the ointment, which Glynn Thomas and I used to use pre-war for that sort of skin trouble, in the post. It's very difficult to obtain. Here it is.

You know I was in contact with David and Anna's schools, before half-term. There are no problems with David. But, you saw how Anna looked. She is much thinner, isn't she? She slept well at Cae Coch, however she is clearly not sleeping at school. Rhys says that she is spoilt and we should try to make her put up with the situation. Overwork makes him irritable. He is sure that there may be more raids on Liverpool. How can we know? I'm of the opinion that Anna should come home and go to school here. Liverpool schools which were evacuated at the beginning of the war are now back in place and continuing to serve the city community. I'm determined about this move for Anna, Maggie.

So, why am I troubling you? Can I be open about this? If Anna does come back here and air raids start again, may I dispatch her, immediately, to Cae Coch? Dad would agree to her living at the farm, I'm sure. I feel, however, that you're doing the lion's share of the work on the farm, as Mother is failing, I fear. Of course I will consult both parents if the occasion arises, but your agreement is paramount, in the circumstances. Let's hope it doesn't come to more raids.

I know you won't worry Dad and Mother with the underlying reason for Anna coming back to Liverpool. They have their cup full at the moment. Rhys and I had a frank conversation with Mother about her heart condition and popped in to see Glynn Thomas, whilst you were taking Anna to see Rachael. The prognosis is not good. How eternally grateful we are that you are at Cae Coch. Thank you. When will this ghastly war end? How many times have we uttered those words?

I'll explain more fully about Anna's unhappiness. It appears that she has been in some trouble not all of her making. Hearing aircraft above the convent, one night, (unidentified, but acknowledged by the nuns), she became terrified and thought they were either bombing us or the school. Elizabeth, aged fifteen, the girl in the next bed to Anna in the dormitory, invited the petrified child into her bed to pacify her. Matron came into the dorm., and ordered Anna out of Elizabeth's bed and reported the incident to the Sister-in-Charge in the morning, accusing Lizzie of being 'immoral'. Anna didn't understand but felt responsible! She thought it might have been a reprisal by Matron – the girls had tried to stay awake to see her undress, when she first did dorm-duty. Matron, who's not a nun, is very fat and ugly! The girls were caught giggling on that occasion, though Anna, who hates her, had been fast asleep at the time. What strange problems this war generates! How does one explain some <u>unexplainable</u> things to children? Anna looks awful, don't you think? She needs to see a Liverpool paediatrician. For that reason I don't want my parents to know how worried I am or why I'm worried. I don't think the Sister-in-charge, who seems to be bullied by Matron, handled the incident sympathetically or fairly. I have every confidence in, and respect for Reverend Mother, she understands children and when I telephoned and broached the subject of moving Anna to a day school, she was sympathetic. Rhys's comment was, 'Roll on co-education; women, especially holy women, seem to have one-track minds'.

We need the Christmas holiday to get Anna back to health and into a Liverpool school; so this is the other reason for us staying here for Christmas. Rhys is up to his eyes, anyway, marking yet another lot of exam papers - this time Anatomy for nurses and physiotherapists, who are much in demand at home and in the field hospitals.

Most importantly, have your letters about Japanese prisoners-of-war to the M.P. and the Red Cross made any positive headway?

I hope Bryan Glynn's rash will be cured with the enclosed ointment and he is back to his usual self, soon. He is a ray of sunshine to all at Cae Coch.

Yours affectionately,

Mary

*

Margaret kept the contents of the letter to herself. For some extraordinary reason, she felt guilty. She hated people in power using their position unjustly. The Morgan family had been so fair in their dealings with her that she had forgotten her family's strange treatment of herself, all those years ago. *Why had they not acknowledged her letters? How and where was Bridget now? Why didn't Bridget ever write to her?* That Anna should be made to feel in the wrong was outrageous. The next time she went into the town, she bought a postcard emblazoned with the words – LEND A HAND ON THE LAND and wrote, 'Yes, Yes, Yes, Maggie' and sent it to Mary. *Should I tell Mary about Anna's attempt to run away? No. I'll leave it for now.* As Bryan Glynn asked her to lift him up so that he could post the card, she was overwhelmed with pleasure in him and forgot about the eggs he'd stamped on, in the yard, that morning; he was becoming a handful!

46

Snowbound

Without the Williams family, Christmas was going to be strange. Margaret and Nancy racked their brains about a plan to make the festival happy and enjoyable for the Morgans. It was the editor of the *Express* who finally made Advent and Christmas as pleasant as any wartime festival could be for Cae Coch and the whole town. He had launched through the paper a special Comfort Fund for wounded troops. His leading article in November 1943, stating his opinion that the war was nearing a final victory for the Allies, pleased his readers. He described the successful advance of the Russians on the Eastern front, capturing strategic cities like Kiev from the Germans. He went on to explain how Allied bombers were targeting industrial sites in Germany at night and in daytime raids, causing devastation and lowering morale. His belief in the long mooted possibility of the Allies opening a Second Front in Europe was his *coup de grace.*

'The article makes the situation clear. All these theatres of war will, unfortunately, result in casualties.' Dai Morgan said as all at Cae Coch read the hopeful, almost triumphant, words.

'Why don't we all plan a Christmas with as many fund-raising activities to meet the need for comforts for our valiant troops,' was Mrs. Morgan's response.

'The schools, the Church, the Chapel and the whole community could all make a contribution. It would be pleasurable, too.' Dai continued, thoughtfully.

An Advent Bazaar was arranged in the Church Hall, with every organization taking part, at the start of Christmas week. Farms in the environs of the town provided holly, ivy, mistletoe and small fir trees. Handy craft stalls were set up. Second hand clothing was displayed to advantage for sale and homemade jams and pickles were auctioned. There was a pre-war feel about the town, which had, recently, become near to despair over the shortages caused by lack of imported food and raw materials.

'I'll be banker,' said the Mayor.

'May I have the honour and pleasure of opening the Bazaar?' asked the editor of the *Express*.

The venture was a resounding success and the astonishing amount of £500 and a few shillings was raised – a fund for the bereaved, the wounded and the heroic survivors. There was immediately a mood of hope. People smiled. There was soon to be an end to austerity.

Margaret was exhausted. She had done too much, adding Bazaar duties to her work on the farm. Bryan Glynn had got over-excited and consequently naughty, he had become so active. The day after the Bazaar she confided to Nancy, 'I feel flat and useless. I put too much effort into yesterday. I would like to sit and cry.'

'Never mind, as the advert says, 'chin up'.' Nancy went on to explain that there was to be an 'Evening of Carols' at Cae Coch with refreshments for the church choir and close friends of the family on Christmas Eve.

'Who will do the cooking?' Margaret asked, tearfully. 'I feel too tired to do anything extra.'

Nancy laughed. 'Well, it's to be a treat for you. Gwyn is to light the fires in the parlour and dining room. Mair who runs the town café is going to provide mince pies, sausage rolls, corned beef pasties, tomatoes and a cake.'

'What do we have to do?' Margaret's tone was weary.

Nancy said playfully. 'We have to put lots of potatoes in the oven of the range; put pickles in those pretty glass dishes and put the plates and cutlery on the table. Will you be able to help me with those difficult tasks, Mrs. Rooney?'

'I'm sorry, Nancy. I'm so down. All the talk of the final push makes me think of Bernie. You know they think he's a prisoner of war.'

'Then he's *alive*? That's grand. Who told you?'

'It's been a secret for some time, but now I think you should know because I've been so moody lately. Bryan Glynn has started to say, 'no' to everything I ask him to do and I feel I can't go on.'

They were in the dairy, cleaning the utensils and Margaret slumped on to the stool by the churn. Nancy looked shocked and said, 'Maggie, you've always faced the ordeal of Bernie's fate with such inner strength. Why now? Please, please tell. . ?'

'I'm sorry. It's all got to me. Let's get into the crisp winter air. A short walk might make me sleep to-night, for a change.'

'We'll go along the lane to the road and back. Promise I won't talk. I'll wait till you feel like it to tell me about Bernie. I won't tell Gwyn either. I really won't, Maggie.'

*

The 'Carol Evening' was a great success. The small choir excelled itself, singing well known excerpts from *The Messiah*, and Welsh hymns. One member had brought a decorated Christmas tree; another placed a hand-made crib on the dresser for Bryan Glynn, who whooped with joy at the sight of it - each piece was carved out of Welsh oak. There was cider cup, home-made lemonade and the promised food was delicious. It transpired that Mair had received a food parcel from America. Cae Coch resounded with the beauty of Bach's music and the familiar Welsh melodies; after the interval for refreshment there was happy conversation. All declared that peace was soon to be a reality.

Nancy who had been very quiet throughout the evening said, 'The country peace of Cae Coch will very soon be the country's peace.'

'Quite the little orator,' replied Gwyn. But for once his tone was proud and not critical.

The fires burned bright with Yule logs of apple – from trees which had been felled to make room for vegetables. The editor made a short speech of thanks to the Morgans, the Joneses and Margaret Rooney as he produced a bag of chestnuts to roast on the fire.

'It's funny seeing The Mayor drying the dishes,' said Maggie.

'What about the Editor of The Express showing Bryan Glynn how to roast chestnuts?' Margaret replied.

'Just as well that we don't have open fires every day,' Dai Morgan commented, 'I hope he doesn't try to roast chestnuts or anything else on my paraffin stove. He's becoming quite adventurous.'

Gwyn had milked the cows as the women were busy entertaining guests. He explained, 'I needed to keep my hand in. It's ages since I milked. Fancy, Susan tried to kick me.'

'So?' Nancy and Margaret said in unison.

'Perhaps at last I know my place.' Gwyn said ruefully.

*

They all woke next day to Cae Coch covered in snow, deep snow. Bryan Glynn was ecstatic, 'Did Fa'r Christ' brought it? D'we always ha' 'no'w on Christ' Day?' He exchanged his Christmas stocking for his wellies, gleefully.

The weather ruled out any excursions to church, but permitted a snow-balling session and caused the stock to be skittish as they snorted at and pawed the snow with mock terror. Only Mrs. Morgan stayed indoors to cook the goose, stuffed with sage and onion, which had been a present from the butcher who had sold the farm chickens for Dai Morgan.

'I hope we haven't broken any Ministry regulations. The snow will prevent any policeman trekking up to Cae Coch to arrest me until the snow clears, anyway.'

'All the vegetables have been prepared by Mair. There's nothing for me to do.' The mistress of the house said in a surprised tone.

'Yes, Flo, there is something you can do. Enjoy yourself.' Her husband replied. He, meanwhile, produced a parcel, which on examination was addressed in Patrick's hand-writing. 'I'll play the part of Santa.' The W.I. theatrical wardrobe had been rifled for the appropriate clothes. Dai Morgan put on a scarlet dressing-gown with a hood, stuck a white beard to his chin and white whiskers as eyebrows. His wife called Margaret, Nancy, Gwyn and Bryan Glynn from the yard into the kitchen.

'Presents, everyone.'

Dai assumed a deep Welsh voice. 'What have I here? For Bryan Glynn, I have a big parcel.'Bryan Glynn was so busy unwrapping his engine, The Royal Scot, and immediately rolling it round the room that he didn't notice Mr. Morgan's absence.

The voice continued, 'To my dear wife, Maggie, this smaller gift.' It turned out to be a Donegal beret and matching gloves. Margaret was delighted. 'Where on earth could Patrick have bought such beautiful things?' Nancy and Gwyn were equally pleased and surprised by their miniature bottle of whiskey and box of chocolates.

'It's a long time since I saw a box of chocolates let alone had one of my own.' Nancy was amazed.

A canvas roll came out of the parcel labelled 'The Morgans'.

'My husband's just slipped out to refill the coal scuttle. On your way to your next family, Santa, could you ask him to hurry in to the house, please?'

Mr. Morgan's reappearance to admire his and his wife's present of an old map of Breconshire was accompanied by stifled giggles, but Bryan Glynn ran to Dai, saying, 'M' Morge, look, look Farth' Chris' sent me Scot engine.'

Nancy was opening her chocolates exclaiming that they were American. 'I've never had anything American before.'

'Yes you have. What about that packet you won, last week, with the Yankie flag on it, which turned out to contain dried egg?' laughed Gwyn.

'Well I gave that back to the Lucky Dip at the Bazaar, didn't I?'

Everyone smiled and even Margaret's expression was content; the anxiety of previous weeks seemed to have been replaced by a feeling of tranquility as she pushed 'The Royal Scot' across the kitchen floor and murmured a whispered 'Thank you' to Santa.

*

Margaret thought it was the wind, which had raged throughout the evening but realized it was a gentle knock on the door of her loft room. She struggled into her dressing-gown as she rushed to open the door – to an anxious Mr. Morgan.

'My wife's had a heart attack. Can you come and be with her? I must clear the lane for the doctor. . . shall I carry Bryan Glynn for you?'

'No, I'll light the night light. He loves that if he wakes. It's out of his reach. He hasn't woken in the night for months. He's safe in his bed if I put the side up.'

'Are you sure?'

'Yes. I'll hear him any way and come back, should he wake. You know, Mr. Morgan, how loud he can be. It's so quiet since the snow.'

She was in her breeches and boots before Mr. Morgan had walked carefully across the yard to the tractor shed.

'Take care on those steps down from the loft, Mrs. Rooney. I'm starting the tractor so I can clear the snow drifts along the lane to the road and further if need be. The doctor's on his way. The lamps are lit in the house.'

'Thank God the telephone is still working despite the snow.' Her words were lost as she closed the door. She muttered a 'God speed,' to the wind as she crept into the farmhouse.

*

Margaret reached Mrs. Morgan's bedroom to find the patient deathly pale and breathing irregularly. At least she was still alive. On seeing Margaret, Flo attempted a smile and co-operated as Margaret put extra pillows at her back and lifted her gently to a more upright position. Despite her assurances to Dai Morgan, Margaret was listening for any sound from Bryan Glynn as well.

'I'll rub your hands, Mrs. Morgan. Nancy was kind and took my hand and massaged it, when I was so ill at Bryan Glynn's birth.' *If only, I'd paid more attention to that talk about First Aid at the Church Hall, last year. I thought the war would be over and then I'd study it when I wasn't so tired. What had Gwyn said about that soldier who'd suffered cardiac failure?*

Margaret sat by Mrs. Morgan, petrified. She stroked her hands, praying silently, asking God to bring the doctor, quickly. *Was it my fault that Mrs. Morgan had had this heart attack? Have I been so desperate about Bernie that I haven't kept my promise to Mr. Morgan about insisting that his wife rested?*

The hands seemed cold and lifeless, but the contact warmed them and Margaret felt overwhelming affection for Mrs. Morgan. An intimacy had developed between the two women recently. If Flo Morgan was going to die, Margaret took comfort from their present friendly relationship. It seemed hours, but Margaret saw from the clock that only half an hour had passed, when the patient relaxed into her pillows and began to doze. As sleep claimed her, her breathing became more regular and Margaret started to worry about leaving Bryan Glynn alone. Thank God Mrs. Morgan had rallied and medical assistance would soon be at the farm despite the snow and the night time freeze.

Light footfall on the stairs announced Dr. Thomas.

'How is she, how has she been?' he whispered, while he was gently taking Mrs. Morgan's pulse. 'I'm sorry I've been so long in coming. I've borrowed a driver and jeep from the Convalescent Hospital and my old friend Dai cleared your lane with the tractor.'

'If I can't do anything more, I'll check Bryan Glynn, if you don't mind. May I come back to hear what you have to say when you have finished examining Mrs. Morgan?'

*

Margaret found her son asleep, just as she had left him. The rhythmic breathing of the sleeping child overcame her and she nearly woke him with her sobs. To wake him and hold him would be unfair.

Back in the farmhouse kitchen, Dai Morgan was handing the army driver a cup of tea.

'The doctor has given my wife an injection. She's too ill to move and the weather wouldn't permit us taking her to hospital, even if there were a suitable hospital nearby.'

'I didn't know what to do. . . I. . . I.'

'You propped her up and your calm relaxed her. That was all you could do. Thank you.'

'May I go and see her briefly, now?'

'Of course.'

In the bedroom Margaret whispered to Dr. Thomas, 'Is she going to be alright, really?'

'Yes, this time. The long term prognosis is not very rosy, I fear.'

'I'll just say 'Good-night' to my friend if I may?'

'Please do.'

As she bent over Mrs. Morgan and spoke to her softly, the other mouthed the words, 'Thank you' and Margaret saw a faint smile cross her pale face.

As she left the room the doctor followed her on to the landing. 'Well done, Margaret. You'll be able to cope with Dai's help until the thaw, I know.'

'I want to see her better.'

'I understand. If you are concerned telephone me. Don't hesitate.'

'I was so frightened earlier. I felt alone.'

Dr. Thomas touched her arm and made her feel calm again by saying, 'Margaret, you're human; the thing about you is that you may be scared but you never show it. You just get on with the job in hand. I'm becoming more and more weary of this war and its miseries. You must feel that too.'

47

Change

Early in the New Year, Mary Williams managed to make a trip to see her mother. 'When Dad rang us on the 27th, my first thought was to take a train to Mid-Wales immediately, but he said, "wait".'

'Your father was beside himself but it didn't stop him having a sensible outlook.' Margaret pointed out.

'I know. He went on to say that mother would have believed that she was dying if the family descended on her bedside.'

'She was a very sick woman for several days. Her breathing varied from hour to hour at first. Then it settled. Dr. Thomas gave her injections. What were they, Mary?'

'Probably he was giving her morphine with other things as well. I'll talk to him.'

'Sorry, I know I shouldn't ask for information about treatment. You're the doctor. I was thinking of you as a daughter, just now.'

'What about her colour?'

'On that first night, I thought that she was almost gone. I panicked a little when left alone with her.'

'I heard from Dad with Mother listening that you were a tower of strength.'

'I might have appeared like that but, Mary, I was so frightened. What if I'd done quite the wrong thing?'

'Being collected and quiet is all a person can do who hasn't the drugs on hand. You had to wait for Glynn Thomas. We found it extraordinary when Dad mentioned the snow. There was not a flake in Liverpool.'

'It seems that it was very local and Cae Coch was unfortunate because it is so high up. The high wind caused the drifting.'

'Thank God it's gone now. I don't like snow. How did Bryan Glynn react to it?'

'You can imagine all the grown-ups played snow-balling and of course a magnificent snowman was made. Bryan Glynn cried when two days later the thaw came and took Mr. 'nowma' with it.'

'Poor Bryan Glynn. I'm going to see Dr. Thomas later, but in the mean time I want to discuss the farm with you.'

'We've managed well this last week.'

'I understand that and I'm grateful but Dad has had the benefit of there not being a Christmas edition of 'The Express'.'

'I hadn't cottoned on to that. I suppose I've been too busy.'

'Dad is concerned that Nancy and you are overworked. Come now, admit it. Something has to go, doesn't it?'

'We'll manage, somehow.'

'There are alternatives to you both claiming an early grave.'

'It seems worse than it is. The truth is; I've not been up to scratch lately. I'm in such a state about Bernie.'

'Quite. You're his mother. It's only natural.'

'Lately, since I've known, nearly for certain, that he's a prisoner of the Japanese, I'm obsessed with the war news from the Far East.'

'Of course. Even so, you're holding this farm together despite your preoccupation.'

'It's good of you to say that. I try to do the work without dwelling on Bernie's fate.'

'I know. Dad suggested to me that he thought it might help if he hired a land girl to help on the farm. How'd you feel about that?'

'I don't know. I'd like to continue to do as much milking and dairy work as possible. A change of milkmaid from Nancy and me might lower the yield.'

'Yes. I think that's a consideration that can't be overlooked.'

'I agree and I'm sure Nancy would like to continue to relieve me in the milking parlour as she does now.'

'Now Mother's unable to look after the house, it would be excellent if you could take over the cooking, cleaning and laundry. You do a great deal of it at the present time.'

Maggie was thoughtful. 'I'd want the farm to be run properly. Some land girls are incompetent and lazy, I've heard.'

'Maggie, I'll be blunt. Would you mind changing your role from farmer to housekeeper? Dad would revert to keeping the workers up to your standards.' Mary couldn't help giving a chuckle as she said the last words.

'I'm being obstinate. Sorry. You mean have a land girl to help Nancy to do the feeding, egg-collecting, mucking-out and checking the pasture, vegetables and arable areas under your father's supervision?'

'Yes, Maggie. You're there at last. That seems a good split. You will be in charge of the house, just as mother was, and the cows.'

'I don't want to usurp your mother's place.'

'She nodded agreement when Dad put the idea to her. She's even agreed to letting the land girl have the small bedroom which David usually has.'

'That's good, Mary. I've got so fond of your mother. I was in a state when I thought she was going to die. I'll do anything to help.'

'Mother is pleased to let you have a free rein. She told me that you saved her life when she had her heart attack.'

'Thank her, please. It's good of her to say that, I tried to do my best. How can we be sure to have a land girl who fits in here?'

'Dad's looking into that, but it requires your prior agreement.'

'The character and personality of a farm help is crucial. She must get on with Nancy, Gwyn, your father and me.'

'The bush telegraph at 'The Express' has recommended a girl who has been working at a farm near Llandrindod, who has asked for a transfer.'

'Why?' Margaret showed some alarm.

'She doesn't enjoy her billet. She has to share with three girls ten years her junior, who are good workers but are 'good-time girls' as well. They're always out in the evening and talking dancing all day at work and Sally feels out of it.'

'So, she's a poor mixer?'

'No, she nursed her mother, a farmer's widow, with cancer until last year when she joined the Land Army. She's a home bird.' Margaret began to see the funny side of the conversation. 'Sounds good. I hope it'll work. I'll give it my best effort.'

'Good.'

'I must admit, it's good from my point of view, too, because Bryan Glynn is becoming too bold with the large animals and needs to be watched all the time. His behaviour is sometimes dangerous. Patrick and I would like him to respect man and beast. I am keen to start him reading and writing his letters and drawing. Perhaps he could start learning to play the piano when he's four.'

'Good. Mother asked whether she could continue reading to him and encourage him to learn rhymes and short poems as his speech develops.'

'Of course. He adores her. He's better behaved with her than with me.'

*

Margaret found that Sally was brisk and silent. She did her work, acknowledged Mrs. Morgan and her politely and taught Bryan Glynn to wink. Only Nancy was put out, saying, 'Maggie, she's so quick, never stops for a natter.'

'The work's done efficiently, then?'

'I s'pose so, but she doesn't even talk to the cattle and the horses, see.'

'Do they mind?'

'No, but I do. Shouldn't we be telling them what's going on?'

*

As an early Spring came, Mrs. Morgan's health improved and she even suggested to Dr. Thomas that she would like to see the heart specialist again.

'Dai, the doctor in Brecon might suggest that I take fewer pills. What do you think?'

'You know, my dear, I'm very happy for you to see the specialist and to pay his modest fees.'

He turned towards Margaret saying, 'It will give my wife a change of scene, Mrs. Rooney, d'you mind escorting her?' There was a smile in his tone.

Margaret agreed with alacrity. She knew from all that had been said since Christmas that Mrs. Morgan was not going to make a dramatic recovery, but she was more than willing to accompany the patient on the train for a day out.

'Bryan Glynn has been fingering my rosary and saying, 'Father'. I think he wants to see Father Anselm again.'

'You have brought a pious son into the world, Mrs. Rooney.'

'No. Father always has a bar of chocolate, but shares it with Bryan Glynn.'

'I see.'

'It's a game. Father gives Bryan Glynn a piece after each alternate sentence of *The Lord's Prayer*.'

Mr. Morgan seemed dumb-founded by the game, but asked. 'Does the priest reward himself, as well?'

'Yes, with a tiny bit. It's all serious until they say together, 'Amen' and they both laugh. Then we go into Mass and Bryan Glynn is very quiet and appears to listen, with a half smile on his face.'

'My wife says he often has a very thoughtful expression when she reads to him. Children must sense the war feeling all around them. You like Father Anselm?'

'Very much. He's revived my faith. I'm not as devout as Patrick, but I feel less guilty about that since I've known Father.'

'The car's coming the day after to-morrow at nine o'clock; the hospital appointment is at noon. I suggest the train home at about four o'clock.'

'Your wife wanted to visit the Cathedral, what do you think?'

'If there's time after a late lunch, but don't let my wife overtire herself, will you?'

'She wants to show Bryan Glynn its inside. She has a pre-war post-card of the inside and outside of the building; picture post cards are a thing missing from wartime Britain, aren't they?'

The planned visit went ahead without mishap. Margaret's dread, that Mrs. Morgan would not have a good consultation with the specialist, was unfounded.

*

Mrs. Morgan told Margaret. 'Bryan Glynn recognized the Cathedral from the photo, but commented on the things in the picture not being there and no flowers.'

'The valuables have been removed to a place of safety, of course.' Margaret was surprised that Bryan Glynn was so observant. 'He didn't indicate anything was different in our church – no flowers and all the statues were draped in black for Lent.'

'Amazing what happens when you have been enjoying a piece of chocolate.' Flo Morgan said with a laugh – a laugh which Margaret echoed.

'How was Father Anselm, Mrs. Rooney?'

'He heard my confession and gave me absolution. Then he turned his attention to Bryan Glynn.' The words were out of Margaret's mouth before she thought of their implication.' Mrs. Morgan's demeanour didn't stiffen?

48

Chatham

'I've obtained a travel permit to visit you and *Bryan'* - as Patrick insisted in calling Bryan Glynn - 'next week,' the letter to Margaret read. She had anticipated the visit with trepidation. Was there more bad news? But as he got out of the car Patrick's expression was relaxed. He had a broad smile on his face and was soon talking animatedly to Margaret, as he played with Bryan Glynn.

'Truth is, Maggie, I've been transferred to Chatham and go there in ten days time.'

Patrick looked well but seemed to have lost weight Margaret thought, but he was full of energy and enthusiasm – a new man in fact.

'I have officer status and will soon be put forward for a Commission. Aren't you pleased for me, Maggie?'

'Of course I am. Most of all, I'm delighted that your commitment to your recent posting has stopped you drinking.'

'Oh! Don't go on about that. You sound like a spokesman for some Temperance Society.'

'I'm sorry. I'm a bit overworked and overwrought these days. I just worry about you. Tell me about your new job, please?' She was delighted that Patrick had come 'into his own', at last. *Why did I have to mention the drink?*

'Fact is I've had an understanding Commanding Officer for the last six months.' Margaret had often wondered whether her husband's slight arrogance and self-righteous Catholicism had worked against his promotion and the recognition of his talent.

'I've become the expert on the servicing of the landing craft, which has been in trials at our base.'

'Good.'

'D'you remember Bernie writing about his pride in ships and their construction.'

'Yes, I do.'

'I've realized that from my Marine Insurance days, I know a great deal about ship building from a theoretical – more an observational standpoint.'

'When we were first married I remember you talked of 'sea-worthiness' and 'ballast'. I found it interesting but I felt you'd come to think that your insurance work was too mundane.'

'I did. When I understood that I could put my knowledge into practice in the navy, I asked to learn to service the craft we are developing and I found that I could do the work – I was a success.'

'That's excellent.' Margaret wondered whether the new found confidence in his ability had made Patrick more amenable.

'For some time now, I've been training recruits on how to service our vessels. I feel that I can play my part in the end game of this war.' The word 'end' was music to Margaret's ears.

The leave was a happy one. Patrick was sympathetic to Dai Morgan over his wife's illness; he didn't tease Nancy too much and he was most attentive to Bryan Glynn, who followed him about the farm, allowing Margaret to do her work in the house and milking parlour with no distractions.

A letter to Patrick and Margaret from the Admiralty interrupted the busy routine of Patrick's leave, either in the house or with the cows. Patrick opened it, whilst Margaret was busy dressing Bryan Glynn.

'Maggie, come quickly. There's good news from the Admiralty.'

'Paddy, is it about promotion for you?'

'No, it's not. It's about our Bernie. Read it - he's definitely a prisoner-of-war.'

'God be praised,' said Margaret. 'What it doesn't tell us is how he is and when he'll be released.'

'He's alive. That's what matters for the moment,' said Patrick as he surprised Margaret by squeezing her hand and kissing her.

'Now I can tell everyone the news without betraying a confidence.' She was pleased but the war was still unrelenting.

Patrick maintained that his daily prayer vigil had worked to save his son, but Margaret still felt that there were great dangers for anyone who was at the mercy of the Japanese. Privately she thanked God that her half-hearted prayers had perhaps been answered. *My constant contemplation, meditation and reflection on Bernie's plight may be a more spiritual relationship with the Almighty than Patrick's frequent use of his rosary. Who knows? I give thanks, whatever.*

As the naval vehicle took Patrick away, Bryan Glynn cried bitterly. He had always waved his father 'Good-bye', gaily, on previous occasions. The tears vanished when Dai Morgan put the 'mascot' in the basket of his bike and rode solemnly down the lane - up the *Yellow Brick Road to Oz*. They returned with smiles on their faces. It was a busy time on the farm, with planting of seed and weeding the emerging crops. Sally was proving a conscientious worker, if taciturn. Flo Morgan was able to do very little but amused the active Bryan Glynn with stories and poems. Her help allowed Margaret to do her jobs quickly and often she managed to take her son for a long walk when all the chores were finished to tire him out and refresh herself. She enjoyed walking by the river; it no longer possessed sinister qualities. Even so, she found an overwhelming need to impress upon Bryan Glynn the danger of running water. *Why do I have this strange relationship with water?*

*

Easter had passed and there had been no visit from the Williamses. Mary wrote to her parents to express her delight at the news about Bernie. She went on to say that Anna, who was now at a day school in Liverpool, was enjoying her school life:

'She has started to play games and loves netball. Liverpool is very different from the city she knew in 1940. There are large bomb sites. Rubble still dominates parts, especially Bootle, where raids caused enormous damage and casualties. I think Anna realizes now that she had to go to boarding school. Other girls in her class – it is a girls' school – had had to go to boarding schools. Three families had been evacuated to Canada!
Anna misses Bryan Glynn. Ask Margaret whether he will send her one of his animal paintings. She loves receiving letters and she and David correspond regularly in term time, which pleases us.
David is still keen to join up, but your pep talk, Mother, did moderate his misplaced enthusiasm. He has won the Memorial Prize for Public Speaking; he will recite his speech, on St. Swithin, at the Prize-giving on July 25th. Neither of us can go to the school. We are working harder than ever before. Is it possible for Dad, and you Mother if you feel up to it, to go and hear David? Please say, "Yes".'

*

'Mrs. Rooney, I have to ask you yet again to hold the fort while I enjoy myself - this time it's a school function.' Dai had passed the letter to Margaret as she came in from the dairy.

'My wife doesn't feel that she will be able to sit in a hot School Hall for the afternoon. Will you look after Flo and Cae Coch, while I'm away, please?'

'You know I will. I'm delighted to hear that David is doing well. Your son didn't attend the same school, did he?'

'Indeed not. Both Owen and Mary went to the County School.' Mrs. Morgan retorted.

'Is David's school not as good as the County School?' Margaret's question was asked innocently.

'It's very well thought of, but it's a Public School, which means that it moulds pupils for high-status careers. Boys gain admission by their parents' ability to pay the fees, whilst the County School requires entrants to be accepted by merit.'

'David is very bright and would have obtained a place at the County School, wouldn't he?'

'Yes. That's right, but I think what my wife means is that he seems to have become a little arrogant, as a result of the Public School system,' was Dai's explanation.

'I'm sure Mrs. Morgan and I would be interested in David's speech. Is it possible for you to have a copy of it?'

'We'll see. I hope it isn't about the genius of Jessie Pope.' They all laughed.

49

Dai Morgan Goes Back To School

Gwyn, Nancy and Sally had cycled into town to a matinee of a film. Nancy had confided in Margaret that she had decided to put up with Sally.

'She looks a bit like a man, so that's O.K. D'you know I think sometimes that Gwyn looks 'funny' at pretty girls. What d'you say, Maggie?'

Margaret felt uncomfortable but assured her friend that she was imagining her husband's 'loose eye'. 'The film's amusing, I'm told. Watch for a simple joke that you can try on Bryan Glynn.'

'We'll make one up if there isn't anything he can laugh at. He does like to giggle. I wish you could come too, Maggie.'

'With Mr. Morgan away for the day I must give my attention to Mrs. Morgan. Recently, we've had some enjoyable chats, especially if her 'darling' is having a nap.'

*

Mrs. Morgan had had a rest before dinner, so she and Margaret were washing eggs whilst Bryan Glynn was having his nap.

'This is a job which is best done when our little helper is not help-ing,' said Margaret. Mrs. Morgan nodded with her 'Bryan Glynn smile'.

'I hope I don't spoil him. Do I?'

'No, of course you don't. You fill his world with imagination and friendship. Did you see the drawing he did of the Leprechaun? Here it is.'

'It's good. I like the shilling stuck on to the little man's bag.'

'How soon will I be able to reclaim it, I wonder?'

'D'you ever consider schools for Bryan Glynn, or is it too early?'

'As things are, it's one day after another. The war is the only cer-tainty I know. I'm so happy that I have Bryan Glynn. And I hope . . . Why do you ask about education, Mrs. Morgan?'

'I was thinking of David. His education is so different from mine and our children's.'

'He has to study hard doesn't he?'

'Yes, but it's as though things will come to him through privilege.'

'You mean, becoming a pilot not just an airman?'

'Yes, I suppose so. Dai and I were talking about it. You see, perhaps we gave Owen a privileged status by encouraging him to ride. He was always here with his grandfather, breaking horses, hunting and exercising unruly animals. He became proficient and then he became an officer at far too young an age, because of his horsemanship and he is no more.' She sighed.

'Forgive me for saying this, but you did try to explain to David what the word duty meant, didn't you?'

'Let's hope he heard, Mrs. Rooney.'

*

Margaret had done the evening milking and had the kettle on the boil for tea, when the three cinema-goers arrived home, full of fun and laughter.

'Look what we've brought you, Bryan Glynn.' A diminutive barrage balloon floated into the kitchen.

'Who said the US army isn't the tops?' said Gwyn.

'She's lovely, her name is Zenobia,' said Margaret, who explained to the others that Anna had known a real barrage balloon named Zenobia.

'Mrs. Rooney has a good memory. There were two balloons tethered in the park opposite my daughter's house – Zenobia and Victoria.' The name didn't matter to Bryan Glynn one little bit – he loved the balloon. Mr. Morgan walked in at that moment and exclaimed, 'What have we here?'

After greetings were said, the cinema party went out to check the stock, leaving the Morgans, Margaret, Bryan Glynn and Zenobia to hear about Mr. Morgan's day at school.

*

'My dear, how was the Prize-Giving? Did David manage to govern his nerves?'

Dai kissed his wife gently on the cheek, 'He discharged his responsibilities well. The College is wonderful. I and other family members, mostly mothers had a guided tour led by two of the boys.'

'What were the boys really like, Dai?'

'Normal young people – they were children. Some dark, some fair, some fat, some thin. What do you want me to say, Flo?'

'Were they aware, sensitive, thoughtful or were they just out of a Public School mould – officer class?'

'You're still concerned about our grandson's pilot ambitions, aren't you?'

'Yes. You know I've become a bit of a pacifist since we lost Owen.'

'When I got to the school, David introduced me to the OTC trainer, Mr. Smythe. He was young, attractive, obviously sporty; he possessed all the attributes that boys admire.'

'And why isn't he at the front if he's persuading his young trainees to volunteer?'

'He was wearing gloves. David whispered to me that Mr. Smythe was a pilot in the Battle of Britain, shot down in flames over Kent with resulting burns to his hands. When he recovered he took the job in charge of the OTC at the school.'

'I'm sorry. I understand now. Youngsters are impressionable.'

'David told me as he served me with a cup of tea, that he was concentrating on his Higher School Certificate exams and, guess what he wants to do as a career.'

'Be a doctor, of course.'

'No, he wants to be a lawyer or a politician. Imagine!'

Dai's incredulous tone resulted in all laughing. Margaret thought of the hesitant though articulate boy, whom she'd first seen in a Liverpool air raid shelter. *Perhaps I'll see him as Prime Minister one day!*

'David recited this speech. Here is the original. He asked me to give it to his grandmother with much love. He said it was you, Flo, who made him keen on Public Speaking.' As he spoke he produced a parchment scroll tied with a ribbon held in place with a waxed seal.

Mrs. Morgan and Margaret pored over the speech.

50

St. Swithin

They read: 'Speech <u>recited</u> by David Morgan Williams on July 25th 1944. On the occasion of St. Swithin's College, Breconshire, Prize-giving.'

To-day is St. Swithin's Day. Do I hear dissent? Indeed, Price Minor*, is it you skulking in the back row? Did I hear the words fifteenth of July?

Due to the Julian calendar being superseded by the Gregorian calendar the day attributed to St. Swithin needs to be augmented by ten days. The name Swithin means 'Pig Man', our saint was, aptly, an animal lover.

This beloved man was priested and became Bishop of Winchester Minster, where he was spiritual mentor for ten years. He was a humble man, who carried out his episcopal duties on foot; invited the poor rather than the rich to banquets and spent his money building and repairing churches, until his death in 862. His dying wish was that his body be buried outside the Minster, 'in a vile and unworthy place' where it might be subject:

> 'to the feet of passers-by
> and the raindrops falling from on high'

What happened in 971, Price Minor*? Yes, I see you are awake. The monks decided to move Swithin's body, canonise him - that is make him a saint - and erect a shrine to him inside the Minster.

Swithin, now St. Swithin was displeased and showed his displeasure by manifesting a heavy rain storm, which lasted forty days. As a consequence rhymes were written:

> St. Swithin's Day if thou dost rain
> For forty days it will remain
> St. Swithin's Day if thou be fair
> For forty days twill rain no mair

or

> If on St. Swithin's Day it really pours
> You're better off to stay indoors

*Price Minor is the apocryphal name given to the 'no good boyo', by the Classics Master.

Honoured guests, members of staff, boys and Price Minor, you poor mortal, may I from my lowly position, exhort you, rain or shine, to emulate worthy St. Swithin, acknowledged, as exemplary, by Pagan, Orthodox, Catholic and Anglican traditions, to labour humbly and rebuild our devastated country and its people, which have been attacked so ferociously by enemy action.

St. Swithin restored, miraculously, an old woman's eggs, which had been smashed by savage workmen building a bridge. Let us restore Britain to its 1939 state, physically and spiritually. May we celebrate enduring peace in Europe and the world, soon? May the victors show compassion to the vanquished?

God Save the KING

"These words were _recited_ by the winner of the _Winston Spencer Churchill_ Public Speaking Prize. The prize is awarded to a sixth form boy, whose speech is less than 400 words and has an element of humour within it. It needs to be well researched."

As the parchment rolled itself up again the only words that could be seen were:-

To my much admired Grandmother,
with love, from
David

Mrs. Morgan's face showed her astonishment as she said softly, 'This deserved a prize. I shouldn't have doubted David. Truly, I don't want him to join up because there is glamour attached to being in a uniform, especially officer's uniform. At the same time I want him to do his duty.'

'I think he's learned the truth about war and peace as well.' As Dai spoke there was a knock at the door and in the doorway stood a man in naval uniform – the Commander who had told Margaret about _Harry_. He looked awkward as he asked Mr. Morgan if he could, 'Have a word?' They disappeared into the dining-room.

51

The Commander

Dai Morgan came back into the kitchen in a couple of minutes. 'Mrs. Rooney, the Commander has come to see you.' His voice seemed choked and Margaret murmured, 'Bernie?' as she passed Bryan Glynn to Mrs. Morgan, took her apron off and made her way to the dining-room.

'I'll be with you in a second but I need to rescue Zenobia, she's stuck on one of the kitchen beams.' Dai Morgan added more words, softly, to his wife, as he followed Margaret.

*

'I was on my way back to Usk where we live, but thought I'd do a detour and visit Cae Coch, Mrs. Rooney.'

Margaret replied, 'It's bad news, isn't it? Is it Bernie?'

Both men looked grave and the Commander answered. 'No, it's not to do with your son, but regrettably, it is, I fear very bad. It's about your husband.'

There was a solemn hush; even the daylight appeared to dim as he went on to say. 'I have the sad duty to tell you that your husband, Patrick Rooney, has been killed.' The words cut into the peace and silence of Cae Coch.

Margaret was numb. 'But he wasn't on active duties, was he? I don't understand.'

'No, he wasn't.'

'Then how. . ?' Her words showed the dread which was engulfing her.

'Are you ready to. . ? Would you like to hear. . . the details?' The Commander hesitated and added quietly, 'my dear.'

Those words released Margaret's silent tears, which rolled down her cheeks to the consternation of the two men. She continued to concentrate, blankly, on the Commander, oblivious of the tears, wiping them away with her hand from time to time. Her mind was in turmoil. *How will I manage? Bryan is fatherless. How will I tell him? Patrick had at last grown up. Now Patrick is dead. Dead.*

'Please tell me what happened? Were you there?'

'No, I was on duty at the Admiralty. An urgent message came in, 'During the unloading of a lorry at XYZ port, a strategic supply vessel HMS ABC avoided being destroyed with considerable loss of life, by the prompt action of service personnel'.'

Mr. Morgan interrupted, 'What alerted you particularly?'

'The name of the vessel, its cargo and the importance of the port alarmed me. I telephoned the officer in charge, and heard a report of great bravery on the part of your husband, Mrs. Rooney.'

'What happened to Patrick? Please tell me?'

'Drums of petrol, ammunition and landing craft were being unloaded from the ten ton truck. Chief Petty Officer Rooney was supervising the operation. The driver had gone on board the ship with some documents. The lorry, which was found later to have defective brakes, began to roll towards the ship and the dock workers on the quayside. Your husband jumped into the cab and turned the steering wheel away from the direction of the ship. The vehicle careered over the dock side and ended up half in the water. When rescuers reached your husband he was beyond help. He'd hit the back of his head on the wall of the dock. I'm so, so sorry, Mrs. Rooney.'

Margaret and Mr. Morgan were dumb. They had both paled as the awful story unfolded.

'I'm here unofficially. I felt I knew you Mrs. Rooney. As I was coming this way on leave, I thought that you'd prefer me to inform you. You'll receive official notification in a day or two. Since the invasion of France I seem to have heard of one disaster and loss after another. This war will be won by us, but the cost will be enormous. May I give you my sincerest sympathy, Mam?' He was standing at attention as he took Margaret's hand.

Time had dried the tears from Margaret's face but her eyes had lost their usual brightness as she said, 'Thank you for coming to tell me this awful news yourself. I appreciate your kindness once again.'

*

Mrs. Morgan passed the sleeping Bryan Glynn, washed and in his pyjamas, to his mother and sat down beside her. After seeing the Commander to his staff car, Mr. Morgan took a chair on the other side of Margaret. No one spoke. It was as though they needed to listen to the child's steady breathing. Did they sit like that for minutes or hours?

'It would be good for us to have a teaspoonful of medicinal brandy in our cocoa, to-night, I think.' Mr. Morgan said, as he took out a bottle of brandy from his overcoat pocket. Both women registered surprise. Did the Commander arrive armed with the bottle? *What was the Commander's name? I'd like to know his name.*

*

'Margaret, my dear, try to get some sleep to-night. There'll be a great deal to do in the next few days.' Mrs. Morgan's words were Margaret's thoughts. She hadn't noticed Mr. Morgan slip out of the house whilst her reverie was elsewhere, until he intimated that the work of the next day would be taken care of by Sally and Nancy.

'It's organized. You'll have to cope with Bryan Glynn. He'll probably sense that something's wrong. He'll need some distraction. The girls will take him out for a bit of fun whilst we three discuss the situation and make some arrangements.'

Margaret smiled at the use of the words 'we three' and was comforted as she said, 'Good night.' *Had Flo Morgan called her 'Margaret'?*

The Eyrie seemed to have something missing from it, as Margaret tied Zenobia to Bryan Glynn's bedstead, put him into her bed and snuggled up against him.

*

'How do we tell Bryan Glynn that he will never see his father again?' Margaret asked. *I don't think he's ever seen a dead animal or bird. Even when we were killing the chickens he was kept out of the way because of the feathers. He's seen the feathers from live birds only. I'm not quite sure where Patrick is anyway. Heaven, Hell, Purgatory and Everlasting Life are concepts that I find difficult to believe; to explain them to a child of three is quite impossible.*

No-one had an answer.

When it was decided that Margaret was to attend Patrick's funeral in Chatham without Bryan Glynn, she said to him, 'I'm going to see your Da and you're to stay with Mr. and Mrs. Morgan and look after the farm. Nancy is going to sleep in my bed.'

'What about Gladstone?'

'He's to stay on the farm with you, but if he tries to climb up into The Eyrie perhaps Nancy won't shoo him away.' The questions stopped there.

*

Margaret was to be accompanied by Father Anselm's housekeeper, Josephine, a widow in her sixties who had converted to extreme Catholicism. Naval accommodation had been reserved for the two women and Margaret wondered which was more agonizing, her grief or Josephine's devotions.

On the train journey Margaret feigned sleep, whilst Josephine muttered her rosary, fingering very noisy beads to the annoyance of other passengers. *Would I have been happier on my own? No, at least I have the comfort of a welcome cup of tea periodically and we're probably on the right train. Without my holy escort I'd have ended up sitting on a strange London platform, looking dazed and stupid, forever.*

*

After unpacking in their shared room, Josephine turned a beaming smile on Margaret and said in a sepulchral whisper, 'Shall we pray together, my dear?'

Margaret replied, guardedly, 'I'm so sorry Josephine, didn't I tell you I was to meet the Naval Chaplain at the Church? He's there at this time to hear confessions.'

'Please excuse me if I don't come with you, I'm rather tired.'

A relieved Margaret said, 'I do understand.'

*

The fresh air was pleasing to Margaret. She looked forward to seeing the priest and the church. Once in the street a familiar tang reached her – was it the smell of the sea, diesel oil and salt spray? A Liverpool scent!

She was walking down hill, of course down to the river Medway. Round a corner, and there were the cranes, the warehouses and ships of Chatham dockyard. She watched sailors going about their business from afar. There was barbed wire and a notice prohibiting her from going any further. She stopped feeling that she was at Liverpool Pier Head. It was such a familiar scene. A naval rating appeared and asked whether he could help her. When she admitted that she was on her way to the Catholic Church, he said with some surprise, 'You're going in the wrong direction, I'll draw you a map.'

Taking and studying the beautifully drawn map, Margaret was touched and explained herself.

'My name is Margaret Rooney. My husband's funeral is being held at the church to-morrow.'

The sailor looked about twelve but his manner was adult as he said, 'Mam, it is going to be an honour for me to be one of your late husband's bearer party for the service. May I shake your hand and offer my sympathy to you, Mrs. Rooney? Chief Petty Officer Rooney has made history in these parts.' They shook hands solemnly.

*

The priest was kneeling at the altar when Margaret arrived at the church. He turned to smile a welcome to her as she knelt beside him.

'You're Mrs. Rooney, aren't you? How are you? Was your journey very tiring? My name is Luke, Father Luke.'

She told him that she was pleased that she'd made the journey.

'I'm glad that I've caught up with you before the service.' He winced as he went on to say, 'Due to all which is going on in France things are a bit disorganized. I'm not supposed to say that, though.'

His accent was Irish and Margaret exclaimed, 'What part of Ireland do you come from, Father?

'Dublin. I was a newly ordained priest in an inner city area of Glasgow, when war broke out. I joined the British Navy, rather than go back to Dublin.'

'I was working there when I met Patrick. He had a job with a Marine Insurance company in Liverpool.'

'Well now. There's a coincidence.' In the next half hour they discussed the funeral, Patrick's accident, Dublin, Cae Coch and Bryan Glynn. Margaret warmed to the priest's humility, humanity and common sense. He wasn't a bigot like the Irish priests of her childhood.

'It's a bit of a secret but the "autorities" are considering awarding a posthumous award to your Patrick.' Margaret was moved by his statement but also his pronunciation of the word 'authorities'. For a moment she was back in Dublin, listening to the Republicans railing against 'autority' in general.

'That's good but I'd prefer Patrick alive to any medal. Nothing will stop Bryan Glynn from being fatherless, will it?' The priest looked crestfallen.

'If I survive the war, I trust that I will work towards compensation for the many fathers that have been taken.' There were tears in his eyes. After a pause he continued.

'Your husband's Commanding Officer suggested that I was to take you to see Patrick. That is if you would like to see him. Are you up to it?'

Margaret uttered a weak, 'I think I'd feel better if I did.'

They walked together to a converted warehouse nearby. A sentry saluted them as they entered the building. *Do the people in here need an armed guard? What can harm them now?*

An orderly uncovered Patrick's body and stepped away, as Margaret mouthed her final 'Farewell' and thanked Patrick from her heart for her two sons. *I suppose you know now where Bernie is?* She kissed the cold cheek, which had no blemish on it and rejoiced that the savage fatal injury was hidden. *Just now, I'm not strong enough to witness that obscenity of war.*

As she walked in silence with Father Luke back to her billet, Margaret thought for the first time since she knew of Patrick's death that she must try to reconcile herself to her widowhood. She must thank God for Bryan Glynn and leave Bernie's fate in God's hands. Patrick was, at least, at peace.

As she tried to get to sleep that night she remembered Father Luke. *A great deal of their time together had been spent in silence but that quiet had been profound – no prayer, no rosary but the presence of something beyond life, time or space – God?* Father Luke was separated from his family in Dublin, had no children nor would ever have the privilege of children but he had known and understood her grief.

52

At Home

Dai Morgan had sent a car to the station for Margaret, but there was no-one beside the driver in it. He was well-known to her and said, 'I had to take one of the soldiers to the station for the other train, so you'll have a quiet drive to the farm. Please accept my condolences. This war's a bad business. When will it end?'

Margaret was delighted by the solitary drive through the town. She saw it with renewed affection after the bustle of Chatham and the emotional strain of Patrick's funeral. The car passed the shops she knew so well and several people waved from the pavement, as the market day traffic slowed the car's progress. How tired she had been when she got off the train, but the country air seemed to have energized her and by the time she arrived at Cae Coch and thanked the driver, she was able to jump out of the car with a feeling of something like muted joy.

As she approached the door it opened as if she'd said, 'Open, Sesame!'

A chorus of, 'Welcome Home,' greeted her, as Mrs. Morgan, followed by her husband and Nancy carrying a squirming Bryan Glynn, who escaped on to his feet to rush to his mother's arms, welcomed her. All three adults shook her hand and showed their pleasure in having her back, even Gladstone appeared to add his purr to the occasion.

As they entered the kitchen, joined by Sally, a tantalizing smell of baking wafted through the door. Sitting proudly on the table was a large iced cake sporting the caption 'Welcome Home'. On it flickered three lighted candles.

'It was my wife's idea,' Dai explained. 'Bryan Glynn will be three in a few weeks, so we decided to combine his birthday celebration with your home-coming. I hope you don't think we're being insensitive.'

Mrs. Morgan added, quietly, 'We attended a mid-week Holy Communion service to-day, where the vicar remembered your husband. He had a recollection of Patrick telling him that he hoped to stay in these parts after the war. His final words to us were, 'Let's make Mrs. Rooney feel part of Wales, now.''

'Let's have a happy meal, Bryan Glynn. Imagine a three year old child before the war who hadn't seen candles on a cake,' was Dai's comment. Bryan Glynn blew his candles out several times and then the others made many feeble attempts without success, at the difficult task.

'You know, Mrs. Rooney, I think, we all needed to see Bryan Glynn smile and laugh didn't we? He was very quiet when you went to Chatham, at first.' Mrs. Morgan whispered to Margaret.

'It was my concern, but you have wooed him with your imagination and thought. Thank you.'

*

After Margaret had put Bryan Glynn in his bed and sung him to sleep she returned to be with Mr. and Mrs. Morgan. They explained that they had planned the 'distraction tea' because they wanted talk of Patrick's funeral to be kept from Bryan Glynn.

'He didn't ask why you'd gone to Chatham. It was as though he knew all about it. We tried to make everything as normal as possible; he wasn't unhappy but solemn. If you feel up to it perhaps you'd like to tell us about how things went.' Flo said.

'I'd like to tell you about my extraordinary, sad day.' Margaret's voice was quiet but she wanted to give her account of the strange time she'd had to the people whom she knew understood her feelings.

'The funeral was very much a naval occasion, which made me able to control my emotions. Patrick's coffin was carried by eight sailors, all young enough to be his sons. The service, a Requiem Mass, was beautiful, sung by a naval choir. I think many, if not all, of them were reservists. Father Luke who celebrated the mass, is a young Naval Chaplain, but dignified with astonishing spirituality – he was born in Dublin.'

'The service was in the strict Roman Catholic tradition? It sounds that Patrick would have been comfortable with all that happened.' Mr. Morgan said.

'I think so. I felt that he was there. He would have loved to have been and was surrounded by many Catholic sailors and about twenty WRNS, as well. Apparently they plot the course of the ships at sea.'

'And Josephine?' Dai asked with a smile which Margaret reciprocated.

'She told me that she had met Patrick once. I think her piety though wearing is genuine. She looked after me.'

'Good.'

'On my way to Chatham, I was unfit to be on my own, but now that Patrick is at rest, I feel stronger and more able to deal with life.'

'Describe Father Luke. Did you have any common acquaintances from Dublin?' Flo Morgan asked.

'No, we had no links from Dublin, unfortunately. It's so long since I was there. Father was slight, fair with fine features. He had a beautiful face which was restful. Unlike many Irish men, he was not talkative, but contemplative and serious. He was a little older than Bernie and said that he prayed for all prisoners of war, including those whom we had taken prisoner.' Margaret noticed Dai smile as she said the word 'we'.

Dai said, 'You must keep in touch with him.'

'I will, he asked me to. Patrick thought priests led a lonely life, dependent on love, faith and trust in God. I suppose he was right. Father Luke had never met Patrick, which was a pity.'

As Margaret rose to go to bed, Mrs. Morgan said, 'Cae Coch is your home from now on, Mrs. Rooney - Margaret. You and Bryan Glynn are our family. Welcome.'

'I don't know what to say,' Margaret mumbled as the couple stood up and both said, 'Good night.' But Dai added, 'Nos da,' pointedly.

*

Widowhood made Margaret reflect on her life. *I am permanently estranged from my folk in Cork. I'm the widow of a man from Liverpool. Mother of a son, who is a prisoner of war in Japan; and mother of a three-year-old boy, who lives with me in Wales, on a farm where all are kind to me. I must thank God for where and what I am and be optimistic.* Thinking of her situation on a walk into the town with Bryan Glynn, Margaret met Dr. Thomas on his way to visit a patient.

'Good morning, Margaret; hullo, Bryan Glynn. And how is the little chap's skin problem?'

'It's completely cleared as a result of the ointment which you recommended. See, how healthy he looks.'

'And you. How are you?'

'I'm busy. The Morgans have been very kind to me since. . .'

'I asked about your health. I'm a doctor.' He said the words with a hint of humour. He'd touched a nerve.

'I have to admit that I have bad dreams, but that is to be expected in the circumstances, isn't it?'

'Perhaps. We're going the same way by the river. Bryan Glynn is safe to run ahead. The fence will keep him from falling into the water. We can talk.'

'I'd like that.'

'Since 1939 I've seen the war through the eyes of civilians and the wounded. A little different from being a medic at the Front, but it has given rise to challenges.'

'I'm sure you're right about that. I feel that I've been in a similar situation, Doctor.'

'Would you like to tell me about the dreams?'

'They're all about The Leprechaun.'

'I'm mystified – if that's an appropriate word to use. Go on.'

'Mrs. Morgan has introduced Bryan Glynn to some Irish folk stories. One of them is entitled 'The Leprechaun'.'

'Yes.'

Margaret's voice was hesitant. 'He's tiny, about six and a half inches high and. . .'

'Interesting. . .'

'He wears old-fashioned clothes and a pointed red hat and. . .'

'Go on.'

'He makes faerie dancing shoes and has a bag to hold the money he earns – it. . . it has a silver shilling in it.' She was beginning to speak quickly but the doctor stopped his interjections and asked,

'What about the dreams?'

'My dream is about a similar Leprechaun, which I imagined and talked about as a child and young adult.'

'Was he bad?'

'No, he was just the opposite. He was a delight. Charming. He occupied a glen by a stream a. . . a stream near my home. I loved him.'

'Margaret, don't be reticent. I'm your doctor. It's helpful if you speak about bad dreams, isn't it?'

'Yes, but. . . my. . . my leprechaun's beautiful little hands, in the dreams, turn. . . turn into evil claws. . . claws and they scratch at. . . at my body.' She was near tears.

'Be calm. The funny chap of your childhood frightens you in his new grotesque form?'

'I wake up scared stiff. It's. . . it's like the feeling of. . . of drowning I had after Bryan Glynn was born.'

'I see.'

'Why do beautiful fun experiences have to become ghoulish and ghastly?' Margaret seemed angry.

'Could your experience be a metaphor for war. Does it mean loss, horror, anxiety and grief? Haven't all your experiences, except for that little fellow, been ugly in this war?'

'That could be an explanation. You see, I can't tell anyone at the farm about the Leprechaun because Mrs. Morgan reads the story to Bryan Glynn.' They both chuckled.

'You've become fond of her. You were a little in awe of her at one time, weren't you?'

'Yes, I was. She is so well-read and Bryan Glynn adores her. Her reading is beautiful. Oh! Bryan Glynn's fallen over in a puddle. Mam's coming, don't cry, little one.'

'Oh dear! Another pair of dungarees to wash, Margaret, but no need for the services of a doctor, I see.'

'Talking of puddles have you had any further dreams about rivers and water?'

'I've sorted that preoccupation out. It's about being a Catholic.'

'I'm out of my depth. Please explain.' Glynn Thomas was amused by his own pun but Margaret continued without a smile. 'We go to Confession and obtain Absolution – it is cleansing.'

'Go on.'

'I have this overwhelming guilt about my rift from my family and about my short-comings as Patrick's wife, the water/river thing goes some way to – is the word 'assuaging'? - the guilt. It's symbolic.'

'That's interesting and probably logical. Thank you for telling me about the dreams. The confidence may stop them happening. I hope so.'

'There is so much to do on the farm with Mrs. Morgan becoming so frail. My dreams and grief aren't important.'

'You know where I am. Don't hesitate to pop into the surgery if you need to have a chat. It's strange that we are talking and walking by a beautiful river.'

'Mr. Morgan told me, recently, the old adage, 'You never cross the same river twice.' It is a hopeful saying and gave me the heart to go on.'

'Yes. For me a river is a metaphor for life. It is smooth, choppy or dark on the surface but beneath it may have soft sand, pebbles or treacherous weed. We don't know.'

'The fact that heartens me is that every river flows into the sea. I rejoice that my Bernie is not at the bottom of the Pacific Ocean.' Margaret's tone was relaxed.

'I'm so glad that he survived the sinking of his ship. I take this left turn here. I must bid you 'Good-day', Margaret. 'Bye, Bryan Glynn. Don't get too muddy.'' The child waved happily. When the doctor had shaken Margaret's hand and raised his hat in farewell, she continued her walk with a spring in her step.

53

Nearly There

An OHMS letter arrived addressed to Mrs. Margaret Rooney. It was from Patrick's Commanding Officer. He wrote:

I have investigated the tragic incident which resulted in your husband's death. I have consulted with all the naval personnel who were present at the time and as a result have decided to put Chief Petty Officer Patrick Rooney's name forward for a bravery award, posthumously.

In addition to the above, I have received a deputation from your husband's unit, stating that it would be grateful if someone from the Royal Navy undertook the task of writing to you officially to thank you for your husband's quick and selfless action. Some of these men were in the area of risk at the time of the accident. I hereby undertake that duty with pleasure.

I understand that you have a young child, a boy. My good wishes are extended to you and your son for the future.

Yours faithfully, etc.'

Margaret was sad, very sad as she read the letter. It had an air of finality about it. It made her realize that Patrick was dead and Bryan Glynn would grow up without a father and perhaps without a brother. She had thrown herself into the farm work and the domestic duties of Cae Coch, since her return from Chatham. The letter reminded her of the lonely life which was her's in the future.

When a trunk with Patrick's effects was delivered, Margaret was beside herself. The fact of Patrick's never again being at Cae Coch hit her forcefully. All the people at the farm saw her plucky exterior crumble.

'Take the trunk and the packages into the parlour, please. Mrs. Rooney will deal with her husband's belongings at her leisure.' Mrs. Morgan instructed the carrier.

To Margaret she said, 'Don't distress yourself, my dear Margaret. I know how you feel. The situation is raw. We all want to help.'

At first, Margaret took one package from the parlour - the box which Mr. Morgan had given to Patrick for his art materials and she opened it in The Eyrie. There, she found the sketches which had enthralled readers of 'The Express' and to her amazement drawings which must have been secret originals for camouflage. She thought that this meant that the war was, really, nearly over. *What a gifted yet flawed man Patrick had been!*

'I will treasure Patrick's works of art forever. What a wonderful inheritance for Bryan Glynn!' Margaret told Mrs. Morgan, who replied. 'You don't need to unpack anything which will upset you. Dai has put the trunk in the box room which David uses, so take things to your room or leave them where they are. Don't feel that you have to deal with memories which will distress you. It's early days.'

Margaret thanked Mrs. Morgan. *She's been in my position. She remembers the pain and the inability to believe what had happened.*

*

Mrs. Morgan had added two more maps to the passage wall between the kitchen and dining-room, at the beginning of the year. One was a detailed map of Europe and the other displayed the Pacific islands including Japan, Indonesia and the Philippines. It was the latter map which engrossed Margaret's attention. Patrick's death had made her avoid the arrows marking the Allied advances in mainland Europe. She was aware of the losses of men and civilians in France, Holland and Belgium; but also felt rage at some of the Allied bombing of German cities where the BBC seemed to be exultant about the thousands of casualties.

Turning her mind to the Far East she scanned the islands with such strange names, wondering where exactly Bernie was. The question, *'Does he continue to live in his hostile prison?' was always with her.* She had started to pray, incessantly, while she worked and when relaxing with Bryan Glynn. Father Anselm had given Bryan Glynn a child's book of prayers, which she read, often, to her darling boy, who carried the little book everywhere with him.

'Mrs. Morgan, tell me all you know about the Far East, please. I was not taught much Geography at my convent school.'

'I'm no expert. I have studied the newspaper a great deal lately. I'm glad my husband has changed our paper from *The News*

Chronicle to *The Times*. There are more informative news items and articles in *The Times*.'

'I don't have time to read any paper, but rely on you to tell me about the important victories. Please gloss over any set-backs, I'm not up to them.'

'One of the problems in the Far East, I gather, is the many islands which have natural harbours which provide places for the Japanese to re-fuel and obtain fresh water and food for their ships and crews.'

'What about our Navy?'

Mrs. Morgan commented, with a broad grin, on Margaret's use of the word 'our', but went on to say, 'I think, it's mainly the American navy which is fighting the Japanese because our ships are deployed in Europe. Read this article in *The Times* – it explains the situation.'

The Far Eastern reports are not as graphic as the European ones – there aren't many photographs – thank God. I suppose it's the difference between a war waged on land and battles raging at sea and who's available to report them. How I hate war! Oh, Bernie!

Dai Morgan was basing some of his own articles on BBC bulletins. He quoted from Wynford Vaughan-Thomas and Richard Dimbleby. He pointed out their bravery in accompanying pilots flying over enemy territory. Margaret thought he probably wished he was younger and could be up in the sky too. *I now know where David gets his love of danger from. Yet Dai Morgan warned his grandson of the need to be cautious.*

*

The harvest was a good one. There would be plenty of hay for winter fodder and there was wheat and barley as well. Even the potato crop was heavy. In Gwyn's absence at the Convalescent Hospital, Margaret had driven the tractor for the first time with the stooking, raking and loading being done by the others. Dai Morgan arrived home in time to put Bryan Glynn on the back of Hywel Dda, the old cart horse who was drawing the last of the hay on the ancient hay wagon. Bryan Glynn was thrilled but obeyed Margaret and Dai's warnings to sit tight, hold on to the horse's mane and look ahead. As he was lifted down he remembered Dai's instruction and walked solemnly to the horse's head and bowed as he murmured. 'Thank you, Halda.'

Mr. Morgan slipped a peppermint into Bryan Glynn's hand and held it palm upwards with his bigger hand. The noble beast bent his huge but beautiful head and as a mother gently kisses her baby, took the reward between his soft lips. *How sensitive and gentle is this large but invaluable animal. I thank God for horses. Were five million, really, killed in the Great War?*

'May this good harvest be the last of wartime? Surely the world will come to its senses, at last.' Mr. Morgan said.

Satisfying the Ministry of Agriculture's and the Milk Marketing Board's demands, made the running of Cae Coch more difficult than ever before. Margaret fell into bed and one night she realized that she hadn't washed Bryan Glynn before putting him to bed. *He's, maybe, all I have and yet I neglect him.*

Nancy, meanwhile, asked about the Americans. She'd met one or two in the town. 'They call me 'honey' or 'sugar'. Will we all speak American after this war, Maggie?'

'That will be the least of our worries. If Bernie comes back, I won't mind if he has a Japanese, a Chinese or an American accent.' Nancy laughed.

*

Margaret lay awake one night after one of her nightmares. Instead of trying to get back to sleep reciting poetry to herself or praying, she decided to analyze her grief. *Have I hidden it because Patrick's death was so unexpected? I want to appear brave but I'm like jelly underneath. Am I doomed - Sean killed violently and now Patrick victim of a tragic accident? No. This war has bestowed pain and grief on most people. I remember the sailor, who had lost both his legs at Dunkirk, and yet he could smile and wink at the pretty nurse who pushed his wheel-chair.* Margaret slipped out of bed and lit a candle. It comforted.

I see Sean's bloodied body by the river and Patrick's broken body in the morgue. Two images flashing through my mind. Patrick, you wanted a lover and a wife to give you children. You gave me the security of your widowed mother's home and soon after, Bernie. I know you would have liked more children. I loved you, Patrick, for your fidelity to me as husband and father. Thank you. Sean hovers in my memory as the perfect passion of my life. Is that because our liaison was so short lived and idyllic? I feel disloyal to you, Patrick, when Sean invades my mind. I have thought that I will find life back in Liverpool, a city, after the war, difficult. I can't outstay my welcome here once the war is over.

Margaret peeped out of the window to steady her emotions and indulge herself with the moonlit beauty of her Cae Coch, with the shadow of the mountain, majestic, in the distance.

Had he survived, would Patrick have reverted to his domineering way of treating me? Drink had changed him and yet he had mastered that demon. He had tempered his over-devout Catholicism recently. Would he have understood the cultural changes in civilian life? Did he, deep down, respect the Morgans, whose Christian lives have been exemplary? Dai Morgan hasn't talked to me about my feelings since Patrick was killed, yet every glance we exchange seems like a sympathetic conversation. He understands. She got back into bed.

I must consider more practical matters. How will I manage Bryan Glynn on my own? He is becoming quite a handful. Here he is among many adults, all of whom nurture him well. Please God let Bernie survive? Liverpool will be possible with him. He will be the man in Bryan Glynn's life. If I'm totally on my own, how will widowhood be? Will money be short? Will I receive any pension? How will I be seen? Poor? Lonely? Or free? I have felt that I am a valued person here in Wales.

I know and admire the drawing of Bernie's ship there on the wall. It is beautiful and reminds me of you, Bernie. Bernie's talent is inherited from you, Paddy. I have been unfair. You may have been right in your criticism of my loss of faith. For our little one's sake I'll try to be more devout in the future. I am a selfish woman. Please God forgive me. I'll be strong minded in future. Margaret blew the candle out.

She woke next morning with a new resolve, she was going to work harder and trust in God. She felt sure that Bernie was alive.

*

'We've been thinking, Margaret. We notice you're not your usual self and you're not eating well. Dai and I wondered whether it would help to sort out some of your practical concerns.'

'I've been told by people in the town that I'll receive a pension from the government, will I?'

'I don't know but Dai's driving Rose to town to a meeting – she'll be stabled so he could go with you to the solicitor's office and get some advice. Would you like to go with him?'

'Could I? Yes. I'd like that but I must pay the bill. You know I've been putting savings from my wages in the Post Office and also buying Savings Certificates. I have a little money.'

'Our solicitor is an old pupil of mine, but Dai will tell him to bill you, if that's what you'd like.'

'Thank you. D'you mind keeping an eye on Bryan Glynn, please? He's taken to 'herding' the chickens. Great fun and Nancy laughs, but it has played havoc with the number of eggs we collect. I'm sorry he's getting so naughty.'

'We'll play a game of counting the eggs. I'll make up a story about a chicken which was chased and how she ran away to another farm where a small boy didn't chase her but read stories to her.'

'It might work.'

*

The solicitor was in his thirties and clearly in awe of Dai Morgan. Dai introduced Margaret and then sat back and let her explain her situation. Margaret felt confident. *Dai trusts me to tell my story coherently. I don't feel like his employee, but his friend and equal.*

'There are two things which have been worrying me, Mr. Davies. The first results from my husband's death in the Royal Navy – I have a three-year-old son, by the way. Will I be entitled to a widow's pension?' *I sound so businesslike and yet I'm so nervous. I've never spoken to a lawyer before.*

'I'll make the necessary enquiries of the Admiralty. Leave the matter with me. Your second concern is?'

'Our house in Liverpool which was, of course, in my husband's name was bombed in November 1940. I filled in the forms relating to a claim for 'War Damage' at the time, but though I left my Welsh address with the 'War Damage' office, neither I nor my late husband has had any communication about compensation.'

The young man laughed. 'I see that all the details are on this piece of paper. I can't promise but I'll start an investigation into this. It does seem that the war is coming to a merciful end, which will mean that people like me will be able to bring the appropriate officials to book. A consequence of this war is not competence, I'm afraid.'

'You'll send me an account to Cae Coch, of course?'

'Mrs. Rooney, I'm a member of the Territorial Army. Your 'War Damage' claim will be the only one I'll ever deal with. It will be a privilege to sort it out. As for your pension, I fear that there are many people in a similar position to yourself. The Urban District Council has set up a fund to deal with these.'

Dai stood up and put his hand out to the Solicitor and Margaret hastened to do the same as she murmured her thanks.

*

'You did well. The rehearsal last evening made it easy, didn't it?'
Margaret was hesitant. 'I sounded so matter of fact, almost hard.'
'Your facial expression and your deportment told another story. Will you do me the honour of having a cup of tea with me? Flo and I always sneak into this café when we go to the market.'
As they drank their tea Dai asked Margaret about Cork, her childhood and family. She was amazed to find it easy to talk about the convent, an 'unsuitable young man', his death, local gossip and its consequence.'
'It's a bit like my history, except I was fortunate in marrying 'my unsuitable young lady'.'
Margaret met his gaze – there was an intimacy in it which made her add quickly, 'anyway, Patrick was a good husband and loving father, so I mustn't complain. I'll miss him, always, and Bryan Glynn will be fatherless.'
'His accident was a cruel act of fate. Don't bottle up your grief.'
'I try not to.'
Offering his cup to Margaret for a refill, it was clear that Dai was enjoying his tea and the conversation.
'I've never had an opportunity to tell you about the highlights of my career, have I?'
'No. I remember you speaking about the Peace Conference of 1919.'
'It was before that. I met Michael Collins in 1916.'
'Margaret was dumbfounded. 'During the first World War? What was he like?'
'Perhaps you didn't know, but he was a prisoner for several months at a camp in North Wales – a place called Frongoch. He was suspected with others of taking some part in the Dublin uprising.'
'I'm interested, please go on. I seem to remember that was the year when the Irish Nationalists seized the Post Office in Dublin. The rebellion's leader was executed.'
'Yes. Were you there?'

'No. I was at home in Cork. The incident provoked anti-English feeling there, I'm afraid to say.'

Dai smiled at Margaret's discomfort.

'Remember, I'm Welsh.'

Margaret nodded.

"I was sent by my paper to the camp to find a story. I found one. Though the camp was primitive the Irish Nationalists didn't seem to care. In fact they looked upon the place as a 'University of Revolution'.'

'That was dangerous, surely?'

'No. Remember, there was a fierce war waging against Germany. These rebels were guarded by soldiers, unfit to fight, and local country people. Very soon those in charge of the prisoners found that they had a great deal in common with the Irishmen - their own language, their own culture, nationalism and a love of independence.'

Margaret showed her excitement, 'how did you meet Michael Collins?'

'It was at a hurley match.' Margaret grinned.

'The rebels introduced that very Irish game to their guards. It didn't catch on but it provided an article for my paper. The news from France wasn't good that week.'

'Michael Collins was a local hero in County Cork. You know that's where he was born. Did he impress you?'

'Indeed yes. He was big, physically strong, cultured and very religious. I'll look out the article I wrote. Would you like me to?'

Margaret nodded enthusiastically. 'Please do. Is the camp still there?'

'No, it was disbanded when it was realized that it was encouraging the very nationalism that it was supposed to deter.'

'D'you consider Michael Collins was famous or infamous?'

'Lloyd-George had great respect for him. If you remember, he negotiated with Collins in 1921; as a consequence, a treaty with the British government was signed but its compromise solution resulted in Collins being shot by his own countrymen in the following year.'

'I read about it in *The Liverpool Daily Post*. It was shocking. He was killed quite near my family home. That was the year my Bernie was born.' Margaret sighed.

'The British government has a great deal to answer for in its treatment of Ireland. The brutality of the *Black and Tans* was appalling. History might have been different had Michael Collins survived.' Dai said very quietly, as he rose from the table and chatted to the waitress as he paid the bill.

'I've enjoyed this conversation. Thank you for coming with me to see Mr. Davies. I must be dependable and think of Bryan Glynn's future.'

'While I'm alive, Bryan Glynn will lack for nothing. You must not fret about the future. Concentrate on your Bernie, Margaret. We all hope that he will come back safe and sound.'

54

More Evacuees

While Cae Coch and Margaret were delighted with the golden harvest, Hitler had a nasty present for London and the Home Counties – the V2 rockets. For a second time Dai Morgan was required to go to the *smoke* to report back to the people of rural Breconshire. He was torn between an increasingly sick wife and his strong sense of duty to his readers.

'You must do your job conscientiously, Dai. Your colleague in Highgate says that North London is safe. Take care. Remember your gas mask. Don't do a David.' Flo's words were spoken lightly, but Margaret knew that Mrs. Morgan hated her husband going away.

'Why's Mr. Morgan going to London, Maggie? I thought that the war's nearly over.' Nancy asked her friend. She relied on Margaret for a run down on war news; she hated hearing the News Bulletins and Gwyn always had the Light Programme on their wireless.

'Mrs. Morgan told me that there was a rumour about more advanced flying bombs beamed on the South East of England.'

'I'm glad the Williams family is in Liverpool, Maggie. London doesn't seem safe, does it?'

'No but when you took Bryan Glynn into town the other day, Mrs. Morgan and I were chatting together over a cuppa. She was very optimistic about victory.'

'How d'you mean?'

'She was very talkative. Telling me that the Red Army, that's the Russians, was advancing in Hungary and East Prussia; and that the British army was having victories in Belgium and Italy backed by the Royal Navy. Her speech was hurried, as though time was short. She'd spent an hour reading the newspaper and had wanted to cheer me up with good war news, she said.'

'Maggie, fancy you remembering all that. You're beginning to sound like the man on the BBC. Is it Alvar Lidell? What about the honeys?'

'Your friends, the Americans, are doing great things in the Far East. But Mrs. Morgan finished our conversation by saying that Mr. Morgan had to go to London, again.'

'And dear Mrs. Morgan with her bad chest, being left on her own. She was being brave, that it?'

'Yes. I think she was worried about possible bombs in London. Mr. Morgan didn't telephone last night. Not that that means anything, with half the lines down across the country.'

As they were speaking, Dai Morgan arrived home. He looked haggard and untidy. He explained that there had been a burst water main and no water in his colleague's flat, so they couldn't wash.

After tea he described his visit.

'These V2s leave devastation in their wake. I went to a place in Southgate where seventeen people had been killed by one rocket. To take cover a person needs to be deep underground – the rocket penetrates the surface. In Croydon four of these wretched things destroyed two thousand homes. I suppose they must have been blocks of tenement flats. Perhaps the reporter made a mistake about the number. I don't know.'

'How horrible! Are V2s different from the V1s?' Asked Flo.

'They are faster, flying at 3,600 mph, while the V1s flew at 360mph, according to one report. That must have been journalistic or War Office exaggeration, surely.'

Margaret asked. 'We haven't heard about them on the wireless, why?'

'That's what concerns me. Churchill kept their capability a secret, hoping that their bases, in the Netherlands, would be destroyed by the Allies, before they caused much carnage.'

'Why would he do that?' The women spoke together.

'Morale is so important just now. I think that the V2s are a last ditch effort on the part of the Nazis, but they are horrific weapons for the people of London and the Home Counties.'

Flo touched Dai's arm as she quizzed him about news of the rumours of the Jewish Death Camps. 'Do they really exist?'

'Colleagues on Fleet Street papers are sure that. . . that. . . millions of Jews and Gypsies have been exterminated in Polish camps, by starvation, gas chambers or medical experimentation.'

Immediately, Flo's breathing became faster, her colour paled as she whispered, 'Naomi Abrahams, a fellow student with Mary was a doctor in Warsaw.'

'I should have been more sensitive in what I said. I'm so tired. I'm sorry, my dear Flo. I remember that beautiful girl.'

All three sat in silence for several minutes. When Mrs. Morgan attempted to stand, she collapsed and spread-eagled over the table in a faint.

'My dear, my dear. . . Margaret, I mean Mrs. Rooney, go and telephone Dr. Thomas and explain that my wife has collapsed, please. Ask him to come quickly, please? I'll bring her round with a little brandy and keep her warm meanwhile.'

*

Mr. Morgan and Margaret spent an anxious time making Mrs. Morgan comfortable. She was conscious but deathly pale when the doctor arrived. He examined her briefly and said that she needed hospital care. Dai went with his wife in the doctor's car and said that he would stay in the hospital for the night. He was worried that this was a more severe heart spasm than before. Margaret was relieved in the morning when the news came to inform all at Cae Coch that Flo Morgan was much better.

Bryan Glyn was most put out, 'Where's Mrs. Morge?' His mother remembered that Mrs. Morgan was the one person who had always been present at the farm, since Bryan Glynn's birth.

'I want see her.' The child demanded.

'She loves the little fellow. Why shouldn't he visit her?' Dai said.

With a favourite book, 'When We Were Very Young', under one arm and clutching a posy of wild flowers in his fist, Bryan Glynn entered Flo Morgan's room in the Cottage Hospital with the biggest smile possible.

'I asked for you to see me and the doctor said you'd cheer me up. Come, sit by me and your mother will take another chair next to you.'

So started regular visits. Stories and poems were taken from Cae Coch for the patient to read to her pupil who gradually mumbled bits by heart, to the amazement of Margaret and the hospital staff. Doctor Thomas considered that Flo Morgan's delight in the shared pleasure of reading with Bryan Glynn had much to do with her steady recovery.

'My daily visits aren't appreciated then, Doctor?' asked Dai.

'You're anxious, the little chap is relaxed and thrilled by the fantasy world your wife invents for him.'

'I know. She's done that for me all our married life.'

*

One good thing resulted from Mrs. Morgan's hospitalization. The Billeting Officer, the town gossip, found out that there were two empty bedrooms at Cae Coch. He suggested that the new wave of evacuees needed placements. Mr. Morgan made the position quite clear – the farm work was a priority and with a sick person in the household there was no chance of evacuees staying at Cae Coch. Margaret, Nancy and Sally laughed.

'What would we do without the German P.O.W.s?' Sally asked.

'We couldn't manage,' was Nancy's reply.

Mr. Morgan left the farm early in the morning on his bicycle, did his work in 'The Express' office, visited Mrs. Morgan at mid-day, returned to the office and returned home late, ate something and went to bed. On market days he went into town with Rose harnessed to the trap as usual. Flo had hitherto gone with him but in her absence the others took turns to go with him. This meant that those left behind had to work even harder.

'Now I have a seat on my bicycle for Bryan Glynn I can take him to the hospital and stay for a short while and cycle back before it gets dark.' Margaret told Dai.

'You're doing far too much. You're exhausting yourself with the farm work, the house and the visiting, my dear.' Mrs. Morgan commented. Margaret assured her that Nancy and Sally helped all they could. She thought to herself that she was exhausted but it meant that she was too tired to think of Patrick and what was happening to Bernie.

Flo gained strength. Rest suited her condition. Her many visitors pleased her. Her anxiety abated. Colour was restored to her cheeks.

'Mrs. Morge better.' Bryan Glynn declared when his idol was out of bed and sitting in a chair. A cloud lifted from Cae Coch and all planned for the mistress coming home for Christmas.

*

Early in December, Margaret was making tea when Dai burst into the kitchen unexpectedly.

235

'Flo's gone, Margaret - Mrs. Rooney. She had a massive heart attack at one o'clock. I was able to be with her before she lost consciousness. It was all over an hour later. Where's Bryan Glynn?'

'He's inspecting the new calf with Nancy.'

Nancy sensed the solemnity of the occasion as she came in. 'What. . ?'

'I'll take Bryan Glynn to wash his hands.' Margaret said.

The house was hushed and still that evening, as Dai told the women that the custom was to have a person placed in the parlour in their coffin.

'My wife wouldn't have wanted that to happen, because Bryan Glynn is too young to see death or be near it. She loved your son, Margaret.'

'She couldn't have been a better grandmother if she'd been a blood relative to Bryan Glynn. Thank you for your sensitivity in the matter of the funeral arrangements.' *Did I hear my Christian name, in the presence of others?*

'It has been agreed that a horse drawn hearse will carry Flo from the hospital to the church. I, Rhys and David together with any male neighbours who would like to be part of the cortege will walk behind the hearse.'

'Gwyn would wish to walk with you if he may?' Nancy spoke emotionally.

'Of course.'

All who had known Flo Morgan were sad at her death but one person grieved more than anyone else – Bryan Glynn.

'Where is Mrs. Morge? Poems? Stories? Where?' He stormed. He cried. He was beside himself. He didn't seem to need an explanation, he somehow knew, but didn't like the knowledge.

'What about the funeral? He's too young to expose him to the sombre atmosphere of the ceremony.' Mr. Morgan said.

'I agree. He'll have to be looked after here. He didn't make this sort of exhibition about his father. Why?' Margaret asked.

'Patrick was often away. Flo has been here constantly during his life, hasn't she?'

The grief stricken boy made himself ill, so was content to stay at Cae Coch with Sally to help her make a cake, when the day of the funeral arrived. His sadness lessened when he found out that David and Anna were to stay on for the Christmas holidays.

Anna assured him that she was going to teach him to read. 'Look I've brought you a book from home, 'The Diary of Snubs, Our Dog.' He was ecstatic.

Margaret put the Obituary of Flo Morgan in Bryan Glynn's scrapbook. At the same time she hid the folklore book which contained The Leprechaun.

55

Victory in Europe

Bryan Glynn was delighted in the New Year of 1945. He had had Anna and David for the holidays, but David was to stay on at Cae Coch. The little fellow's grief was relieved by David's presence. He stopped looking for Mrs. Morge in all the rooms and buildings of the farm.

'Why is David to attend the County School in the town, Mary? I thought his boarding school was very good.' Margaret was mystified.

'We had chosen that school for David because it had an excellent science department; we assumed that he'd want to study medicine. We were wrong.' The words were said with a slight shrug.

'Don't you like the idea of a lawyer or politician in the family?'

'I'm flabbergasted. Dad has always been interested in Politics because of his job but Rhys and I haven't any leanings in that direction.'

'Why this County School?'

'David's history master joined up in November. The headmaster suggested that David would do better in Higher School Certificate exams if he studied with the renowned history master here who is following the same syllabus.'

'I see.'

'It was decided in the summer but we had to give a term's notice and Mother's health was so uncertain that we thought that David could be of use here.'

Margaret was a little shaken, 'I didn't know anything about it.' *I thought I was supposed to be family.*

'I should have discussed it with you but I assumed that Dad would tell you about it. He is so close to you, we thought he'd have spoken about it.'

'I understand. Life has been so chaotic here that we all thought only of your mother.'

'I know.' *There's an atmosphere. I must try to improve the situation.* 'I did grow to respect your mother. That respect turned to affection, now I grieve for her. Bryan Glynn couldn't have had a better friend and ally.'

'You certainly removed her anti-Irish prejudices.' They both chuckled.

'It was odd, Mary, your mother's war pre-occupation was the plight of the Jews and the Gypsies. She often mentioned your university friend, Naomi Abrahams.'

'That's another thing that I haven't told you. It's awful. Naomi, her husband, Isaac and their three children were put to death in Auschwitz, the notorious concentration camp.'

'Oh, Mary.'

'The news blocked out everything else for a time, I'm afraid. A Polish Catholic priest wrote to a Jewish doctor in Liverpool, who told me the devastating news. I'm glad I didn't tell mother. Naomi was special to her and when we were students she was my dearest friend.'

'I think your mother knew without being told. She spoke to me of Naomi when she was in hospital.'

'What did she say?'

'She told me of an afternoon walk by the Wye. She and Naomi were discussing the Old Testament. She asked your friend, 'Do you consider you belong to a Chosen Race, Naomi?' Naomi had replied, 'Doesn't that depend on who does the choosing?' Apparently they faced each other and laughed.'

'Mother could get away with that question. I couldn't.'

'Your mother's comment was, 'if you are in tune with another, the two minds embrace,' she went on to explain, 'the physical embrace can be misleading, the mental embrace has a divine quality in it'.'

'You know, Maggie, latterly you knew Mother. I often found her difficult to understand.'

'Your mother understood Bryan Glynn better than I do.'

*

Margaret felt that she owed a duty to Flo Morgan to continue tracing the allied advances on the wall maps. The course of the war was still the only topic of conversation but Dai Morgan clearly liked to argue against David's fresh opinions on strategy. Margaret was delighted to hear Dai's condemnation of the bombing of Dresden, and was surprised by David's support.

'It will shorten the war.'

'Is it ever justified to kill civilians?' Margaret wanted to shout, 'Hooray! Well done, Dai!'

David's views were moderating. *This is why his grandfather wanted him to be at Cae Coch. Had Dai not spoken to her about the change of school because he knew that she'd influence the decision and might fall out with Rhys and Mary about the local school?*

All the people of Cae Coch followed the race of the Western armies to liberate Berlin, in May 1945. They were glued to the wireless. Even Dai Morgan welcomed the killing of Mussolini and the suicide of Hitler in April which had led to the surrender of Germany in the following week. Margaret found Dai looking at her as she searched the newspaper for news of hostilities in Japan.

'It won't be long now before your Bernie's released. Have faith, my dear.' His endearment was unprecedented and Margaret treasured his concern about her son.

VE day was not celebrated in the town. The mayor had proposed that no civic parties would be held officially until Japan surrendered.

David's exam results, on the first of August confirmed his place at University College, Aberystwyth to study Law. This was most important and was celebrated with an iced cake, made by Margaret.

'Your grandmother would be delighted; you'll make an argumentative lawyer but I approve of people having their own opinions. Listen to another but don't necessarily agree with them.' Dai said that evening.

'I do miss Granny. It was her love of language which made me interested in the written word. Mrs. Rooney has the same love of books.'

'I hope I do, too, David. Recently I have had to be careful in my articles. The copy had to be pro-British and encouraging to our forces. Soon I'll be able to be free in what I read and write.'

'I'm off for the cricket practice. Are you coming to the cricket match on Saturday? The captain asked whether you'd start to write about the team, now the war is won.'

Margaret was surprised at Dai's reply. 'It isn't won. While the war in the Far East still continues, I'll be writing about that not cricket. Give me time.'

*

Margaret had finished washing the dishes and was about to rescue Bryan Glynn from the dairy, where he was 'helping' Nancy when Mr. Morgan came into the kitchen.

'Did I startle you? You seemed to be far away.'

'No. I was thinking that it would soon be bedtime for Bryan Glynn.'

'I'm glad that David has taken to village cricket. Would you and Bryan Glynn like to come with us to the Saturday match? I thought we'd go to the library on the way there. You don't seem to have had time to read recently. A new book might make you sit down for an hour or two and there may be a book about Wonk for Bryan Glynn.'

'I'd love to go to the library and watch the cricket. A pity that my son will never play hurley.'

How does he know that I long to read; to feel the smooth surface of the pages of a poetry book or novel between my fingers? How I miss my chats about books with Mrs. Morgan.

'I used to read a great deal. I'm afraid I've become a war bore. It's the job. Journalism will be more exciting once peace comes. It won't be long now and your Bernie will be here.'

'I do hope so. When I was in the grocer's yesterday, I met Evan Lloyd.'

'What did you think of him?' Dai enquired.

'He's had a distinguished war career. What will he do in peacetime?' *He was talking about the harvest and the price of wheat. He must want to come back to run Cae Coch.*

Dai Morgan reached for the brandy bottle from the top of the dresser. *He must need Dutch courage to tell me that Evan Lloyd will be in charge of the farm. They won't be my cows any more. Dai will probably move to the town to be nearer the newspaper office and the library. I'll be just a housekeeper.*

Dai poured a little brandy into a glass and motioned to Margaret to ask whether she would like a drink. Margaret shook her head. *He knows I don't drink.*

'Evan Lloyd would like to return to Cae Coch. He spoke to me about possible college courses he could take as part of the Government scheme for ex-soldiers.'

Margaret felt that her expression was blank as she muttered, 'I see.'

'I thought I should discuss Evan Lloyd's intentions with you, but that's not important, just now.'

Well it is to me. Bryan Glynn would hate to move from Cae Coch or away from you.

'Margaret, I always think of you that way, I may call you Margaret, mayn't I?' She bent her head. She couldn't look at him.

He looked embarrassed and sat down at the table where Margaret was folding the laundry.

'Margaret, I have to say something. Please forgive me if it offends you?'

Margaret found that she was turning a pillowslip inside out instead of folding it. She tried to face Dai.

'You look worried, my dear. I've been thinking during the last couple of months. I'm concerned about you. . . I. . .' He broke off, but took her hand, then continued.

'Could you, would you overlook my age, my religion and my mediocre scholarship and consent to be my wife?'

Margaret was astonished and speechless but noticed that the hand with which Dai was holding her hand, she was caressing with her thumb. After a long pause she whispered. 'I. . . I'm so surprised at what you've just said. I...I. . . respect you and have always admired you. You have always been so open and honest with me. I love Cae Coch. However, I feel unworthy of taking Mrs. Morgan's place as. . . as. . . your wife.'

'That's nonsense. D'you think you could consider it in time?'

'I don't know. You know I'm obsessed about Bernie's survival. I can't help it. . . I. . .'

'Can't we share that anxiety?'

'I suppose so. Do I sound unemotional - cold? I don't mean to be. . . I. . . do. . .'

I'm holding Dai's hand, I'm squeezing it, while I say these dispassionate words. Why? Is it because I think of him as my employer not as a man? Not as a lover? If I'm honest, he's a person that I've always felt an affinity with – a man whom I have found attractive.

*

A week later, news was announced from Tokyo that an atomic bomb had been dropped on Hiroshima.

Dai and David bowed their heads at the wireless. Nancy put her arms round Margaret as they listened, stunned by the news.

56

Atomic Bombs

'It's eight o'clock in the morning here. The hay's all in; the wheat and barley are being threshed but our great American allies have dropped an atomic bomb on the Japanese city of Hiroshima, killing thousands of civilians and servicemen, destroying the whole city and leaving thousands of men, women and children with radiation sickness.' Dai Morgan was standing in the middle of the yard of Cae Coch speaking in a loud but controlled tone of voice.

'There's sad - the gentle Mr. Morgan raising his fine voice. It's the yanks and their nasty bombs. They're not honeys after all.' Nancy muttered.

All the workers, including Hans, gathered to listen intently and with great wretchedness. They had heard the news in outline the evening before. They hated it.

Dai continued, 'Margaret is distraught. I've asked Dr. Thomas to call on his rounds. Nancy and David, can you look after Bryan Glynn, he's with his mother but he can't understand her anguish.' There was a chorus of, 'Of course,' which Margaret heard from the kitchen.

'I'm going to the newspaper office to glean all the information I can about this wicked inhuman act of war, which has been perpetrated on Britain's behalf.'

There was a hushed silence. Dai went back into the house, picked up Bryan Glynn, gently, saying. 'Hywel Dda needs a good grooming. Would you like to help David make him beautiful?'

'Yes please, Mam not well.'

A few minutes later Dai was sitting by Margaret. He took both her hands as he said. 'I will telephone the Commander. My editor will contact Fleet Street and the News Agencies.'

'Thank you, but the situation in Japan is chaotic. Bernie may be anywhere, dead or dying in Hiroshima. How can news get out?'

'I know. Remember, the Government knows more about our prisoners than they tell us. This horrific act of slaughter may make it issue a statement, giving details of where prisoners are. Leave it with me for now. Trust me, cariad.'

Margaret smiled. *How young Dai looks when he is on a mission.* She said, 'I do need you, Dai. I do love you. Thank you from the bottom of my heart.' She added, 'Without you, my dearest Dai, I couldn't live.' Spontaneously, she jumped out of her chair and flung herself into his arms. *He's desperate to be away in search of news of Bernie and I choose this moment to be demonstrative.*

'We'll have some news by nightfall. Have a chat with Glynn Thomas while I'm away.'

He kissed her cheek gently as he moved towards the door.

Margaret kept herself busy until Glynn Thomas walked into the kitchen. She replied to his enquiries, 'At these times of stress, I always think and dream of County Cork. You must be tired of hearing the same old story. This time I look for cleansing. The Leprechaun is American, I'm Japanese and I'm searching for the river. Am I mad?'

'All the reports state the enormous heat which the bomb generated. A longing for water to sooth and to drink would be natural, wouldn't it? You're thinking of Bernie being there, aren't you?'

'Yes. How can any power do such an inhuman act?'

'I have a feeling that even the Yanks wouldn't drop a bomb of that magnitude where it was known that there were allied prisoners.'

'You don't seem pro-American?'

'No. I have felt no affection for our US allies since yesterday.' He shook his head.

'I don't like your response to stress being so severe and so Cork-related, by the way. Would you take the advice of the consultant psychiatrist, Dr. Hughes? Didn't he suggest that as soon as the war is over that you would benefit by a visit to Eire?'

'Yes, Doctor. I've written to my sister. Dai would like us to marry and tour Ireland as a celebration, but I must know Bernie's fate.'

'I understand. The Irish visit is a good idea.'

'It's too far ahead. You know I can't think of anything until I know Bernie's alive. And now there's this development.'

'Maggie, I must finish my round. I'm sure Dai's enquiries will be fruitful. Keep in touch by telephone, please. I'll take a peep at the little chap.'

'Bryan Glynn senses something's wrong. I try to be my normal self. It's so hard. He's with David in the stable.'

'Come into the surgery to-morrow if your anxious state continues - a walk will do you good. I'm thinking that there'll be news by then. Good day to you, Maggie.' He took her hands in both of his, with a lingering gesture.

*

The morning seemed endless. The workers each came in and checked on her. The last to come was Nancy who asked her to see some great sight – Hywel Dda groomed to perfection with David aboard with Bryan Glynn snuggled into the horse's massive mane in front of David.

'Mam, mint please.'

She obeyed and produced two mint imperials. One she gave to the noble beast and then reached for her son who with no prompting stood, fearless, in front of the great horse and thanked him, giving him the second sweet. *We use animals, we exploit them but they show us such love and respect. We humans are supposed to be intelligent but we develop weapons which will destroy us and our world. A horse is incapable of inventing a bomb.*

At that moment Dai Morgan's car came into the yard. He was smiling as he jumped out, saying, 'All prisoners of war were well outside the area of risk caused by the bomb. The fact will be announced by the BBC.' He hugged Margaret, Bryan Glynn and Hywel Dda. Nancy's smile was broad as she whispered something to Sally.

A few days later more gloom descended upon them when a further atomic bomb was dropped on Nagasaki. This atrocity resulted in the Emperor of Japan surrendering. He said on a Japanese broadcast, which was translated as:

'Should we continue to fight, it would not only result in the ultimate collapse and obliteration of the Japanese nation but also it would lead to the total extinction of human civilization.'

Within days a telegram came from Bernie to say he was free and in Australia. A long letter followed.

57

A Letter from Australia

Dear Da and Mam,

I'm told that you would have received my telegram. I am free at last and in a Rehabilitation Unit run by the Australian Navy. I can't wait to see you both and my brother. I am so impatient.

I don't like writing this but the naval psychiatrist has directed all the ex-prisoners to write an account of their capture. This is for service records and for the history books. In addition, this expert in mental health is of the opinion that by remembering our capture and prison experiences we will be able to deal with them, more effectively, when we return to civilian life. We discussed the matter for some time and we all, with the exception of one man, agreed that we were willing to record our involvement with the enemy, if our memories could, in any way, help others or prevent acts of inhumanity in the future. It seems that the man who refused to co-operate with the naval doctor had had nervous problems before the war. The medics also considered it was useful for our families to be made aware of our prison experiences.

You will read or, perhaps, already have read accounts of prisoner-of-war camps in the newspapers and seen pictures of the horrific conditions and the atrocities which prisoners and civilians have suffered, in camps both in Japan and Germany. The group here in Australia, where I am now, agreed that personal stories would be less harrowing for our families than versions written by the press or filmed by commercial companies, which might exaggerate some of the details. Da and Mam, you were both in my mind throughout my years in captivity and it was your loving, spiritual upbringing which was a constant reminder to me of my duty to those around me. Throughout I longed to meet Bryan Glynn.

The day, March the first 1942, was the day which changed my life. I told you in my letters in 1941 and 1942, how pleased and proud I was to be in the navy. I was and still am sure that the war was a 'just war'.

In February 1942, we had been engaged, with the enemy, on and off for days. It was war, alright. It was the battle of the Java Sea. I was on deck with a stretcher party, ready to evacuate any casualties to the sick bay. We were all exhausted, but morale was high because we had amazing commanding officers, whom we trusted.

'Action stations! Action stations!' The command was precise, authoritative.

Suddenly, there was a deafening blast; we were on our backs; the man next to me was screaming with pain and drenched with blood. I felt as though I'd been thrown in the air like a juggler's ball and missed his hand as I dropped back down. I checked my body – yes – I still had two arms, two legs and just cuts, burns and bruises inbetween. I touched my mate, but it was useless, he was in a better place. I hope that I'll be able to contact his family when I come back home.

'Prepare to abandon ship! Prepare to abandon ship!' The voice had unmistakable urgency in it. I looked about me but could only see destruction; I could only hear crashes and explosions; I could only smell acrid smoke and cordite. The beloved ship had been our home for nearly two years, she had been invincible, we thought, but now every man looked to the emergency life rafts and concentrated on the exodus from the burning deck, soon to be a wasted wreck. No-one spoke; all followed a much practised drill. We had never imagined that we would use these well-rehearsed skills. Escape was paramount.

'Abandon ship! Abandon ship!' The words came with urgency – the tone desperate. I thought we had defied the Japanese ship which had been pursuing our cruiser. Every terrified hand on our proud warship was at work. I remember wondering why every command had to be repeated. It was extraordinary that we could hear anything above the noise of the sea and intermittent gunfire. Then, an explosion deafened us but, we saw the result of the detonation; it was unbelievable; it seemed to be astern only. Silence for a moment. Then the sea erupted behind us, but the ship seemed intact – another bomb had been dropped into the turbulent waters. With horror the gun crew, still at their stations, aimed at a glinting, gliding enemy bomber circling and sweeping the sky in the early light of dawn. It avoided the shells and returned to aim its hellish ammunition on our dearly loved ship. This time there was an explosion on the deck itself and the ship felt as though it was leaping out of the water and around me were heaps of debris, floating in oil and water. For a moment there was an eerie quiet and then screams of men but that plane was diving again at its quarry. As the smoke cleared, fire erupted from all directions and the steady voice of the captain, 'Man rafts! Abandon ship with speed!'

I found myself in the water, I don't think I jumped, I believe the ship had broken in two and I'd been catapulted into the hostile sea.

Looking back I saw fire raging on the fragile remains of the decks and men running, jumping and bleeding into the water; their bodies looked like actors on a metaphysical stage with the fire appearing as an evil spotlight, picking out their faces, ready to destroy them.

What would happen to the casualties below? Those heroic men, who'd been the first to suffer shrapnel wounds and burns from previous raids, had no chance of survival. I remember praying that their deaths were quick and their pains were cured, forever. The docs had injected them with large doses of morphine as we had gone back on deck. Their faces filled my mind but I had to concentrate on trying to swim avoiding the burning oil and small, sharp, pieces of metal and wood. At the same time I became aware through the spray and foul-smelling smoke, of other survivors, some were known to me and all were ours. No-one spoke, all knew that the aim was to find a raft; a piece of debris; anything large enough to hold a man's weight; to escape from the area around the ship, which now seemed to be in two awful shapes. It must sink and its bulk would displace tons of sea water. We all appeared to be in some aquatic competition to race from the scene of our home of many happy months to an uncertain watery future. Eventually, the noise of the ship's immersion into its deep and final grave, was frightening. The spray was like a giant fountain, intent on reaching and drowning the clouds. The horror lasted minutes and then a silence, followed by the sound of frantic swimmers and at last gasps of relief.

Miraculously, all but one of the watch I'd been working with, were there. Some were panting; some were vomiting; all were tiring but none were dying, yet. Others, from the hundreds who had been on board, became our new comrades. All of us knew that we were the lucky ones. We were alive. As if to compensate for our loss, we witnessed a crippled plane – Was it the one which had destroyed our vessel? It had ceased to drone and its fuselage smoked like a steam train. Suddenly, it fell from the sky. It dived elegantly into the sea and sank quickly beneath the turbulent waves. A muffled cheer broke out from our disparate group.

A few life rafts had been washed overboard, but it was difficult to board them as the sea was rough and it was necessary to avoid taking the polluted sea water into one's mouth. There was oil everywhere.

A hand reached for mine and I was hauled onto a raft and noticed that others were similarly pulled out of the water. We all gasped for drinking water; there was none. Our rescue had been a miracle but as hour followed hour, and day followed day, it seemed that this rescue was only prolonging our ultimate destiny. At dawn of the second day a ship appeared. It had a Dutch name so we christened it Amsterdam. It was not a warship but a hospital ship. Somewhere on its deck I remember a Red Cross, suggesting its neutrality. The flag with its blazing sun on a white background told another story. All of us were pulled up on the deck – hundreds of men appeared from the inhospitable sea. Some didn't realize that they were captive, until a Japanese group of guards with rifles and fixed bayonets marched between us, pushing men into columns with aggressive gestures. Though we were wet, hungry and thirsty, we had a curiosity about our captors; few of us had ever met a Japanese person! What would the future hold?

I looked over the side of the ship at the water, which had gobbled up our cruiser two days previously, and remembered a quotation about the sea from the last book I had read,

'It is deeper than one imagines, and fuller of memories.'*

*

My journey from this ship to a prison camp was full of misery rather than horror. Food and water were short and my body like all the other prisoners' became slow and uncomfortable. There was a fear of violence but our guards understood that wounds and dead bodies would make progress slow. Their language was peremptory and the words in Japanese were clearly uncomplimentary and abusive. Within the week of transit, we arrived at a camp, which was our home for three years.

I was fortunate to attract attention early on in my imprisonment. A Japanese guard had a silly accident and sustained injuries. He lied about the cause of his accident – he had obviously been drinking alcohol, against regulations. I had gone to the man's aid as I was nearby. His colleagues thought I was about to kill the man and advanced towards me with knives at the ready. When they saw me examining the patient, with obvious expertise and compassion, they held back. My calls to other prisoners to help the unfortunate man resulted in four of us, one being a doctor, propping the man up and communicating with the astonished guards, the need to bring water and dressings to clean and dress the head wound. We hid the man in our hut for a day. We thought between ourselves that if the circumstances of the accident had become known to the Japanese prison commander all the guards would have been punished. After that we were given more respect, especially those of us who demonstrated some medical knowledge, for we were able to treat our fellow prisoners and reduce the illness and death rate.

I look back on those years and come to the conclusion that insanitary conditions and poor diet were bigger killers than the brutality

* 'The Princess' by D.H.Lawrence

of the Japanese. Of course the hard labour forced upon us for the furtherance of the war took its toll. I was fortunate to avoid this often, when it was considered necessary for me to tend to the sick, of whom there were many. This will amaze you – I even learnt some Japanese!

This letter will give you both concerns, but, I hope it will stop you imagining that I will be an invalid for the rest of my life. Remember this, Da and Mam, I have survived and I am determined to be fit when I am repatriated. I have an ambition to be a doctor, in a peace-time era. Still!

I hope we'll all be able to return to Liverpool and be a family again. I look forward to hearing your news. A photo would be good, too. Please write. I know letters take ages to get here but I want to know everything that's happened while I've been otherwise engaged.

How I long to see Cae Coch and meet all the people and animals. How is my old friend Gladstone?

I enclose some drawings for my brother. The drawings are of a boomerang; an Australian bush hat; a kangaroo and numerous horses.

Much love,
Bernie

58

A Reply

'My dear, dear Bernie,

Thank you for your long letter and your drawings for Bryan Glynn. I enclose a photo of him and one of Cae Coch. Welcome back. I long to see and touch you. Bryan Glynn talks of Vernie all the time.

Though I found the account of the ship being sunk and your awful capture by the Japanese harrowing, I was proud to read your account of it and how you have dealt with your dreadful experiences.

Strangely, Dr. Thomas, the doctor in this town, comforted me, when I heard you were a prisoner by saying, 'A person who has medical or nursing skills is treated well in confinement because they are useful to their captors'. It seems he was right.

Dr. Thomas looks after Bryan Glynn's health – he, BG, is very fit and active but suffers from some slight skin trouble. When I told the doctor that I had had a letter from you, he advised me to be very open in my response. Here goes!

Your father was injured early in the war but went on to do some amazing things, as indeed you know. His work included creating a complicated camouflage and testing and servicing a special landing craft. His artistic and mechanical talents were always in demand. He was active in preparing craft for France in the D-day landings. During June 1944 he was involved in loading a ship with fuel and ammunition for France – I'm coming to a sad incident, sorry Bernie. A badly serviced stationary lorry started to roll towards the ship at the quay. Your Da saw the possible horrific consequences, jumped into the cab and diverted the vehicle away from the vulnerable ship averting catastrophe. The resulting crash caused the death of your heroic Da, instantly. I have chosen to tell you this now because the incident has been widely reported and I would hate to think that you read about it from anyone but your mother. Your Da has been recommended for a bravery award. I am so sad, for you and Bryan Glynn to have lost a gallant and loving father. The shocking news tore me apart. All the people at Cae Coch have been kind, helpful and understanding. When we met at Plymouth, I told you about Gwyn and Nancy being an invaluable part of the Cae Coch work force. At the present time Sally, a taciturn land girl, and Hans, a German POW have joined us – we all work flat out - the Ministry of

Agriculture requires more and more productivity from the land. Recently, it's been worth it.

After your father was killed, I found the future daunting but soon afterwards news came that it was thought that you and other POWs were alive but still imprisoned. This bucked me up. Your Da was certain that you had survived all along!

My sorrow was followed last December by the death of Mrs. Morgan. She had been ill with heart disease for some time but had soldiered on. Her most endearing quality was her love for Bryan Glynn, whom she adored.

I have been in charge of Cae Coch for more than two years – both the farm and the house, since Dai Morgan's journalism has taken him away from the farm most of the time. I have grown fond of the place and of Wales. After all, half of Bryan Glynn's name is Welsh and he speaks both English and Welsh – neither well yet! I want you to love him as I do – he is ours.

Another surprise. Two months ago Mr. Morgan asked me to be his wife. My reply depended and will always depend on your repatriation and settled health for the future. Your letter suggested that you had worn well in captivity and a healthy and able life was assured for you. Even so, I want to see you in the flesh to know that 'all is well with our Bernie'. I can't wait for you to come back to Britain. Work hard at becoming super fit.

Make the most of your time in Australia and thank the Australians for their share in our victory over both Germany and Japan. Remember that your health is paramount and put aside our selfish longing to have you with us here. We'll have to wait.

Bryan Glynn has drawn a picture for you. In case it isn't obvious, may I describe the scene – it is Hywel Dda, Mr. Morgan's, Dai's cart horse lying in his stable asleep, with Gladstone curled up on his flank. This is a regular sight on the farm. Amazing! We can learn from the animal kingdom, can't we?

Fondest love always,
Mam'

*

Bernie sent a telegram by return.

SAD NEWS ABOUT BELOVED DA STOP *SHARE LOVING CONDOLENCES* STOP *AM A1* STOP *SHE WHO HESITATETH IS LOST* STOP *CONGRATULATIONS* STOP *LOVE TO YOU BRYAN GLYNN AND ALL MORGANS* STOP BERNIE

*

To Dai and Margaret the first day of September was memorable. They stood before Father Anselm in the Brecon Roman Catholic church with Mary, Rhys, David, Anna, Nancy, Gwyn and Bryan Glynn to make their marriage vows.

*

'Skirts suit you, Maggie.' Nancy blurted out enthusiastically. They were all enjoying a post-wedding tea with homemade wedding cake, in the eminent Wellington Hotel in Brecon. It was indeed a celebration as they wore Sunday best and drank excellent tea from bone china cups. The happy couple was toasted and all spoke highly of Father Anselm who had welcomed the party so wholeheartedly.

'I was quite surprised. Catholic churches are just like Church of Wales ones except they do have lots of statues and they do smell funny.' Gwyn said with an air of shock.

'Can I have a skirt like Father Anselm, now the war's over?' Bryan Glynn asked his mother.

59

Peace at Last

After a brief pause at Flo Morgan's grave, where each person placed a bloom from the Cae Coch garden, in the stoneware urn, the whole party continued to the celebrations in the town. The combined VE and VJ parties had been planned for after the harvest. It was late September.

There was a band playing all the Welsh tunes. Margaret loved the *Ash Grove* whilst Dai Morgan enjoyed the hymns, which were sung loudly but harmoniously by choir members, and everyone else. In the much beloved hymn, *Guide Me Oh Thou Great Jehovah*, an impromptu descant echoed across the crowd. A bonfire roared on the river bank, the flames lighting the faces of the merrymakers and the water reflected the sparks as though it too was celebrating. The excited children danced in the shadows of the flames, putting the privations of war behind them. There was more fun to come – fireworks. The food seemed to deny the existence of rationing, but of course it was autumn and local apples had become toffee apples and cider flowed from jugs straight from farm presses.

To Margaret, at first, the cracks and bangs were frightening; her mind went back to the blitz but as Anna grabbed her hand, trembling, she realized that her fear was shared and she must try to appear to be brave.

'Look at the colours and the trees reflected in the river. What a beautiful sight.' Margaret looked round to see Bryan Glynn, who was ecstatic as he experienced the exotic festivities, squealing with delight, as he was passed between Dai and Rhys like a parcel. 'Let's sit down on the riverbank, Anna'

'Nobody will notice if I jump at the bangs if I'm sitting,' replied Anna.

'Tell me about your new school. Is it better than boarding school?'

'I can't say enough good things about it. You know that this term I've been in the seniors. There are twenty of us girls in each class. All of us have had to pass a scholarship. D'you know some of the girls come to school by train? The headmistress is very strict: we have to wear our uniform, including our ties all the way home. Someone reported one girl for eating an apple in the street! Granny would have approved.'

'What about games, do you have a playing field?'

'Yes, I play Netball, and Lacrosse. Inside we do Gym, with rib stalls for climbing, a vaulting horse and a lovely floor for practising dance and music with movement.'

'Are you applying yourself to your academic studies?'

'Now you're sounding like Granny.'

'In a way I am your Granny now. I wish all the same that I hadn't become related to you as a result of Patrick being killed and your real Granny dying.'

'I know. There has been so much sadness as a result of the war. A girl in my class has lost her father; he was in the army at Tobruk. Our Form Mistress said to each of us privately to be careful about asking too many questions of other girls because some had had relatives killed or injured in air raids, others had more than one member of the family maimed or worse at the front or in prison camps.'

Anna bowed, her companion realized that she had become silent because of Bernie.

'You can talk to me about Bernie. I'm so pleased he is alive. You know that he is in Australia recuperating. His camp was the first to be liberated after VJ Day. He has written to me. They were all given four pieces of paper. Bernie doesn't change. He used half of one of his to draw horses for Bryan Glynn.'

'Did BG like them?'

'He said 'Verny draws ponies not tunters'.'

They giggled at the judgment of the four-year-old.

'Can I write to him? I'd like to tell him about Bryan Glynn. How he laughs when I tickle him and how he tries to be a farmer – feeding hay and carrying his milk churn and the extraordinary noise he makes when he spills the milk.'

'In a bit I'd love it if you wrote, but at the present time I have just acquainted Bernie with recent news. His father's death must have been a terrible shock to him. What's more he was ignorant about my possible marriage to your grandfather. I had written to him about it and a telegram came back with words of encouragement, 'Don't delay, say yes'. As you know we didn't delay.

In my letter, I enclosed a photo of BG, as you call him, and one of Cae Coch – the one that will be in The Express next week accompanying Dai's article entitled, 'War and Peace'.'

'I'm like my mother aren't I? I speak before I think. I'm sorry. Of course I'll wait to write to Bernie. He'll be delighted with those two photos. Do letters take a long time to get to Australia?'

'Yes. That's one of the problems.' *Bernie was a person, whom Anna had never met. How would she respond to an ex-POW sailor? Was she thinking of him in terms of glamour? How damaged would he be? But the new school in Liverpool had made Anna thoughtful and considerate.*

'Pinny, I can still call you that can't I? I'm so pleased that David was too young to join up. He was so mad about being heroic that I feared that he would be a casualty once he enlisted.'

'Choosing to study Law instead of Medicine surprised me.' *Anna's learning.*

'Granny loved him reciting poetry, public speaking and debating. Doctors have to be more down to earth, don't they? Look at him, now, he's in quite a heated discussion with the Mayor. Probably he's talking about Capital Punishment or some ethical subject.'

'Let's rescue your mother, who's doing a voluntary surgery with those women – the three of them are always in the doctor's waiting room with some dreamed-up ailment.'

Anna laughed and pulled her new granny to her feet. Margaret noticed how well Anna'd grown. She had remained dark like her mother, with well-defined features and the expressive blue eyes of the Celt; she was tall for her age and had Rhys's athleticism. *Five years had turned a frightened child into a bright articulate girl. What memories would she take into adult life?*

The festivities went on until almost midnight – a time of day when hitherto the whole community would have been in bed. Nancy looked very happy and asked about her high spirits she confided in Mary and Margaret that she was pregnant and the doctors thought she would carry the baby to full-term. 'Gwyn and I plan to name the baby Victor or Victoria.'

The two older women spoke in unison, 'That is great news. Congratulations to you both. Be careful, Nancy, all babies will have those names next year.'

Nancy laughed, 'We hadn't worked that out. We were just so pleased.'

'All those lovely things you made and didn't use, which Bryan Glynn had, will be used for the Jones baby after all.'

'I know you've washed them and stored them in lavender. Thank you.' Nancy yawned. 'We're all going to be sleepy to-morrow. Farming people aren't used to celebrating like this.'

'I know. I'll volunteer for early milking in the morning. I have a feeling there will be quite a cross little son with me. He's never been up so late in his whole life.'

'He's never been cross in his life,' said Anna as she joined her mother.

'So you're the volunteer nursemaid at 5.30am to-morrow.' Mary commented, with a wry smile.

*

The Williams family returned to Liverpool, the following day and missed 'The Express', which had the article by Dai. It was a masterly piece of journalism, regretting the losses and privations of war but exhorting readers to make every effort to regenerate the countryside. There followed, in the next edition, a correspondence on the 'Letters' page, which complimented Dai for his tireless work throughout the war as a newspaper man, as a charity worker and as a farmer. Margaret cut out the relevant extracts and pasted them into Bryan Glynn's book holding his father's drawings and the recent Bernie sketch from Japan. *How will Bernie respond to Dai? For the two men to like and respect each other is my dearest wish.*

Dai Morgan spent many afternoons at his beloved Flo's grave. He ate and slept little but Dr Thomas assured him that Flo would not have liked to live an invalid life at Cae Coch.

He said, 'Look to the future, to peace, knowing that David and Anna will not be sucked into the vortex of war.' Dai heeded the doctor's advice and turned his mind to writing and Cae Coch.

Margaret murmured, 'Amen. Brian Glynn will grow up in peacetime. I mourn and miss Mrs Morgan. She and I were women of war. We both understood loss and grief but she taught me to hope and I'm grateful for that message.'

60

October

Bernie was in the first group of prisoners to be brought home from Australia and repatriated. They had flown part of the way and sailed from the Mediterranean to Plymouth to a hero's welcome. It had been arranged that Bernie would be brought by naval transport to Cae Coch – there were two other sailors who were to be taken on to Liverpool.

Margaret was relieved that she didn't have to go to Plymouth, though she wanted to have the first glimpse possible of Bernie. As Bryan Glynn had never confronted crowds she wanted to be sure that Bernie saw him at his best.

The vehicle slipped into the yard earlier than expected and it seemed that Bernie was deposited quite impersonally from it, together with his luggage. Margaret was glad that there was no need for hospitality for the driver and his two other ex-prisoners. They were in a hurry. She was overwhelmed with delight at the wanderer's arrival and could think of nothing else. She found herself alone with her son in the familiar kitchen. It was as though he belonged there. As she embraced him she found that far from being a pale, ex-prisoner, Bernie seemed to be tanned, fit and handsome.

'I didn't expect the 'Welcome Home Bernie' banner across the yard which I recognize from the photograph of the farm. It made me feel important.' Bernie's impish smile flashed on to his face.

'To everyone in this house you are important.'

'Mam, you look younger than you did when you saw me off those four years ago at Plymouth.'

'To-day, I feel younger. The war is over and I, a good Irish woman can say, 'God Save the King'.'

'Now where's that cup of tea, and is that the smell of some Welsh delicacy and do I spy a grey tabby cat, as ever, asleep?'

Margaret laughed. 'When I arrived here in 1940 there were Welsh cakes on the table. Their spicy smell and taste made me feel at home. So, I thought I'd play the same trick on you.'

'Well if everything Welsh is as good as these I'll be happy.'

'Bernie, let me touch you one more time to be sure I'm not dreaming.' He rose from the table and gave his mother a big hug, at the same moment Dai appeared in the doorway with Bryan Glynn on his shoulders. The two men grasped each other's hands.

'Welcome home, Bernie. I suppose you don't know who this small person is?'

Of course, Bernie put his head to one side, assumed a quizzical expression and murmured, 'I don't think we've met.'

'I'm your brother, Verny. I'm Bryan Glynn Rooney. I'm four.' Their embrace was far more boisterous than Bernie's greeting with his mother.

There was an atmosphere of a family united in goodwill. *My mind goes back to my first day at Cae Coch. Then I was full of apprehension. Bernie seems to be relaxed. I hope he isn't as apprehensive of Dai as I was of Flo Morgan'.*

'I have to admit that for a young man my habits may appear strange. I get very tired quickly. Forgive me.' *Is he alright?*

Dai stood up immediately and asked Bernie whether he'd like to see The Eyrie.

'Have you eagles on the farm?' Even Bryan Glynn chuckled.

'No, it's the name your mother and father gave to the loft above this room, which they occupied until recently. We thought it would give you privacy. What d'you think?'

'Lead on, Mr. Morgan.'

*

Later that night Dai told his wife how he'd discussed Bernie's needs with him.

'He addressed me as 'Sir'. I laughed and told him that it was I who should show reverence to a person such as he, who had survived shipwreck and incarceration.'

'What is Bernie to call you?'

'It's very modern but I insist that he calls me Dai. He agreed to this reluctantly.'

'How did you leave him?'

'I explained that the doors of this house are never locked and we wouldn't consider it odd if he slept and ate at strange times. I also mentioned how Glynn Thomas would be willing to take over his health care now Bernie's been demobbed.'

'My dearest Dai, you think of everything. Bryan Glynn behaved as though he'd known 'Verny' forever.'

'Children are a bit like animals. Hywel Dda took to him as though he'd known him since he was a colt. That horse can be positively indifferent to strangers.'

*

The next few weeks were spent making Bernie's application to Medical School, a process he'd started in Australia.

'Why not combine a visit to Liverpool University for Bernie's interview with a trip to Cork?' Dai suggested.

It was arranged.

Bernie had flash-backs from his years of imprisonment but after a little persuasion he agreed to discuss them with Dr. Thomas and Dr. Hughes. Some days he seemed to Margaret to be carefree and content and at other times he was depressed, moody and withdrawn.

'I can't understand the British supporting the Americans in their use of Atom Bombs against Japan.' He said this as though the residents of Cae Coch, personally, approved the devastating act.

Margaret replied, 'I was appalled by that and its everlasting consequence, but I couldn't stop it.'

'Mam that's not good enough. I want to work, when I'm a student and when I qualify, in a Peace Movement to ban such weapons internationally.'

'Dai would be one of your keenest supporters.'

'D'you know, Mam, when you wrote to say that you wanted to marry Dai, I felt very jealous. Then I thought of what you'd done in the war, moved, worked as a farm labourer, brought up a child in a strange place and been a lot of the time on your own. I suddenly understood your need for companionship.'

'You're reconciled to my marriage, then?'

'I'm delighted. Dai's a good man. He loves you. He admires you and he'll see that Bryan Glynn is educated properly, as you and my Da did for me. Most importantly, he understands my need for freedom, quiet and getting on with my life. I've even agreed to sing in the Church of Wales production of The Messiah on Christmas Eve.

How's that for a good R.C.?'

'That's a surprise. I'm pleased. How are you to-day?'

'It's a good day. I'm sorry about the bad ones.'

'They'll be fewer as time goes on. Sorry, Bernie, but it's your turn to read to Bryan Glynn. He's waiting patiently in his new bed upstairs.'

61

A Holiday

'Dai says that he should stay here and supervise the farm. You, I and Bryan Glynn will be fine without him. He'll come next time we visit Ireland and we'll spend some time together in Dublin, Kerry and Cork when we have you and David here to look after the farm.'

Bernie was hesitant. 'I feel that he should come with us or he should go instead of me.'

'Nonsense. It's all arranged. Passports and a bed and breakfast in Cork booked for a night either side of the visit to the farm in County Cork. Bridget and Ciaran seem happy to put us up at the farm.'

'Why do you use the word 'seem'?'

'Water under the bridge, Bernie. It helps that you survived the camp.'

'What does. . .'

'Remember, I left Cork under a cloud.'

'Please, Mam, let's have an end to all this mystery. Families fall out; countries fall out. Let's have a bit of peace around us.'

Changing the subject quickly, Margaret said, 'D'you know, this is the first holiday I've ever had?'

'What about the night you spent in the nurses' home when Dad was recovering from his escapade.'

'I was worried stiff.'

'And, what about the night you spent in Plymouth when you saw me off to wherever and ultimately the Java Sea.' His tone had an element of jokiness about it. Was he being impish, Margaret asked herself?

She laughed and sensing his playful mood, she retorted, 'Of course, you had three years holiday, courtesy of the Japanese Government.' She regretted her words immediately, but they worked.

Smiling he said. 'I don't know how one would classify that in hospitality terms. I've been giving the matter some thought.'

'And. . .' Margaret wished she'd not encroached on to sensitive areas.

'Seriously, one of the officer captives was a Politics graduate – we used to talk about our predicament – he said, 'Karl Marx wrote, 'to regret experience is to deny development.' I think I've got the quote right.'

'D'you mean that you were all glad that you were taken prisoner?'

'No, but I don't want to dwell on it for the rest of my life. Now that I've been offered a place at Medical School, I'll work at my studies with more enthusiasm than I might have done without the horrific experiences of the prison camp.'

Margaret was silent, but she gave Bernie's words some thought. She considered the people whom she'd lived among for the last five years: they'd all impressed her, with the exception of Gwyn. And he – well. . . even he, had changed, due to his war work, hadn't he?

*

At four, Bryan Glynn was a bright child. Margaret wanted him to see Ireland through a child's eye. She knew that Bridget would endear herself to him and the meeting between her and Bridget, after so long a time, would be made easier with Bryan Glynn present. Had Dai, - a Welshman - been with her, the visit might have been difficult. *Even so, hadn't Dai spoken of Michael Collins with admiration? Hadn't Lloyd George been saddened by Collins' murder? The Welsh had sympathy with the principle of nationalism.* On the other hand, Bernie was adult and had survived a prisoner of war camp; he filled Margaret with pride tinged with apprehension. How would her family read him? She worried whether in Ireland, that supposedly neutral country, people would feel ambivalent about the war. Bernie himself was naïve about politics. He thought no further than in terms of war and peace. As yet he was blinkered concerning the need to put forward coherent policies for peacetime. Margaret knew that the Irish person's love of education would, probably, be satisfied by the news that Bernie was to go to Medical School and his part in the war would perhaps be forgotten. She longed to see her nephews and her niece.

*

Hans had made application to become naturalized, and was to do all the heavy work on the farm, under Gwyn's supervision, in Margaret and Bernie's absence. Nancy's pregnancy had surprised all. Her duties would be to run the dairy and look after the chickens and cook for Dai Morgan, whilst Margaret was away. Gwyn was winding up the Convalescent Hospital, but his time there was minimal; it was due to become a smart hotel. He had told Dai and Margaret that he felt at a loss, his war work had made him want to work amongst people in future. Was there any opening in medicine for him in post-war Britain? He'd asked this question of Bernie several times, in front of Margaret, who'd, in turn, discussed the matter with Dai, who'd made and continued to make enquiries around the county. Margaret thought that one of the sad consequences of peace was the unemployment of the very people who had made the war winnable. Dai had jokingly teased her by saying that she should write a book entitled, 'Ironies of Life'.

*

The three travellers were to go by train to Liverpool, stay a day and a half with Will and Jean, whilst Bernie had his Medical School interview and then take the ferry to Dublin and on to Cork by bus. Bryan Glynn was excited. He had his beloved brother, his mother and a little case with B.G.R. printed on it, but Gladstone had to remain at Cae Coch.

Dai Morgan promised that he would take on the onerous duty of looking after Gladstone. He had never fed a cat, hitherto.

*

Declan, Con, Theresa, and Bernie had taken Bryan Glynn up the hill, where the Irish sheep, belonging to Ciaran, were. As they left the farm, Margaret heard her son say, 'I like Ireland. Who's peat? Mam said you burn him on the fire.' She didn't hear the reply and wondered whether Bernie would have to translate a Welsh accent into English that the Irish cousins would understand.

Bernie and Bryan Glynn's smiles had broken any coldness that might have existed with their cousins, when they arrived at the farm. Bridget and her family had all been outside the house as the taxi had driven up to the door. Ciaran and Bridget had said, 'Great to see you all. Welcome home.' Ciaran had excused himself, after having a cup of tea, as he had to pay an urgent visit to a neighbour who was unwell, but suggested that his sons and daughter walked with their two cousins, up to the top of the hill, a vantage point, to see the surrounding area for miles around and look at the sheep at the same time. He seemed to Margaret to be proud of his flock. She remembered his kindness from years ago.

As the back door closed, Bridget offered her sister another cup of tea but her tone was nervous.

Margaret replied, 'Please, I'd love another cup. I'd forgotten how delicious tea tastes when made with Irish water. It's such a treat to see you all. Declan was Bryan Glynn's age when I last saw him.'

'Tell me about Patrick, Bernie and Dai. What an eventful life you've had – so much anxiety and sadness but some joy as well, I hope, Maggie. Tell.'

'What about you? Con seems so like his Da, at that age and Theresa is so beautiful.'

'I think she's like you, Maggie. She has your red hair but she's not so tall nor so broad shouldered.'

There was a pause and Margaret thought that she must broach the subject which lay between them, unspoken. 'Bridget, sometime you must tell me about Da and Mam. I've longed to know about the family, and the village. There was that awful estrangement when I left here. I wish. . .'

'Things might have mended but you married Patrick so soon after and he was a Protestant!'

'He converted soon after and became more devout than me.'

Bridget replied quickly, 'We never knew that. There are things that have gone round and round in my head about you leaving us. The parents were a little bigoted.'

'I was their daughter, Biddy.'

'You were always so secretive, Maggie. I never stopped loving you. Are you still a practising Catholic?'

'Sort of. . . yes, yes – I am. Bernie and Bryan Glynn are too. I have so much to be thankful for. When we married, it was Dai who decided the wedding was to be in a Catholic Church and nowhere else, I just wanted to marry him.'

'That sounds so romantic.'

'No, Bridget, it's real, rather than romantic. We've both been through so much during the short time we have known each other.'

'Yes, you told me about the ups and downs of the years since you left here in your letter.'

'Bridget, it must have been strange to be outside the World War, wasn't it?'

Maggie was careful to remember that she must not remind her sister of the reported incident of German submarines being re-fuelled in Cork. Did Bridget know about that? Probably not. Was that just a bit of anti-Irish propaganda? Bridget's reply explained her stance.

'What could we do? We were just pawns of the government. A few Dublin men went over the border and joined the British army, but Cork has never been very fond of England. Remember the savagery of the Black and Tans. Sorry, Maggie.'

'I know. . .' said Margaret thinking back to Sean's English mother. How she must have been ashamed of her English nationality when those loathsome volunteers imposed violence, murders and executions on those seeking independence.

'When you wrote about Bernie being a prisoner of the Japanese, we were horrified. Japan of all places.'

Margaret wondered what Bridget meant, so she nodded in agreement, but changed the subject. *Ireland hasn't moved into the twentieth century. It will now the war's over.*

'Bernie looks well and he's so handsome.' *Had Bridget any idea about the scars left in a person after three years of incarceration?* Pleased by the compliment, Margaret asked, 'What about his brother?'

'He's a darling. As I told you in my letter, I only had the three. Like Mam I had several miscarriages.'

'I'm sorry. Bryan Glynn was a bit of a surprise to Patrick and me, but he's been such a wartime joy to all at Cae Coch. Remember that's the name of our farm.'

'Would you like to see round our farm and your old haunts?'

'Good idea. After seeing all the changes you've made, could we walk down to the fairy glen by the river?'

'Surely you don't want to go to the place where you had your accident?'

'That was moons ago, I'll be fine. What did happen, anyway? Why was I banished? Please tell me, Biddy?'

The two women, one tall red-headed with flecks of grey beginning to show, the other short, dark but lacking the intelligent spark of her sister, set out to inspect the familiar surroundings. Their ready smiles reminded the observer that they were indeed sisters. As Margaret looked at Bridget, she thought that the hard grind of maintaining and extending the farm had taken its toll; Bridget must have had to work as hard if not harder than she, without the benefit of mixing with so many interesting people. Cae Coch had the advantage of the town nearby. Ciaran and Bridget were living in very rural surroundings, isolated from society. Their experience must have been narrow. Bridget was a bit like Nancy – she didn't read, she sewed and enjoyed making a welcoming home for her family and anyone who dropped by. She was content. Margaret thought of Patrick, Dai, Bernie and Bryan Glynn – *All in all, God hasn't treated me badly.*

62

The River Bank

'So many alterations have been made, since I left all those years ago. The cow shed used to be next to the house, but it's now where the pig sties were.'

'Declan is a genius at building. D'you know, Maggie, that we own the house and ten acres with it?'

'Great. How did you manage that?' Margaret showed her admiration with a whoop of delight, she felt family all of a sudden.

'When the big house was sold at the start of the war, Ciaran went to the auction and bid next to nothing for our place; no one else was showing an interest in a place which was tenanted – they must've been drinking or at Mass. He was surprised at his good fortune.' *Margaret marvelled at Sean's parents' generosity.*

'How many acres do you rent?'

'Seventy,' said Bridget proudly.

'You've got a tractor now, I see. Do I spy tackle to go with it?'

'Con's the mechanic round here and he does contract ploughing and harvesting, all over the district.'

Observing the pigs, the chickens and the cattle, Margaret was amazed at the good condition of the stock: walking over to the fields, this impression was confirmed. The fencing was well-maintained and the grassland was in very good order. As a child she remembered that it had been a struggle to breed and rear good animals as the fodder and stock available to her family was of poor quality. Her sister, Ciaran and their children had, clearly, excelled in their management of the farm. *Had the fact that Eire hadn't been in the war helped the Irish farmers?*

'Now you've seen your old haunts, Maggie, what d'you think?'

'It's stunning. You and Ciaran have transformed the farm. Shall we walk to my favourite bit of the river?'

'Lord help us, Maggie, you don't really want to go there.'

Margaret laughed. 'It's where I sneaked away with a book in my pocket when I was supposed to be doing some holy duty for Mam, or saying a hundred decades of the rosary as a penance.'

'You didn't. . .'

'Not exactly. Remember my destiny was the convent. I had to store every experience I could before I took the veil. I read copies of poems there and committed them to memory, after doing my penance.'

'I'm so glad I wasn't a scholar. Mam made sure I'd always be here to skivvy. Thank God for Ciaran.'

They were on the path to the river when Margaret felt uneasy. *Had she been too glib?* 'You haven't told me about the accident. I can't remember a thing.'

'Mam was in a mood. You'd gone off somewhere – not turned up for milking so Fergus had to do it.'

'She used to get furious if she saw me go out with a poetry book. She was hard, but her life had been hard.'

'Poetry books and Sean, Mam never made that connection—nor did she stumble on your affair with Sean. Nobody guessed. Thank God. After all he was half-English!'

'Looking back on it and having experienced family life, it seems awful to say, but then the quiet and reverence of the convent was tolerable.'

'You were Mam's only hope. None of the boys did well at school; Denis and Fred were lured into horse-racing stables in County Kildare and only Fergus stayed at home to work.'

'You and Ciaran were here. I adored Fergus. He was always sticking up for us girls. I felt his presence in the kitchen just now.'

'He helped me nurse Da and Mam through the 'flu' and then succumbed himself. We had a funeral for all three together. I'll never forget it.'

'I wept when I read in your letter about Fergie's death. He was too good to die. Mam and Da were old, after all. I wished that I could have helped you look after them. I'm sorry. I should have been there despite everything.'

'I longed for you but Mam said you were dead to the family.'

'Oh Biddy I wish I. . .'

'No, Maggie. Don't feel guilty. Mam told me after her final confession that she'd forgiven you.'

'Oh. . .'

'I prayed that you were alive, then, and ever since, and have asked God's blessing on you. Thank you for finding out about us when the war ended and writing so kindly to us. We didn't deserve it.'

Margaret wondered whether she should have discussed the family tragedies when she and Bridget were first alone. She had longed to be in the fresh Irish air, drinking in the quiet, not talking about the past. She couldn't change what had happened.

'Let's enjoy our walk now. How did I manage to have that stupid accident?' Her words were spoken lightly. The memory of her childhood frolics with Bridget and later her trysts with Sean touched her. The beauty of this part of Ireland overwhelmed her – it was idyllic. The loveliness of Cae Coch was home.

'Ciaran and I found you in the river. You were up to your waist in water. Your neck was scratched and bleeding from the sharp rocks. Jesus, I thought you were dead, but Ciaran took hold of you and murmured, 'She's unconscious.'

'Had I fallen?'

'We never found out. You had no memory of what happened.'

'I've never remembered anything about it, except having a recollection of being terrified and longing to bathe and cleanse myself in cold water. Where or when, I don't know.'

'It was a week after Sean was killed. Only Ciaran and I knew about your affair with him. Possibly his mother knew. It remained a secret. D'you know that after Sean was shot, for a while suspicion fell on local men – even our brothers! Sean's family was very magnanimous to us. His Da left no stone unturned until the gunman was caught in Cork city.'

'That should have removed Mam's anti-English prejudice, did it? Sean's Da was always good to me, though I never saw him after Sean's death. That week, I had tried to act normally. I remember going to confession – that was hard. Strangely, Sean's death had reconciled me to the veil.'

'When you were recovering I insisted on looking after you, in case you rambled on about Sean. You didn't. You seemed numb.'

'And then. . ?'

'The news got round that you'd lost your mind as a result of the accident. Some people believed that you'd thrown yourself down onto those rocks to avoid the convent. What shame! Attempted suicide is a mortal sin.'

'As if. . ? Isn't gossip cruel everywhere?'

'Mam, having her brother a priest, was angry and unforgiving about the gossip. She kept saying that you'd let the family down; the order wouldn't accept you; you'd have to be put in a home for lunatics.'

'I wasn't mad,' Margaret was outraged.

'No, but Father Mark made it worse by saying you had a divil inside you, which needed exorcising...'

Margaret interrupted, 'Jesus Christ, his Catholicism was so extreme.'

'So will I just be getting on with it now?'

'Sorry, please do, Biddy.'

'Maggie, I had to find a middle way. You'd spoiled your chances of going for a nun, thank God, and I wasn't going to let you go to a mad house. I wrote to Aunt Theresa in Dublin, secretly, and begged her to ask Mam for you to help in her shop in the docks.'

'God be praised. You saved me. Aunt Theresa never told me about your letter – bless her memory. In Dublin I met Patrick. Without him I wouldn't have Bernie and Bryan Glynn. Thank you, Biddy. I understand it now.' Margaret's relief was palpable. She squeezed her sister's hand.

The path wound round mounds of rock. Suddenly, they could hear the rhythmic bubbles and splashes of the water. As the two women continued downwards, they became accustomed to the lulling melody of the river. Walking under the welcoming hazel trees of the riverside copse, the sound of the river became quieter but as they stepped up the steep grassy bank, they were aware of the surging torrent below. They could see the frothing, swirling stream. A rocky outcrop barred the water's flow, below, making a deep pool surrounded by savage crags.

Bridget pointed, 'You were there, Maggie. We thought you had fallen because you had a small book clutched in your hand. It was a book of poems, sodden with water but the inscription, 'To Maggie, with all my love, Sean' in large letters jumped from the watery page.'

Margaret whispered,

'*If God choose, I shall love thee better after death.*'*

As if not hearing her sister Bridget continued. 'We burned the book. We had to. It would have explained too much.'

---

* Elizabeth Barrett Browning 'Sonnets from the Portuguese'

Margaret gasped. 'I would never have done away with myself. I wanted to help his little crippled sister, Maeve, who I'd read with for years, with Mam's approval. That girl loved him to distraction.' As she spoke she felt dizzy and put out her hand to Bridget. 'Sean used to say that our beloved friend the Leprechaun inhabited this bit. . . our bit of turf, but I. . . I saw an evil form just now. My legs . . . are going. . . I'm falling. . . I'm frightened. . . hold me, Biddy.'

'What is. . . who can you see, Mag. . . don't faint. . . I'll. . .'

'It wasn't Sean, it wasn't the Leprechaun. . . either would be welcome but. . . I remember, so clearly. It was here. Biddy take me back. . . before. . . I collapse . . .'

'Tell me . . .'

Margaret's voice was hardly audible, 'It was the devil, himself. I shouldn't have come here. Biddy, I don't need to go into the water; the cleansing water. Please, please don't let me fall this time. . . I . . .'

*

Margaret felt disorientated. *Where am I? I can't be in Cork, can I? How is it that I seem to be in my parents' bed? No it's a modern bed, a sprung mattress – not a feather bed. Where are the pictures of the Madonna? I can hear a man's voice, an Irish accent, outside the window. My Da's? No, I remember I am Margaret Morgan, wife of Dai, on a visit to my beloved sister Bridget and I've had an awful shock. I've seen the truth. The Welsh psychiatrist was right to advise me to visit the home of my childhood, the place from which I was driven away at seventeen. I am free, I am cleansed at last.*

Dr. Hughes had said, 'So much happened to you at a very sensitive age. Go to the place and meet your family again. There may be a mystery to solve. The nation has peace now. Perhaps you need a personal peace.'

She dozed. It hadn't been a dream. *Should I tell Biddy? Does Biddy know? There was something that Biddy was not telling me.*

Bridget's knock on the door roused her. The delicious smell of an Irish stew brought Margaret back to life. She was so hungry.

'I've told the others that you're exhausted. I've brought my supper up here as well as yours. Bernie's washing Bryan Glynn ready for bed, and has promised to read him an Irish story which Theresa has found. The two sisters ate their meal slowly, but comfortably, without saying anything to each other. 'That was so good,' said Margaret as Bridget put the plates on the tray by the door.

'Maggie, it's time for the truth, however unpleasant it is. If you can remember, now, please tell me what happened all those years ago? I could guess, but I might be wrong.'

'I'll explain. Whenever I have a high temperature I become delirious. I had an alarming illness when Patrick was posted missing; a fever that I developed when Bryan Glynn was born brought on another bout of terror. It happened again when Patrick was killed – I developed a high temperature and was aware of disturbing horrible things. The doctor referred me to a psychiatrist who traced the sequence back to my illness after the river incident. I was asked whether I'd suffered some awful experience which had brought on that fever. I said. 'I can't remember.''

'What did the psychiatrist advise?'

'He suggested that I visited you. The funny thing is that I had already answered your letter accepting your invitation.'

'I'm so glad you're here. Go on.'

'I knew I'd never have another episode. My marriage to Dai made me feel at peace. How wrong I was. This afternoon all the pieces of the jigsaw fell into place.'

Bridget felt Margaret's brow – it was very hot. Sweat ran down her face. She was in a trance and her voice was hardly audible.

Margaret managed to whisper, *'The Leprechaun, Sean, both always disappear and reappear as a devil, today the monster took on human form – physical, menacing and repulsive. This man, with whiskey and tobacco on his fetid breath, bawled obscenities at me – 'whore', 'harlot', 'slut', 'prostitute', 'bitch'. The Leprechaun's artistic hands became filthy finger nails. These talons clawed my neck, pulled my hair round my throat, about to throttle me. Then my body was brutally devoured from the outside and savagely destroyed from inside by the devil lying and lunging on top of me, like a rampaging bull, squeezing life and love from my very existence. As I began to faint, I saw the evil creature's face and realized that the devil was my uncle, my mother's brother, Father Mark. The priest who had only recently smiled as he gave me absolution at confession.'*

'Hush now, Maggie. It's over, over. My neck is scarred as well. I wondered about what happened to you but daren't mention violation, even to Ciaran. After that divil assaulted me, Ciaran threatened to kill him and would have done so, had he known what happened to you. I wondered and watched. When it happened to me, Ciaran became a server, monitored all uncle's movements. He was present in church whenever confessions were heard. D'you remember?'

Maggie nodded. Her sister continued, 'People commented on his religious devotion. Huh! I thought over the afternoon you had your accident. Father seemed to be under scrutiny all the time. There was, only, a half hour when Ciaran had to drench a sick sheep. I was certain sure there wasn't time for that evil one to be by the river to hurt you.'

'Where is the filthy demon now?'

'When Da and Mam died in '38, I went to the Bishop and told my story. I was surprised that he believed my tale, but Father was Mam's brother and the Bishop realized the family shame that Ciaran and I had shared for years. The wretch was recalled to the Priest House in Kerry, but no criminal charges were made. We were relieved because our decent saintly mother's memory will never be besmirched.'

'Oh Biddy, I thought that only tyrants like Hitler and the Japanese did evil things, but there is wickedness even in the Holy Mother Church.'

'Maggie, our uncle is dead now; he must answer to a higher authority and we can now forget and be at peace. You and I are together again.'

*

There was laughter and a loud knock on the bedroom door.

'May a clean little boy and soon-to-be medical student, come and wish their Mam, "Goodnight"?'

'And their aunt. Please come in, Bernie.' Bridget's voice was happier than Margaret had ever heard it. *She mused on the irony of three of the four people she loved and honoured most in her life being in her late parents' bedroom, without the Madonna.*

'Tomorrow, we're all going to the market. Margaret Morgan is going to telephone her husband from there to tell him how well and happy she feels, and how right he was to encourage her to come to visit her sister in Cork.' Margaret said, grinning at Bridget, as she hugged Bryan Glynn and caressed her Bernie's hands.

'I'd like to speak to my brother-in-law, too, and say, 'Amen'. May I?'

Edward Gaskell
publishers
DEVON

Lazarus Press
Bookprinters
DEVON